A NEW BEGINNING

"Ye've said yer future lies in America, in some gold field," Ellen said fiercely. "If ye've a mind to go, Danny, then sell the cottage at once. Caitlin and I are not yer concern. I'll not have yer charity stretchin' across the sea."

He walked over to her slowly and took her shoulders in his hands. "There is no charity in how I feel about you, woman. Don't you see? I'm giving you the cottage so you can come to me in California. When I've made my fortune, I'll send for you and we can be married."

"Truly, ye would marry me, even now, with Caitlin and all? Tell me honest now, Danny. I can take no more lies in my life."

He touched her face gently. "I'm asking you now, a man too full of love to put the words properly. I'm asking that you let me love you, share my bed and my children, share all my life. Say you'll marry me, Ellen. Say you'll come to California when I send for you, and be my wife."

He bent his head and, for the first time, kissed her. It was not the passionate kiss of his dreams, but a gentle kiss, to break the steely bond that constricted her heart. That bond was the lessons of her past, hard and unyielding, but as their lips met, she felt the fetters of it fall away, and she was free of the past, free to give love, and free to receive it. . . .

CATCH UP ON THE BEST IN CONTEMPORARY FICTION FROM ZEBRA BOOKS!

LOVE AFFAIR (2181, $4.50)
by Syrell Rogovin Leahy

A poignant, supremely romantic story of an innocent young woman with a tragic past on her own in New York, and the seasoned newspaper reporter who vows to protect her from the harsh truths of the big city with his experience—and his love.

ROOMMATES (2156, $4.50)
by Katherine Stone

No one could have prepared Carrie for the monumental changes she would face when she met her new circle of friends at Stanford University. For once their lives intertwined and became woven into the tapestry of the times, they would never be the same.

MARITAL AFFAIRS (2033, $4.50)
by Sharleen Cooper Cohen

Everything the golden couple Liza and Jason Greene touched was charmed—except their marriage. And when Jason's thirst for glory led him to infidelity, Liza struck back in the only way possible.

RICH IS BEST (1924, $4.50)
by Julie Ellis

From Palm Springs to Paris, from Monte Carlo to New York City, wealthy and powerful Diane Carstairs plays a ruthless game, living a life on the edge between danger and decadence. But when caught in a battle for the unobtainable, she gambles with the only thing she owns that she cannot control—her heart.

THE FLOWER GARDEN (1396, $3.95)
by Margaret Pemberton

Born and bred in the opulent world of political high society, Nancy Leigh flees from her politician husband to the exotic island of Madeira. Irresistibly drawn to the arms of Ramon Sanford, the son of her father's deadliest enemy, Nancy is forced to make a dangerous choice between her family's honor and her heart's most fervent desire!

Available wherever paperbacks are sold, or order direct from the Publisher. Send cover price plus 50¢ per copy for mailing and handling to Zebra Books, Dept. 2556, 475 Park Avenue South, New York, N.Y. 10016. Residents of New York, New Jersey and Pennsylvania must include sales tax. DO NOT SEND CASH.

MEREDITH MORGAN
EMERALD DESTINY

ZEBRA BOOKS
KENSINGTON PUBLISHING CORP.

ZEBRA BOOKS

are published by

Kensington Publishing Corp.
475 Park Avenue South
New York, NY 10016

First printing: January, 1989

Printed in the United States of America

This work is dedicated to my husband, Johnny, whose love sustained and encouraged me throughout the writing of this book. May he too find his dream.

ACKNOWLEDGMENTS

The completion and sale of a novel is never done alone. I wish to thank the many people important to that process for this book. First among those, my teacher, Gloria Miklowitz, who first saw something worthwhile in my writing and made invaluable introductions for me— every writer should have such a friend; my agent, Florence Feiler, who took on this beginner and worked chapter by chapter, encouraging me whenever I despaired throughout the writing of this book; my editor at Zebra Books, Carin Cohen, whose belief in this work has brought the characters to light; the fellow writers in my group, for their suggestions and pats on the back when needed—may they all succeed; my mother, whose love of writing led me irrevocably down this lane; my son, Christopher, and my daughter, Lisa, who had to take care of themselves while their mother wrote, and who complained only a little; and lastly, my eldest son—the writer—Terry, who pushed me into taking a class, and got the whole thing rolling; I thank you.

Part One

Dougal and Moira
The Lovers

Chapter One

It had been threatening rain all morning. The ground was hard as rock and the chill went through the thin soles of his shoes to the numbness that was his feet. Dougal arrived just as Moira finished preparing the dinner tray. The broth was steamy hot, and the soft new bread was warm from the oven.

"You're here late this night, Dougal O'Shay," said Moira. "Come in quickly now before that cold blast you've brought with you chills the tray complete."

Dougal stepped into the room, snatching the hat from his head. He stood then, in the great white kitchen, twisting his hat between his hands as if he had nothing to say.

"If you've business with Aunt Rebba, you've come too late. She'll not see you tonight," Moira offered, bothered by the silence of the man.

Catching up his pluck, he started in. "I've not come all this way to be speakin' with yer aunt, Moira. 'Tis ye I've come to see." He said it bold as brass.

It wasn't what was said, but how it was said that made

Moira turn around. "And what would you be wantin' with me?" she asked, stopping where she stood.

"Sit a while with me, Moira, will ye then? I have somewhat I care t' speak with ye about," the man replied, setting his cap on the counter with a firm and resolute hand.

"You'll be doin' me the favor if you'll come to the point, so I can get this tray up before she upstairs starts yellin' the rafters down around my ears."

"I'll not keep ye long," he promised. "Will ye sit here beside me?"

"I'll stand, thank you kind," came the reply.

Not knowing how else to make her attend to what he had to say, he began at once. "Ye know what sort of man I am, Moira. Ye've known me all yer life. Like most folks hereabouts, ye've counted me very little. I'm not much to look upon, a fact I've learned the hard road. I'm not more than a dirt farmer, and no great family have I to inherit from. There's just myself in the world to look to and see about," he told her, growing ever more easy with the words.

"I cannot imagine why you're tellin' me all of this, Dougal O'Shay. We've all got our own trouble in this world, and that's more than enough, sure," the woman remarked, thinking again how odd he was acting. It made her snippy with him, for she could not get the drift of what he meant.

"Let me finish what I've come to say, woman," he shouted, "and put that blasted tray aside the while." He took it from her hands and set it down.

Moira looked at him in stunned silence. Her interest peaked.

"I'm not," he resumed, "a very young man. The plain

face of it is, I'm thirty-six today. The other plain fact is, I've lived as much of my life as I care to alone. I cannot recall a day when I've been truly happy, and I'm tired to death of it. All my life, I've worked for near to nothin', and look to continue such. It was today," he explained, "bein' my birthday and all, somethin' came over me. I knew I couldn't go on any longer as I was. I gave myself a present. The present bein' to come here this night and ask ye for yer hand in marriage." Having had his say, he drew a long cleansing breath.

Moira sat down then, and gazed in wonder at this unexpected suitor. It seemed to her the scene was a fantasy, and she and Dougal the players. She waited, speechless, as though expecting him at any minute to break out laughing and tell her it was only a joke. Their eyes met and held, but she could think of nothing to say. As chance would have it, Aunt Rebba took this moment to shout down from upstairs at the delay of her tea. The stream of insults was hearty for the fragile woman she claimed to be. Still, Moira stood her ground and did not go up at once. Dougal had not laughed.

"Why ever would you pick me to ask? As everyone knows, I'm a spinster past her youth, and never much to look upon even when young. I've known it all these years, and it's no comfort to me to say it, but I'm not blind to the truth. Why then would you be askin' me?"

He came a step closer to her. It was the hardest thing he'd ever done, and the finest. "Who would ye I be askin' then? Some fine lady with a courtly air and a dazzlin' smile? Someone fair as Candlemas? Or should I look for a rich lady perhaps? What would someone like that see in me, I ask ye? What have I to offer a lady like that? Even if someone were foolish enough to accept me, she'd learn to

13

hate me soon enough, for what I could not be. I've known enough unhappiness. I'll not be seekin' more."

His words revealed his lonely life, and they touched her with the sadness they evoked, a sorrow much like her own. They were two of a kind, it seemed to her, the misfits of the world.

"I know yer life too, Moira," he went on. "Ye're like me. What little joy have ye in life? Ye live here, a pauper in yer aunt's charity. Are ye thinkin' ye'll ever inherit a penny of her wealth when she dies? Ye won't. It will all go t' her son in America, who cares not a whit for her. A spinster ye are, as ye say, and not a ravin' beauty. All this ye know too well. What have ye t' look to? So, I say t' ye, could life with me be worse?"

Moira was intent on the man's eyes, watching them as he spoke. It was an odd proposal. It was a pitiful proposal. It was the only proposal she'd ever had.

"I'm lookin' for a woman t' make my house a home. Someone I can come home to of an evenin' and talk to of the day's events. I want someone who'll do for me, and let me do a bit for her. I've a need to share my life and make it worth somethin'."

She was studying him as he spoke. She'd known him all her life, but had never thought of him as someone she could give herself to. He made it sound so cold, yet she would rather have cold honesty than fanciful lies. He kept talking quickly, as though if he stopped, he'd fumble and never restart.

"I would be a husband to ye in all ways. I will not promise ye wild, romantic love, but a mistress in yer own home ye'd be, with no one to yell insults at ye." He pointed above, where abuse was still being hurled with great abandon. "I'd treat ye with proper respect, that of a

14

man for his wife. And someone ye'd have who'd care a whit for ye if ye ailed." He moved close beside her now, and spoke face to face. "Children I could give ye, and you t' me. I'd want no home of mine barren long. I would fill it with happy voices ot those of me own flesh. There, the love will come," he said, looking down into her eyes, "in those children." They were lovely eyes. He hadn't noticed, until that moment, how lovely her eyes were. "It's life I offer ye, woman, a chance at life for both of us."

He stopped then, having said everything he knew to say. He had put his life before her, the pain, the longings, and the hope.

Moira sat quietly, still as midnight in her thoughts. She was trying to see the man behind the words. A chance at life. She repeated the words in her mind. Some part of her that had grown closed and hard with the years of rejection began to ache with longing. Take it, woman! a voice within her cried. Never will it come your way again. It was hope, where hope had died.

"I see I've said too much at once," said Dougal, mistaking her silence for doubt. "I'll be goin' now and give ye the long night to decide. I'll come around again, tomorrow mornin', for yer answer."

He started for the door, but turned back again when he heard her call. It was like a star coming out of the velvet black. "Wait, Dougal," she whispered, holding a hand to her breast, as if to still the beating of her heart. "All you've said is true. I need no time to think. I will marry you, and proud I'd be to be your wife." Her words were a gift between them. "Since you have made your fine promise, now I'll make mine. A good wife I'll be to you. Never will folk look down on you on my account. I'll keep

15

your house in all tidiness, and share whatever you give me to share. I'll not ask love of you, but well will I give of kindness and caring. And if God will grant it to so old a spinster woman," she added, mocking her thirty-two years, "a house full of children will I bear you."

In three hesitant steps, Dougal came over and kissed her fully on the lips. Both were painfully shy, but a spark had been lit this night to carry them over their awkwardness.

"I'll call on the priest on the morrow then?"

"That would be fine indeed," agreed Moira. And so, it was settled.

On the way home, Dougal stopped at the cottage of Tommy Gray. They had been friends since earliest boyhood.

"What are ye up to, lad?" Tommy called up the road when he saw Dougal approaching. "Ye're in fine cloth for this mucky weather." The rain was pelting down generously. Mud had spattered up the sides of Dougal's boots, dulling the hard-earned shine. A spigot of rain had found its way beneath the collar of Dougal's coat and iced his back on its way down. "It must be something special t' make ye trudge up here in this downpour," Tommy remarked. "Come inside, man, Ma will make ye a nice cuppa steamy."

Dougal came into the house and shook the wet from him like a spaniel. The heat generated by the blazing peat fire enveloped him in an instant. The little cottage held the heat so well that when Dougal removed his sodden coat, he could see the steam rising from it. "Ye're warm enough here," he allowed, straight-faced.

"Aye, man, ain't it awful." Tommy grimaced. "Ma's got the arthritis pretty bad every rain. Says the heat's all that gives her ease. What else am I t' do, Dougal? I stand it long as I can, then I hie out the door for a fresh breath of clean air, like a suffocatin' man. Don't say nothin' of the like to herself now, will ye?" Tommy cast a glance toward the kitchen door.

"Not a word of it."

Mrs. Gray brought in a tray of tea—the big earthenware pot, three mugs, sugar, creamer, and three slabs of her soda bread.

"I've come here, Tommy, to ask a favor of ye," Dougal began.

Mrs. Gray's interest in the conversation picked up. "What trouble are ye bringin' my boy?" she demanded. After all, it was her house.

"No trouble at all," Dougal reassured her, seeing the track of her mind. "I'm gettin' meself married. I want Tommy t' stand up with me at the church."

"Married!" choked Tommy, aghast and sputtering his tea. "Who'd marry ye?" Mrs. Gray's face was standing open.

"Moira Monahan," Dougal answered carefully, his voice a low breath in the quiet house.

"Who?" Tommy stood up, sloshing hot tea against his pants leg. "The spinster Monahan—niece of that old drone Rebba Cleary? Are ye mad then? The woman's gone with age, man. She's not for marryin' anymore. Mother of God, she's not even rich!"

"Tommy!" his old mother spoke sharply. "Keep a Christian tongue in yer head, or I'll skelp ye a lesson in religion. And don't be slanderin' the poor girl. She's not a bit t' look at, that's true, but likely she's got a good soul."

Tommy could not contain himself. "A soul's not much t' warm yer bed, though, is it? I'd hate t' think of lyin' beside that nice clean soul on m' weddin' night."

"Shame on ye, ye scandal!" Mrs. Gray scolded him. "Shame. Such talk. I'll not stay to hear such from me own son." She rose with great dignity, carried out the tea tray, and closed the door. Both men knew she had her ear plastered against the door's other side.

Dougal rose too. He was angry, so angry he wanted to knock Tommy down.

"I had it in m' mind that ye would stand up with me at m' weddin', but I see that won't do. Since ye feel as ye do, I'll thank ye to stay away. We won't be needin' ye. We'll marry if there's none but the two of us."

"Dougal, ye fool!" Tommy shouted.

"Enough," Dougal answered, taking a step toward Tommy. "I've not asked yer advice. Keep yer warnings t' yerself. From this day, ye're no longer m' friend."

"I'm that sorry then," Tommy answered, but Dougal had already gone—the door left standing open and all of Mrs. Gray's heat going out after him.

Chapter Two

They were married by Father Liam, after the third reading of the banns. There was no throng of people to witness the event, for Dougal had no family and Moira had only her aunt, who refused to come to a marriage that would shame the family. They had only each other, but that was crowd enough, for both of them were still shy of each other.

Father Liam blessed them, wishing them God's bounty of many children. It made Moira blush a deep scarlet, clear to the neck of her gown. Dougal could not help but see.

As it was daylight still, Dougal offered to buy their dinner at the village inn. The price was dear, the food dry and tasteless, yet Moira thought it heaven.

Think of it, she mused, the man sitting at my table, buying my dinner, is my husband. The words floated in her mind like a lovely dream. It had happened so quickly, yet there they were, man and wife. She had stopped dreaming long ago that such a day would come to her. Now it was here, unlooked for, unasked, shining like a

19

wishing star.

For Dougal too, it was a thing to wonder on. For the first time since he'd asked her to marry him, he'd caught her in a smile, and oh, the change it made. When she smiled, it lent a sparkle to her eye and her whole face lit up. In that quick look, you could see the young and pretty Moira, the girl she might have been had not her life battered her down as it had. The look was over in a twinkling, and she drew back to the face she normally presented to the world, but Dougal had seen it in that instant, and tucked it away as a keepsake.

At last, when neither of them could think of any further excuse to delay it, Dougal brought Moira to her new home. They were alone, riding up to the farm in the cart. Neither talked very much, for both were as nervous as cats about to litter, jumping in their skins. All of Moira's possessions were packed upon the cart, with room left over. It was a light burden, for the possessions were few. No welcome light warmed the sight of the cottage. No field hand came to greet them, for Dougal worked the farm alone.

"It's not much of a farm, I know," Dougal said, wanting to make it seem better for her, "but I've some improvements in mind I've been wantin' this long t' do. There never seemed reason before now."

And that was true. It had been a cold and lonely place, never asking anything of him but to break his back turning the soil and pulling the harvest from the land. Never had it urged him to add to the house, or mark out a cottage garden. There had never been a need until now.

Moira was silent, taking it all in, the look of it, the cottage and the land. There were laurel trees, and a wide oak to shelter the house. The land sloped down to a little spring, then ran out to pasture land for the few cattle. The field lay to the left of the cottage, green with sprouting life. There were straight rows of green heavily laden with goodness. They needed only a hand to nurture them that they might grow stronger.

Off to the right was the cow byre, and nearer the cottage a newly added-on room. "What's that ever for?" Moira asked him.

"'Tis the new chicken house I built for ye. Folks round here are wont to keep their fowl in the cottage of a winter. I've always thought that a bad business. 'Tis but a little luxury I wanted ye to have over some."

You could see he was proud of it with both eyes closed, she thought.

"I thank you for it, Dougal. A fine gift it is," she told him. The wonder of the man.

He helped her down from the cart. "It'll not take me long to put the stock to rights," he said. "Go on in and make yourself comfortable. The tey's in the larder."

It was a comfortable cottage. It had four rooms and a loft above. Though Moira did not know it, it had been recently swept clean. Peat had been laid out for the fire. Plates and bowls rested on the open shelf.

Moira found a large lamp in the kitchen and lit it, and a smaller one beside the bed. She stared hard at the bed for some minutes. In this bed, she thought, his wife I'll be, and here my children will be born. This house will be my home and this fine land will give us crops and strong, healthy cattle. It's a treasure I've found. Unable to hold back the torrent of emotion any longer, she sat down and wept. A wild, sweet joy she had never known before overwhelmed her.

Dougal, hearing her weeping, came running in. He

21

knelt beside the bed, awkward with his new feelings. "Don't be weepin' so, Moira m' own. I know it's never so fine as yer aunt's house, but give me some time, woman. I'll make it grand for ye, sure. Don't cry now, for it breaks m' heart to see ye so." He gathered her into his arms and rocked to and fro.

"No, Dougal," she cried, "'tis the grandest house I've ever known, and you the grandest man. 'Tis all so much. I cannot tell you how I feel."

She kissed him then, with her lips, her heart, and all that was hers. Then he in great joy returned the kiss, and all the love so tightly bound all the long years came flowing out of both of them.

"Ye might as well know the truth of it now, Moira mine," Dougal said, turning away from her to hide his face. "I'm as much a spinster as yourself, for I've never been with a woman in all me days. M' legs are shakin' at the thought of what's to come this night. I'd not be wantin' to disappoint ye. Ye must think me a great daft fool."

"It's an honest soul you are, my man, and I the grateful one for the tellin'," she answered, turning his face back toward her. "All this while my thoughts were on myself. How will it be? How will I look to him and such. Now I see well, 'tis both of us a-cowerin'. Come here to me then, Dougal, my great mannie. I've courage enough for both."

He came into her arms, and she held him and kissed him. Then standing, she took off the dowdy dress her aunt had given her for the wedding, and even stepped free of the shift beneath. Completely innocent, she stood before him.

Dougal felt great unbounded joy as he looked at her,

for she was beautiful in the moonlight, with her hair falling down across her shoulders and her arms outstretched inviting him. In that moment, he forgot he was Dougal, poor farmer of no account, meaning nothing to anyone in the world, and knew only that at last he had come alive, with all the yearning of the long, lonely years behind him. No coaxing did he need this night, nor any other. He came to her a full man, glorying in their love, for passion born of loneliness is great.

He touched her gently, as he had never touched a woman, as he had always dreamed of touching a woman. He bent his head and kissed her breast as he knew other men did with their women, and his heart thrilled. She was not shy with him, and everywhere he longed to touch, she allowed and welcomed him. His fingers stroked and caressed her, learning her. And when he took her hand and brought it hesitatingly to himself, she did not pull away, but touched him too.

"I would never want to do you any harm, Moira. Will it hurt you, the first time?" he asked, concerned for her even in his growing need.

"I am told it may," she answered, "but what is hurt to do with me now? What can any hurt take away from this? I would have this hurt, Dougal. I would welcome it, and never be a spinster again."

He was gentle. The pain was a sharp moment, tearing away all the past, and opening a world of love to her. She felt it, and said, "Hold me tighter still."

When it was ended, this first night of their lives as man and wife, he whispered to her, "Proud I am that ye are my wife."

She answered in return, "A woman you've made me this night, Dougal, and I'm grateful." They slept the night away, cradled in each other's arms.

The tea was made before he arose. A fire was laid on the hearth, and it warmed the room with its crackling light. The hanging table had been brought down and set with platter and porringers. Everything is laid out grand, thought Moira. Even the smell of new bread was wafting on the morning air.

It's a fine morning. It's a lovely morning, thought Dougal to himself. He was almost willing to stay in bed, just to feel the coziness settle in around him. It was the first time in his life he'd awakened with pure and utter happiness in being alive.

"Did ye rise with the chickens then this morning? Ye've been up and about so long," he said, smiling up at her.

He sat at the table then, and she began setting the food out, steaming hot and smelling so to make a man's stomach growl in anticipation. She was tidy, he saw. Everything had been set out in its proper place, even the spotless tablecloth and linen napkins. These had been her mother's. Now they were hers. It was the first time she had used them. They, along with the gold band on her finger, said she was a wife.

"Sure it's too grand to eat," he said. "Let me just settle meself a while and breathe it all in."

"You won't be startin' your day with nothing to warm your insides," said Moira, blushing at his praise. No one's ever praised me much, she thought, and never for so simple a thing as setting a table out proper. It pleased her that he noted little things, for to be truthful, she had taken great pains with it. It had to be special.

"I hope the tea's to your liking."

"It is and more," he said, full of himself and the joy of her. "But where's yer cup, for sure I don't see it sittin' in all this glory."

"I thought to be eating after I served you yours, while it's still hot," she answered, holding out the platter heavy with johnnycakes.

"Ye'll do no such thing," he insisted, searching out the cup. "Ye'll not be a servant in yer own home. Here ye'll share m' meals as well as m' bed, and no argument will I hear on that. Sit down now and eat with me. Sure ye've earned it."

She blushed at his mention of having earned it, and thought he meant what had happened during the night. "You'd think I was made of fine porcelain," she muttered, but she sat.

"I've a bit of somethin' I want t' ask ye," he began. "Now then, there's a matter I've been meanin' to see about these few weeks. I've learned the farm across from our own is up for sale."

Our own indeed, she thought, wondering at the goodness of the man. Her own father had never consulted her mother over any decision to be made for the family. Dougal, it seemed, would be different.

"He's been plantin' pratties there since his father's time and the soil is near given out. 'Tis Joe Flarity's place. Well, the point is this, I've a bit of money set aside. I've not needed much, livin' alone as I have. Till now, I've had no one to spend a shillin' on but meself. So that bein' as it is, I've set some away.

"Now here I come to the trouble. I know how much store women set on frills and the like, and I'm after givin' ye the fine things ye've done without so long. Could we manage, do ye think, for a bit longer with what little we have now, and buy this farm of Joe's?"

She sat for some moments, hardly knowing what to say. She had never expected to be asked her opinion on how to manage their goods. Her own father had run his home with a loud voice and a strong arm. He had never brooked any interference. She had expected it was everywhere so.

"You're askin' me what to do? Sure it's your decision. 'Tis your farm and money and all," she answered.

"No, nay. I'll not have that," said the man. "The house and all I own is yours too, now and evermore. It's little enough I can give ye. I'll not decide a thing like this without yer consent. There's but the two of us. We'd best do right by t' other."

"Well then," said she, pouring out another steaming mug of tea for him, "it sounds a fine idea. The cattle could spread out the more and fatten on the winter grass. We could even plant a bit o' grain for them, and leave the pratties go.

"As for me yearning away for fine bits of frill and nonsense, I've not a notion in my head. I'm content as that old coween in the byre. You're after spoiling me with all your grand ideas."

"Ye need some spoilin', if I'm a judge," he told her, pleased with her answer. "Then, as you agree, I'll go this day and see to Joe."

He did go. Joe drove a hard bargain, like any true son of Erin, but in the end, the land was theirs. It marked a good beginning for their first day of married life.

Chapter Three

The days went on as sweet as summer. Dougal tended to the farm and the cattle, while Moira saw to the baking and the cleaning, and tending to her man. No one ever tried harder to give happiness to another soul, and Dougal returned it all, in little ways of kindness and caring.

On Sundays they left the work, and went down to the village in the cart for Mass. Everyone who saw them together could see the glory shining round them, for they were so content with each other. They did not have a care, until some, who were only busybodies, began to notice more than their happiness.

The old women began to laugh behind their hands at them, making jibes about Moira's womb being closed so long now, it would never open, no matter how long Dougal came pounding at the gates. Some pieces of this and other such remarks came back to Moira, and she grieved over it in her heart, but said not a word.

It happened that Dougal too was wondering why, after six months' time, her womb had not opened and life quickened within. He kept his own council on it, and they both dwelled on it alone. That great thought lay between them at night, as cold as a harlot's kiss. So by and by, a silence grew between them. The cottage became a quiet house in those days. You could almost hear the shadows of gloom creep in about them.

Moira, unable to keep her pain to herself any longer, took her troubles to Father Liam in the secrecy of the confessional.

"I cannot go on like this much longer, Father," she whispered. "The women are all talkin' gossip about us. It's shaming him, and I'm to blame."

"Now how would you know a thing like that?" he pointed out. "It could as well be Dougal."

"Oh no," she dared correct him. "Never. He's a good man. God would never do that to a man like him. He'd never."

"It's a sin to be thinking you know exactly what God would or wouldn't do, I'll remind you."

"Yes, Father." Her childhood training was much too strong to go against the word of a priest more than once in a single day.

"All of this is premature anyway. You've only been married a few months. All you need is time."

"But that's it, Father. There isn't much time," she interrupted. "Don't you see? I'm not young, and Dougal wants children while he's still young enough to be a good father to them. He married me for that very reason. I'm spoilin' his hopes for them."

"Nonsense. My father was forty-five when I was born, and lived to be seventy."

"And you became a priest," she answered impulsively,

28

then realized how it must have sounded. "Oh, I'm sorry."

It took Father Liam a moment to regain his composure. "I believe I understand your concern, though I am surprised at your attitude toward the religious life."

"Oh, Father!" she moaned, ashamed to her core.

"Never mind that now. Put your worry over this behind you, Moira. If you let nagging tongues plague you, you'll never have any peace in this country. You mustn't listen. Do you hear?"

"Yes, Father," she answered meekly, too humbled by her recent brush with shame to give further argument.

He blessed her then, and she left the confessional. There was no feeling of relief, no lightening of her spirit. Three women stood in line before the confessional, waiting their turn. They looked at her as she passed, and then back at each other. Moira knew that nothing the priest had said had made any difference. They would go on talking about her, and she would go on listening. She hurried from the church, and ran home.

"Oh, Devil take this needle!" cried Moira, throwing her sewing to her lap. "I'm no use to you at all. I cannot, even so much as mend this poor worn shirt, it seems. Can I do nothing right?"

"Leave the shirt go," soothed Dougal, taking it from her hands. "'Tis the poor light at fault, and not yer stitchin', if I'm a judge."

"Nay, 'tis not the light, nor even my needle. 'Tis me," she insisted, not allowing him to put the blame elsewhere. "A great wife I've been to you this long while.

29

I cannot sew a proper stitch, it seems, nor cook a decent sort of meal, nor even give you the one thing you want the most. Don't be shaming me by denying it," she cried, her eyes ablaze with hot, angry tears. "I've seen how you've watched me for signs. Well, there's nothing to watch for! I cannot seem to do that right either." Throwing the sewing from her, she ran crying from the room.

Dougal sat, biting hard on the stem of his pipe. "Life's tricks," he muttered darkly.

After a bit, he got up, meaning to go in and comfort her. It means not a thing, he would tell her, although the words would leave a bitter taste in his mouth. He opened the door, a man swimming the low tide of life, and he was shocked to see her packing her few belongings in the old valise.

"What's this?" he cried, puffing full of indignation.

"'Tis plain to see I'm leaving," she answered, her eyes swelled and red from crying.

"Why?" he asked her, incredulous at her actions. "Haven't I been good to ye?"

"Good you've been and more. A blessing on you for your acts of charity. The trouble is, I'm one that likes to do her part and pay her way, and there, woe t' tell it, I'm not able. So, I'm clearing out to give you room to find one that is. I'll ask the priest for an annulment. That being turned down, you can always marry a Protestant."

A proper insult Dougal knew that was, and him the innocent one entirely.

"Hold on," he said to her. "Don't be runnin' out o' here like fleas jumpin' off a dead dog. I never wed ye for breedin' stock, ye know. 'Tis a wife I wanted, and that ye've been t' me. When I want t' increase m' stock around here, I'll buy a proper favored cow."

"Don't compare me with a cow!" She turned on him, eyes ablaze. "I know why you married me. I remember well what you said about children. 'Tis only to free you that I'm going, so don't be making it the harder." She brushed past him to the outer room.

It hit him then that she truly meant to go. The idea of living without her, now that he was so used to having her about, was like an unexpected death. Jumping up, he followed after her and called out, "Wait a bit, Moira, ye cannot go and leave me like this."

Her ears, it seemed, were deaf to him, and she kept to her packing. In short order, she had finished, and was set to go. "It's for the best, Dougal. The whole of the town's laughing at us. I cannot bear to see them do that to you." Her hand rested on the knob of the door.

"I don't want ye t' go," he said, his voice crumbling within him.

"Why not?" she asked, her heart a butterfly, a whisper away from flying down the road to light somewhere dark, alone, and die.

"I love ye," said he, the words sounding to her like Christmas angels. "I never knew it meself, till now, but now I know it sure. I don't care about the babies. It matters not t' me." He heard the echo of the very words he had meant to say to her before, but now, it was so changed. He meant them, every one. "Never leave me, Moira mine. I'll love no one but you in all this weary world."

"O' my great, lovely man," she cried, tears streaming down her face. "How ever can I leave you now? I've loved you like a schoolgirl since the day you brought me here. My heart has grown to you more with every passing night. Now, the partin' from you would pull it from me sure. Now then, you say you love me. I feel I'm home at last."

They fell into each other's arms, and that night made love with special tenderness. They whispered lovers' phrases like babies trying out new words. They were man and wife at last, as God had meant them to be. And on this night, Brendan Michael O'Shay started his long journey into the world.

Chapter Four

Bearing a child is young woman's work. Moira was no longer young. For her, the act of bringing life forth was costlier in what it demanded from her than for most women. Many times during the course of her labor, she despaired of ever bringing her child to light, so agonizing was it. Yet, if nothing else, Moira was a courageous woman, and in the end, the mother's cry came forth like a herald to the new awakening life. A cry of glory it was.

It was a son she bore. She heard him crying aloud his presence on this earth. Then, bundled, he was placed beside her, tiny hands and feet flailing the air in wild and frantic seeking. She touched her finger to his tiny hand, and it was captured by this, her son, captured as was her heart. The frantic searching ended, for she helped him to find that which he had sought. They were content then, both of them, and in their peace, drifted off to sleep.

"A brave woman you have," said the tired old doctor.

"That I know well," Dougal replied, hearing again in his memory the muffled cries that had gone on all day and half the night. To hear such piteous cries and not know how to help her, that had been the cruelest thing. She had sounded so tormented. Guilt overwhelmed him. Was this the blessing of love?

He had prayed for her, as he had never prayed for himself, as he had never prayed for anyone. It was all a man could do—pray, worry, and listen to the anguished cries. He would gladly have run from the sound of those cries, but there was Moira's face upon the pillow, Moira's eyes looking to him for help, Moira's voice calling to him for all eternity. A man could never run from that. He had stayed beside her, bathing her forehead with cool water, holding her up so that she might breathe between the pains, and whispering words of love to her.

"It's always harder on them when they begin at her age," continued Doctor Clancy to the daydreaming man. "A good-sized child she's had. That being God's blessing for the baby, but little comfort to the poor woman who must bear him. A healthy, strong son you have, it would seem. God be thanked," said the man.

He readied his belongings to take his leave of them. He had been called out to the O'Shays in the early afternoon. Now the sun was brightening out the new day. Doctor Clancy was sixty-five that year, and felt every day of it weighing him down that morning. Why was it, he wondered, a woman could never bear a child at a reasonable hour of the day? It was always four in the morning, or just as the sun came rising to the sky.

He looked forward now to a good strong cup of tea, something hot inside his stomach, and hours of undisturbed sleep. From experience, however, he knew the most he could hope for was the tea, and maybe a bite to eat, before the next crisis called him out again. In a village the size of this one, with only one doctor, it was always the same. I'm getting too old for this, he thought, stopping at the door.

"See that she gets all the rest she can, man. I don't much like how weakened she is," he said to Dougal.

"I'll do that, Doctor, and thankful I am to ye for all ye've done this night."

"'Tis your wife that deserves the credit, I'd say. Go in and see to her now. Go on with you."

Dougal waited until the horse and trap had pulled away, then tiptoed back into the bedroom. Moira lay so still among the folds of white bedding. Her face was nearly the color of the linen. How much she had given him, this woman. How much she had given them both.

He lifted the sleeping child from it's mother's arms and lay it down upon the coverlet resting in the cradle. He had made the cradle as a gift for Moira more than a month ago. It had lain empty and cold-looking that small while. Now it was alive, with blankets kicking and one small fist swinging in the air. A tiny face looked up at him, trying gamely to stuff the whole of his other fist into his mouth.

What was a man supposed to feel, he wondered, in this quiet moment of seeing his firstborn? Many of the lads he'd known had seemed to take it as a common thing. "Another mouth t' feed," they'd say. For Dougal, it could never be so easy a thing, being a father. He was a future, this squirming little son of his, a reason for having lived. It was an awesome thing.

He knelt beside the cradle, speaking softly to the child. "Hungry are ye, little man? That hand will have t' do ye for a bit, for yer mother's that worn out and gone with sleep. Ye made a fine lot of trouble comin' here. I wonder, was it that hard for ye too? Poor boyo."

He touched the little fist, swinging to and fro, and Brendan's small hand closed around his father's finger. It was the softest touch, that innocent baby's. It was a helpless little soul, needing him. It moved him as nothing in his life had ever done.

"Ye've a strong grip, m' lad. The next thing ye know, ye'll be learnin' t' box," he joked, overwhelmed by the raw emotion he felt.

"Bring him here to me, Dougal," Moira called from the bed. "I'll not have you making a prizefighter of him before even he's weaned."

"I didn't mean t' wake ye," he said, feeling foolish now that his wife had caught him talking so to the child. "I was just gettin' introduced to himself." He lifted Brendan up like the finest china, and lay him down beside his mother.

Moira held him close, nestling him within the crook of her arm. Men's arms were made, it seemed to her, for hard work, strong and muscled, but a woman's arms were made to hold a child, soft and yielding.

"Hello, my little Brendan, angels guard you forever," said the mother, giving a kiss to her child. "Are you hungry then?" She unbuttoned her gown and brought the child up closer to her to nurse. Rubbing and rubbing, he searched her breast until he found its hold.

Dougal watched this small event, embarrassed and thrilled at the same time. Moira smiled up at him, and there was gold in that smile, filling the room to overflowing.

"Thank ye for my son," Dougal stammered, the words choking in his throat, knowing they could never tell the way he felt. His chest felt ready to burst with joy. Long he sat beside them and filled his heart with watching. Like an empty vessel, the love from them flowed into him and made him strong.

Later, when Moira slept, he went to the outer room and reached under the old oak dresser for the bottle of fine whiskey left to him by his father. He had never been much of a man to drink, but this day deserved a toast. He poured himself out a generous glass, lifted it to the air, and said, "To Brendan Michael O'Shay, my son and heir." He drank the long draught, and contentment flowed through him like the warmth of the whiskey coursing its way.

Chapter Five

"Have a caution, my Brendan," called Moira from the doorway of the house. Her arms were floured up to the elbow from turning out the bread. "Those hens will nip you if you plague them so."

One hand reaching out for a hen's tail feathers, Brendan toddled after them as fast as he was able, encumbered as he was by the long, dainty dress he wore. He'd grown to be a beautiful child, with the look of Ireland in his rosy cheeks and golden curls.

"Look now, Brendan," said Moira, scooping him up into the folds of her apron. He lay there happily, like a wiggly sack of flour, as she hugged him to her. She had never gotten used to having the child, and each new day was full of wonder at his antics.

"Do you see your da comin' cross the field?"

"Pony, pony," cried the boy, pointing out his favorite of all the animals on the farm.

They were gray and brown, the ponies, and sturdily built. Dougal used them for the plowing, but to Brendan, they were his own special toy. Often, after long hours in the field, Dougal put them to carrying Brendan about the cottage land before they earned their night's rest and reward. Nothing delighted the child so much as sitting astride one of the small, hairy beasts and calling out, "Hie, Hie!"

It was understandably a great disappointment to him then when he saw his father head the animals directly into the barn. He set up a howl which scattered the startled chickens back to the hen house.

"Hush now, ye wild pagan," said Dougal, catching him up in his rough, worn hands. "Can ye not see it's threatenin' rain? Yer ponies would not thank ye for a bath, I'm thinkin'. Climb up on me back if ye must have it, and I'll give ye a quick pony ride meself."

This mollified the child, and soon he was laughing and shrieking in mock fright as his da galloped across the cottage green. Moira, watching from the window, stood wondering at the energy of the man. After so long a day in the field, he still had time and strength left for the boy. Seeing the big grin he wore, she knew it was energy born of love at being with the child.

The first big drops of rain began to pelt the ground, and the two riders dashed inside just before the full force of it was on them. "More pony. More pony," Brendan began.

"That's enough galloping on this steed, my lad," his mother answered. "He looks near ready for the knackerman's hammer. Your dinner's ready to take up, besides."

Dougal stood before the window, staring hard at the glowering clouds building up outside. Quiet these country storms could be, he knew, but fierce in the destruction they could carry. Great claps of thunder crashed overhead, and lightning played against the

39

evening sky, a warrior's dance to the gods of old. He stood so for a long time, watching the rain turn to hard pellets of hailstones. Watching too his field, where the tender young stalks, barely standing out from the ground, were beaten down and broken against the merciless storm. All the work of a season was being ravaged by one night's hellish weather.

"How bad is it, then?" asked Moira, slipping up beside him.

"Be glad we have the cattle," he said. "If this keeps up as now, we'll lose the heavy portion of the crop. The pratties, even, will rot in the field, so sodden it is. God's pity on those with no more than that this night. It's comin' down ruin. Ruin."

"Come away, lad," she told him. "It's no good watching it. It'll take the heart from you."

The candles were lit long before the hour Moira usually brought them out, for it was so dark without. They sat down to their supper, and with each mouthful, they heard the beating down of all the life-sustaining plants they had nurtured so carefully. Each mouthful of food brought thoughts of the hunger which almost certainly would come.

The hail continued throughout the night, and heavy rain into the following evening. When at last the silent sound of sunshine brought a respite to the new day, Dougal was out the door to the fields to see what might be done. Moira, bundling Brendan in a shawl, ran after him, ankle deep in the mud. They went to the heart of the field. The wreckage lay about their feet, green shoots lying broken in the mud as far as they could see. The work of the season was wasted, and the profit for the next season's crop gone too. All the struggle and back-breaking toil of those long months of labor—so useless now. It lay heavily on Dougal's shoulders, pulling his spirit down into the muck with the poor broken plants. It was not only his crop, he knew, but the crops of nearly every farm in the valley.

"It's starvation comin' for the valley this winter," he prophesied, "that and maybe worse." His voice was a mirror of his mood. "How will we make it?" he cried, despair taking him. He looked at Moira, and his eyes came to rest on his son, sheltered in the nook of her shawl. God help us, he thought. I canna' think of me child sick and starvin'. I've got t' see m' family through this. Somehow.

"There's still the cattle, remember," Moira said softly. The words were a spark of hope to see him through the dark.

"Aye," he answered, pulling back from dim despair, "the cattle will save us." His words were a fervent prayer. Then seeing the fear in Moira's eyes, he took her hand and kissed it. "The cattle will save us, sure."

Joy is short and sweet, but despair is long and enduring. That is how the days went by after the rains brought their ruin, long and full of despair, with people trying their best to endure them.

The time of harvest passed unnoted by the crops rotting in the fields. The pratties—potatoes—lying beneath the soggy mess turned spotty and sick. They were fit for neither man nor beast. A desperate farmer here and there tried to feed them to his stock, only to have the beasts sicken on them. They were useless for seed eyes for a new season's planting, out of fear that the new crop would also be blighted.

A few farms scattered across the valley were spared the blight, and they that were hid the fact well, knowing the hunger that was already on the people. If a man had any provender, he hid it well and talked poor.

It was hard for families to believe a crop like potatoes could spoil and sicken. Every farmer in the valley depended on them in one way or another. For most, it was all that got them through each year. Some had pigs and chickens. A few had cattle.

Like the others, Dougal had turned his thoughts to what might pull him through the long winter and spring. For him, it was the cattle. He and Moira had tramped the ground, gathering up all the fit grain they could glean. They would use this for themselves through the winter, for the grass was plentiful to nurture the cattle. The rain had brought a wealth of verdant pasture to the sloping hills. His mother had always said, "It is a bad wind indeed that does not blow some good." In this case, it was so.

They had milk from the cows, and eggs from the chickens. A hen once in a while would see them for fresh meat. They resolved not to butcher the cattle, for with them lay their hope of survival. Many of the heifers would calve in early spring. Those calves could be sold for seed money. What little cash was left must see them through to the first harvest.

With all of these concerns, Moira had another worry. She was again carrying a child, and this she kept to herself. Their meals were lean enough, with the finest piece always going to Brendan. She and Dougal were misers to themselves, eating only enough to get by. If Dougal were to learn of the child to come, she knew he would cut his portion by half to see her fit and strong. It would be known to him soon enough, she knew, but every day she kept it from him gave him the gift of it. So she held the secret within her, and said nothing.

Living meagerly as they were, they were still far better off than many of their neighbors. Bordering either side of their land were small farms with big families to feed. Padraic O'Reilly had seven children, and his wife was carrying the eighth. Kevin Kennerly was father to eight, although one had gone to America. These men were potato farmers, solely. The hunger of the winter loomed darker over them by the day. The pinched faces of their children gave mute testimony to the fare at home.

Dougal found that he had to guard the chickens of his coop. At sunset, he and Moira gathered the hens into the cottage and penned them in the kitchen, in spite of his earlier resolution against such a practice. They were a great nuisance too, but there was nothing else to be done for it, if they did not want them secreted away during the night. A hungry man must feed his family somehow, Dougal knew.

Little Brendan had fresh eggs for his dinner, and good cow's milk to wash it down. Moira was still able to make soda bread and good, sweet butter. Once every two weeks, she killed a fryer, and so carefully parceled out the meat from it, it would last them until the next. It always proved a good soup pot.

Moira kept the secret of her child well into the fifth month of her pregnancy. Dougal was too concerned with daily getting by to guess. Already she had felt the first stirrings of life within her.

An hour past supper one evening, the eldest of the O'Reilly children came knocking softly on the door. Just sixteen, Ellen was the daughter of Padraic and Kara

O'Reilly. It was plain from the look on her face that something was wrong at home.

"I've come t' ask yer help, Mrs. O'Shay," she began. "'Tis for me mother, who lies near to death at home. Her time is on her, the eighth she's brought into the world, only this one will not be born, it seems. My father asks for ye t' help her if ye will."

"Whista then, won't she be wantin' Doctor Clancy, child? I've borne but one bairn, and was no fit witness to that."

"We canna' have the doctor, Missus. We've no extra to spend on doctors now. Please, ma'am," she said. "She was that bad when I left her. We waited till the last, so as not t' be wastin' yer time."

The look in Ellen's eyes was grim. It was plain she feared returning home, feared seeing her mother in such pain.

"I'm ready to go with you, Ellen, but I'll need you here to watch my Brendan. You know what fathers are," she added aside, giving a low-opinioned look in Dougal's direction.

At this reproach, he sat up smartly, wondering what great crime he'd done to be slandered so. "Here now," he rebuked them. His pride stung, he settled in to seethe.

Ellen, in contrast, visibly broke out in relief. She loved her mother fiercely, but the ordeal of watching her anguish, and hearing her fearsome cries, brought the fast-approaching years of her own motherhood and childbearing years too close to her tender spirit.

Moira slipped out into the night with a prayer on her lips for Kara O'Reilly. She asked for an easy childbearing, for she knew her skills at midwifery were limited indeed. It was a long walk to the O'Reilly farm, and she was tired from hurrying. She felt her own infant kicking vigorously in protest. She knocked softly on the door, not wishing to disturb the quiet of the night.

The hard, tormented face of Padraic O'Reilly met her at the door. "Come in quick," he told her, "before the chill air sweeps in the more." The look of fear was on him. "God's blessing on ye for coming to us this night, Missus."

He fumbled with the latch of the door, and Moira looked around her and saw the faces of the six remaining O'Reilly children. They seemed like little urchins, thin and hungry all. Their eyes were big with fear for their mother, and looked all the more pitiful in their gaunt little faces. The mother's heart in Moira was moved to tears for them. How would it be, she wondered, if her own little Brendan were starving, or that unborn child of hers, as these poor children surely were?

A ragged scream came from the bedroom, abruptly breaking the mood. Moira gasped in spite of herself, and little Mary Elizabeth, the youngest, began to cry again, holding her hands over her ears. Moira had expected some cries and moans—she had made some herself when bearing Brendan—but this high-pitched shriek was unnatural.

"My God, man! How long's she been like this?" she asked, the question itself a horror.

"'Twas yesterday mornin' the pains took on in earnest. This afternoon she took worse, like this," he told her. "At first we thought it was a good sign, the more quickly to be over for her. But it has gone on so long now . . ." His voice began to break. "God! I fear she'll die of this I gave her."

"Hush, Padraic, you mustn't say that. You must call

on Doctor Clancy for this. She's gone bad sure. I never heard anything like that in all my life."

"I canna," he answered with what little pride was left to him. His face had gone hard and stony. "Clancy's gone, retired or sick, or somewhat else. A new doctor there is to the village now, and a meaner man never drew breath. His name's Mallon, and he don't treat the poor. He knows we canna pay, with the stinking blight and all. I even offered him the farm, but he wouldna' listen. Said t' get a woman for her. There's but you and I t' help her, Missus. Ye've got t' help us. I don't know what else t' do." The man was begging her, tears standing pools in his eyes.

Another nerve-jarring shriek rent the room and set Moira into action. "I will need hot water and clean toweling, a sharp knife, twine, soap. Hurry now."

Kara O'Reilly's room was dark, with only the light of three small candles illuminating the wreck of a woman lying twisted in the bed. At first glance, Moira wondered if perhaps Kara had already died, for she was so unnaturally still. Then softly, like the ruffle of a butterfly, Kara's eyes fluttered and opened.

"Who's there?" a voice crackled with the long hours of suffering whispered.

"'Tis Moira O'Shay, Kara, come to help you."

"There'll be no more need t' help me soon, Moira. Dying I am, and this poor unborn babe with me. Only thirty-five am I, and all me poor starving bairns to leave motherless."

Moira stared in disbelief. The woman before her looked in her late forties. "I'll not listen to that sort of talk, Kara. I am strong-willed and stubborn, and not

46

ready t' give up on you yet. Never could I look those children in the eye if I did."

With acute embarrassment, Moira lifted the hem of Kara's shift and put her fingers within the woman to check the progress of the child. Kara made no protest, in too much pain to care. She could feel the stretched opening of the birth canal, and the flesh of Kara's baby wedged tight against it. It was soft, like a hip or stomach, and not the hard feel of a skull.

"It's layin' wrong, Kara, stretched across, I believe. If I could turn it straight, I believe it could be born. I mean to try, else no fight of yours will be to any avail. Will you let me try?" She waited for the answer, wanting yes—not wanting yes—afraid, unsure, but ready.

"Aye," Kara answered. "God help us both."

With the next pain, Kara held back from pushing, biting her knuckles until they bled. Moira reached in and grasped the infant in four fingers, pushing hard to the side. Twice more, at the next contraction, she reached in and pushed, until she felt it move. Kara screamed again and again, and Moira kept saying Hail Marys loudly, to drown out the awful sounds. The body slipped from her fingers' touch, and she forced her hand deeper up the canal, grasping at last what seemed to be an arm or leg. Two fingers gripped the appendage and pulled. The little body shifted, and a loud sucking sound followed. The opening was so tight now, Moira's fingers could not move. She pulled them free, and felt as they drew away the unmistakable form of a chin and head.

"It's turned. Now push hard, Kara, and you'll have your child at last," she said, hope bringing heart to her voice.

"I've no fight left in me. I canna'. I canna'," cried Kara O'Reilly, bereft of strength and exhausted to the soul.

"Hold to me now," said Moira, refusing to let Kara quit when they had come so far. "Look at me! Listen to what I'm saying!" she ordered. "Now, Kara! Now, and you'll have it over. Try! Try for those children who need you. Now! Good. Now again! Again!"

The mother cried out long and low, her torment over. The child slipped from her body, and lay squalling on the sheet. It wailed so furiously, Moira laughed and cried, uncertain of which she felt she needed more.

"It's another son, Kara, and he seems fine and strong. Can you hear him cryin' out at all this madness? He's angry, he is, over this long wait he's had to be born."

Kara lay quiet and still, in that excellence which is release from pain. "I hear him, Moira, but I can scarce believe he is alive. That is thanks to you for that," she said. "Both of our lives we owe you."

Moira cleaned his mother's blood from the infant. It squalled in anger at the touch of the cloth.

"Give him to me, Moira. Let me see this child who nearly cost me my life. I pray God he may be the last. Now there," she sighed, taking the wriggly body into her arms, learning the look of him with her eyes and the touch of her hand. "What a beauty you are."

Remembering her manners, she turned again to Moira. "You've done more than I thought possible tonight, more than I can ever thank you enough for. What can a poor woman give you, things bein' what they are? God have mercy on us all."

"You mustn't fret yourself, Kara, my friend. We all have all we can do to get through this winter. There's no shame in that. Things being as they are, you can soon be returning tonight's favor by standing beside me, four months hence, and seeing my child into the world," Moira answered with a smile. "You're the first to know of it."

Kara nodded, knowing now she could repay this night's help in like kindness. "That I will, girl, and gladly. You have a friend in me and mine, from this hour on."

Padraic stood up from his place before the fire when Moira came out of the room. He did not turn around to face her, but stared into the flames.

"You have a new son, Padraic."

"Aye. I heard him," he answered stiffly. "And me wife? Is she . . . ?"

"Turn round man and go to see her for yourself. Kara is well. You have not lost her."

A sound of choking came from the man, and the hard, straight shoulders shook with sobs. "I wanted t' run out and kill meself, listenin' to her screams like that. I thought . . ."

"You were wrong to think that. What would have become of your bairns with no parent between them and starvation? You're worn out with worry, Padraic, that I can see well enough."

"I'll never touch her again. Never will I bring her to this night again, by God! I'll castrate meself before I'll ever do this to her again."

"Padraic, you're frightening the children with your ravings. It would be as well if you kept your word on this, as you have sworn," she added softly, beyond the hearing of the children. "I believe another child will kill her."

"Aye, I will," he swore, but Moira knew, even at that moment, that it was the passion of the moment which he swore by, and that when the fear was off him, some months hence, he would seek and expect his wife's love in bed again, just as before.

"Don't look so scared, chicks," she told the children, "your mother's fine."

She hurried to her own home then, and told Ellen the glad news. She sent the girl on her way with a smile on her lips and a lilt in her heart. That same night, she told Dougal of their child to come, but kept the horror of the night's events to herself. She protected him from the fear which now assailed her. It was a heavy burden, the weight of it oppressing her and pulling away at her thin reserve of courage. The fear grew like a parasite within her, and all but consumed the strong woman she was.

The day after Kara's child was born—Brian Andrew, he was named—Dougal took one of the milk cows and gave the use of it to the O'Reillys. The cow needed only the good grass of Ireland to fatten on, and of that there was plenty.

"I only hope they don't butcher it," he remarked to Moira, but she scarcely listened, for she could not have rested a moment remembering the hunger on the faces of the O'Reilly children had they not done something to help.

The winter drew long and bitter through the valley. Families butchered and ate all the stock they possessed, being brought to this extreme act by starvation. Few vegetables survived the blight, and many were forced to subsist on turnips and parsnips, which they had formerly fed to their pigs. By early spring, most families had depleted all the extra provender they owned. A few sound potatoes had not been touched by the black hand of blight. These, saved through the hunger of winter, were now cut into small seed eyes and carefully planted. Watched over like jewels, they were watered and tended by men whose hearts pleaded with them to grow healthy and feed their starving children. The white flowers of these precious plants bloomed in gay contrast over the fields, giving hope to all who saw them. Surely now, it was thought, the worst was over and families could get back to the business of living.

Dougal and Moira came through the winter well enough. Two calves were dropped, a bull and a heifer, both strong and healthy. One more calf was due soon. When all the calves had fattened, Dougal planned to sell them. With this precious bit of real money he would buy the grain for planting.

Into this bit of hope and renewal of their world came James Connor O'Shay. It was an easy birth, as women tell it. Moira, feeling the burden of fear lifted from her at last, rejoiced all the more at her robust little son. James Connor he was named, after Moira's father, but Jamie he would always be.

Dougal, having a farm of his own, a wife, two strong sons, three milk cows, two calves, two bulls, a scattering of chickens, and not an extra shilling to his name, felt the wealthiest man alive. Life seemed good again.

Chapter Six

The famine which had swept the valley made beggars and thieves of honest, honorable men. Their hungry families called to them in pitiful voices. Only a heart cut of stone could have borne so much suffering and not taken every means necessary to remedy it. Still, begging was looked upon with intolerance, and stealing was severely punished. As often as not, a man caught stealing in order to feed his starving family was sent away to prison, leaving his dependents in far worse straits.

The old ones, without a son or daughter to shelter them, died of hunger in their cottages, quietly as the passing of a cloud. Their fierce pride often kept them from admitting the desperate conditions in which they lived. One day they would be standing at the fence, nodding in gossip with their neighbors, and the next, they would disappear into their cottage, to await death with dignity.

Infants born into a family already overburdened with life to support starved—a lingering death. Nursed by mothers who had no milk to give them, being so emaciated themselves, the little beings clung fiercely to life as long as they were able, breaking the hearts of all who bore witness to their struggle. In the end, they would waste away, until as skeletons they would die, cradled in their mothers' arms. Women who had borne hunger and suffering with such endurance broke under the strain of the loss of these children. Insanity was added to all the other afflictions.

Men were murdered for the theft of a chicken or a cow. Mothers smothered their own children rather than see them slowly starve. Some went to their death in violence and rage, and some slipped away silently, in suicide.

Families were pushed to extremes. Older sons worked their passage to emigrate to other countries, hoping to find the means to gain back their hold on life. Their anguished farewells to fathers and mothers, whom in most cases they would never see again, broke the spirits of the families. It was a sorrow many a parent had to bear. It was a black time, full of the desolation of the human spirit.

It was all the more wondrous then when autumn brought its clean bounty to the starving land. Turnips and parsnips, carrots, squash, and new potatoes, miraculous in their purity, blessed the land. Empty bellies could now be filled with the life-giving stuff. The baneful time had passed. Now was the time of harvest, and of the renewal of life.

On the O'Shay farm, the crops yielded up their plenty, the cattle fattened, letting down their rich, wholesome milk, and the two O'Shay children grew strong and healthy. Even Jasmine the cow joined in the spirit of abundance by dropping two calves. One was a bull calf, destined for fresh meat, and the other was a heifer, for the continuance of life.

Thanks be to God, we have come through, was the constant thought in Dougal's mind. He went about the work of his day whistling in good cheer, a man so pleased with life, the joy of it seemed to radiate from him. Like the steam rising from a teakettle, his cheery whistling could not be restrained. A small peat fire welcomed him home at the end of each day. It was his own fire, in his own house, spotlessly clean, with his own wife and sons to people it. Life, he thought, was grand.

At the end of one particular day, Moira had the pull-down table laden with good things to eat. The smell of new bread, hot from the baking, filled the room and made his stomach grab with pangs of hunger for it. Hanging his cap on the peg, he called out, "Woman mine, where is the king for this feast? Or is it that I mistook the path to me own cottage and lost in fairyland am I?"

Moira came around the corner then, Jamie resting on her hip. A stray lock of hair fell curling over one eye, making a picture lovely and sweet. His heart swelled with love at the sight of them.

"There now, Jamie my love. Didn't I tell you your da would be home soon? There he is now, poor mannie, calling on the little people to sit supper at our table this night. Fie on you, Dougal," she teased. "Would you have them sharing table knives with your own sons? Go on, lad, behave yourself now. Wash up, then we'll sit supper while it's still hot."

Fresh minted carrots, potatoes in their soft, buttery jackets, new baked bread, and cabbage with pork bits to flavor it graced the table. The swirling steam of hot, sweet tea rose up from their mugs, flavoring the very air. Little Brendan could not get enough of the still warm bread, and loaded it with sweet butter and wild strawberry jam. The mixture dripped between his fingers and ran down his chin.

Moira finished setting out the tea, and sitting down at last, pulled the big, white envelope from her apron pocket and brushed the clinging flour from it. "This wonder came today," she said, and handed it to Dougal.

Turning it over and over, he tried to guess the contents. In the corner were the names: Anderson, Polli, and Gregor, Counselors at Law. What mischief can this be now? he wondered. He took special care opening the seal, and took sheet after sheet of lettering out. It began:

Mrs. Moira O'Shay (nee Monahan):

This is to inform you of the passing of your aunt, Mrs. Rebba Cleary, formerly of Twenty-one Dobbin Lane. We are saddened to inform you that Mrs. Cleary left this life on August third of this year. The physician at hand attributed her death to a failure of the heart.

Mrs. Cleary had engaged our firm two months prior to her death to draw up her will, bestowing the entirety of her estate on Mrs. Moira O'Shay. This change in her will was the result of the untimely death of Mrs. Cleary's son, William, the original heir to the estate, due to an influenza epidemic in America, in the spring of this year.

Mrs. Cleary wished the entirety of her estate to go to her only living relative, Mrs. Moira O'Shay.

55

Our firm is at your disposal to discuss the terms of the will, and provide you with the titles, deeds, and monies of the estate.

Yours sincerely,
David Polli
Counselor at Law

"Blessed saints and angels," breathed Dougal, standing up to better take the weight of the news. "We're goin' to be rich, m' boyos," he shouted. He lifted Brendan up and swung him around and around, laughing and dancing with him around the room. "Come here to me, Jamie lad, and dance a jig with your da this fine day. Yer Aunt Rebba had some good in her at the end after all. Who'd of believed it?" he cried, laughing and swinging Jamie around until on the twirl, his eye caught sight of Moira, sitting at the table still, turning the great white pages slowly and carefully.

"Can ye believe it, Moira mine?"

"Aye. I believe it all too well, Dougal. They're gone, the both of them. Aunt Rebba was my own mother's sister. She was old, and crotchety, but she took me in when my mother died."

Dougal bit his tongue to keep from saying, "Aye, she took ye in as a hired girl, and that's the whole of it." One look at Moira's eyes made him solemnly decide to keep his peace.

"William was my cousin," she said. "I played with him as a child. They were all the family I had left to me in this world, and now they're gone."

This was too much for Dougal to swallow. "Ye're missin' the forest for the trees, love. Here, in this house, are all yer family. Ye have two sons, and a husband who loves ye. Ye'll never be alone in the world while we're about."

She stood up then, reached for her shawl on the peg, and swept it around her.

"Where are ye off to, without even a bite of this fine dinner?" he asked her, wondering at the odd way she had taken the news.

"I'll be at church, praying for the souls of my aunt and cousin. Being their only relative, I owe them that."

"Ye're goin' then, I see, and I'll not stay ye. Sure, they're both blessed saints in heaven by now, though a bit of prayin' was never known to hurt in guidin' one's footsteps up the right path."

He watched her go down the road, until she turned off at the crossing, then swooped up his boys, and began again to dance and sing. "Who'd of believed it, lads? That old crow wasn't quite so black after all." The boys laughed and shouted with their father, although not knowing why. He was happy, and that was enough for them.

Then, just as suddenly as he'd begun, he stopped. It seemed too much, overwhelming for a man to be blessed with the love of a good woman, two fine sons, a good plot of farm land, cattle and crops, and then a wealth of money to crown it all. In the midst of his glad singing, tears of joy overcame him. They coursed down his face as he hugged his sons close to him.

"Are you cryin', Da?" Brendan asked, confused.

"Cryin'! Of course not." He set his sons down.

Taking a great gulp of air, as if to still the wild beating of his heart, he stood up. "Lord, 'tis Dougal O'Shay speakin', wantin' to thank ye for all the bounty ye've brought m' way, and askin' yer pardon for all the mean and low things I said about ye in years past. 'Tis marryin' Moira that turned m' life around, sure, and her believin' so strong in ye that's brought about all the goodness ye've shown me. For her then, Lord, I'm thankin' ye, for givin' me Moira."

He wiped his face on his sleeve then, and settled again at the head of the table. "And now, boyos," he said, "let's do justice to yer mother's fine meal." He ate the food, and his heart sang the lovely name—Moira.

Moira began her third pregnancy in the big house on Dobbin Lane. True to her word, she had indeed begun to fill their home with children. It was a wonder to her, and a delight. When carrying the boys, she had been unreservedly well, feeling young and strong, but this time, her pregnancy was harder to bear. She was nearly always uncomfortable. It seemed to her that there was something wrong, with either the child or with her.

The house itself was like an added weight to her. Dougal had insisted that the family move up from the farm and occupy the larger house in town. He thought it would be easier for her there, without all the work of the farm. He leased their farm to a family named Leed.

Try as she might, Moira could not seem to feel at home in her aunt's house. It would always be her aunt's house to her. It held too many unpleasant memories for her, of servitude and loneliness. The cottage where her sons had been born was her only home. It called to her, in her heart's yearning, and beckoned her back. Her first night as Dougal's wife had been there, and it was home to her as

58

no other place would ever be. In the big house on Dobbin Lane, she felt the shackles of the past. She had always been an unwelcome servant there. Then, and now, it was so. She was unwelcome to the very walls. She told herself the feeling would pass, but after six months in the house, it seemed all the more real. Her longing for her little cottage home was all the more intense.

Dougal purchased an interest in a local textile mill with part of the Cleary legacy. He was gone a large part of every day, looking out for their interests in it. Moira was left alone to cope with the unfriendly neighbors of their city home. Most of them looked down their noses at the O'Shays. Moira and the children spent many lonely days remembering their cottage home. For Brendan, it was the memory of chasing the squawking chickens about the cottage green. Most of all, he missed riding the gray and white pony. Jamie, hearing about all the things Brendan missed, pouted, and thought he missed them too, even though he had been too small to remember.

It was such a big house, and hard for Moira to keep up alone, notwithstanding the way the pregnancy was making her feel. It was as though the child, having been conceived in this house, was of this house, and not of her, fighting against her always. It was a superstitious thought, she knew, and she kept it to herself. Still, she believed, women carrying life within them are more attuned to the inner voice which speaks to them.

Dougal pushed her hard to hire a girl to help with the cooking and the cleaning, now that they had the Cleary money, but Moira fought it. "Another woman under my roof, cleaning my house, cooking the meals my family eats? Never. That far out to pasture I'll not be pushed." Since she had nothing outside the house to occupy her, the busy work became important to her as a means to pass the long hours of the day.

A new, young doctor, Adam Wescott, had examined her when it became obvious that her pregnancy was not proceeding as it should. He prescribed bed rest and little strain. Dougal took him at his word. He hovered over Moira when he was home, and wouldn't allow her to carry as much as the tea tray. At such times, Moira felt suffocated by the restrictions put upon her.

The unnatural pregnancy was not only hard for Moira, but for Dougal too. Moira, normally a warm and tender lover, now turned coldly away from him at night. She felt too ill to be loving. Oversensitive as well, she'd fly up at him in a rush of tears at the slightest wrong word. He soon learned it was better to keep away during the day and leave her alone, so he lingered in the pubs until nearly dark each night, long after he might have come home.

Determined to convince her to hire a girl for help, and being Irish and therefore a little crafty, he made up his mind to send a letter to his old friend and neighbor, Padraic O'Reilly, asking for the loan of his eldest daughter, Ellen, for the remainder of Moira's confinement. Ellen O'Reilly would be about eighteen now, he reasoned. Taking her out of her father's house would be a blessing for the O'Reillys: one child less to feed. Dougal intended to see that she took home a good bit in the way of wages, to help her family when she returned. Surely, he hoped, once Ellen's here, Moira will have to give in and let her help with the housework.

Thinking of that, he remembered the first time he had seen the O'Reilly girl. It had been on the occasion of her brother Brian's birth, with Moira the uneasy midwife. He

60

remembered how Ellen had stayed at the cottage and played games with Brendan. He recalled how childlike she'd seemed, rocking Brendan to sleep, like a little girl playing at being grown up.

"Well, Ellen," he said aloud, "I hope ye're grown up now."

Chapter Seven

For eighteen years, Ellen O'Reilly, eldest daughter of Kara and Padraic O'Reilly, lived in a four-room Irish cottage with seven brothers and sisters, several chickens, and an occasional piglet. Now that she was eighteen, it was thought to be time she moved out to a home of her own and made room for baby Brian, her mother's youngest. "I had you before I was sixteen," her mother often told her, in mild reproach at her unwillingness to marry and start a family of her own.

Like her brothers and sisters, Ellen had received no formal education, but she could read and write and figure, due to her lessons from the hedge schools of Ireland. These lessons were literally taught behind a hedge by some wandering scholar, at no cost to her family other than perhaps a meal now and then. The hedge schools, a good tradition, kept many an Irish child from illiteracy.

Ellen, at this prime of her youth, had the beauty so often found in the backcountry boglands. It was as though the Lord, having given them poverty as a trial, gave them beauty to sustain them and give them heart. Fair-skinned, like most Irish, Ellen had black, curling hair, as a striking contrast. Her body was as well rounded as a woman's, and her natural grace of carriage made her startlingly beautiful.

Had not the hand of fate intervened, Ellen would surely have married an eldest son from a family in her parish, settled down as her mother believed she should, and borne six or seven children by the time she was thirty. Her fragile beauty would have been bled from her in the early years, with the hard life of a cottage wife, and old age would have come rushing to her even as her last child was weaned.

That is not to say that the life of a cottage wife and mother was all bad. For the first few years, before the crowding came, it could be peaceful and beautiful. The little cottages could be lovely and sweet with their thatched roofs—providing it didn't rain too often, which it always did—and their stone walls—providing there were no gaping spaces in them for vermin to crawl through, which there always were.

On a good day, the sun would shine jewels on the lush, green grasslands. Pert little fairy flowers would bedeck the hills and valleys, so called because of their habit of closing up and dying as soon as they were picked; put there, it seemed, only to gladden the eye and lighten the step, and never to be removed from fairyland. The days were soft, with the mild Irish mist hiding any sharp glare and lending the whole scene an aura of timelessness.

The wonder of all this wealth of beauty would warm the heart of any true daughter of the old sod. And too, a young Irish husband in his prime could not be matched in all the world for handsomeness and rugged manliness.

The true glory of Ireland, however, lay in her children. Nowhere in the world was there such an abundance of such lovely and angelic faces as those seen daily in the cobbled streets and country lanes of Erin's emerald isle. Round, glowing, pixie faces, crowned with flaxen curls, soft as silky down; mischievous eyes, dancing with secret merriment, looking out on the world in innocence. Fiery red-haired Viking brothers stood firm astride the world, looking each man straight in the eye and hanging their heads to no one. Dark Druid lasses with gypsy eyes of mystery awakened dreams of elvish kings beneath the sleepy mountain. With these jewels, an Irish mother's crown was made. No richer crown was ever worn by any nation's queen.

After the first ten years, though, the cottage wife's life was very different. If, being average, she had borne a child every two years, she would have by then filled the little four-room cottage with five lively children under ten. Perhaps a loft or small room had been added to absorb the overflow. The care and feeding of a family of this size—not to mention caring for the livestock, making butter, baking bread, washing and ironing, and tending to the cottage garden—was enough labor to exhaust the hardiest of women.

Since she was a good Catholic, and bore in mind the Church's stand on submitting to her husband's rights, these would not be the last of her children. She would go on bearing children well into her forties. Eight or nine offspring were all too common. The general rule was, the later in your family's line you were born, the less likely your chance of survival. This applied to all but the last child, who was usually spoiled and cosseted by all. Often, it happened, the oldest child would raise the youngest.

Many an Irish cottage wife would end her days bringing the last of her children into the world. An old and beaten-down woman at forty-five, she simply could take no more.

This most certainly would have been Ellen O'Reilly's lot, as it had been her mother's before her, if fate had not intervened, but intervene it did, in the form of an invitation from Dougal and Moira O'Shay to work for them. This being gratefully accepted by her parents, the course of Ellen's life was irrevocably changed.

Driving for the first time into a large town, in pony and cart, was an exciting experience for a young woman, just off the farm. Ellen had been to a large village once with her father, but that was so long ago, it was hard for her to remember. Her brother Connor accompanied her now, and drove the cart.

Town was so different. Shops of every description brightened the wide thoroughfare. Lampposts stood at every corner to light the way at night. Cozy-looking pubs were snugged into quiet streets. The names of these were delights to be wondered at: The Cannon's Staff, The Boar and the Drake, The Unicorn's Horn.

Ellen saw women in stylish dresses browsing through the shops along the boulevard. Imagine, she thought, not a worry or a care in the world but for picking a new bonnet or a fine bolt of cloth. There were nursemaids pushing prams about in unhurried fashion, here and there. They strolled languidly, with no greater need for their time than taking the master's son out for a breath of air. It all looked so restful to Ellen's eye, another kind of place from what she'd known. Another kind of people too, she knew, and she felt herself grow small with the newness of it.

The most interesting part of all came when the town and all its shops dwindled out, and the majestic houses began. Since she was accustomed to a cottage of five rooms and a loft, it was an awesome thing to see, one after another, three- or even four-story mansions. The first they came to was English Tudor in its design, its exterior black and white. Massive beams joined cunningly, making a picture frame for roughly plastered expanses of white. A three-turreted chimney rose above the house, smoke curling to the heavens.

"Oh, the lawns and flowers," Ellen pointed out to Connor. Lining the walk before the houses were myriad-hued fairy primroses and lavender hedges, with roses of every description flanking the walls. In the side gardens, if she craned her neck, she could see yellow-headed trumpets of daffodils, purple crocuses, bunches of butter-colored freesias, tall spires of crimson snap-dragons, beds of marigolds with their thick sweep of color, and many more flowers the names of which eluded her. She thought the whole of it lovely and enchanting.

"Look, Connor!" she cried, as further down the way they came to houses of stone, aged and regal in their weathered grace. Homes of brick, with their muted tones ranging from soft pink to deep red, sturdy and massive-looking, demanded her attention to their presence. Like miniature castles, each seemed a realm of its own. More houses of wood followed, Victorian in design, to capture the mind's eye in endless fantasy. With elegant fretwork beneath the roofline, cutouts and clever patterning seemed to drape from every ledge. Windows of every shape—hexagon, oval, rectangle, or diamond—somehow fitted into the gay, madcap fashion that was Victorian, and pleased the eye. Stained glass fitted into doors and windows marked the houses like jewels glittering in the sun. Ellen was captivated by each one.

Connor pointed out a Georgian manor, square with no nonsense about it, save for the brightly painted door After it came one house after another, each a visual delight, until at last they came to 21 Dobbin Lane, the home of Dougal and Moira O'Shay.

It was a sensible house of brick, with aged beams joined as a V along the front. Its massive chimney bore the initial C for Cleary. Connor began to count the rooms that he could see from the street, and stopped at sixteen, not including attic and basement. It was a stately, reserved-looking house. To Ellen, it was a wonderland, ready to open up on strange delights and flights of fancy she had never imagined, but to Connor, it was a formal, unnerving place, a realm so far apart from the world he knew, his discomfort in it was acute. Stepping down from the cart, he handed down to Ellen the old valise, which was his sister's only baggage. A low whistle escaped his lips as he looked at the mansion before him.

Ellen's head turned this way and that, as she craned her neck to see it all. "Can ye believe it?" She inhaled deeply. "Me livin' in a place like that?"

"Ye'd not find me livin' there," Connor answered with a shrug. "The kind of folk lives in that place, I don't know nothin' about. They'd not be my sort, I'm thinkin'."

"Connor, ye're daft and backward. Come on then," she hurried him, and started up the walk.

"Nay, I'm off home now, Ellen. Ye can certain sure carry that little bit of naught t' the door yerself." He moved to climb back in the cart, anxious to be away.

"Hold on, little brother." She grabbed him by his shirt. "What if no one's at home? What am I t' do then? Sure, ye must see me to the door an' all, what would they think of us elsewise, just droppin' me off like a load of wood. They won't eat ye, ye know," she teased him, and then tugged him along with her to the door, knocking with ladylike gentleness.

"Coor, they've gone for sure," exclaimed Connor. "We've come all this way for nothin'. Well, let's be goin' now." He turned to walk away, but Ellen had not released his shirttail, and hung on, knocking loudly this time with her free hand. A moment later, the door opened and there stood Moira, Brendan, and Jamie. Ellen smiled, and waited to be welcomed. Connor stared hard at his battered, dusty shoes.

The surprised expression on Moira's face told Ellen she clearly hadn't expected them. For a moment, Moira simply stared at the two of them in confusion. This alarmed Connor so, it was all Ellen could do to hold onto his shirt and keep him from backing down the stairs.

Ellen spoke quickly. "Excuse me, ma'am, but it's Connor and Ellen O'Reilly, come to visit, as ye asked."

Recognition dawned on Moira then. "Ellen O'Reilly? Ellen O'Reilly! Oh, how you've grown, just look at you. You've come to town to visit us, you say? Well, come in. Come in. All by yourselves, are you? I'm that glad to see you."

They were ushered in ceremoniously. Connor, hanging back, whispered to Ellen, "She doesn't know. She wasn't expectin' us at all." Ellen shushed him.

"Dougal, come and see who's here," cried Moira. "It's the children of Kara O'Reilly, can you believe it?"

Dougal came then, and in a moment, explained away

68

the mystery of it all. Ellen was shown to her room, and Connor asked to supper, which he resolutely refused, making one lame excuse after another for why he had to leave at once. Ellen did not dispute him.

Free of it all, at last, and on his way home, he muttered, "Never could I have swallowed a bite in that grand house and not choke meself, m' mouth was that dry. Scared the swallow right out'a me. Nay, Calla, m' lovely," he spoke softly to the pony as she clop-clopped along. "Give me m' own hearth with a toasty fire, an' a bit of meat simmerin' in the old black pot. That's what I call home. Them mansions are for queer folk. Ye dare not even put yer feet up and take yer ease. 'Twould put a mark on the shiny, grand furniture. Give me our own settle by the fire, and the little low stool for me feet, and' I've more comfort than all their money can buy."

He was a farm boy, in heart, mind, and temperament. The city, with its glitter and its wealth, held no lure for him. "Hie up now, Calla, m' beauty. Give us the fast ride home."

Chapter Eight

The days after Ellen came blended one into another. Her role in the household became one of nursemaid, housekeeper, sometime cook, and most important of all, companion to Moira. The two of them filled the house with the sound of their ringing laughter. No class structure laid a boundary between them, for their friendship was that of sisters.

Moira's spirit, floundering, refreshed itself in the clear innocence of Ellen's naïveté. For Ellen, the excitement of the city and living in a great mansion was enough to lift the heavy yolk of poverty from her heart and set it singing.

Brendan and Jamie benefited by the arrangement as well. As a playmate, Ellen could not be matched. She played endless games of cowboy and Indians with them, swooping down on their hideouts with blood-chilling war whoops, before letting them capture her. She told them stories of the Indians in America, over the sea, embroidering every detail. These stories were the boys' special favorites, for Ellen always believed her own tales.

Brendan and Jamie had no trouble picturing the red men in heathen war paint, for they could see them clearly through Ellen's eyes. Both boys went to bed shivering just a little in the delightful horror of it all, grateful that Ireland was not a place where, as Ellen put it, "such godless creathurs lurk." They loved her, almost at once; and for her, the boys became like the brothers she had played with and cared for in her own home.

Everything, it seemed, was in perfect harmony—except for Dougal. For him, there was a battle waging within, and Ellen's presence only struck blow after blow against his moral scruples. From the moment he set eyes on her again, on the day of her arrival at the house on Dobbin Lane, he became a man obsessed by a great desire. She was not the Ellen of his memory. She was a child no more. Whenever they stood both together at once, Moira and Ellen, he saw the contrast between them—Moira, matronly and dowdy in her pregnancy, and Ellen, fresh, exciting, and beautiful in her youth. It made no difference that he knew the shameful sin his thoughts represented. He could not put thoughts of her from him. In the oddest moments of the day—while opening the mail, or listening to his banker, or worse, while making love to his wife—he would be flooded with thoughts of Ellen, and find himself drowning in the clear blue of her eyes. When this happened, more often than not, he was useless to business, banker, or wife.

It is a sin so heavy, he thought, I feel it pullin' me down to hell. Like the demon it was, he fought it. Battle after battle he waged, slaying the beast in him, only to have it rise up anew, an unquenchable demon, at a lilting laugh, a touch of her skin brushing against him if they passed each other, or the sight of her face, fresh and lovely in the morning. Hardest of all, it played about his mind in the night, keeping him from sleep, and laying torment on his soul.

Never in his life had Dougal been near to anyone as lovely as Ellen. As much as he loved Moira—and truly, he vowed to God night after night, he did love her—it had never been a love begun of beauty or passion. Passion had come as a yearning, needful thing between them. He had never been struck breathless at the pure golden sight of her, her arms outstretched, twirling, playing with the boys in the sun; nor had he ever been kept awake, dreaming of the way her shining hair dressed her face, the way the light was captured in her eyes, the soft rise of her breasts.

He loved Moira for her goodness, for her love of him, her need of him. He loved her for the children she had given him, and the life they had made together. But this feeling for Ellen was different, a need never before awakened in him. It was not a flame of love, as it had been with Moira, but an all-consuming blaze, and he was trapped within the flames. If Moira guessed how he felt, she gave him no sign. And so he hid it deep within him, a dark, unclean fire, burning away the heart in him, and singeing his very soul.

When did I change? Ellen stared into the mirror above the dresser. I came here as a girl, timid and full of silly fancies. Everything's so different now. All the colors in the prism are brighter, more urgent. Is it really the colors, she wondered, or have my eyes begun to see life more clearly? Every day I wake up with the sense of rushing. Hurry, dress. Hurry, see it all. Hurry, live all the

72

life you can.

Looking in the mirror, she saw a stranger, familiar but not known, a woman. The eyes, they look like mine, she thought, but hers are lit within with a passion shining through, like torches in the night. Hers know a hunger, and what they hunger for, the child I am still cannot say. But the woman knows, and she holds the knowledge secret, like a babe within her. It grows, this secret, nurtured with every stolen glance, every tempting smile, every coveted touch.

"How long have I loved Dougal?" the child asked the woman in the mirror. There, she thought, I've said it. Who would have thought such a simple truth could be the torment of a soul? "I must go to confession and lay it all before the priest," the child decided, but the image in the mirror knew the futility of that act, and passed it over as inconsequential. She in the mirror knew. A season unlooked for had changed her, and all the forces in nature drew her to its final bloom. The girl within the woman cried out in fear, in guilt, but the woman said, "Be still. It can be no other way."

Her mind played round its corners, drawing memories to its hold. What sort of look was that he gave me, when none could see but I? A pain, it fell between us, cutting through the masks we wear to the truthful core within, touching . . . touching. A mark it left, burned forever in the deepest part of me, plain for all the angels, spirits, God and Ghost to see.

Into this sin, I would gladly walk, blessing it and holding it dear. What am I then? A soul turned coldly from its light, drawn on like emerald moths to flame, to singe my wings upon the pyre of love and like the lovely moth, fly boldly to the heart of it?

73

Realizing the coldly stated truth, she knew she could never go back to that place of her childhood, to the days of a child with her father and mother. She was a child no more. Like a sword, this consuming fire within had cut that part of her life from her. It was gone, like her innocence.

Here my future lies. Here is my destiny, whatever it might be. All other ways are closed to me. Like the sacrificial lamb, I am led to the altar of my heart. "Lord have mercy. Lord have mercy. Christ have mercy."

The house was still, unnaturally still. There was no sound of children running through its halls, for Moira had taken them with her on a day of shopping. Brendan must have new shirts and pants, for he had grown so quickly. What she did not say was that she needed to be away from the house for a while, for there was an air about it these days, disquieting and uneasy. She could not name its source.

Dougal, swamped by business he had neglected, had decided to remain behind. It was a web so sticky, could it not be seen? Moira had tenderly kissed him good-bye, and Ellen, he saw, had then turned her head aside, not wanting to see the goodness in that kiss and the easy intimacy between them. He'd seen her do it, and he knew she was caught up in the web as he.

And so they were alone. Ellen found an errand in the room where he sat reading, reading, but never seeing the words. She lingered there, drawing out the task, moving slowly, sensuously.

"How can ye bear to read so much?" she asked him. "I've never had a mind for words and books. Ye'll hurt yer eyes in this light."

"Oh," he sighed, "I'm not much for it this day. Me mind rebels," he admitted, laying the papers aside. "I cannot seem to make sense of the words."

A force was building. Even so, she dared not risk a look.

"Have I told ye, Ellen, what a blessin' ye've been to us?" he began, testing the water. "The way ye are with the boys, they both adore ye. What we all could have done without ye, I'll never know. Moira was gettin' swamped with all of this." A smile passed between them, saying nothing. It was an empty smile, like screens before their faces. "Have ye been happy here these months, or are ye longin' for yer home again?"

She turned sharply then, faced him, guard down at last. "I've never been happier than here. It's like a second family, with Moira, the boys . . .you." The words dropped upon the air with the impact of a heart stopping.

A breathless space of seconds passed between them, daring, holding back, and then at last, daring all of heaven's wrath. When he spoke, it was as a man borne to his fate by some unstoppable force.

"Oh, God, Ellen," he began. "I've felt yer presence here as no married man should. From the first day ye walked through the doorway, I've fought a battle with m' soul to keep from ye. Every day has been worse than the day before, and the yearnin' grows harder to bear. I've dreamed of ye as I lay in Moira's arms, longed for ye as I watched ye playing with the children. At night, seein' my wife's body swollen with child, my child, I've thought only of you. Yer beauty has drugged me as liquor never could. I can think of nothin' else but you. Nothin' but pullin' ye to me, and holdin' ye, as I've so longed to do.

75

"Sweet Jesus," he whispered. "What kind of man is it I am? What sort of cursed love is this I offer ye? Won't ye say somethin'? Don't let me go on drownin' before ye. Tell me ye hate me, if ye will, and let the flames of hell burn me for the damned soul I am. I would understand, for I feel it singein' m' feet even now. Or if ye will," he added softly, "tell me ye love me, as I love ye, and turn me from this purgatory I've found m'self within." He turned away, unable to meet her eyes.

"Can ye truly wonder if I hate ye?" she asked. "Are ye blind as that, then? If ye're damned for wantin' me, then damned I am as well. I can barely breathe, knowing it now that ye've wanted me as I have wanted you. And ye said ye loved me. If it truly is a cursed love, then I go to it willingly. God, I go to it joyously. I never practiced sainthood. I know the hell ye speak of, I've lingered there a while. Still, I'd rather step boldly into the fires of it than bear the slow and living ember burnin' out the heart of me were I to turn away from you."

Her hand stretched out to him, across the chasm dark and fearful between them, passing forever the sheltered cottage of her home, the sure security of her faith, the friendship of Moira and the boys, and the last moment of her childhood . . . and touched a kindred soul.

Drawn by bonds of human will for human will, they met in passion fierce with need. Burying his hands in the wealth of her hair, he pulled her to him and kissed her. That kiss, singeing through him, burned away all restraint. A low, mournful groan escaped him in his desperation, and he took her there, the image of her face etched upon his soul . . . forever.

Seeing her after, he touched her as men will touch that which is precious to them. The thoughts which floated past his mind were errant and aimless. She was the only reality for him. She was a woman whose needs matched his own.

He held her gently, breathing in the fragrance of her. In their closeness, he felt his need rise again within him, for he could not have enough of her. He took her once more, slowly this time, quietly learning the way their bodies blended together, drawing out the pleasure, until at last, he held her to him, complete man and complete woman.

Her eyes fluttered open, tranquil butterflies, and looked out upon the world with sight grown older. All that her eyes beheld had somehow changed. The man beside her, once a phantom of her dreams, now lay against her, skin touching skin, her lover. A cat's smile of contentment crept across her face.

"You are mine, Dougal," she whispered. "You are mine."

Chapter Nine

December 28th: In the early hours of morning, Moira began her labor to bring her third child forth into the world. She was ensconced in the luxury of the master bedchamber, with its down coverlets and its fine linen, and attended by the learned Dr. Westcott, but the powers that be ignored the rise in Moira's station, and bestowed upon her the same equality of pain as that of the lowliest of cottage wives.

The family stood vigil far into the day. Dougal stayed with the boys, soothing their fears, for it was frightening to them to hear the agonized sounds which came from the room above them. It was their mother, they knew, and that made it all the more fearful.

Doctor Westcott left Moira's side twice, and came down to speak with Dougal. In tones of superior authority, he demanded hot water, soap, toweling, and hot tea from the unnaturally subdued Ellen. It rankled Dougal, the way Westcott spoke to her, as if she were no more than a servant to be ordered about, but Ellen seemed not to notice. Dougal noted with alarm that she was distant, and had withdrawn into herself.

The busier Ellen kept, she found, the less her thoughts would wander to the second floor, and the less the guilt would weigh on her shoulders. With every cry of Moira's, she felt the pain of it cinch tight against her heart. How long she suffers, and her so innocent, Ellen thought. What fate then waits for me?

She and Dougal had been together many times since their first lovers' tryst. They had been cautionless and foolishly free in their lovemaking, abandoning all restraint. How much longer will my secret go undetected? she wondered. My turn is next for this, only it is a poor bastard child I'll bear. Will he desert me then? When he knows my secret, he might rapidly regain his senses, and return to the open arms of his family, shutting the harlot out.

Ellen dwelled on this, and other such dark and cloudy thoughts, alone in her imagining, with the sounds of Moira's cries above her head. At six o'clock, Dougal sought her out, needing to assuage his own guilt-ridden conscience. Try as he might to gain a bit of comfort from her, she would not speak, nor even look at him, but hurried away to do some unneeded task. Her heart was too tight with dread. She could not speak.

Midnight came and went, the downstairs clock striking out the hour with pitiless exactitude. No one wished to be reminded of the hours that had passed. It was enough that every few moments were punctuated by the piercing animal cry of pain which echoed down the stairs with all its nerve-jarring intensity. At a quarter to one, Doctor Westcott came from the room. His face, haggard and worn of all its youthful elegance, was sobered by the struggle of the woman in the room above.

"The child's turned wrong," he began, darting his eyes away from Dougal's frank stare. "I've tried my best to turn it, but it won't shift. If something doesn't happen soon, I believe we'll lose them both," he said, as though Dougal might know some means to correct it. He was already beyond his medical powers to assist Moira. The rest was only waiting to see her die.

Ellen had ventured quietly into the small downstairs room as well. She sat in the near dark, nursing her thoughts. Neither she nor Dougal wanted to confront each other with their thoughts. Remorse was stronger than love. Remorse beat at them with every pulse. It was the constant weight upon their soul.

Doctor Westcott, finding no solace in either of them, returned to his patient. Her tormented face now haunted him, like a mask of horror. Nothing in his life had prepared him for these scenes. Every time he lost a woman in a long and grueling labor, some part of him denied his own professional competence, and indeed his very maleness. He felt he should be strong enough, and wise enough, to prevent such senseless deaths.

As if some inner voice were speaking only to her, Ellen suddenly responded to what Doctor Westcott had said. Turned wrong . . . lose them both, he had said. A moment from her past jumped vividly in her memory. Her mother had nearly died of a breech delivery when her brother Brian was born. Moira had been midwife then. So strange to think of it now. She remembered how Kara, her mother, had told her that if Moira had not turned the child just when she did, she surely would have died that night, and Brian with her, for she was so weak and broken and had no will to live.

Perhaps Moira will die, her tormented mind reflected.

Listening to Moira's suffering, she thought it would be easier. It all began to come together and make a sort of sense. She'll die, and then Dougal will be free to marry me. It must be meant to be so, she concluded, exhausted to the soul, for God would not take Moira otherwise. Dougal loves me, I know he does, and then we can be married, and our child will never be born a bastard. It was all so clear now. It was perfect for them both. If only Moira would give up and stop this fighting. She must die, Ellen rationalized.

In a frenzy of excitement, begun in the certainty of her newly gained knowledge, Ellen came and knelt at Dougal's feet, took his hands from his face, and forced him to look at her. It was so simple. She began to tell him all that she had thought out.

"Ye must not grieve so, Dougal. It's all right now. Everythin' will soon be all right. Moira must die, don't ye see? It's the way it's meant t' be, for us. It's all so much better this way. Now she'll never have to be hurt by our sin against her. It will free ye to marry me." Her eyes were unnaturally bright, a wild current running through them.

"Good God! What are ye sayin'?" he cried, pulling his hands away from her. "Are we not deep enough in sin, we two, without covetin' m' wife's death? It's madness ye're talkin'. How could I ever forgive m'self if she were t' die? How could I ever look at ye again?"

He turned away, shaken to the depths by the cold frankness in Ellen's voice when speaking of Moira's death, as if she were no more than an obstacle in their way, an obstacle to be done away with. Unnerving too was the mad glint in her eye.

"If nothin' else, I owe her loyalty. In truth, I could

never leave her. Look at what she's given me"—he gestured in a wide sweep about him—"my children, the love she's given selflessly, the child she's dying trying to give me now. I used to count m'self a man of some honor. Never could I look at m'self in a mirror again if I so dishonored her. I love her, and I cherish her. Merciful God," he cried, letting his head fall back into his hands, "she must not die!"

Then, only then, Ellen knew. In that sudden realization, she saw the falsehood in their love. Was it ever love? Could it be called that now, against the greater declaration she had just been witness to? The shallowness of what they had given one another struck her like an icy hand, at last awakening her senses and clearing out the cobwebs her plotting had woven so neatly.

"Ye love her," she said, her mind at last grasping it. "What was I to ye, a need to be served? And itch to be scratched? I've been a fool, a naive, stupid fool. If ye loved her so, ye should never have let this happen. Damn ye and yer honor!" she cried, hitting him as hard as she could. With hot tears of hate running down her cheeks, she ran from the room.

Dougal wanted to go after her, wanted to somehow take the hurt from his words, but he was held by a stronger grip. He could only think of Moira now. She needed him. He owed her that much. Ellen would have to understand. It was Moira who needed him now.

"I could never abandon ye," he whispered, and fell back into the chair, repeating a fervent prayer for the life of his wife—whom he loved.

Medical record of Dr. James Westcott:
3:00 A.M. December twenty-nine. Case record:

Mrs. Dougal O'Shay (Moira). After an unusually long and difficult breech labor, delivered Mrs. O'Shay of an eight-pound, four-ounce girl. Mother and child expected to recover. Suggested to Mrs. O'Shay that this should be the last childbirth she should attempt.

The child had lovely, soft, auburn-colored hair and alert, blue eyes. They named her Bronwyn Anne, after Moira's mother. In the old country church of his childhood parish, Dougal O'Shay knelt in prayer. Tears glistening on his face, he repeated again and again the litany of his heart, "Thanks be to God."

In another sector of town, within the fashionable Saint Michael's Cathedral, Ellen Gwenhara O'Reilly knelt before the beautiful Botticelli statue of the Virgin, whose arms held out the loving hope of comfort. In Ellen's hands she held a rosary, her fingers passing quickly over the beads as she said the Our Fathers, Hail Marys, and the Apostles' Creed from the rote memory of her childhood. Over and over, she said them, praying that some feeling would come with the words. Her eyes looked pleadingly into the eyes of the Botticelli statue. "Mother Mary, help me. What am I to do? Can ye hear me? Do ye hear me?" she cried, but the eyes of the statue remained unchanged.

In despair, she rose, and cast the rosary beads on the floor at the feet of the plaster Virgin. Leaving the beads and her innocence behind her, she set out into the night, alone within a world grown unforgiving and cold.

Part Two

Danny and Ellen
The Seekers

Chapter Ten

The candles flickered in the dead woman's room. The black-robed priest anointed her head with a cross of holy oil, and recited the prayers for the dead. The glow of the candles showed warm, yellow light upon the crucifix above the bed, marking a circle around it, like a halo.

A young man of twenty knelt beside the bed, in the candlelight, still holding his mother's hand. She would never feel it again, the touch of the son she loved so well. He was the last of the four children she had borne, and the only one left to her at her life's end.

Her name was Bridget O'Mally, and her son was Daniel Rourke O'Mally, now the last of his family, orphaned of parents and siblings by the irrevocable hand of fate.

"Your mother was a good woman, Daniel," said the priest, "and sure, she's earned her place in heaven after the trials of this life."

"I've no doubt of that," Danny answered, rising from his knees at last.

"You must not be turning your thoughts inward now,

lad. Look out at what's about you. There's rare beauty in the world, and a place for a wise young fella like yourself. Your mother here would never want you giving over to grieving. She saw her share of death in this world, and I shared the pain with her for nearly all. She sought comfort in the world to come, Daniel. She stiffened her back and looked forward, never back. A brave and faithful woman she was, and you are very like her. A man is never conquered until he gives up, son, remember that."

"I don't mind the dying so much," Danny said, trying to explain the turmolt of his feelings. "I believe she never dreaded that. But why must it be so hard?" he asked the priest, his eyes seeing again the pain which clouded his mother's face.

"The world is hard, lad, and a struggle in both living and in dying. That's the way of it. But life is generous as well. Like a tease, we get a taste of its riches, and then callously, it seems, the rug is pulled away beneath our feet. Even so, Daniel, it's all we've got. The world is ours in all its anguish and all its joy. And although it's bitter little that we gain of it, life is precious even so. Although you've a bitter portion now, son, remember that we're ever turning, turning. No one knows what blessing awaits them, even an instant away. Have the courage, lad."

"I'll not stay here," said the young man, in the voice of conviction. "My future lies as far away as I can go on the money gained from selling this land my father worked away his life for, the land that claimed my brothers and sisters in its harshness, the land where my mother had to die before she could claim her rest at last. I want no part of it! You talk about the beauty. It kills what beauty there is in life. It sucks away your strength and your youth. No.

I'll sell up and go. I've had enough."

The priest had seen many such scenes in the last few months. The young were fleeing the death and hardship they saw around them. "It may be that you're right, lad," said the old priest as he paused at the door. "I'll not try to change you from your course. God go with you, on whatever path you walk." He couldn't blame Daniel for hating a land that had been bought with so much pain. In sadness, he closed the door behind him. Out into the night he walked, the rain beating down upon his cassock, his head bowed from the sting of it, and bowed too from the weight of the world's sorrow.

The funeral was held on Saturday. It rained all the day through. A few black umbrellas kept Bridget's son company for the short service.

Danny stood bare-headed in the downpour, glad of the rain to hide the tears he could not hold back at seeing his mother put into the earth. A few old women, friends of his mother's, patted his hand and offered their words of comfort at the end. Then huddling beneath their umbrellas, they hurried back to the shelter of their own turf fires at home, and only Danny was left to stand over the freshly dug grave.

The gravedigger stood off to one side, impatient to finish his work and get out of the rain. Danny was unaware of him. His eyes and his mind were on his mother's coffin. A loud cough from the man brought Danny's head about to see the bedraggled fellow trying vainly to wipe his runny nose with his wet hand. It was clear the man wanted to get on with it.

"I'd not be rushing ye, sir," the man said.

"Sorry," muttered Danny. He gave the coffin one last look, and then he turned away.

He walked and walked, quite alone because of the rain. It pelted him in the face, the pain of it feeling good in the cold abyss of his soul. Miles passed in this fashion, until at length he began shivering so violently, he was forced to stop. A little church stood across the courtyard from him, with lovely candlelight glowing through the lead-paned windows.

"It would be good to go inside and light a candle for my mother's soul," he resolved.

Within, the nave was nearly dark, illuminated only by the tiny flickering lights beside the altar. Blue candles and red, dancing colors in the darkness, seemed to him like tiny, live spirits. Striking a match, he lit a blue one for his mother's soul, and watched enraptured as it leapt to life. Making certain that the flame burned steadily, he took a seat a couple of rows back. His eyes blurred in the soft glow the candles lent the church. Only then did he see her.

She was curled up in the first pew nearest the statue of the Blessed Virgin, a form so still and lifeless, Danny took her for dead. He looked around quickly, casting his eyes about for some sign of a priest or parishioner; but no, they were alone. "Holy Mary!" he whispered, more a talisman than a prayer.

On feet of quiet, he stepped across the nave and stood before the still figure of a young woman, wet as himself and shivering in the chill church air.

The statue of the Virgin seemed to look down upon the girl as though with pity. Danny looked from the statue to the still woman, and felt himself shiver. A strong sense of protection seemed to be directed at the girl from the lovely painted eyes of the Virgin. It was as though she sheltered her.

He bent and touched the woman's arm. She awoke at once, to his great relief, and jumped up and drew away from the stranger, a look of wariness aflame in her eyes. In the dim light, he could see now what was not obvious before. She was great with child. Her clothes were soaked and heavily soiled. Her hair needed a wash, and her feet were bare. It seemed he had come upon a gypsy of sorts, whose luck, he believed, had failed her.

Feeling that he must say something to break the strange silence between them, he began lamely. "Don't be afraid, miss. I mean you no harm. It was only that I thought you were . . . sick." A better choice of a word, he thought, than "dead." "I only meant to help you. Now I see you're fit, I'll be going."

He meant to turn away and go. He did. It was just that she looked so unfit, a mockery of his words. Lord, she must be starved by the look of her, he thought. How thin her arms and legs were, he noticed, compared to how great she was with child. Her face was like hunger to look upon, so little flesh it carried. Something about her look kept him, and would not let him turn and go.

Whatever made him say it, he could not tell. Whether it was pity of her, the candle lit for his mother's soul, the loving eyes of the Virgin, whatever it was, the words came tumbling from him like oil spilling from a broken jug.

"My name is Daniel O'Mally. My mother was buried this day. There was just she and I. Her bed is empty now, an empty space that fills the cottage with loneliness. You look near done in," he blurted out, without thinking how it would sound. "What's your name, girl?"

91

"Ellen," she said, the word a whisper, solemn in the stark, quiet church.

"What are you doing out on such a night?" he asked, knowing well the answer before he heard it.

"I've nowhere else t' go. I was so tired," she said, sitting down once again. A single tear slid quietly down her cheek. She took no notice of it, as though long past expecting anyone to care. The sight of that tear, that single shimmering jewel of water-light, conquered all his doubt and led him by the heart.

"Then, if you've truly no place to go, you must come home with me this night. You cannot stay out in this damp. It isn't good for the child." His glance dropped awkwardly to her waist. "I've plenty of hot food, if you're hungry." That question could go without answer. It was only for politeness and the sake of her pride that he stated it so.

"I could eat," she said.

"Can you cook then?" he asked as an afterthought. It would be a help to have someone about the house who could cook, for he made a poor stab at it.

"Aye, I can," came the reply.

"Good," he allowed. "Then it's settled."

The woman made no move to follow him, but remained seated and stared down at her feet.

"Are you coming then?" No answer. "What is it?" he asked, truly not knowing. No answer. Her eyes would not rise to meet his. "I'll not touch you, if that's what's holding you here. You're big with child, remember. I'm not that dauncy. It's only the shelter I'm offering, nothing more. Well, will you come or not?" His patience was gone, and he was beginning to feel like the greatest fool. His foot turned for the door, eager to be free

92

of his moment's folly.

"I'll not sleep with ye," she stated flatly, "but if ye meant what ye said, I'll come." Her eyes met his in a steady gaze.

"Hush, woman, remember you're in church. It's a long walk. We'd best be setting out."

She followed him up the aisle. At the door she turned and looked around, as if there was something she'd forgotten.

"What now?"

"I was but thinkin'," she began. "I'm sorry about yer mother."

"Aye," he said soberly, and pushed the heavy door ajar.

"Look, the rain's gone," he said, the voice of hope.

"Likely only settlin' in a hidey-hole," answered the voice of experience.

Down the lane they walked, the orphan boy-man and the near-mother girl. Neither saw the candles all alight at once, bathing the wall with a halo glow, beneath the gentle face of the Virgin

Chapter Eleven

In over a fortnight's time, all that Danny knew for a certainty about the woman in his care was that her name was Ellen and that she was due to have a child sometime very soon; which meant he knew no more then than he had five minutes after he had met her. She would give him no last name, and grew afraid whenever he asked her, or tried to trick it from her. He stopped trying soon, not caring what her name was, or her past, but only caring about her.

She did prove an admirable cook, and very clean in her habits and person, which was a pleasant surprise, considering the first impression he had had of her. She was quiet, almost to a fault, speaking only when necessary. Still, he had to admit, she filled the empty space in the cottage with her presence, and the hollowing loneliness that had come to him when his mother died had not returned. They were a comfort for each other, each in his or her own way.

There was talk in the village about the impropriety of two unmarried young people living together, and Bridget

O'Mally's friends often shunned Danny in the streets, thinking the worst of him. It rankled him to think that they would turn against him in this way when he was only helping the woman. Besides, in her condition, she was far from a sexual lure. Still, they saw it the way they wanted, and they would talk. He expected a visit from Father Donnally any day. Let the old hens cackle, thought Danny. Let them see sin where there is none, if they will. Within himself, he knew there was no wrong in it.

Ellen, on the other hand, had learned a great deal about Danny in a fortnight's time. He was kind and honorable, keeping his word about all that he had promised. It was still hard for her to accept, a total stranger giving so much of himself and asking for nothing in return. He was gentle in his ways, good-hearted and generous, and attentive to her, always trying to draw her out. He heaped praise on her for the little things she was able to do for him. After the months of hardship she had known, the world had grown a softer place, it seemed.

During that time, since the night she had left Dougal's house, she had wandered aimlessly, providing for herself at first by chance work here and there, and then, as her pregnancy became more obvious, from the charitable handouts of cottage wives. No mistress wanted her around for long. They seemed to find her state distasteful and threatening.

The last month, she had lived solely on what she could steal. When Danny found her, she had come to the end of her strength, physically and mentally, and could go no further. She had stopped caring too what would become of her. Life was a survival game, played one day at a time. For all her suffering, she would not go home. She would have died a nameless woman, by the side of the road, rather than go back to her parents with a bastard child swelling out before her. And she could never go back to Dougal. That part of her was dead, never to be reborn.

In Danny, she found calm strength. It was what her wounded spirit needed, serenity, filling the emptiness within her with its healing. Her spirit, so much steeped in fear these last months, began to rest, and prepare her for the task of bearing a child. If she did not speak often, it was because she was resting in the quiet of her mind, casting all worry from her. Yet she was watchful of all about her, and took in the little acts of kindness that Danny did for her.

She slept in his mother's room, although she had said a pallet would do, in the kitchen. But on this, he had insisted. In the night, when she lay upon his mother's bed, she felt comforted and welcome by the old woman's spirit. Every night, before she slept, she prayed for the soul of Bridget O'Mally. She prayed too for Danny, but never for herself.

She lay awake in the night, thoughts crowding her mind, fighting restful sleep. For the first time, she began to wonder about the child so still within her. How would she ever care for it, and what would she feel toward it? If there were no child, she could go home to her family. If there were no child, she would not be where she was, living in the charity of a stranger. Even without the child, she wondered, could I ever go home again? All was so different now. Surely all of them, her parents, her brothers and sisters, could see how she had changed. No, there was no going back.

In the midst of her musing, a sudden vise gripped her, the shock of which made her gasp aloud. She lay back in its passing, a prisoner of nature, for it resolved to do with her what it had done to womankind since the beginning of the world. She was not frightened. Rather, she was alert, like a watchful animal. She lay still and waited. A few minutes later, she felt again the unyielding grasp upon her being.

Through the long, sleepless hours of the night, she labored with the child, thankful for the warm room and soft bed to bear it in, instead of being, as she might have, by the side of the road, like an animal. With each pain, she held back the cry that came choking to her lips. Her hands bore the marks of her teeth as she struggled to endure without a sound.

She thought about the father of her child. Would he care about her struggle? she wondered. Had Moira survived the birth of their child? Would God punish this child, making it an imbecile or a cripple, because of the sin she had committed against Moira, that innocent woman?

Pain raged at her. With each contraction, she tried to say a Hail Mary, as she had heard her mother do on her childbeds. It was no use. The words sounded hollow and futile to her ears. In her mind she knew God and His mother had turned away from her. There was no one to help her or her child. And so, she bit down the cries of pain and suffered, alone.

In the early hour of morning, she felt the nearness of the birth at hand. At last, she let her cry come forth, satisfying a need so basic, so human, that the very act brought her relief. Hearing her cry, Danny ran into the room. He stood before the bed, his mother's bed, the bed she had borne him in, and took in the scene at a glance. He turned to go.

"No! Don't leave me alone!" Ellen cried.

"I'll go and get someone to help you," he said, his face pale.

"No! Don't leave me. I want no one else, only you." Her eyes closed in pain, her breath short and panting. "I think it will be soon," she breathed, her eyes wild and bright. "Stay with me, Danny. I fear only bein' alone."

"What should I do?" he offered, knowing that this was madness, but knowing too that he would not leave her.

"Have ye never seen a baby born?"

"No." He shook his head, and shrugged. "I am my mother's youngest."

She sighed. "Clean hands, twine, a knife and toweling, no more, only stay." She watched him while he did her bidding and gathered what she needed. He stayed beside her then and spoke what words of comfort he knew, and she gleaned a measure of ease from them.

As dawn broke fully upon the new day, so came the child, with the morning. Until that moment, Danny had never seen the privacies of a woman, but there was no time for hesitation or embarrassment. He did what was needed. Into his own hands he delivered the infant, a girl. The child's cry trilled as Danny held her for Ellen to see. He smiled at Ellen, and she returned it, a shared, triumphant smile.

"You've a daughter, Ellen, perfect made, and strong by the sound of her." He looked the baby over again, to be sure. "Tiny fingers and toes, but all the right amount. Aye, she's perfect." He cleaned the child with the toweling, and laid it beside its mother.

Ellen's face was white, and her eyes were so deeply sunk with fatigue they bore a look of being lost, but her lips bore a smile of welcome for her child. She nuzzled its soft face, stroked its hair, and kissed the tiny hands. "My poor baby. My poor little baby. God help us both."

Danny watched this small scene, and it made him want to cry. The two of them looked so vulnerable.

Ellen looked up, and saw the look on his face. "We did it, Danny. We did it."

The morning opened up and settled in his heart. A tightness constricted his throat, so all he could say was, "Aye. Aye."

He settled himself beside them, and watched as Ellen got acquainted with her daughter. A feeling of warmth and peace came over him, like nothing he had ever known. The child slept, and after a while, Ellen's eyes closed as well, but he watched. He felt a guardian of them both, a part of them, in a way he couldn't explain.

The child awoke, and Ellen with her. "Have you a name for her then?" he asked.

"I thought to call her Caitlin Mary."

"And what family name?" he added, as if an innocent afterthought.

"None." Even now, her walls were up, and she was firmly resolved in her silence.

"What! Will you deny her a proper name? How can she go about being only Caitlin Mary?"

"Same as I go about bein' only Ellen," she answered, putting the matter to a close.

"Well," he said, picking up the squalling child and walking around the room with her, "I've seen my first birth, and my first unclothed woman, all in the same day. It's been quite a morning.

"Poor little bit," Danny whispered so Ellen could not hear, "only half a family, only half a name. Ah, but," he said to soothe the child and make amends, "'tis a lovely half a name."

Summer arrived mellow and golden. The earth, turned over by the plough, lay yielding and soft, ready to shelter again the renewal of life.

So too was Ellen ready. Six months had passed under Danny O'Mally's roof, and nearly six months old was Caitlin, child of her heart. The natural yearnings of her youth, which she had thought long dead, came flooding over her at times, without a whisper of a warning.

She and Danny had lived like loving brother and sister, and not as much as a single kiss had passed between them, although they had lived and slept under the same roof that long time. The scandalmongers of the village had pegged her as his mistress from the first week, but it didn't matter. She would have lived with Danny had the whole world shunned them. She had never known such peace.

Father Donnally visited them many times and saw the innocence of it, although he said such things to Danny as: "You must begin to look for lodgings for Ellen, Daniel. Living together, almost as though you were man and wife, is tempting an occasion of sin."

"It's no different than if she were my housekeeper, Father. I live alone now, and need a woman to cook and clean. She needs the shelter for herself and the child. I see no sin in it, and neither should anyone else."

"But you must think of the child, son," the priest added. "There's a great deal of talk over the little one already. Imagine how it will be when she's older. It would be best for Ellen to live and work where there's a chance she'll meet a man who might wish to marry her and be a father to her child. Living here, no man will ever think of marrying her."

"She seems satisfied enough for now, Father," Danny answered. "I'll not tell her how to live. I'll take care of her and the child as long as she's willing to live here, and that's the end of it."

"Daniel," Father Donnally went on, "another thing's been troubling me."

Hostile now, Danny didn't want to hear anymore, but could not force himself to be rude to the priest. "What's that, Father?"

"'Tis just this, lad, I've known you since your mother brought you to me in her shawl for baptizing. You've grown up in the shadow and the blessing of the Church. I've never known you to abandon your faith, Daniel."

Danny could feel the small hairs rising along his neck, for he knew well enough what the priest was leading up to.

"I say I've never known it before, Daniel, but I cannot remember the last time I've seen you in confession. You've stayed away since Ellen came to live here. Could it be the thoughts you've been having, concerning Ellen, have been keeping you from your duty?"

Danny had never lied to a priest in his life. To him, it was craven, and would have been dishonorable to do so. He knew also that if Father Donnally believed him to be in danger of committing a mortal sin with Ellen, he would never flag in his determination to prevent it. Knowing this, he weighed his answer carefully.

"Since my mother died," he began, "I've felt a heaviness of spirit weighing on me. I've dwelled on my loss, and not thought much on any occasion of sin. I've been to Mass as usual," he added.

"You have. You have," Father Donnally agreed. And he dropped the burdensome subject with these words. "Although I don't actually approve of this situation, I believe I do understand the necessity for it, and I'll do my best to hold the cackling gossip hens at bay."

"Did he say I should leave?" Ellen asked Danny after the priest had gone.

"No. He said nothing of the kind. I told him it's like you were my housekeeper, and he saw that clear enough," Danny explained, afraid that she might feel obliged to leave him.

"Oh, I see," she responded slowly. She said no more about it, and kept the odd way the term "housekeeper" had made her feel to herself.

The sun was warm upon her face, and her baby's lips soft upon her breast, and there was Danny to nourish not only her body but her spirit as well. He had kept his word and never come to her bed, although in the long nights of the last weeks, she had begun to wonder how long that would last. Her feelings were changing daily, as gentle caring and security softened the cold stone of her heart.

Danny spent the long, rich days of summer in the village. A carpenter by trade, he filled the hours from dawn to dusk laying floors, fitting out window frames, building a kitchen hutch, or table and chairs. Danny made most of inexpensive wood, for the cost was dear, but his craftsmanship was lovely of line and form. An occasional job at one of the large manor houses enabled him to put a little cash aside once in a great while. Although the villagers were not wealthy, there was always work for a carpenter. Even the job of coffins for their dead came his way.

In his own cottage, there was ample evidence of his keen workmanship. The heavy outer door with the brass-handled knocker was his, and indoors, the weathered oak mantel above the hearth bore hand-carved birds and vines in a cunning design. The cottage table was not the flimsy stuff the village farmers dined upon, but polished mahogany, shiny as glass. Although small, the cottage lacked nothing. The beveled edges of the tabletop and the table's hand-turned legs seemed so delicately made, they were almost out of place in a country cottage. Against the far wall stood a matching sideboard, lending an elegance to the room. A neatly carved rose graced its twin doors, and heavy brass pulls adorned its five drawers. Danny had made it as a present for his mother the Christmas before last. The inside of the drawer bore her initials and the date: B.O'M. 1847.

He had begun a matching hutch to house his mother's few good pieces of china and pewter, but her illness and death had taken the heart of it from him. He was finishing it now, in secret, as a surprise for Ellen. A pane of beveled mirror would be the back, with three tiers of delicate shelving on either side. Three large cabinet doors would stand at the bottom. He had carved an oval on each door, and within each oval frame, a rose. On the back of the first door, he had carved the word Ellen, and placed it in an oval frame.

For Ellen, there was one piece of his work dearer to her than all the rest, and there her daughter was kept each night. A week after Caitlin was born, Danny gave it to her. It was hand-worked, an ornately carved cradle, a home for the child and a warm welcome. She had cried when she saw the dear lambs worked into its head and foot. Her child lay in it now, feet kicking the air, as

Danny came home from his day's work.

"Hello in the house," he called, pegging his cap to the wall in a sweep. "Ah, there's my darlin'" he cooed, picking up the squiggly bundle which was Caitlin. "Have you a laugh for a tired worn man?" he coaxed, swinging her up above his head.

Ellen stood at the bread board, kneading the dough. "Ye're overlong this night. Caitlin was near asleep."

"Then I'm glad she waited up. She knew I'd be along, I expect."

"I've kept yer supper warm. I'll get it now."

Onto the baking sheet went the two circles of dough. Crisscross went the knife across the tops, and then they were set aside to rise. Ellen's Irish soda bread was one of Danny's favorites.

He sat at the table, the child on his knee, and began to eat some of the lamb stew set before him. "Ah," he sighed, savoring a mouthful, "I've been tasting this in my mind all the long way home."

Ellen watched him eat, pleased that he enjoyed her cooking. He broke off a great chunk of bread, and sopped up the meaty juices. Round and round the bread went in his bowl, until only a smallish piece of bread was still held in his fingers, with a drop or two of broth still settled around the edges; then, swish, swish, swish, the bowl was clean and the morsel popped into his mouth as neat as you please. He looked up to see Ellen smiling at him.

"Ye're a good old dog, Danny, always leavin' yer bowl clean. Shall ye have another?"

"I will that, and no remarks, I'll thank you," he answered, grinning, bouncing Caitlin up and down.

"What was it kept ye so long this night?" she asked,

setting the steaming bowl before him.

"I ran into a couple of the lads on the way home, and stopped for a pint." That was nothing unusual to Ellen, for Danny was popular with the men, and often stopped at Dwillim's public house to raise a mug or two with his friends. She had never seen him even middling drunk, and he was nearly always on time for meals.

"There was this sailor fellow, home visiting his mother. He was showing round a news gazette he brought with him from across the sea, from a place called San Francisco, in California territory."

"That must have been interesting," she noted mildly, taking up the child to nurse.

"Oh, more than that," he corrected her, standing up, his movements, Ellen noted, restless and fidgety. "If what that gazette said was true, there's riches to be made by playing about in a wadie stream. There's gold, it says, nuggets of it, laying scattered about the river bottoms. All a man need do is stoop to pick it up. There's been a strike at a place called Placer Canyon, and men are selling hearth and home to take a chance at it." His eyes flashed with excitement as the spell of it took hold of him.

She stopped rocking, and looked straight at him at last. "Ye don't believe that ballyhoo, do ye?"

Seeing the stricken look in Ellen's eyes, Danny quickly covered his excitement. "No, no," he said, "sure, it's some miner's drunken swill, most likely."

Ellen sat back with a relieved sigh.

"Aye," said Danny, putting the folded paper into his pocket, "that's all it is, sure."

But this time, Ellen caught the look in his eyes, even as the last words were spoken. The look put the lie to the sureness in his voice. A pall began to settle over her, and a chill crept in on the warm summer air.

It was past ten o'clock. Ellen sat still as still in the fireside rocker. She had watched for him at sundown, watched through the gloaming, as the land gently darkened, and still he had not come. She had bathed and fed Caitlin, and at last put the child down without sight of Danny. Supper had been kept warm until nine. After that, she had let the embers in the fire die out, unwilling to move a hand to rekindle the flame.

She knew where he was, Dwillim's Pub. Since the first night, when the sailor came, Danny had been drawn, ever more often, to their gold-fever talk. Every evening his step was later at the door. "I was at the pub," was all he would say, and she knew she had no right to question him. They never spoke about the gold found in California again.

He would leave her, she knew. The cold certainty of it enveloped her. She could not think beyond it. She dwelled on it in the dark cottage, for she had let the candles burn out. The dark was easier on her thoughts, which were hard to face. When, at last, his hand turned the latch, it was as if he had already left her.

"Anyone still up?" he called softly into the shadows of the room.

"I'm here." Her voice sounded colder than the fire.

"Ellen, I thought, by the dark, that you'd gone to bed. Why are you sitting in this black? Might you not have left a candle in the window, for me to see my way home? Where's Caitlin then?"

"In bed these four hours ago," Ellen replied, an icy

edge lacing her words.

He let that go. "Does a man who's worked the whole day get nothing to eat at supper?" he blustered. It unnerved him, the queer way she was acting. It made him sharp with her, when he had not thought to be.

"It's on the hearth," she replied, not moving.

"Aye"—he put a finger to it—"and it's cold as sea'y clams."

"Now it is," she agreed.

"A fine welcome home you're giving me, Ellen. I'm not sure why I came," he muttered, sitting across from her in the dark, and not lifting a hand to put a light to a candle. His own thoughts were dark as well, and it was easier for him to stay hidden.

They fell silent and sat a while, like solid stone souls, apart from humankind. After a time, the emptiness of it was too much for him. He brought a box of matches from his pocket, and flicked one to life with the edge of his thumbnail, to light the small lamps on the mantel.

Her voice came clear, like truth, with the light. "When are ye goin', then? Well I know ye're bound t' leave."

He stopped himself, his tongue ready to lie. It would be so much easier to deny it, but he couldn't deceive her. "The *Condor* sails from here in three days. I'll be on her when she does." The words spilled from him like a dammed-up stream, bursting loose.

"So soon," was all she said, the rocker moving slightly now, the tension broken.

"The captain of the *Condor* has offered me passage to America in return for my carpentry work on board the ship. I can't refuse this chance," he said pleadingly, willing her to understand.

"Nay, Danny, ye cannot," she agreed. "Does he offer

107

ye return passage as well?" she asked, merely going through the game, knowing full well the answer before she spoke.

"No return," he said, the words too hard to float the air alone. "I'll not be coming back, Ellen. Ireland has ended for me. Whatever I have left in life lies there, across the sea."

"So far away, I'll never see ye again," she whispered. Then she set her shoulders straight. "After I've set the house to rights, Caitlin and I will be on our way. We'll not hold ye up on sellin' the cottage. Have ye a likely buyer?" she asked, too calmly, already thinking of another woman inspecting the house, and hoping it would pass, her cleaning of it not thought wanting. Mad to be thinking of that now, she thought, when my heart is breaking. What lame-headed foolishness, worrying about what some woman will think when my world is crumbling before my eyes.

"Now why would I be after selling the cottage, when you and Caitlin are here to keep it for me? I've seen a lawyer, this very night, and signed a waiver giving over this house and land to you." He spoke the words simply, not building up their worth. "I've spoken to Father Donnally as well. He's promised to give you your food and necessities in exchange for your tidying up the rectory for him. Of course," he added quickly, "that's only until I have some cash money set by to send you. I'll save out only what I must have to live, and the rest I'll send to you and Caitlin, to put away toward coming over when I'm settled. Then you're to sell the cottage for what you can get, and cross the sea to join me. Caitlin will be that much older then," he emphasized, thinking it a favorable point, "and more able to stand a long sea journey, don't you think?" The words seemed to her long practiced and repeated often for this one performance.

"What nonsense are ye sayin', man?" asked Ellen, brought to her feet at last. "Are ye daft, givin' away yer inheritance at the scratch of a pen? Ye've too much faith in humankind, and too trustin' are ye by half." Her words sounded harsh and scolding, but he saw her lips were trembling as she spoke. "Ye're such an innocent, I'm near afraid t' let ye go off alone to that enormous country.

"Ye've said yer future lies there, in some gold field. If ye've a mind t' go, then sell up at once. Caitlin and I are not yer concern. I'll not have ye playin' the fool, leavin' us this and leavin' us that. Ye've been a good, kind friend to us, our very lives we owe ye, but here's an end to it. I'll not have yer charity stretchin' across the sea."

Her words stung him. "You're wrong, Ellen. 'Twas never charity that made me do this. Was it charity that drove me out into the hammerin' rain the day my mother was put into the ground? There was no charity in the heart that trod those miry miles, only emptiness, dark and vast and overwhelming." He turned then, and laid some more peat on the embers in the hearth. He struck another match, and they began to smolder. "Did you think it charity, me bringing you home with me, cold and near starving as you were? It was selfishness entirely. Only when I had you to walk the empty miles with, only when there was you to light the darkness of the cottage and drive the pall of death away, only then could I come home. 'Twas you brought me back home, and not the other way around."

The fire kindled, and the darkness lifted in the room. "You've made a home for me, you and Caitlin. How can

109

you talk of me not being responsible for you? I am responsible, and I welcome it."

He walked over to her slowly and took her shoulders in his hands. "There is no charity in how I feel about you, woman. I think about you all the day, when I'm gone. I can see your smiling face, laughing with the child. I can see your soft eyes looking down with wonder at her when she's asleep. And at night, when you've gone to bed and closed the door from me, the way I think of you then has not a bit of charity to it." She tried to turn away, but he held her fast.

"I lie staring at the door between us, willing it to open, willing you to be standing there, arms outstretched, inviting. I imagine you coming to me, of your own will, and me meeting you with a kiss I've dreamed a hundred times. And then you come to my bed, Ellen, and I love you, as I've wanted this long while. I've kept my promise and never touched you, but you must know how hard it's been. I've stayed away only for fear of driving you away from me."

She wrenched herself away from him then, and her eyes, which looked at him, were blazing fire. "In the end, ye're all the same, aren't ye?" accused Ellen, bitterly. "So ye want t' bed me, and maybe father another nameless bastard child before ye leave for the seas and the gold fields, a notch on yer belt of manhood? I'll not stay here like some cast-off thing ye've grown tired of. Nor will I lay down with ye in payment for m' keep. Sell up the cottage when ye go. Never will I give m'self again, unmarried, to any man—and certain sure, not for the price of a crofter's cottage." Unreasoning rage boiled up within her. She ran from the room, bolting fast the door behind her.

"Don't you see?" he cried, pounding his fist against the unyielding wood. "'Tis why I gave you the cottage, so you can come to me in California. When I've made my fortune, I'll send for you and we can be married, away from all the wagging tongues of here. I'd not take you in shame, Ellen, but as my wife, before God. Come out of there now, and say you believe me."

A long moment passed, and then the bolt slid back and the door drew open. She stood, staring up into his eyes, searching for truth. "Truly, ye would marry me, even now, with Caitlin an' all?" asked Ellen, fully aware of her shortcomings. "Tell me honest now, Danny. I can take no more lies in m' life."

He touched her face gently, the barest touch. "I'm asking you now, a man too full of love to put the words properly. I'm asking you to live with me, for to live without you is no life at all. I'm asking you to be my wife, for even now I'm a husband to you in the way I feel. No churchish words would make it more. I'm asking that you let me love you, share my bed and my children, share all my life. Say you'll marry me, Ellen. Say you'll come to California when I send for you and be my wife."

He bent his head, and for the first time, kissed her. It was not the passionate kiss of his dream, but a gentle kiss, to break the steely bond which constricted her heart. Something out of the past was that bond, hard and unyielding, but as their lips met, she felt the fetters of it fall away, and she was free of the past, free to give love and free to receive it.

She looked up at him, tears standing pools in her eyes. "I will marry ye, Danny. If ye send for me, I will."

"Will you never trust me?" he said softly, holding her gently, in innocence, his heart an eagle against a

111

sparrow's breast. "I love you, Ellen," he whispered. "I love you so." And through the long night, he held her, whispering words of what their life would be.

For the next three days, he kept at home with her, going out only once, to make his farewells to the graves of his mother and father, and those other few graves with markers that bore the name O'Mally. He would never return, he knew, and it grieved him to think that no one would attend to their graves after he was gone. He felt that in some way he was betraying them, betraying all they had suffered for. "Forgive me," he said aloud to them all.

He walked away from them then, from the past, from all that had gone before, down a new road full of dreams and promises. On the day the *Condor* sailed, he went with it. A new life lay ahead. He sailed with his back to Ireland, ready to meet that life.

And in the cottage of their home, before the fire, Ellen sat remembering the words he had left her with, and waited.

Chapter Twelve

The clipper *Condor* sailed from Dublin Harbor, June 8th, 1849. Captained by Phineas Samuels, the *Condor* was bound for Boston, Massachusetts, for its first port of call. Once a swift tea clipper on the China trade, the *Condor* now sailed as a passenger-emigrant ship between the coasts of Europe, England, Ireland and the eastern seaboard of the United States.

"These are your quarters," the first mate had said.

Danny's bunk, like those of the other members of the *Condor*'s crew, was in the bow of the ship, and open to the great chains which held the anchor. A fine spray of water misted in from the porthole, and Danny wondered how they would keep dry. A series of squalls two days out of Dublin gave him his answer, soaking the bunks with cold, briny spray and making the men too miserable and soggy to sleep.

The following day, the weather turned mild, and for over a week there was blue sky and gentle water. The men dried their clothing, and blankets hung from the ship's rails like pennants.

Danny, as ship's carpenter, was kept busy repairing the fo'c'sle decks, resetting the mizzenmast with wedges to hold it firmly seated, relaying the rotted planking of the hatch steps, and mounting a new Chinese paneling in Captain Samuels's cabin. The work was hard, and at the end of each day, Danny's back ached with the unfamiliar strain. No one called him Danny anymore. The captain called him Chips, as did most of the men.

"I never saw such a farmyard of animals in all my life," Danny said to a crewman beside him as he repaired the deck. The ship carried livestock for provisions, penned on deck: twenty-five pigs, two milk cows, two bullocks, ten sheep, and a hundred head of ducks, geese, and chickens.

"No," the man agreed, "and I never smelled such a smell either." It was a memory they would both carry long after the voyage had ended.

Working among the men, and eating his meals beside them in their hard wooden bunks. Danny listened to their stories, and heard their sea chanties as they worked the sails. They were lonely, sad songs, sung to the rhythm of their labors.

O mark for a west wind, the oceans we rove,
to sail to America's mountains of gold.
Well, hail thee to Boston, we're bound for your
   shore,
then off to the forties, we'll stand to your roar.

O hie the winds westerly, westerly rove.
O hie the winds westerly, westerly rove.

Now land me in Frisco, your hills all a-gold,

to seek for America's riches to hold.
You'll rob me, you'll cheat me, your women are
    cold,
but I'm a poor sailor, a-brazen and bold.

O hie the winds westerly, westerly rove.
O hie the winds westerly, westerly rove.

The rum is all drunk now, the bacon's gone bad.
There's bugs in the mealy, not fit for a lad.
If ever I get back to the port of my home,
I'll never no more for the oceans to roam.

O hie the winds westerly, westerly rove.
O hie the winds westerly, westerly rove.

A good head wind carried them in their second week
off the Grand Banks, as the ship tried to run above the
Gulf current and down the shallow coastal waters off
Newfoundland and New Brunswick. At a point just
outside the two landfalls, the cold Arctic current crossed
the Gulf current, and a storm blew up. Mountainous
waves buffeted the *Condor*. Heavy rain slashed a mad
torrent, threatening to broach the ship, casting it on its
beam ends.

"Storm's worsening! Tie yourselves to the ship!"
bellowed Captain Samuels, his voice nearly drowned out
by the howl of the gale.

Danny clung to the mast as great, headsome waves
broke over the bow, dipping the *Condor* perilously low in
their wake. Heeling over, the waves hit keen to the
forward side, sending an ocean force across the gunnels.
With a loud rent, they lost the main topsail yard, and the
mizzen topgallant mast. It snapped, like the sound of a

firecracker, and crashed to the deck below.

Danny, standing near the main hatch, could hear the passengers below deck, trapped in the wooden belly of the ship, screaming in fear. They had no portholes for air, being below the waterline, and the top hatch was securely battened down to keep the sea from rushing in and filling the hold. With the hatch closed, it was dark within steerage, there being too great a danger of fire in such a heavy sea for even the light of a single candle.

Danny was moved to pity by their cries, and shouted, "Captain, we must open the hatch!"

"Get away from there!" Samuels ordered. "Open that hatch, and you'll sink us all. Get back to your post, and tie yourself well to it."

If we go down, Danny thought, they haven't a chance in there. From the way the ship was bucking, and the noise the timbers were making, it seemed sinking was a very real possibility. The steep pitch of the deck convinced Danny to tie himself to his post, or be washed into the sea with the next wave. Still, he promised himself, if the *Condor* began to list irretrievably, he would open the hatch as his last act before jumping into the sea. He stood ready to do so throughout the storm, his muscles tensed and aching against the pull of the waves which crested the deck.

The crew fought for the gain of every nautical mile that freed them from the storm. The waters swelled off the shallows of New Brunswick to a froth of spewing foam, threatening to smash the hull as they had so many other ships in this graveyard of waters. At the first break, Captain Samuels ordered the raising of the upper and lower fore-topsails, and the mizzen sail crossjack, to catch the wind blowing from the north and carry them out of the teeth of the gale.

The *Condor* ran before the storm, down the Atlantic seacoast, and once out of the tangle of the Grand Banks, threw full sails to the winds. Captain Samuels shouted over the roar of the blow, "Hang the Queen's laundry!" and a full set of yards ran up the masts, billowing out like clouds across the sea. "Open the hatch now," Samuels called to Danny, his face well masked against a show of feeling for the men and women in the hold. Black-bearded and beetle-browed, he presented a visage of dark, unyielding authority to his men. Danny had watched him through the storm, and had seen how well he knew his ship, and that he did not willfully risk his men's lives. He had gained a measure of respect for Phineas Samuels, and for men like him who made the sea their home.

"We're in American waters now," one of the crew told Danny later that same day. The thought sat with him all that night. He had come so far.

Two days of clear sail brought them safely into Boston. There, Danny took his leave of the ship. He had a little money, left to him by his parents, and that he took to the Exchange for a trade into American currency. He hoped it would be enough to pay the rest of his passage, and see him through his first weeks in California. Unwilling to spend the long months at sea it would take to go around the Horn, Danny resolved to find a Panama steamer to take him on the shorter route, across the Isthmus of Panama and up the Pacific coast. He walked along the waterfront, excited to be in America. Ships of every sort were anchored in Boston harbor, steamers, side-wheelers, China tea clippers, whalers, and a fair assortment of sloops and barks. The waterfront was a busy thoroughfare, with the announcements of arrivals and departures spreading among the hopefuls like wildfire. Every sort of packet was overburdened with more anxious men than it had ever thought to carry. Billboards outside each vessel declared its rates and date of departure. Most rates were blacked out, indicating there were no more berths available.

What surprised Danny most was how many derelict-looking vessels there were jamming the harbor, and how many men had signed up with them. Some looked to be taking on water right there in the bay, yet the men fought over space on them, and thought themselves lucky to have beaten out their fellow travelers. Danny passed them by, afraid of the frenzy that drew men to them. His life was worth more to him than that. He stopped before the billboard of the *Nantucket*, a Panama steamer. The billboard read: "The Finest American Steamer on the Eastern Seaboard. Cabin passenger and steerage. Departs—June 28th." June 28th was just two days away, perfect for Danny. But the rates were blacked out, indicating the *Nantucket* was full.

"You there!" a disembodied voice called from the ship. "You a swabbie or a miner?"

Danny spoke up loudly, wondering who he was speaking to. "I'm a ship's carpenter. A chips," he added, hoping it sounded right.

"Are you now?" The voice sounded interested. "Looking for a berth going to Panama?"

This seemed too good to be true. He grew cautious. "I might be."

"Well, then, come aboard. I could use a good

118

carpenter. If you're a hard worker, I'll take you to Chagres. If not, I'll drop you in New York, like so much excess baggage."

A man appeared on the gangplank, a short, burly fellow with a sandy-colored beard. "I'm the captain of this steamer, Gilbert Miles. And who am I addressing?"

"Daniel O'Mally. I take it from your billboard that all your berths are filled."

"Oh, they are, filled and overfilled," Miles answered.

"Then how . . . ?" Danny began.

"Don't let that worry you. I have more passengers than I want. What I need is a good crew, and a chips like you. Come aboard, Mr. O'Mally. We'll find you a berth, even if we have to kick one of them pickaxed miners overboard. Damn nuisance they are too," he added, and led Danny up the gangplank. "Now, let me show you what needs doing. . . ."

That night, Danny slept aboard the *Nantucket*, in an empty four-by-six-foot cabin. It was hard to sleep. The sounds of the city seemed too loud after weeks at sea. So many thoughts filled his mind. There was so much still awaiting him. There would be weeks of testing, he knew, before he reached the gold fields. They were thoughts to keep a man awake. The ship rocked gently, and Danny lay looking out of the porthole at the stars, dreaming.

Danny's cabin aboard the *Nantucket* held eight men, with four berths available for sleeping. The berths were allotted on a first-come, first-served basis, with the late arrivals sleeping on their packs on the floor. Each morning, as Danny got up, he had to step gingerly over lumps of packs, and lumps of men, and hope he chose the right place to put his foot.

Second-class cabins held twelve to fifty berths. Steerage consisted of wooden bunks, stacked three or four high and crowded with as many as possible in the hold. Space was at such a premium, some men even agreed to sleep in the lifeboats.

Danny was kept busy in his two weeks aboard the *Nantucket*, repairing the bunks in steerage, some of which had fallen in on the occupants below them, and recaulking the planks on deck by chipping out the old hemp and filling the cracks with new sisal and tar. His whole body ached with a kind of misery even sleep could not ease. Still, he was glad of the work. It kept his mind busy. When idle, he thought about Ellen. He wondered if he had done the right thing, leaving her behind in Ireland. The thought haunted him—will I ever see her again?

Uneventful weather brought the *Nantucket* safely into Panama, at the mouth of the Chagres River. Once a Spanish trade route, the sixty-mile isthmus was little more than river, swamp, and jungle. The village of Chagres was the most pitiful place Danny had ever seen. Overrun with hard-faced men of every description, it was the kind of town where you watched your back and slept with one eye open.

"Where can I rent a boat?" Danny asked one of the idlers beside a monte tent.

"You can't," he replied. "Wouldn't be sitting here if I could get hold of a boat of any kind. The natives have the only boats—bungoes, they call them—a kind of canoe. There're only so many. The way my cards are coming today," he added bitterly, "I expect to be broke by the time the next one pulls in."

Broke was what Danny would be too if he had to wait long in Chagres. He went back to the *Nantucket*. "Will you sell me the planks of my bunk and those below mine?" he asked Captain Miles.

Miles considered the idea. "It wouldn't pay me to do so, son."

"I'll give you a dollar a board," Danny offered. "They're not worth that, and you know it. The timber's rotted, and won't hold up much longer. You'll have to replace them anyway, when you get back to Boston. You won't need them going back. The cabins aren't full then."

Miles thought it over, speculating on his profit. "A dollar a board," he agreed, and laughed inwardly at the money he was making on the gold-rush trade.

The raft took the better part of one day to build. Danny kept the nails with the boards of his bunk, and so had a way of holding the planks together. Nails were a scarce item in Chagres. He made two poles for moving the raft along out of the width of one plank. He laid out his belongings on it, ready to leave with the early morning light.

"That's a verra fine raft you've built," a young, red-bearded man behind Danny said. Tall as Danny, but more angular all over, he had the pale skin so many redheads had. "My name's Griffin McTaggart." He offered Danny his hand in introduction. "I've been sitting aboot in this place for over a week, waiting for a way oot. I canna get two miles doon that river on my own. I ken you need some help poling that raft."

"I don't need a partner," Danny told him bluntly.

"You do now," McTaggart argued. "You do that.

121

You canna navigate that river and watch your back too."

"I'll take my chances."

"Either you're a fool man, or you dinna ken how bad it is on that river. There's tropical fever here. I can help you if you sicken. I know a bit aboot jungle fevers. Besides that, I want oot of this place as fast as I can get oot."

Danny looked back at him then, despite his earlier caution. Fever was the one thing that worried him. If McTaggart did know about jungle fevers, he might be worth taking along. Deciding by instinct, he stuck out his hand in agreement.

"I'm Daniel O'Mally. This is my raft, and I say where we go on it, but you're welcome to come along."

"I'll just go and get my gear. You've Griffin McTaggart watching oot for your skin from this day forward," the Scott declared solemnly, returning Danny's handclasp with a firm grip of his own.

They set out the next morning, July 14th, in the sweltering heat of the tropics. Within the hour, they were in the thick of the jungle, crowded on either side by outcroppings of plants and the choking grass which clogged the riverway. It was heavy going, poling through the swamp. Sweat poured down their faces, and stung their eyes with its salt.

After five hours of such toil, they came to a narrow in the river, so choked with marsh grass both Danny and McTaggart had to wade into the slimy mass and pull the raft along behind them. They could make no headway with the poles.

"Are there snakes in the waters here, do you think?" McTaggart asked, easing his booted feet into the murky morass.

"It's thinking I'm trying to avoid," Danny answered, gingerly lowering his own feet into the water. It was the worst feeling he had ever known. Every step filled him with the most loathsome thoughts of blood-sucking leeches, fanged snakes, and the oozing, decaying grass that twisted around his legs. They traveled this way for three more hours, and then came to a freer passage of water. Climbing back up onto the raft, they collapsed with exhaustion.

"How far do you think we've come?" Danny asked, laying flat out on the raft.

"I doot it's over twenty miles," McTaggart reasoned.

They had come just under eight miles from Chagres that day. The land around them was ever climbing, and they were working against the current.

The jungle after dark was worse than any nightmare Danny had ever known. Mosquitoes attacked them on every bit of exposed flesh. Hordes of them floated in the air above their heads each time they tried to tie up on shore. The sound of their wings beating by the thousands filled the air with an awful whine.

"Throw me that tarp!" McTaggart shouted. "I'm being et alive!"

They covered themselves with every piece of clothing available, but their torment was still so keen they couldn't sleep, despite exhaustion. Muscles burning with strain, they pushed their poles back into the sluggish water, and drove themselves on.

Sometime before daylight, they felt a jolt as something drifted under the raft. "Are we grounded?" McTaggart asked.

"I think we've hit something," Danny told him. He scratched a match to light on his thumbnail, to peer into the dark water. A second later he blew the flame out and pushed hard on his pole, bearing the raft along and away from the blockage.

"Did you see what it was?" McTaggart pressed him.

"A body," Danny answered, his voice tight. "I think it was a man, or what was left of one."

With the light, they spelled each other, one man poling up the river while the other man slept. They traveled in this fashion for four days, sometimes wading back into the river to pull the raft along.

In the late afternoon of the fourth day, backs and faces burnt and blistered and eyes half blinded by the glare of the sun on the water, Danny and Griffin McTaggart reached the river village of Cruces, and the end of the Chagres River. Twenty miles of overland trek remained, through swampy jungle, and then the high mountain pass to Panama City and the Pacific.

"I'd as soon travel with you the rest of the trek, if you've a like mind," McTaggart said.

"We've made a better team than I expected," Danny agreed. "Besides you're the one who knows what to do for fever, as you said."

"Oh, weel, not so much as I'd carry on aboot," McTaggart admitted, looking awkward.

"Oh?"

"The truth is, I hinna a whit of an idea what to do aboot a fever. 'Twas only so you'd take me on that I said it. I'm verra glad you dinna come doon with one,

124

Dan'l, or you might have ended up deed. You're not mad aboot it, are you, man?"

Danny thought about all they'd been through, wading in infested swamps, back-breaking days of endless poling, mosquitoes eating them alive, and the awful heat. Mc Taggart had shared all of it. And he had been worried about fever! He began to laugh, glad to have something to laugh at, even for a moment.

"You might have told me," he said. "No, Mac, I'm not mad."

"Weel that's a worry off my mind," McTaggart said, giving him a big grin of relief. "I'd be proud to be your partner, even if you're not a Scot."

"Partners," Danny agreed, feeling sure of himself for the first time in weeks.

In Cruces, Danny sold the raft and the poles for a horse. McTaggart bought a horse and a pack mule from one of the natives. The horse looked badly used, but the mule seemed sound.

"Good-looking mule," Danny remarked, casting a dubious glance toward McTaggart's horse.

"He'll live long enough to see me to Panama City," he said, and gave the animal a second look himself. "I only hope I do as weel, riding him."

They began the trek at daybreak of the fifth day. Rain was now coming down hard, making it slippery going for the horses. The ravines were full of water, with mud up to the horses' bellies. Danny and Mc-Taggart had to lead them up the steepest inclines, and pull on their reins as the animals slipped backwards down the muddy slopes. Every slide cost them precious time. The horses were blowing hard with the effort, but the men drove them on. Soon, the rain was coming down in a torrent.

"I canna see the path before me," McTaggart called out over the sound of the storm, and the whinnying of the frightened animals. "It's all awash."

By nightfall, they reached the first outcropping of stone. The rain cleared, and the men made a hasty camp with no fire, for there was no wood dry enough to burn.

"How old are you, Mac?" Danny asked, huddled beneath his sodden blanket for warmth.

"Twenty-four. Why'd you want to know?"

"So I could scratch it in the marker if you don't get out of this alive," he told him, in mock sincerity.

"You're full of kind thoughts I'd as leave do withoot," McTaggart answered him, and scowled at such an idea.

"Why'd you come, anyway?"

The Scot didn't answer for a long time, but then he said, "I got this idea caught in my mind, a quickfire I couldna put oot of my head. There was nothing to hold me in Scotland. I had no family. I felt it call to me, all the way across the ocean."

"And now, do you feel it still?" Danny asked, his thoughts wound up with Griffin McTaggart's, in his own fervent dream.

"Oh, aye," the man answered, "like a fever I canna shake." That was how Danny felt too. The thought quieted them, as they waited out the rain.

The morning of the sixth day saw them picking their

way over a crumbling precipice, and up sheer cliffs. They traveled over a narrow spine of rock, legs knotting in the pull of unfamiliar muscles. At dusk, they reached the summit. Both men and beasts were exhausted, but there was nowhere to make camp on the ledge of rock. They pushed on.

The land sloped downward now, leaning at a crazy angle. Once the horses slid on some loose gravel, their legs under them, into a small canyon of crumbled stone. It was twenty minutes work getting them back up, and moving down the path again. Precious moments of daylight had been lost.

"I'm not verra keen on this night scrabblin'," said Mac.

"When we get to the flat, we'll rest," Danny promised him. But there was no flat. For two more hours, there was nothing wider than the width of one horse. Then suddenly, they cleared a narrow overhang, and there were the lights of Panama City below them, campfires and lanterns twinkling like earthbound stars against the black of the sea. The road widened there, and they could have stopped at last and rested, but the draw was too strong.

An hour out of the city, they began to hear voices and see groups of travelers in drunken revelry. Empty bottles of whiskey littered the pathway along with the discarded remains of verminous supplies. A gunshot was heard in the distance, and the sound of a girl's laughing—a high, bawdy shriek. Danny and Mac shared a long, tired look. They had come to civilization.

*   *   *

127

The rain stopped the morning after they arrived in Panama City. They woke to a view of a mud hut village, overburdened with miners' tents and the ramshackle sheds of several hundred restless men waiting for a vessel, any vessel, to take them on to California. After the mad rush to get this far, risking even the fevers of the Panama jungle, the wait for a ship was an agony, eased only by gaming tents and brothels.

Danny checked with the owner of the town's biggest bar. "How long until the next ship?"

The man shrugged, indifferent to the problem. "Maybe tomorrow. Maybe next week. Maybe not for a month. The mail packet was due a week ago. More and more steamers are coming here now, even some old fishing boats." He laughed, a hard sound. "You're likely to be here a while. Might as well relax and enjoy it."

Relax was the last thing Danny wanted to do. McTaggart sold his horse and mule to the stable that rented animals to travelers going east. Danny sold his horse to the owner of the town's biggest brothel. At least, he thought, the horse will get fed and have a shelter from the rain. Its sale brought him a good price, which he added to his savings, hoping he would have enough to pay his passage on the steamer.

After that, there was little to do but wait. Danny and McTaggart camped out on a hill overlooking the harbor. Two days later, the bark *Rebecca* sailed in. Descending from their vantage point overlooking the bay, Danny and McTaggart were the first men in line to buy their tickets for the Pacific passage. Behind them, nearly 400 men crowded the small pier, threatening to collapse it with their weight. Fistfights broke out

128

over places in line, for the *Rebecca* could hold only 250 men.

Leaning over the railing aboard the ship, Danny saw the latecomers run for the bark as if death were chasing them. Desperate, some tried to force their way on board, only to be shoved into the sea. The *Rebecca* sailed out into the bay that night, away from the panicked crowds in Panama City. It anchored there until morning. At dawn, July 25th, she hoisted anchor and raised her sails for the Pacific passage north. Hugging the rugged coastline, in summer's tranquil water, she sailed north, carrying a crew of 50, 250 passengers, and something more—cholera.

Like an ink stain blacking out a map of the world, it had begun in the Ganges region of India, laying waste to the populace. It had found new victims in China, the Middle East, and Western Europe. From there, it had come to Russia in the summer of 1847, and a year later, had moved like a scythe across Germany. By the fall of 1848, it was filling the cemeteries of France and England, taking a total of over a million lives. Brought out of France into New York City on the ship *New York*, it quickly took its toll in the congested quarters of that town. It went with the men aboard the steamers, to Chagres, across the Panama isthmus, and into Panama City. Knowing only that they felt unwell, with painful, spasmodic cramps, a few miners boarded the bark *Rebecca* and brought cholera across a continent to California.

Rapidly worsening, they spent their first full day at sea suffering bouts of repeated vomiting, diarrhea, and an agony of thirst that seemed unquenchable. Afraid of being put off the boat, they kept their illness silent, until weakened to complete prostration, they developed convulsions. The ship's doctor was called in at that point, and the word quickly spread among the passengers and crew. Cholera.

By the evening of the second night at sea, two men had died, and twelve others had fallen ill. With no major seaport between Panama City and San Francisco, where they could obtain medical help, there was little to do but continue on, treat the sick with what supplies they had, and hope for the best.

Still a week from San Francisco, every day Danny noted the events on board in a journal he was keeping. A real sense of danger alarmed him now as nothing had before. He wrote:

"August 2nd: Three days have passed since the last death from cholera. We all fervently hope that this is the end of our sickness on board this ship. It is a desperate feeling, knowing that men are dying of this, that any of us could be next, and yet we are unable to get away from the contamination. There is no way to fight it, as I would another man who threatened my life. It remains with us, like a poisonous viper in our midst. These men have come so far, only to suffer such ignoble deaths.

"August 3rd: Today is the ninth day of our passage. Today I have witnessed three more burials at sea, a sight I wish never to see again. With so many sick and dying, the ship's doctor has run out of medicines. There is little he can do for them but bleed and purge. Some rally with little treatment, surviving on their own strength, I believe."

The journal was silent for three days, then Danny wrote this entry:

130

"August 7th: Today is our thirteenth day aboard the *Rebecca*. Our captain is hopeful of arriving in San Francisco tomorrow, or the next day. No more deaths have plagued our ship, but we are low in spirit. Many are ill with the ravages of cholera, and not expected to live. There is so little we can do for them. A continuous sound of moaning comes from the dining hall, where the sick lie on cots. It is a sound I hear even in my sleep, and cannot get away from.

"August 9th: McTaggart and I have agreed to be mining partners when we reach California. I believe a man has a better chance with a friend to back him up. Last night, we talked about Ellen. She is always in my mind. He seemed to understand how I feel. Perhaps he has a loved one too he has had to leave behind. This waiting is endless. It draws on my nerves like tight wires. I am anxious to begin whatever California has in store for me.

"August 10th: On this eighteenth day of our voyage, we see the outline of San Francisco Bay, and the sharp rise of her hills. I have packed my belongings in readiness to flee this vessel. God help me, I am wild to get free of it. How many miles have I come, I wonder, from that one dear face? Here, most of all, where my real adventure is about to begin, I feel her presence beside me. She is with me, as surely as if she were by my side."

The white hulls of the ships in the harbor reflected off the water, and the sound of a megaphone in the distance announced the arrival of the bark *Rebecca*. Daniel O'Mally, son of Ireland, had come to the end of his long journey—home to his new country, America.

Chapter Thirteen

Dearest Ellen,

I take my pen in hand to announce my safe arrival in California. Standing on the pier beside the bay, I look up at the hilly land of San Francisco. Our ship, the *Rebecca*, lies snugly anchored in the harbor, a sight to see from this side of the water.

It is now two and a half months since I last saw you and Caitlin, and every day of it I have thought of you. This day, most of all, I miss having you here beside me.

I have kept a journal recording my crossing, as a keepsake for you. I will only tell you now that there were times I wondered if I would ever see California. When you come, you must go by Cape Horn, and on no account attempt the Panama Crossing. Still, I am well, and have not been injured, and for that I am grateful.

San Francisco is a hurly-burly town. It is all so new and hasty-looking, not at all like our villages at home, weathered and settled. It is a camp, really, with tents dotting the land like a carnival. We are nearly all miners here. Even the sailors try their hand at it, although the captains talk it down, so many of their crews have they lost to these hills. There are a few wood-frame houses, trying their way at permanence, but for the most, it is roughly thrown up tents and shantytown dwellings. We are a city which changes daily, a new tent today and two gone tomorrow. Neither are there any rooms to be had in this overburdened place.

The talk is of the gold fields north of here, in Yuba County. Tomorrow I will head out for the fields to try my hand. I am anxious to see where they are finding the gold. You would not believe the prices in this town. Today, I bought a pick for $2.50, a shovel for $2.50, one pound of tea at $2.25, a sack of flour at $14.00, five pounds of sugar at $2.00, ten pounds of beans at $3.00, and $6.00 for the sorriest-looking piece of pork ever to sail around the Horn. I had better make a strike soon, or I'll starve at these prices.

In spite of this, excitement runs high in this town. The latest strike is all the men talk about. I have seen some of the nuggets taken out of the fields near here, and know there must be a rich vein of it still waiting for me. There's so much gold washing hands hereabouts, it can't be long, I'm thinking, until I'm rich as a lord, and can send for you and Caitlin. Every other day, it seems, I hear of another miner who has found a nugget as big as his thumb.

In the midst of all of this, I keep you and the child ever in my thoughts. I close now, for tomorrow I must rise early to get a good start before the heat of the day. The sun here is murderous at times. It saps your strength. I pray this finds you and the child well. Keep to me, my Ellen, as I will surely keep to you.

Your loving,
Danny

It was six months before the letter came into Ellen's hands. Caitlin passed her first birthday without notice, but for Ellen's noting the date and the soft lamb she stitched for Caitlin to cuddle. She was too alone in the cottage. The heavy winter rains pelted the thatching on the roof, and here and there the drips came through. Were Danny here, she knew, he would never have countenanced it, but she let it go. What did it matter?

The good wives and mothers neighboring the cottage kept stiffly away from Ellen, never as much as nodding their heads to her when she passed by. She knew what they thought of her, that she was Daniel O'Mally's whore, and that she had borne a bastard child of some man who was not her husband—maybe Danny himself. Well, what of it? she thought. They were partly right. There were some who took their delight in snubbing her when she did her shopping in the village. She let their remarks, and their rude silences, fall away from her like so much rain. There were worse things than the women of this town thinking she was Danny's mistress, and she had lived them. Still, it meant she had no friends. There was only Father Donnally to talk to.

Three times a week, she went to the rectory to clean for him. She and Caitlin lived on the small wage he paid her. It was enough. She had no rent to pay, living in Danny's cottage. Caitlin was too little to have many wants, and

Ellen could think of nothing important that she lacked for herself. When the letter from Danny came, and she had read it, she took it to Father Donnally and let him read it too. She was too full of happiness to keep it to herself.

"So, you've heard from him, have you?" he said, taking it from her hands. He read it through, folded it carefully, and handed it back to her. "I've known that young man all his life," he began, "and I've never known him to lie to anyone. What a journey he must have had! Here," he said, pulling out the atlas, "let me show you where he came through." Together, they charted Danny's Atlantic voyages, his trek across the isthmus, and the journey up the Pacific coast to California. "Here is where he is," Father Donnally pointed out, "about here."

"But that says Yerba Buena," Ellen noted.

"It was Yerba Buena, until two years ago," he told her. "They changed it to San Francisco then. There's a Catholic mission there. That's how I know. There's a whole chain of missions in California. How exciting it must be for him to be a part of this gold rush they talk about. He was never meant to be a farmer, our Danny," he said, and smiled at her.

His smile eased her loneliness. At times, he was all that stood between her and black despair. Danny was so far away, and the months were so long without him. Still, she would not let herself think anything but that truly he would send for her as he had said. If only she could hold onto the dream until then. "Keep to me," he had said, "and I will surely keep to you." At night, she repeated the words like a litany, to ease her mind to sleep.

*   *   *

A month after the first letter, another one came. Her hands shook as she opened it.

Dear Ellen,

I greet you from Yuba County. I have struck a small claim here with a fellow miner. His name is Griffin McTaggart, a Scot, who I first met on the isthmus crossing in Panama. We have been through a lot together, he and I. Someday I must tell you more of him, for he is quite a character. A man needs a good partner here, to protect his claim and his back, and Mac is truly that. I count myself lucky to have him.

We've worked some color this week, rocked sixty buckets of sand, and claimed seven and a half ounces of gold dust. We've seen no nuggets yet, but the dust sells for $18.50 an ounce, which I count as good wages for a week's work. Some, I hear, are bringing in much more higher up on the river, but we plan to stick here until the vein is played out.

From sunup to after dusk, we are at it, and I am hurrying the work the quicker for missing you. It is hard being alone.

McTaggart believes when we hit bedrock, we will take the gold out in buckets. We break our backs at it, day after day. For all the wild excitement it brings when we spot a bit of color, it is a lonely life.

There are no women here, save for a few Mexican girls who work in the gaming houses, and a few Indian squaws who work for some of the miners. It is a land of men. How I miss you.

I enclose $25.00 for you and Caitlin. You will know best how you must use it. Spend it if you need the cash to live, or put it safely aside toward your passage fare. I will send you more as soon as I am able.

This day, I finished my first sluice box, called a long tom. It operates by a force of running water washing the dirt through the box, over ridges at the bottom, where nuggets and the heavier gold dust settle. It is a wonderful time-saver. McTaggart and I have moved more dirt through it in one day than we could have rocked in a week. Got ten ounces today alone.

I must end this now, for I am bone tired. I will dream of you tonight.

Your loving,
Danny

The long days of winter blended one into another. The end of December was near. The nights were long beside the peat fire, the rocker slowly keeping time with the wind song playing about the roof.

In the hill country of Yuba County, the nights were cold and lonely. The stars glittered brightly, and the plaintive coyotes howled. A man had time to think and dream. How far away she is, he thought, another world away. Will she ever come, he wondered, across the sea, to this wilderness, to be with me?

The night bird called to its mate. The coyote lay quiet, at last. Only the stars were there to answer, and they, in regal haughtiness, declined to speak.

Chapter Fourteen

Christmas Eve, 1850: In the darkened nave, Father Timothy Donnally stood facing his congregation. He had just finished the recital of the story of the Nativity, from the book of Luke. The parishioners stood, flickering candles held in their hands, the light of which brought a blessed brightness to the dark church, transforming the dark night. It was just after midnight, the Christ Child's hour. A statue representing the holy infant was placed in the manger. Singing filled the room.

The priest thought, as he always did on this night of nights, how rich and fulfilled his life was, and how grateful he was for the part he was able to play in people's lives, bringing them closer to personal peace, bringing them closer to God. How fortunate a man I am, he thought. On such a night as this, every soul should be as content as I.

He looked out over the faces before him. Families sat together, some for the first time all year, but joyful now in their sharing of this most precious night. Large, and for the most part devout, Irish families, eagerly awaiting the ritual birth of Christ into their world. Happy children, faces scrubbed clean, and best clothes gingerly worn, looked out upon the Christmas scene with awe. Mothers with infants in their arms gazed from the Holy Child to their own, most loved child. Christmas brought the unifying love of Christ to all of them.

Yet, in sadness, Father Donnally knew that not all in his parish were happy this night. He glanced in their direction, and once again felt their pain, the wound of which he carried personally. It hurt him like a physical torment to see the suffering of their spirits. Yet, like a magnet, he was drawn to them. He watched them, saw their pain, and was troubled.

Colin Muldair sat in the back row with his three young children. No wife sat beside him, for his wife, Annie, had died a year ago giving birth to the youngest Muldair child, Elizabeth. They sat in the midst of the celebration, listening to the Christmas story, but, thought Father Donnally, it did nothing to lighten their suffering. In all the world's great joy, the Muldairs were excluded.

This was a sight the priest, whose calling dealt with life and death, had often faced—the incomprehensible loss of a loved and vital life which left a hollow in a family that could not always be mended. It was one thing for the old or pitifully ill to die. Families could bear the parting then, were prepared for it. But when death snatched up the very heart of a family, as it had with this young mother, then the wound was hard to heal.

For Father Donnally, it was a personal anguish. He needed to help them through their grief, fully as much as he needed to say Mass. His commitment to the priesthood was to both God and man. It would be a poor priest, he thought, who served only one.

He watched the Muldair family with mounting anxiety during the remainder of the Mass. Poor man, he thought. He is too alone, with too much pain welled up and trapped within him. He needs to marry again. His children need a mother, and he needs a spark to light the flame of his life again. What chance had he, though? What woman would think him a catch, poor as he is, with three motherless children into the bargain?

The call to Communion began. A sense of duty, warmth, and love spread through the congregation, and nearly the whole of the assembly came forward to share in the spirit of the Host. Mothers and fathers led their littlest children, or carried them in their arms, to see the lovely manger set before the altar rail.

There was one notable exception to the throng of people at the rail: Ellen and her daughter, Caitlin. They sat quite alone at the back of the church. Ellen could not partake of Communion, or the comforting bond of faith it offered, since she refused the sacrament of confession. Confession would mean telling Father Donnally about Dougal.

Father Donnally looked at Ellen, alone in the great expanse of empty pews. It was, to his knowledge, the first time she had ventured into the church since he had known her. He rejoiced in her return to the fold. She had come back to God of her own will and her own desire. It was a Christmas gift for him, rich beyond compare.

For not the first time, he wondered, how may I help her? She is always alone, with never a friend or family to speak to. The neighbors shun her. Except for Daniel O'Mally and myself, she knows no one. And Daniel, now there is a puzzle. He's been gone almost a year. She's had two letters from him, and even a bit of money, but will he

140

never send for her? Shouldn't he have done so by now? Are you through with her then, Danny? thought the priest. How much longer must she go on waiting for someone who may never be coming back, and who, in all likelihood, will never send for her?

The man kneeling before the Communion railing looked up at Father Donnally. It was Colin Muldair, a young father, a resolute Catholic, although at the moment a strained and grieving one.

Wait now, thought Timothy Donnally. Why couldn't this be the answer for them both? Colin would make a fine husband for Ellen, and a good father for her child. Caitlin's almost of an age with his own Elizabeth. He's an honest, reliable man, not wealthy, but fine-looking. He clearly needs a wife for his home, and Ellen is after wasting her life waiting for Daniel O'Mally. She could do worse than Colin. It was perfect, really.

He lingered on the thought, distributing the Host to the people before him. Here was Thomas Flannagan, the town's cobbler, dressed in his brown worsted best. Good fellow. And here was Mary Margaret, the Halsteds' maid, in what he was sure was her one good dress.

He glanced at the image of the Christ Child, lying in the manger, circled with soft candle glow. It filled him with the strongest sense of love. Then, in that instant, it came to him—the way to bring them together, Ellen and Colin. What good mother, as Ellen surely was, could ignore the needs of three motherless children? Surely such a family needed help with this or that, cleaning, cooking, laundry. A bargain could be made, and wages offered. He could arrange it himself. Once Ellen saw how much the Muldair family needed her, and once Colin saw how much Ellen and Caitlin needed him, the solution would take care of itself. Only let her see the sadness of that house, Father Donnally thought, and her heart will fill with pity. There's a lot to be said for pity. If often leads us down the very road to our own happiness.

The matter was settled in his mind, and once more, he turned his attention to the beauty of the Mass. It was Christmas, he reminded himself, and the sense of perfect love filled his thoughts and his words.

All about him there were smiling faces, radiant in their once-a-year joy. Even the children were happy, thinking of the gift they would receive, or a special meal for the family.

For Father Donnally, the sign of peace and love had come to him from the image of the Christ Child in the manger, he had no doubt of that. He was a simple man, sure of the goodness of mankind, and immovable in his belief of God's will among us. Even the thought that had just come to him, about Ellen and Colin, he was sure had come from God. It made him happy to believe his Lord cared so much about two lonely people.

In sincere love, he offered the closing benediction. He blessed them, all the people he cared so much about. Filing from the church, he genuflected before the altar, a man radiant in the beauty of the human soul.

Chapter Fifteen

My Darling Ellen,

I hope this letter finds you and Caitlin well. I am fitter now than I have been ever before. This life does that to you. Either it kills you off, straightaway, or it toughens you up, considerable. My skin is getting brown as an Indian's, for the sun is so fierce at times.

I would tell you more about the life here, but there's other, more important news that won't wait patiently to be told. Eureka! We have found a vein lousy with gold! McTaggart and I worked it all this week, from the long tom. We took out nearly 105 ounces. I feel certain there's more there, if we have the stamina to stay with it. There's some talk of the miners north of here picking up nuggets as big as a pound. I've seen a few of the big ones with my own eyes, so I believe it's true. It seems to me, the higher you get in these mountains, the coarser the gold gets.

The Indians around here are a curious lot. They

believe in the practice of burning their dead on a high, trellis structure, instead of burying them. I witnessed one such funeral rite a week ago. It was an old man, I think. His squaw kept wailing, and yelping, and pulling at her hair, and then rubbed ashes all over her face. She was carrying on like a banshee. For the most part though, they're a quiet lot, and keep clear of the miners hereabouts.

I went into Sacramento with Mac last week. Drunken miners everywhere. The town was swimming in gold dust. We bought one horse for $65, and paid $75 for the bridle and saddle. Everything here is double and more what it should be. The town reminds me of a circus, with tents for gaming at every turn. The miners lose back their hard-earned gold to the monte tables, but still they come, for it's something to do, away from the back-breaking labor of the gold fields.

Ellen, I enclose $300 toward passage money for you and Caitlin. I've met a fine man, Captain Rawlings of the *Yankee Clipper*, and he has promised to deliver it into your hands in person. I don't trust the mails.

I bought a piece of land for us, in San Francisco, and I'm seeing about the building of a house for us there. Mac thinks the value of land will go sky high soon, and he's been right before. Anyway, you will have the comfort of a real house when you come here. Around me, all is still rough and ready, more camp life than any other, but I can see a town beginning to emerge.

Mac has encouraged me to invest in some of the cheap beach lots for sale near the harbor. I admit there's a wealth of people coming here every day, but I can't foresee people living on such land as this. The tide sweeps in at night. Still, I've gone along with his judgment and purchased a few of the better lots, and even bought a partnership in a business or two. I doubt that those will be bad ventures, for business is booming here. At least it gives me something to fall back on if the gold plays out.

I must close now, as Captain Rawlings is waiting for my letter. The months apart have been hard for us both, Ellen. Have good heart, we need wait only a little longer. We will be together soon, I am sure.

Your loving,
Danny

In good faith, the letter was sent, the money vouchsafed with Captain Rawlings. The gale winds which toppled the *Yankee Clipper*, and the deaths of Captain Rawlings and his crew, could not be held Daniel O'Mally's fault. Still, for the woman in the cottage, the letter looked for with such urgent need never came. The hopes and plans so far away, and silent, in California, were unknown to her.

She would not be the first forsaken sweetheart left in Ireland, she knew. All over the land, men were going from the place of their birth in what was called the Great Abandonment. Nearly every mother's son of them had a sweetheart he left behind, and some, a wife and children. Still, they left. They promised to send for their sweethearts, their wives, and meant every word of their speech on this side of the sea, but the distance was so far, and many never found the riches they hoped for. So many were never heard from again. Yet Ellen nurtured a hope which fought against dying. She held to her belief in Danny, until the dream would die.

Even Father Donnally, her one true friend, began gently suggesting that Danny, being so far away, might have abandoned her. He said, "A man might be ashamed to write such news to his sweetheart, and take the coward's way out, in silence. It wouldn't be the first time a man did that," he added, shaking his head sadly. "There's so much you could do, in the meantime," he told her. "There's a family I know of in our parish who could use your help very much. The mother died a year ago, and the three children are alone much of the day, while their father, Colin, is working. The baby, Elizabeth, is of an age with your Caitlin. They need your help, and you need a diversion to keep your mind off your worries. There'd be a salary in it too that wouldn't hurt."

Ellen let the arrangements be made, and began work at the Muldair house the next day. Every weekday morning after that, Ellen walked up the path between the houses, carrying Caitlin on her hip. The house itself wasn't much to clean, only five rooms. She cooked the meals for the family, and mothered the children, laughing with them and playing baby games with Elizabeth and Caitlin.

In the back garden, the two girls played barefoot upon the soft, cool grass. Colin's Elizabeth was too good. She never cried, a silent little being. Ellen thought of her as a shy flower, afraid to show herself in the glaring gaze of the world. She never whined or acted naughty, as Caitlin did, but was solemn and still, afraid of her father.

The older two children, Matthew and Kerry, were the heart of their father. He showered his attention on them. For baby Elizabeth, however, he had neither smile nor kiss to offer. Elizabeth's birth had been the cause of his wife's death, and he still held the child to blame for what she could not help. His own hurt and pain kept him from loving this child who needed his love so much.

Only a few days after Ellen began caring for the child, Elizabeth gifted her with a little bird chirp of a laugh, showing off four shining new teeth. It was a wonderful, happy sound. Ellen laughed too.

"Elizabeth, what a cunning little whisker ye are, playing hidy-face with those solemn looks. There now, I've found ye out, little elfin girl. Ye're a high laugher, ye are. A whole smileful of teeth ye have too." She gave the child a tickle to giggle her up. Both babies, Caitlin and Elizabeth, fell about cushy and roly-poly on the cool green grass.

Slam! It was the cottage door. The dark figure of Colin Muldair stood framed in the passageway. "Is this how ye idle yer time away on my good wages? Playing patsy-cakes with babies? Have ye no thought to Matthew and Kerry's supper, or any but playing with that one?" He pointed at Elizabeth. His eyes, scowling, were black as his mood. He turned back into the house, and slammed the door behind him.

Ellen, caught off guard by the suddenness of his anger, had said nothing. Now she pulled Elizabeth over to her and kissed her cheek. How could the child's own father treat her this way? It made her furious with him.

"Poor little duck," she said to Elizabeth, "yer da's lucky to have a little charmer like ye, though he doesn't know it. We'll just have to make him see it. He's a great, daft fool, and needs a good awakening, he does."

Sometime later, Colin came out of the cottage, his head hanging downcast as a schoolboy's. Despite her anger,

Ellen felt pity for him, the way he looked. It was like a pin had punctured all his hot air and left him a sad, withered shell.

"I had no right speaking to ye as I did, just now. I don't know what made me do it. I'm sorry, an' all."

"Ye forget this one's yer child too," snapped Ellen, "though ye never seem to think so. As for Matthew and Kerry, their supper's on the stove, which ye'd have seen if ye had eyes in yer head instead of that black cloud ye carry with ye always."

"It's just seeing her so happy and laughing, I couldn't help thinking of Annie, my wife." The words were painful to him, Ellen saw, like needles sticking to his skin. "I remember sometimes how she was, bringing that one into the world. They had to pull the child from her, covered with Annie's blood, squalling and squalling as Annie was slipping away. They couldn't stop the bleeding. I can see it sometimes, is all. It might have been better if that one had died with her." He looked at Ellen, his eyes reflecting his pain. "When I let myself think of it," he said, "I get hard with the child."

The confession spilled from him; the hurt of losing his wife, the horror of watching her die, being helpless to stop it, and the child who took her from him. When she heard it, the anger drained away from Ellen, washed clean in pity for him.

"I believe ye're a good man," she began softly, "a man who loves his family. 'Tis hard to lose someone ye love so fierce. I've been that road, I know. Only, Elizabeth never meant to cause such grief. She's a child who needs her father's love. She's a pretty child, like yer Annie, I'll wager." This was only a guess, but from his look, she saw she was right. "Ye mustn't blame the world's pain on her.

She's too young to shoulder that burden. Would ye maim her back, loading it with heavy weights?" she asked.

"No, of course not. I never meant to hurt her," he answered quickly. "It's only, I cannot seem to love her as I do the other children."

"But in not loving her, man, ye maim her spirit as surely as ye would her body. Too heavy a load is it for a child to bear, this grief ye nurture so well. In keeping it alive, ye think ye can keep yer wife alive, if only in this pain. It's time ye face the fact yer wife is gone, Colin. Know it for God's will, not this innocent child's."

"All ye say is true," he said, "but how can a man change how he feels? If the love's not there, how can I give it?" Tears welled up in his eyes.

"Begin with small steps, like a baby learning to walk. Learn to kiss her good night, a small step. Hold her on yer lap after supper each night, another small step. Play horsey, or peek-a-boo, or any such nonsense, as ye must have done with Matt and Kerry. All are small steps that will lead ye up the path to loving yer daughter. One day, it'll be there, without the trying. Ye'll kiss her cheek because it's soft and smelling sweet and clean. Ye'll hold her on yer lap because it makes ye happy hearing her small prattle, her laugh. Ye'll play such games with her because they make her smile. Her smile will lighten yer heart with love, for ye will love her then."

She picked Elizabeth up and brought her to her father. "I know ye'll try, Colin, for ye're a good man, as anyone can see. I'll just get my things now, and be off home. 'Tis settlin' dark without."

Colin held his daughter against him, a stranger he had known, yet never known at all. He saw a look of uncertainty on her little face. Something in that look made him want to die inside. She feared him, her own father. She barely knew him, except for that fear. At last he saw her as his own, not Annie's child, but his. She was part of him.

"What soft blond hair ye have," said the father, touching his child with wonder. "Poor little mite, can ye not smile? What have I done to ye, little girl?" He rocked to and fro, holding his daughter close. He sobbed, painful, shuddering tears, in long last release.

Ellen, watching from the door, saw it all. She kissed her own Caitlin, quietly closed the door, then walked down the road to home, humming.

Chapter Sixteen

The heavy March rain pelted the ground, turning the earth to slush. The miners' claims were washed out by the deluge, which laid down sand and gravel over all. The creeks, swelled by the rain, ran high up the banks. There was little to do but wait it out. Nights in the cabin were cold and damp. Restless men, trapped by rain, by mud, grew lonesome.

While the rain danced rhythms on the roof, Danny lay sleepless on his cot, seeing far away. His mind wandered to the green valleys, brightly dotted with wildflowers, the thatched-roofed cottages nestled snugly against the land. The very smell of the earth was different. Lying still, he tried to remember the green, growning smell of Ireland.

His dream took him to the village of Aberthyne, to the old women in their shawls, the old men in their jaunty caps, the tousle-haired children running across the green. He saw the steeple of Saint Anne's, the long black cassock of Father Donnally. It was Sunday. The people were coming to Mass in families: fathers clean-shaven and dressed in their stiff-collared shirts, with their freshly blacked boots; mothers in their best wool dresses, brooches tidy at the neck; rows of children with clean faces, with hair so neatly slicked their mates would hardly know them. The church bell rang, like a voice calling, "Come, come, come." He saw, and heard it all, the things of home.

He could almost hear his mother laughing as she kneaded the soda bread. He could see the cross she marked on it, and smell it as it came out, hot and fragrant from the oven. She smiled at him, as she had when he was a boy. How he missed her. The vision went on. He was awake, yet dreaming.

The rain came thundering loud, threatening, violent. Great cracks of lightning slashed the sky. McTaggart slept through it all, unmoved by its savage beauty. Like the wildness of the winter storm, Danny felt a tremor running through him. Closing his eyes tightly, he could just see her. She was as she had been that last night, never changing. Her lips said she believed him, believed that he would send for her, but all the while, her eyes mourned him, filling her soul with a last look at him.

She had been so vulnerable, so fragile in her faith in him. It troubled him, knowing how hollow a love he had given her—letters from far away, a bit of money sent, the interminable waiting. What am I doing to us both, my Ellen? It's time you came to me. There's more than enough money now. The house I promised you is nearly done. No more waiting will I give you. No more. Too long have we been apart. Things can come between a man and woman in so much time, he thought.

Like the beating of the rain on the roof, his dream played on. He saw them married. He saw their wedding night. She would come to him, her long, lovely hair falling across her bare shoulders. A fire began to burn in him, filling his soul with longing. All the nights that had lain fallow between them were a torment now. He had been much of a boy before, innocent in his love of her. Time and hard work had made him a man. Although he loved and cherished her, no locked door, no honor would ever keep him from her again.

All the night long he lay in the lone and empty dark, certain that the time had come to send for her. Again and again, he watched the visions, the pretty scenes of how it would be between them. Yet there was the nagging fear in the corner of his mind: Was it too late?

In the gray light of morning, he wrote the letter, long before McTaggart rose with the dawn.

Dearest Ellen,

I will not tell you how slowly the gold dust comes, or how muddy the rains have left our camp. I have no care or thought for these things. If you do, you must ask friend McTaggart when you come. They are of great importance to him.

My only interest now is you. I find I can wait no longer to be with you, although the fine house I promised you is not yet finished, nor am I as rich as I might yet be. None of it matters now. I am a man sick with the fever of longing for you. I enclose $1500, which will more than cover your passage fare when put with the bits I have sent before, especially the money I sent on the *Yankee Clipper*. It should be enough for first-class passage. The captains here say the clipper *Flying Cloud* is the swiftest ship to port in Dublin. She is a finely fitted-out vessel, I'm told. You must make your inquiries in Dublin about exact arrival and departure dates. See about selling the cottage now, with all haste. I'm not anxious that it sell for a good price. Father Donnally will arrange for a driver to take you and Caitlin to Dublin, with your belongings. I have written a letter to him as well, and sent him money toward this purpose.

I am told the *Flying Cloud* has been known to make the trip with good sail, in as little as 121 days. How far apart I have put us, Ellen. When I think of how difficult it was for me when I came through Panama, I can only hope that the journey is easier for you. You must bring warm clothes, for Cape Horn is fiercely cold. Now that I have written for you to come to California, it is so hard to think of waiting all the time it will take for this letter to reach you, and then the time for your ship to make its crossing. I must try to be patient. When you have your departure date, write to me at this address to let me know the possible date of arrival:

Daniel O'Mally
P.O. Box #76
San Francisco, California
United States of America

As you can see by the address, we have recently become a state of the Union. Our California flag now flies beneath the flag of the United States on the Court House building here in San Francisco. It gives our state a permanence it didn't have before, belonging to the Union. I find I am attached to this country, in a way I never thought to be. I'm proud of its successes, and protective of its freedoms. This is the country where I want my family to be born, and grow up in. There is a strength in this land that is contagious to its people. Now, you will not only be coming to California, but to a whole new nation.

I will be there to meet you in San Francisco. Come swiftly to me, my own Ellen. Never will I willingly part from you again. God speed the *Flying Cloud*, and set His hand beneath you to protect you.

Your loving,
Danny

Danny's letter was sent by the Pony Express, the fastest way of mail available across the country. The price for a letter was dear, but the dangers to the riders were high. From San Francisco to St. Joseph, Missouri, was two weeks of hard, non-stop riding, with changes of horse and man set up at points along the way. The riders risked Indian attack, exposure to all weather conditions, the danger of their horses falling lame, or breaking a leg and leaving them stranded, even robbery or murder, for it was well known that the Pony Express riders often carried large amounts of cash in their saddlebags.

From St. Joseph, the letter was put aboard a mail car and taken by train to New York, a journey of another two weeks. There, it was loaded in the belly of a clipper ship bound for London—three weeks more. In London, it was routed by train to Sedgewick Ferry, placed in mail bags, and transported across the Irish Channel to Dublin. The letter sat in Dublin Annex for a full fortnight awaiting transport to Aberthyne. In Aberthyne, the postal clerk was ill, and did not deliver the letter until after he had fully recovered from his bout with influenza, a period of yet another two weeks. In all, it was three months from the time Danny, in all urgency, mailed his letter to Ellen to the time she received it.

With the passing of Caitlin's second birthday, Ellen felt time slipping by her, as if she were not living at all. She hadn't heard from Danny in over a year, and found it harder by the day to still cling to the hope that he would send for them. Why hadn't he written? Had something happened to him? Had he changed his mind? In the night, while Caitlin slept, Ellen lay awake, tormented by thoughts of what was to become of them.

"Danny," she said aloud. "Danny! Why don't ye send for me, as ye promised? Keep me, or let me go. Only tell me. Tell me soon."

The next day, when Ellen took Caitlin with her up to the Muldair house, she was gladdened by the sight of the changes taking place between Colin and Elizabeth. He showed his affection to the child in so many little ways, ways that Elizabeth reacted to with the unqualifying love of a baby for anyone who loves her back. What a quick little handful she had become, daring to be as naughty as Caitlin was sometimes. What a pair they were, climbing the walls out before the cottage, watching to see if Ellen saw them in their mischief.

It was a comfortable place for Ellen, for the long days of waiting with no word of Danny. Matthew and Kerry reminded her of her own brothers and sisters. It was as if she was in a big family again. They liked her, she knew, and that made it seem like a home. It was good for Caitlin to have other children to play with, other people to care about. She and Elizabeth were more like sisters. Matt always had something funny to say, a smile in his eyes and on his lips. Kerry needed someone to mother her. It gave Ellen something to do, and people to care about. In recent days, she had even warmed to Colin. A feeling of pity had grown in her for him. At first, she had been angry with him, for how heartlessly he treated Elizabeth, but as she learned the reason for his hardness toward the child, she also saw his pain. His was a terrible loneliness. The very heart of his family had been taken with the death of his wife. Now, after their argument over Elizabeth, Ellen felt a break in the wall he had put up. He was more open to her now. Often, after supper, he wanted to talk about the children, or what he had done that day. He seemed so animated, and glad of her company, as if starved for conversation.

Colin was a steel monger by trade. He handled the white-hot billets of metal at the company yard at Aberthyne. Sometimes, when his shirtsleeves were rolled up, Ellen could see the evidence of his trade, the marks left by burns on his arms and hands from bits of hot steel. He was a rough-hewn man, though, and the scars suited him. Ellen began to relax in his easy company.

"I'm thinkin', Ellen, how natural it seems, you sittin' there at the end of the table and all the children scattered in between us. Does it seem so to you as well?"

"Ye've made us very comfortable here, Colin. Caitlin thrives in the company of yer children."

"Good. That's good," he said. "The way I see it, the children are very fond of ye, but I suspect ye knew that."

"I can see it," she answered, "and I'm glad they are. I'm fond of them too."

"Are ye, Ellen?" he asked. She nodded. "Oh, well,

157

then. I'm not puttin' this so very well," he said, pushing his chair away from the table, and standing up. "I'm not a man for words. I feel like a blatherin' child tryin' to recite his piece at school. I'm tryin' t' tell ye how I feel about ye, how I have felt for some time. I don't rightly know where t' begin." He ran his rough hand across his mouth. "Shall I tell ye how it is now, comin' home of an evenin'? For a year or more, I did it like a lead soldier. Something in me was dead, never to feel joy at life again. Now ye're here, I hurry home, knowing ye'll be here when I come in the door."

"Colin," she said, stopping him, "ye're talkin' like we might be sweethearts an' ye know we're not that. I'm promised to another man."

"Oh, I know all that," he said, brushing her warning aside. "Father Donnally told me about it when ye first came t' work here. Said ye might be leavin' sudden like. It hasn't happened, though, has it? He hasn't sent for ye as he said he would. How long has it been since ye've heard from him? Do ye know if he's even alive? That's a rough place, remember."

She turned her face away, angry at his words.

"Now I've gone an' made ye angry, an' I never meant that. I only wanted ye t' see that waitin' for him, maybe, was a fruitless task. Ye might be waitin' forever. An' there's Caitlin t' think about," he added.

"What about Caitlin?" she asked him, defiance shining in her eyes.

"Aberthyne's a small place. A child like Caitlin growin' up without a father's name is bound t' bear the ridicule of other children. The young are sometimes cruel. The way it is, ye're makin' a hard road for her."

158

"Caitlin'll be fine. She won't have to depend on this place or these people for her happiness. We're not stayin' here anyhow. As soon as Danny sends for us, we'll be gone, wipin' the dust of this place from our feet." She was angry, angry at the knot of fear his words produced in her. She could bear the shunning of their neighbors in Aberthyne, but Caitlin was a child. It was a raw pain to Ellen, thinking of Caitlin having to suffer it. Damn Colin for making her think of it.

"I wonder if ye might want t' marry me," Colin said.

Ellen couldn't think what to say.

"I know ye don't love me," he told her, "but ye might learn to . Ye've made me feel alive again, as nothin' has in so long. Only say that ye'll think about it, will ye, Ellen?"

"I don't have to think, Colin," she answered, standing up, and going for her things. "I won't marry ye, because I don't love ye, as ye say. It wouldn't be right, don't ye see? A marriage like that would be a dead, hopeless thing. If ye feel alive again, Colin, it's 'cause yer time of mournin' is over. It's time for ye to look around, and find a wife—but not me. I'm not that one. I'm sorry if ye thought I was."

He said nothing more, his teeth clenched hard in his jaw. She got Caitlin and left the cottage, walking the short distance up the hill. It was bitter cold out, and dark earlier now that it was winter. She hugged Caitlin to her for warmth, and bundled her shawl around the child, leaving her own shoulders bare.

The events of the night troubled her. What will I do now? How can I go on working for Colin after this? Why did he have to say that about Caitlin? She was worrying about it all when she opened the cottage door and stepped

159

into the dark room. Her foot slipped on something on the floor.

"Who's puttin' things under our door?" she said to Caitlin, worrying about her unfriendly neighbors.

She felt around blindly for a candle, and a match to light it. She brought the single flame close to the floor, peered down, and picked the object up. A letter.

Chapter Seventeen

Life is like a ball of twine, unraveling, rolling along in its own set course, marred by occasional knots and tangles, and ending only when the twine is spent. Once again, the course of Ellen's life was altered by the arrival of a letter. Danny had sent for her at last. She could have been Mrs. Colin Muldair with four children to fill her house before she ever touched the marriage bed. A simple life, an ordinary life. But now, Danny had sent for her, and all that she had hoped for would be. The dream she had carried like a child within her for two years was being born at last.

She made up her mind to tell Colin at once. Putting it off would only make things worse between them. If he hated her, well, then, let him hate her for the truth, for that was all she'd ever given him.

He was waiting for her when she came walking up the road, standing outside in the garden with Elizabeth on his shoulders. It was a nice scene, the two of them together like that, but Colin looked exhausted, as if he hadn't slept the night through. His eyes were sunken in, and even in the bright daylight, his skin had an unnatural pallor.

"I've been waitin' for ye, this mornin'," he began. "I wanted t' tell ye that I said too much last night. Not that it isn't how I feel," he added, "but I didn't mean t' say it so sudden like." He looked as if he'd been practicing that explanation all night, like a schoolboy reciting his piece. "I don't want ye bein' mad at me still. Are ye?" he asked, looking even more like a little boy.

"No, Colin. Ye shouldn't have worried over it. Ye don't look well to me. Have ye had any sleep last night?"

"I can sleep any night," he answered lightly. "I liked havin' someone t' worry about," he confessed.

"I got a letter from Danny," she said, straight out.

"Ye never did," he argued. "How would ye have gotten a letter when ye told me yesterday that ye hadn't heard from him?"

"It was there, under the door, when I came home last night. He's sent for us, Colin, sent the passage money an' all."

Colin was silent for a long time. He put Elizabeth on the grass beside Caitlin. When he looked at her, it was with eyes hard and cold. "So ye're goin'?"

She nodded.

"I wish ye'd never have come at all. Ye've made a fool of me, haven't ye?"

"Ye know that isn't so. I never meant to hurt ye."

"Makin' a man come alive with longin' for ye, an' then castin' him aside when ye're through with him. Does yer boyo across the sea know how ye've been carryin' on behind his back? No, I'll wager not. Go on then, and damn ye!" he shouted. "I'll not be beggin' ye t' stay." He walked out of the yard, leaving the children wide-eyed, staring after him.

"Colin, wait!" she called after him. "Colin!" She ran up the road, but he was gone. She came back then. The children were staring at her, their mouths open in surprise.

She couldn't leave them alone. They were frightened, their father going out like that. He was gone all that day. That night Ellen made them all supper, and put Elizabeth and Caitlin to bed.

He was drunk when he came in, she could smell it on his breath. "Go to bed, Matthew, Kerry," she told them. They were frightened, she could see. "I'll talk to him. Go to bed, an' stay out of his way." They hurried away, casting worried looks over their shoulders at their father, slumped in the chair.

"Go home," he said to her, not looking up from the floor.

"I've made ye a plate of supper." She set the plate before him, hoping the food might sober him up enough for her to leave.

"Do ye think I want anythin' from ye!" he shouted, throwing the plate against the wall, where it shattered and broke into a thousand bits.

"Stop it!" she screamed at him, horrified at what was happening.

He stood up, looking as if he wanted to kill her with his own bare hands, and said, "Why don't ye just leave? Will ye leave a man no dignity? Take yer brat an' get out of here."

"Yes," she said, trembling. "I will. I will now." She started for the room where Caitlin slept, and had gone but two steps when his hand reached out to grab her and pull her to him. He crushed her against him so tight, she could not breathe. She struggled to push away, but his arms held her like a vise.

"Colin, let me go!"

He pulled her closer, and kissed her. "Don't leave me, Ellen. I'll die if ye leave me. I can't hurt ye," he whispered softly. "I can't even hate ye." His arms went slack, and she stepped back from him. "Please don't leave me," he said again, but there was something about the way he looked. It was more than being drunk. He was trying to control his balance, putting his hand out to catch her shoulder for support.

"Colin, what's wrong with ye? Are ye sick?"

"I . . . I don't know. I feel so . . ." His hand slipped off her shoulder, and he fell to the floor.

"Colin!" she cried, putting her hand to his brow. "Ye're burnin' up with fever."

"It's all right, Ellen." He tried to rise up from the floor. "I'm just drunk."

"It's not all right. Ye're sick. Let me help ye." She put her shoulder beneath his arm, and helped him to his feet. She walked him to his room, helped him to lie down, and covered him with a thin blanket.

"Don't leave me, Ellen," he pleaded, chills replacing the fever.

"Try and rest, Colin," she told him. "I'll be here when ye wake up." He closed his eyes and slept.

Through the night, Ellen sat beside him, bathing his face with water when his fever was high, and covering him with blankets when he shivered with chills. His skin was so hot, at times, she thought he might die, and she resolved to get the doctor for him in the morning, no matter what it cost. She would use some of Danny's money if she had to. She couldn't just stand by and let Colin die.

164

At times, he was delirious, calling out things that made no sense, and once he called out his wife's name. "Annie!" he said, in a loud voice, as if calling to her to come back. Sometimes the fever would leave him, and he would look at her, clear-headed.

"I'm sorry, Ellen," he told her. "I never meant t' get ye into this. Go on home now," he urged her. "I'll be right enough in the morning. I wish I hadn't kissed ye," he added. "I never would have done it if I'd known I was sick."

"I'm not goin' anywhere till I know ye're well," she answered him. "Don't be worryin' about me now. Close yer eyes and rest."

By morning, the fever was constant. "I'm goin' for the doctor," she told Matthew. "Stay out of his room, all of ye."

There was but one doctor in Aberthyne, Josiah Royce, a young Englishman contracted by the steelyard to treat their men, and only secondarily the other inhabitants of Aberthyne. Being English, he was not always trusted by the men. Ellen had heard Colin speak of how the men thought his ideas too modern, too radical, for them. They preferred the more familiar remedies of purging, blistering, and bleeding, as their old Irish doctor had treated their ills before he died. Colin had let Kerry's swollen tonsils go by two months ago, without calling in the doctor, preferring to treat it himself rather than take a chance with his child on this English doctor. Still, Ellen thought, he's all we've got, and Colin will hardly know he's there anyhow, so gone with fever is he.

"I've come about Colin Muldair," she said to Dr. Royce when she was allowed into his office. "He's bad sick, brewin' a fever all night."

"Are you his wife?"

She shook her head, silent and shy in this room full of books and medicines on the shelf.

"Well, perhaps I'll come by this evening. I've got office hours to keep this morning. If you could bring him in . . ."

"I can't be bringin' him in! He's lost in fever, I tell ye. Ye need t' come with me right now, if ye're a proper doctor, as ye say. The men of this town wouldn't think too well of a doctor who won't treat one of their own from the mill," she added, hoping to pressure him to come.

He seemed to be weighing that. "All right. If he's as bad as you say, perhaps I'd better come now."

He drove them both in the buggy back to the Muldair cottage. They could hear Colin shouting before they opened the door. He was raving at Matthew, half sitting up in the bed.

"What'd I do?" Matthew asked Ellen, tears filling his eyes. "He took on so, like he hated me."

"Ssh, Matt. It's the fever talkin' with yer da. He don't know what he's sayin'."

"I'm glad ye're here, Ellen," he said, hugging her tightly. "He was actin' mad. He scared Kerry," the boy told her, unwilling to admit his fear.

"I've brought the doctor, Matt. He'll soon have yer da well again. Take the children up to my cottage, there's a good boy. I'll depend on ye and Kerry to mind the babies for the day. I'm trustin' ye with a lot of responsibility, 'cause I want to stay here and help yer da." She brushed the shock of hair out of his eyes, as his own mother might have done.

He reached up, in that instant, and kissed her on the cheek. "I love ye, Ellen," he said.

166

Her throat tightened with the effort to keep the tears from her own eyes. "I love ye too, Matt. Now go on up to the cottage, and keep a sharp eye on the little ones, won't ye? Off ye go," she hurried him.

Colin had quieted again, and was very still when Ellen came to the doorway of the room. Dr. Royce was leaning over him, looking in his mouth, and poking around the outside of Colin's throat.

"What's the matter with him, then?" she whispered, afraid to disturb Colin again.

"Diphtheria, it looks like. There's a hard patch of fibrous growth at the back of his throat. I scratched at it with a swab, and it held on tough as flesh. I scraped it away, and it's bleeding now. That'll help him breathe for a little, but it'll come back soon enough. If I can keep his throat clean and clear for the next few days, he's got a chance of making it. Otherwise, the membrane will close right over his airway, and he'll die."

"His neck's so swollen," said Ellen, coming closer. "Is that from the membranes too?" It made her feel a sharp stick of pain in her own throat, thinking about how that tough, hard mass could cling to your throat and shut off your air.

"No, the bull neck's not from the membranes, but from the swelling of the glands and muscles around the larynx. What we must concentrate on first is getting his fever down. Might I have a glass of cool water?"

Ellen brought him one, and he mixed a white powder into it. She watched him carefully, inspecting everything he did.

"It's all right, I won't poison him."

"What is that ye're givin' him? Shouldn't ye bleed him?"

"Bleeding will only make him weaker, and he'll need all the strength he has to survive this. This compound is quinine. It will help control the fever."

"Quinine?" she said, filling her mouth with the word, as if it were a tablespoon of cod-liver oil.

"What do I call you?" he said, wondering at her relationship to this man.

"Ellen's my name."

"Well, Ellen, I know the men from the steel mill don't trust me because I'm English." She had the grace not to argue with that. "I am a qualified doctor, though, and I'm going to do my best to try to help this man. I'm younger than the doctor who was here before me, and I've learned more recent treatments for diphtheria. Will you trust me enough to do what I ask when I need your help?"

"I will," she answered, without hesitation.

"Good," the doctor said. "Then he's got a chance."

Colin worsened during the day. By evening, his breathing was ragged and sounded as though it was being sucked through wet wool. Dr. Royce kept the kettle boiling all day. He'd added a tea of fine ground leaves to the pot, pungent and strong-smelling.

"What is it?" Ellen asked. "Such a smell."

"Eucalyptus leaf, from the Orient," he told her. "It's helpful in opening up the breathing passages. The clipper ships bring it in with the tea."

She wrinkled her nose at the smell, but said nothing more. She was watching the rivulets of water drip down the windows and walls, like a storm within the house. It pearled the glass like jewels, from the constant steam. The air was thick, and hot, and moist, as though she were

168

breathing through a fine mist. The room was quiet now. The quinine had brought the fever down lower, and Colin slept.

"Go and see to those children," the doctor told her at six. "You can spell me when you come back."

The air outside the cottage was sweet and clean, fresh and light. She sucked it in greedily, and made her steps slow to have the joy of it longer. Exhaustion heavied her step, and worry was her companion. Her own throat felt sore and tender, from the strong scent of the eucalyptus, which she still carried in her nostrils.

"Is my da all right?" Matthew asked first, when she came into the cottage. Kerry stood close beside him, waiting to hear too.

"His fever's better, but he's still very sick. I'm goin' back to him after supper, if ye can put yerselves to bed."

"We're not bairns," Matt answered, looking insulted.

"I know that," she assured him. "Eat yer supper now, so I can get back to yer father. I must give the doctor time to go home and have his own rest."

"Ellen," Matt asked her quietly, while the others were eating, "our da's not goin' to die, is he?"

"I hope not, Matt," she answered him truthfully. "We're doin' our best for him." If Colin dies, she thought suddenly, Matt, Kerry and Elizabeth will be orphans.

Caitlin cried when Ellen left her, but Elizabeth sat very still, her thumb firmly in her mouth and her large eyes watching Ellen leave, turning inward again to her old silence. It broke Ellen's heart to see her do that. What would happen to the child if Colin died? Would she shrink inside herself, and never be whole again?

Instead of going to the Muldair cottage, she went to St.

169

Anne's and knocked on the door of the rectory. Father Donnally came out.

"What is it, Ellen? Why are you here so late at night?"

"It's Colin, Father. I think he's dyin'. Can ye come?"

"Wait there," he told her, without a moment's hesitation. "I'll get my things."

Father Donnally stayed with Ellen, while Dr. Royce was gone. Ellen listened as he gave Colin the last rites of the Church, and saw him mark Colin's head with a cross of holy oil. With Colin so quiet, drugged with the opium Dr. Royce had given him before he left, he seemed already dead, but for the sound of his labored breathing.

"Shall I stay with you a while?" Father Donnally asked.

She shook her head. "No. I'd like to be alone with him for a while."

He left her then, promising to come back in the morning to check on them both. What else can I do for ye, Colin? she thought. I've brought ye the doctor, foreign though he may be. I've brought ye the priest, for yer soul's sake. Now, must I watch ye die?

Dr. Royce was gone for several hours, during which time Ellen sat beside Colin, wringing a wet flannel in a basin of cool water and wiping his face and neck with it. Tiredness dragged at her. This was her second night without sleep. She talked to Colin, though he could not hear her, to keep herself awake, and to give herself company against the fear of death in the room.

She was alone with him when he started to strangle. The sound was awful, short, staccato gasps which brought no air. Ellen sat him up higher in the bed, pounded on his back, and then watched in horror as his skin turned red, and then a wine blue. His eyes went wide in panic, and his fingers tore at the skin of his throat, as though trying to find a way for the air to break through. His head slumped, chin to his chest, unconscious.

"Colin!" she screamed. What was it Royce did? She fought her panic to remember. The swabs were all in his medical bag, which he had taken with him. Something to break through an airway, she remembered. What! Revulsion vied with horror as she stuck her fingers into Colin's mouth. The candlelight in the room was too dim to see his throat. She had to feel her way, along the roof of his mouth, to something hard at the back. She slid her fingers lower. Something thicker there. What if it's part of his throat, she thought, and I poked a hole through it? Would I be guilty of murder? "God help me," she prayed, and pushed two fingers hard against the thick, slimy-feeling mass, and then harder still, with a great force. It gave, embedding her fingers in its mass, like poking her hand through a rotten potato.

There was an audible hiss when her fingers broke through the hard mucus plug, and air rushed into Colin's lungs. Blood poured from the wound. So much that Ellen feared she had killed him. She was still wiping the blood from his mouth when Dr. Royce came back to the cottage.

"Have I kilt him?" she asked, holding the candle high above Colin's head, while Dr. Royce staunched the wound.

"You did just right, girl," he said, with a firmness to his voice that was authoritarian, and resolute, and English. "You did better than I might have done myself."

She cried then, giving way to the tiredness she felt, and the roughness of her own raw throat. He had come so close, with only her between him and death. "Will he live?" she asked, when the tears were ended.

"I can't say. The disease is at its worst the first four days. After that, the membranes shrink and disappear. If he can survive the next two days, then he'll make it."

Ellen slumped in her chair, worn out and sick at heart.

"You go on to your home now," Royce told her, helping her up. "Go home and sleep."

The fresh air was no comfort to her as she walked down the hill, for the weight of the world was dragging her down. The children were asleep, and the fire in the grate was banked and low. She lay down on her bed, and before a thought could come to her, she was asleep.

Chapter Eighteen

Ellen awoke to the sound of coughing. It invaded her sleep and pitted her consciousness with its barrage of sound. Colin! Then she remembered where she was. Standing up, still fully clothed from the previous night, she went out to see who was ill.

Kerry was sitting at the table, her face red with the strain of coughing. She was crying softly, and looked miserable.

"Kerry," Ellen said gently, coming over and laying her hand on the child's forehead. Hot, as she'd feared. "Ye should have woken me and told me ye were sick."

"I feel so bad, Ellen," Kerry said, and cried again with the pain. "My throat is achin' me, worse than when my tonsils were so bad, a ways back."

"I wish ye'd have told me sooner," Ellen said again. "This didn't come on this bad so sudden, did it?"

"She's afraid of the doctor," Matthew said, speaking up for his sister. "Kerry's always been afraid of doctors, with their nasty medicines and their leeches, ever since our mother died."

Kerry wailed in earnest now, more afraid than ever after Matt's words.

"Stop that, Matt," Ellen hushed him. "Kerry's got enough on her plate, without ye addin' more t' her fears." She hugged Kerry to her, and felt the heat from Kerry's skin burn through her own thin dress.

"Are ye still gonna leave us?" Kerry asked her. "Are ye still goin' t' America?"

For the first time that day, Ellen thought of Danny, and the new life waiting for her in America. If she could only take her child and run to it, before it was too late. "I'm not goin' anywhere till ye're well again, don't ye worry," she told Kerry.

"I'm scared, Ellen. I'm real scared," Kerry said, and started to cry. "I wish my ma were here."

"Come here, Kerry," Ellen urged her, and held the girl in her lap and rocked her as she thought Kerry's mother might have done. God help us, she thought. God help us all.

By evening, Ellen had brought all the children back to the Muldair cottage. Kerry was very ill, trembling with high fever, and Elizabeth and Matthew showed signs of being ill too. Ellen had no time for anything but spooning broth into Kerry's mouth, sponging fevered bodies with cool water, making tea for the doctor, and carrying soiled flannels and swabs and cotton out to the fire, to be burned. Colin was desperately ill. The skin on his face seemed to have sunken, and now hung on his cheekbones. Worse, his color was gray. He had regained consciousness, and moaned in great pain.

Father Donnally came again. He gave last rites to both

Kerry and Matthew, and sat again with Colin, talking to him softly. Ellen guessed it was a last confession, and stayed clear of them.

Dr. Royce looked exhausted, and Ellen felt herself about to drop with fatigue. Father Donnally came up to Royce and said, "I'll stay with them for the night, Doctor. You go to your home and have your night's rest. I can see you're worn out. Ellen, you'd best lie down yourself. You'll not do anybody any good like you are."

Royce left them then, and Ellen lay down beside Caitlin for a few moments. She couldn't rest. The children were crying, and suffering terribly. Pulling herself away from her child, she went back to the sick children who needed her.

"I thought I told you to lie down," Father Donnally said roughly. "Haven't you enough sense to know when you're about to drop, woman?"

"Don't, Father," she said, stopping him. "I can't go to bed and close m' eyes to sleep when these children are hurtin' like this an' callin' to me. I'm not made of stone. Leave me be. If I drop, I drop."

"I'd say Colin Muldair got more than he bargained for with you, Ellen," he told her, admiring her loyalty to this family.

"No, Father," she answered, thinking of how Colin had asked her to be his wife. "In fact, I'd say it was a little less."

Despite Ellen's constant bathing of her, and despite Dr. Royce's quinine, Kerry's fever rose uncontrollably, until the child was laying limp as a rag in Ellen's arms, her eyes scarcely seeing.

"Mama? Where did ye go, Mama?" Kerry said to the vision only she was witness to. "I've been so afraid. I feel bad, Mama. I feel so bad. Come an' kiss me, Mama. Come and kiss me and make me well."

The mother bent and kissed the child, and only Kerry knew if she saw Ellen, or her own mother. It didn't matter, for at that moment, Ellen was her mother, and her tears fell against Kerry's cheek, as Annie's might have. She held Kerry, even through the terror of the convulsions which came of the fever; even after, when Kerry lay so still, scarcely breathing; and even when she was very sure that Kerry breathed no more. She held her close, and let her tears fall.

"Let me take her now, Ellen," Father Donnally insisted. "She's beyond our help now." He laid Kerry Muldair in her bed, and began the prayers for the dead.

Colin Muldair was a strong man. His body was hardened by his work at the steelyard. It took more than the fever which killed Kerry to conquer Colin. It took the strangulating membranes of diphtheria to choke the life from him. Three days he had struggled. Every breath was a battle that he fought, forcing his body to make the exhausting effort to draw in another torturous breath of air. Ellen watched him in his struggle, knowing that he fought the harder for his children's sake. If he gave up, stopped fighting, and let himself die, his children would be orphans. I wonder, Ellen thought, does he know that Kerry's dead? Would he struggle so if he knew?

Four days. Ellen remembered Dr. Royce's words. If he lasted four days, the membranes would begin to recede of their own. He had made it through three. "One more day, Colin," she told him. "Hold on one more day." His eyes, when they looked at her, said they would try.

Dr. Royce returned on the morning of the third day of Colin's illness. His first duty was to sign the death certificate for Kerry Muldair, and see to the removal of her body from the cottage. Ellen watched in mute grief as he bound Kerry's body in a sheet of linen cloth, laid her body on the back seat of his buggy, and drove her to the small mortuary in Aberthyne to await burial.

When he returned, it was to three very ill patients. Matthew and Elizabeth were in a rage of fever. Matthew whimpered as he tossed fretfully on his sheet, but Elizabeth screamed in pain, her voice hoarse with the agony of it. Ellen carried her in her arms the whole of that day, for when she laid the child down, mucus choked her and Elizabeth would start to strangle.

"Give her to me," Dr. Royce said when Ellen looked too exhausted to move, but she only shook her head.

"She doesn't know ye. It would only make her cry the harder. I'm fine. See to Matt."

Holding Elizabeth, Ellen felt herself sinking. It was as though something pulled at her, dragging her down. She had to struggle to hold on to her strength. They all needed her. Elizabeth slept on her shoulder, and for one blissful moment, Ellen let herself dream. It gave her courage, this dream. It made her strong. It was a dream of love, clean and sweet. Love which had crossed an ocean, and yet held to her with its promise of future. There was hope in that love. She clung to the hope it gave her, and pulled herself back from the drag of defeat and bought another night to fight against death.

The morning of the fourth day dawned, with Ellen asleep in the chair, holding Elizabeth against her. She had slept an hour, maybe two, and awoke, startled to see the light of the new day in the room. She could hear

Colin's breathing, sounding clearer than it had during the night. The fourth day, she remembered. It's the fourth day. He's going to live.

"He's better?" she asked Dr. Royce, who had sat beside Colin's bed all night.

"His breathing's easier. Even his color's better," he told her. "We may pull him through, if we're lucky."

"An' how's Matt?" she asked, a kernel of belief that things might turn in their favor began in Ellen. Surely, Colin was not spared to be bereft of children. Matt and Elizabeth must survive, with their father.

"Diphtheria's harder on children," he told her. "Hardest of all on that one you've got there." He pointed to Elizabeth, in Ellen's arms. "I don't know how she's lasted this long."

Ellen knew. It was her own heart which kept Elizabeth alive. Her own will. Lying against her body, Elizabeth could feel Ellen's heart beat, and her own beat in answer to it, and her own breath drew strength from the sound of Ellen's breathing. If there was such a thing as a power of will, Elizabeth Muldair was alive because of Ellen's.

"I'll give Matt some broth," Ellen suggested, wanting to do something to help the boy.

"He can't swallow it," Royce told her.

Unwilling to accept what Dr. Royce was telling her, Ellen pulled her chair beside Matthew's cot. The boy lay flat as the sheets, his face colorless. He looked so alone, so fragile in this body racked with disease. Her Matt—always a look about him full of mischief. He was a little sprite—a changling, his father called him—so different from the rest of his family, so alive. And now . . .

"Ellen," he said to her, startling her out of her remembrances.

178

"Yes, Matt?" she said, picking up his hand and kissing it.

"Am I dyin', Ellen? Am I dyin' like Kerry?"

Something in her heart grew so tight, she almost couldn't speak. Her eyes burned with the need to cry, but she held the tears back, knowing they would frighten him.

"Course ye're not dyin', silly. Ye're very sick, I know, but ye're gettin' better. Dr. Royce says ye'll be well soon. Only rest now, Matt." She stroked his hair.

"Where's my da?" he asked her, his eyes frightened.

"He's very sick, Matt. I'll take care of ye, don't ye worry. We mustn't bother yer da right now. I'll be right here all the night through, so ye hold my hand, and I'll tell ye a story about the kings of Ireland."

He closed his eyes then, and listened as she weaved a dream for him, a lovely dream to chase away the thoughts of death. She spoke to him until she was sure he was asleep, and still she went on, afraid to stop the tale, afraid that when she did, he would die.

Hours later, Dr. Royce checked the boy again. "He's better," he said to her, incredulous at the change in the child. "He's passed the crisis. I think he's going to live."

Only then did she let the tears she had been holding back all night fall. Only then did she pray. It was not a prayer of asking, for she believed God had turned away from her petitions, but a prayer of gratefulness. "Dear Father," she said, "thank you for sparing his life."

He woke then, eyes staring up at her in concern. "Don't cry, Ellen. I'm not so sick anymore. Please don't cry."

She laid the palm of his hand against her cheek, and kissed the inside of it.

"I love ye very much, Matthew Muldair," she told him, tears streaming down her cheeks.

"I love ye too, Ellen," he whispered, and then closed his eyes again and slept.

Ellen sat beside him all of the night through. Like a guardian, she watched over him. She turned her head to see her own child, Caitlin, sleeping peacefully, unharmed by the illness in this house. God protect her, she thought, surprised at herself for asking such a boon. "Dear God, protect her," she said aloud, reaching into the hollows of her own soul at last, "protect us all."

Dr. Royce was gone to his home when Colin awoke. He had other patients that he must see, other cases of diphtheria in the town that must be treated. He hoped it would not be an epidemic, for he was ill prepared to care for many such cases. Colin rose up from his bed, with only Caitlin awake to see him. She watched him move around the room. Only Caitlin, of all the children, had not sickened. Colin moved purposefully through the cottage, first to Elizabeth's bed, then Matt's cot, and then to Kerry's empty bed. He tore the bedclothes from it, calling, "Where's our Kerry? What's happened? Kerry! Where are ye?"

"Colin, come back to yer bed," Ellen called out to him. "Ye're not well enough to be walkin' about."

"What's happened to my daughter?" he asked, eyes wild with fear. "Where's m' child?" He didn't wait for her answer, but began calling again, his voice harsh sounding with weakness. "Kerry! Kerry, child! Where are ye, little girl? Where are ye, Kerry?"

"Colin, she's not here," Ellen told him, her eyes

unable to meet his own.

"Not here? Where is she then?" He turned to her, and saw his answer in her downcast face. "No!" he cried. "Not our Kerry. No!" he shouted, and went running to the door.

"Colin! What are ye doin'?" Ellen called to him, in real panic, for he was out the door, and running like a madman down the road. She ran after him, but he was wild in his need to find his child. She couldn't leave the other children alone in the cottage, especially with Matt and Elizabeth so sick.

"Colin, please come back!" she cried out once more, with none to answer her call but the stillness of the night. Caitlin began crying, afraid to be alone in the house after all the yelling and screaming. With one final look down the road where Colin had gone, Ellen turned and went back to the cootage.

"We found him," Dr. Royce told her when he arrived the next morning. He had come to check the children, and pronounced them much improved.

"How is he?" Ellen asked quickly.

"Dead, I'm sorry to tell you."

"What?" Ellen couldn't believe his words. "But that can't be. He was getting well. He ran out of here on his own strength. He was better," she insisted.

"I know. I know. But it was his heart, you see. Diphtheria's hard on the heart muscle, weakens it badly. When he raced out of here like he did, just up from his sickbed, it put too much of a strain on it. He didn't get two miles down the road, poor fellow."

"Oh, Colin!" she cried, head in her hands, weeping for

him, for his children, for all of them. She thought of all the suffering he had known, first Annie, then Kerry, and knew that their losses had been too hard. He had not strength enough to bear it.

"Go home now, lad," she whispered, tears blinding her eyes. "Go home, Colin."

Chapter Nineteen

"Now, Ellen, be sensible," Father Donnally urged her.

"I am being sensible," Ellen argued. "I'm taking Matthew and Elizabeth to America, and no one's going to stop me." She had never spoken to a priest like this before in all her life, but something in her was more determined than unnerved. Her love for the children prompted the words.

"I can't allow it, Ellen. You're not even a relative. You're not married. You're going to another country, where who knows what may happen to them. No, it's too much of a risk."

"Risk! Do ye think it's less of a risk leavin' them to live their young lives in an orphanage? What sort of a life is that? Will the orphanage care for them as I do? Will they love them? No, they won't. Orphanages are for children who have no one. Matt and Elizabeth aren't orphans. They have me." She put her arms around the children, as if daring anyone to take them away.

"But what about Danny?" he reminded her. "What if he refuses them?"

The thought had occurred to her too. It was more than she should ask of him, but what else could she do? How could she make him see?

"He won't refuse them, Father. I know he won't. He took Caitlin and me in, didn't he? He'll understand how I feel about the children."

Father Donnally looked doubtful.

"If the worst happens and he won't accept them, I'll work and support them myself. There aren't many women in California. There must be a great lot of work I could do, cooking and laundry. I'd do whatever I had to do to take care of them, that I promise ye."

"I don't know, Ellen. I just don't know," Father Donnally said, rubbing his brow as if to ease the worry from it. "I know the love you bear the children, and they you, but this seems such an impulsive act. So much could go wrong. I'm responsible for their welfare. I can't make this sort of decision lightly."

"Ye won't leave us, will ye, Ellen?" Matt cried. "We'd hate it in Dublin. I know we would. Don't leave us alone. Take us with ye, please take us."

Elizabeth began crying then, not because she understood what was being said, but because Matt looked so afraid and he was shouting. She clung to Ellen, her little arms wrapped tight around Ellen's neck. Even Caitlin began to cry, frightened by the loud voices and the tears.

"Shush now, all of ye," Ellen said, trying to comfort them. "No one's bein' left behind. We're all stickin' together, just as I said we would. Now stop that wailin'. Matt, give Elizabeth yer handkerchief, there's a good boy. Don't ye worry. Everythin' will be fine, won't it, Father?" she asked, looking imploringly at the priest.

Matt spoke up again. "If our da was still here, we could

stand Ellen going away, but we've got no one else. Please don't send us to the orphanage, Father. Please don't."

"I don't know how I'll manage it," Father Donnally began, still rubbing his brow in that peculiar way. "I may be the greatest sort of fool," he allowed, "but I do believe in you, Ellen. I believe in the love you have for these children, and they for you. I trust you'll do everything you can to see them safe in your care. If I'm a fool, then it's the same sort of foolishness that brought me to the priesthood in the first place, a belief in the goodness of people. You will go to America, Matthew and Elizabeth. I'll see to it."

He smiled at them then, and Ellen hugged her children to her, for they were her children now, all of them. "It's all right, chicks." She kissed the two little girls, and dried their tears. "We're a family now. We're really a family."

"Then, we can go?" Matt asked, hardly daring to believe it.

"And didn't I tell ye we would, Matt?" Ellen whispered, and smiled encouragingly at him. "Of course we can go."

He looked at her with eyes so full of trust and love, she felt warmed by them. "Ellen?" he asked shyly.

"Yes, Matt?"

"Can we call ye Mother, then?" He wouldn't look at her. His eyes stared hard at the floor.

"From this day, Matthew Muldair"—she lifted his chin, to look into her eyes—"ye are my son, and Elizabeth my daughter." His lip trembled and his eyes filled with tears. "None of that now." She hugged him to her. "This is a happy day. Come here, m' darlin' boy."

"I'll do my best to be a good son. I promise," he told her. Someday I'll make ye proud of me. Someday I'll

185

repay ye for all ye've done for us."

She hugged him to her all the more tightly. They all had so much love to give, and so much love they needed too. The look on Matthew's face just then, and the way he held her as if afraid to let her go, told her that what she was doing was right. Somehow it would work. Somehow they would make it, together.

Dear Danny,

I send you my love. Before anything else, I send you that. We have missed so much of each other's lives, but this one thing, my love for you, hasn't changed.

So much has happened to both of us since we have been apart. I have read your letters from California with amazement. To think you have found gold! I must tell you now, the money you sent on the *Yankee Clipper* never arrived. You must discover what happened to it.

I have been working for a family here. Father Donnally suggested that I might be able to help them, since their mother had died a year before. There is so much I might tell you, but I will tell you all when I see you. For now, you must know that there has been terrible sickness in this family, diphtheria. I stayed and nursed them during the sickness, and so missed sailing on the *Flying Cloud*, as you said. I could not leave them so ill, with no one to care for them. Despite the doctor's and my best care, the father, Colin Muldair, and one of his daughters, Kerry, died of the illness. Matthew and his sister, Elizabeth, survived.

Matthew is eleven, and Elizabeth is two, the same

age as Caitlin. I am bringing them with me to California, Danny. I know this is a shock to you, but I can see no other way of dealing with the situation. They love me, and I love them. I cannot leave them.

We are sailing on the *North Star*, leaving Dublin on July 10th. I am told we may arrive in San Francisco as early as November 20th. That seems a very long time to me, but each day will bring us a little closer.

Caitlin is well, and has grown so much, you will not recognize her. She and I remained well, when all else were so sick.

I long to see you again, Danny, and pray that you will be there, standing on the wharf to meet us when we arrive. I have asked so much for you to understand and accept of me, and now I ask this too. I come to you with the hope that you will accept us all, but if you cannot, I understand, and release you now from your promise to me.

With greatest love,
Ellen

It was raining when Ellen mailed the letter to Danny, raining when she turned away from the cottage that had been her home for so long. She was grateful for the rain, letting the tears which welled up in her eyes fall and mingle with it. It was sad leaving all the furniture Danny had made behind in the cottage for someone else to use. She couldn't take it with her on the ship, not even the cradle he had made for Caitlin. All of it was sold with the cottage. Father Donnally sold Colin's cottage too, and added the money to Ellen's, toward passage for the children. They would have enough for first-class fare.

She and the children said their good-byes to Father Donnally, and received his blessing. "It hurts me to see so many of Ireland's best people leaving her," he said to Ellen. "So many of you will never return, and that is Ireland's loss." He laid his hand upon the crown of her head. "May the Lord keep you in His care for all your life, and bring you happiness at last. May your children rise up and call you blessed."

She could only stand and let the tears mark channels down her cheeks. She took his hand quickly and kissed it, then turned and helped the children up into the cart taking them to Dublin. "Go now," she said to the driver. "Please go."

"Good-bye," the children shouted, excited to be going on a journey. "Good-bye." They waved at the lone figure who watched them drive away. Ellen turned and saw him standing there, long after the cart was far down the road, waving to them still. In her mind, that image would stay with her forever. It was Ireland, saying good-bye.

On the deck of the *North Star*, on the morning she sailed, Ellen stood at the rail, her thoughts filled with memories of the country that had been her home for all her life.

"Good-bye, Ireland, land of poets and kings," she said to the silence around her. "Good-bye, Mother, Father, brothers and sisters, all. Good-bye, old cottage—may the fire never go out on yer hearth. Good-bye, Dougal, father of my child. Do ye ever think of me? I wonder. Do ye ever wish . . . no, that was a life ago. Good-bye, poor Colin, and little Kerry. In a way, I take part of you with me.

Good-bye to all of you. Good-bye, Ireland, good-bye."

Pulling herself away from her sad thoughts, she gathered her children to her. They were her country now, her family. The *North Star* pulled away from Dublin Harbor, and they sailed with her, a new life to begin.

The crash of the waves against the ship created a rocking motion that was to be common for the next four months. At first, Ellen's stomach rebelled, but soon the odd movement became as natural to her as it was to the crew climbing the rigging.

Ellen shared a cabin with the children, four berths in a smartly fitted-out room of satinwood and mahogany panels and trim. Caitlin and Elizabeth spent part of each day taking turns at the porthole, watching the sea birds or simply looking at the pretty curl of the waves. For their safety, Ellen spent most of her day in the cabin. When she did take them out, she held them both tightly by the hand, as though the next wave might tear them from her. Without a hand to steady herself against the rail, she and the girls sometimes went rolling with the ship.

They were good companions, Caitlin and Elizabeth. Hours were spent playing with dolls and sharing silly little games. Matthew was allowed the freedom of the ship, as long as he didn't get in anyone's way. He quickly made friends with the crew and a few of the children in steerage.

It wasn't unpleasant, once Ellen got used to the rocking. In fact, it brought a kind of peace to her. The terrible time they had been through so recently was eased by the quiet days of open sea and rest. Finding means to keep the two-year-olds busy occupied most of her time.

In the nights, she lay awake long after the children were asleep, thinking about Danny. She wondered, what will he think of such a letter? Will he be there for us, as I hope? What will I do if he isn't? Have I thrown away my only chance at real love? She looked at the children lying near her, and knew she could have done nothing else. Still, the thought haunted her: Will you be there, Danny? Will you?

Twenty-one days out of Dublin, they arrived in Boston. Ellen came off the ship with the children, and made a short tour of the city. In the shop windows, Matthew saw signs offering employment. In smaller letters, below the rest, the signs read: "No Irish Need Apply."

"Why do they say that, Mother? Don't they like Irish in this town?"

"I don't know, Matt, but I'm glad we'll not be livin' here. Danny has said nothin' about such unwelcomeness in San Francisco. Don't ye worry. It'll be different there, sure."

They boarded the ship again, and the *North Star* left Boston early the next morning. For the next few days, the coastline of the distant land was in sight. They ran south, passing the port of Rio de Janeiro in their haste to reach the Horn before the foul winter weather set in. The farther south they sailed, the colder the weather came. The children huddled together in their cabin for warmth. It was the coldest Ellen had ever been. The two girls cried with the fierce cold, but Matthew bore it quietly. As the weather worsened, snow flurries fouled the *North Star*'s deck.

They passed the Straits of La Mare, with a calm wind at their back, stopping days later at Valparaiso for fruits, vegetables, and fresh water. Ellen brought the children off the ship to walk along the beach, a treat to sea-weary legs. It took some getting used to, walking on land again. Ellen picked up a few seashells as a present for Danny. It was strange to think of him so close now. A feeling of belonging came over her. It was home she was going to, a new home, different and a little frightening, but still a belonging place. It came to her then how anxious she was to see Danny and how long she had borne this loneliness.

"Never again will I be set apart from ye, Daniel O'Mally," she told the lapping tide about her feet. "A man may have his need for wanderin' when he's young, but when he's married, his wanderin' must come to an end. I've a mind to settle, like a broody hen."

"Will he like us, Ellen?" Matthew asked. She hadn't heard him come up behind her. "Will he be angry, do ye think, that we've come?"

"He'll like ye, Matt. How could he not?" she said, smiling reassuringly and ruffling his hair.

They went back to the *North Star* then. All was still. Nothing had changed—but she had changed. An excitement lying dormant for so long had awakened in her. An eagerness to be gone, to be on their way possessed her. Hurry, she thought. Hurry.

"Wait for me, Danny," she whispered, hugging her arms to her chest in the lonely cabin. "Wait for me."

The ship ran north, up the Pacific coast, past Panama, Nicaragua, and around the Baja Peninsula of Mexico. On the eighteenth day of November, the boy-mariner standing on the rigging of the main skysail called out, "San Francisco!" to the captain. Passengers jammed the bow rail to see the distant outline of San Francisco Bay.

"Look, children!" Ellen said to them. "There it is, at last." The 21 days from Dublin to Boston, and 107 days from Boston to San Francisco—4 months and 8 days of rocking sea, cramped quarters, and a building loneliness—had brought the *North Star* home to port, and Ellen, her heart a hammer in her breast, home to Danny.

Let him be there, she held her breath and prayed. Be there. She scanned the groups of men waiting on the wharf, their faces hidden by their hats.

"Where are ye, Danny?" she said, trying to still her fears.

"He isn't here, is he?" Matthew asked, a line of worry across his brow. "It's because of us, isn't it? He didn't come."

She couldn't answer him. It wasn't true. Danny wouldn't just abandon them. The gangplank was down, and people were coming off the ship. There was so much movement on the wharf, it was hard to see the faces. At the foot of the gangplank, a man was waving and waving, his hat in his hand.

"Mother," Matthew said, "There's someone over there, calling you." He pointed to the waving man. "Is it him?"

She looked to where the boy pointed. The man was bearded, and she did not recognize him. "No," she said, "that's not him." Then she heard his voice calling her, and she knew it at once. "It is him!" she cried to the children. "Danny!" she called back to him. "Oh, Danny!"

Chapter Twenty

"I can't believe you're really here, at last," Danny said, holding his hat in his hand. He hadn't kissed her when they met at the foot of the ramp. That worried Ellen. Was it he was shy with her before these children, or was it something more?

"I wasn't sure ye'd be here to meet us," she told him honestly. "I didn't know ye when I first saw ye, with the beard an' all. Ye look so different now, Danny."

"Not too different, I hope." He smiled then, and she saw the Danny she remembered in that smile and in his eyes. "You thought I wouldn't be here? I've been waiting here in town for a week, hoping you'd be early. I never knew a week to go so slow." He was staring at her, his eyes holding her with their gaze, as if he had something of desperate importance to say.

She was staring at him too. He looked so much more of a man than she remembered. His skin was browned by the sun, and his hair and beard had flecks of gold and copper glittering among the darker shade. There was nothing of the boy she had loved about him. He was a man now, and

193

the difference was overwhelming.

He bent down to the child before Ellen. "Hello, Caitlin, darlin'." Caitlin watched Danny, her eyes wide with suspicion. "She looks like you on the day I first met you in the church. Do you remember?"

"I remember everything," Ellen answered softly.

"Have you a hug for the man who loves you, Caitlin?" he asked, holding his arms out to the child. With only an instant's hesitation, she ran into his arms. When Danny picked her up, she hugged him tightly, pressed her face against his cheek, and stroked the beard on his face.

Ellen watched them, amazed at the actions of her child—Caitlin, who was so shy of strangers. They looked so natural together, as if Danny really were her father. There was something about the way Danny looked as he held her too, as though he loved her, as though he loved them all.

"And you're Matthew Muldair," he said to the boy, still standing behind Ellen.

Matthew stepped out then, barely daring to look up. He had never been so afraid in all his life. What would this man say to him? What right had he or his sister to be there? He knew he should say something, but he couldn't speak. Suddenly, all he wanted to do was be back in Ireland, anywhere in Ireland. He'd been all wrong to come here. He swallowed hard, afraid he was going to cry.

"I'm glad you came, son. You'll be a big help to us at the diggings, a strong-looking boy like you." Danny put his hand out to Matthew. "You're welcome here, son, you and your sister. I mean to make a good home for you"—he turned to Ellen then—"for all of you."

She loved him at that moment, more than she'd ever loved anyone in her life. She watched as Danny put

Caitlin down and took Matt's hand. He pulled the boy to him then, and hugged him. "We're going to be a family, Matt. That's the way it'll be. Nobody's an outsider here. We're all of us a little bit of strangers. I'm glad you're here, boy. I mean that. I'm really glad."

When Matthew looked up at him, it was with eyes which saw Danny O'Mally as his hero, and always would. "Did ye mean it when ye said I could help ye with the mining?" was all he could think to say. He wanted to hug Danny back, but was too shy. The death of his father, and his loyalty to him, was too fresh in his mind.

"If you're willing to work hard, you can," Danny told him. "It's not easy being a miner, but there's gold to be found, even by a boy as young as you. What say you, Matt, will you help me?"

"Course I will," Matt answered, his face a smile from the top of his head, to the tip of his chin. At that moment, there could have been nothing on earth he would have liked better than the idea of gold mining with Daniel O'Mally. All thoughts of going home to Ireland left him, and never returned.

"And you're Elizabeth, are you?" Danny reached out for the other child, but Elizabeth drew back and cried for Ellen. She buried her face in Ellen's dress, and refused to be touched by this big man with the bushy beard.

"Elizabeth, you stop that!" Matt scolded his sister, ashamed that she was carrying on so and afraid Danny wouldn't like them because of her.

"It's all right, Matt," Ellen said, and she picked Elizabeth up and held her in her arms. "She's just frightened. She'll get to know Danny better later on."

"She's likely tired as well," Danny added. "I'd better get you all to the hotel and let you get some rest."

Ellen nodded, grateful that he understood. The children were tired. It would be good to rest in a real bed, one that didn't rock.

Danny loaded their bags in the cart, and lifted the children up into the back of it. He and Ellen sat at the front. He drove them through the town, to the Hotel Franciscan.

"I'll never forget how kind ye were to Matt," Ellen whispered to Danny as they rode along. "I know he was afraid, meeting ye the first time." He looked at her, and a feeling of such intense longing to be held in this man's arms came over her, she had to look away.

Even on the short ride to the hotel, there was much to see that was new and exciting to them. The people here were so different from one another. New England whalers walked beside serape-clad Mexicans, or Indian women in their striped blankets. There were Irish, Germans, New Zealand bullyboys, and even a Kanaka from the Hawaiian Isles. Matt kept pointing, and whispering, "Look, Mother, look!" They passed wooden shanties and adobe brick houses, and in between the Hotel Niantic, a salvaged windjammer hauled up on shore to serve for housing since wood was scarce. Being foreign seemed common. Nothing brought more comments from Matt, however, than the pigtailed Chinese. San Francisco was home to an enormous number of Chinese. Twenty-five thousand of them would arrive in 1851 alone.

"Those men are wearing plaits!" Matthew shouted.

"They call it a queue, Matt," Danny explained. "They consider it part of their honor."

The hotel was comfortable. Ellen shared a room with the children, and Danny had his own room down the hall.

They all had dinner together at the hotel that evening, and then Ellen put the children to bed in her room and asked Matt to watch over the girls while she talked to Danny. The girls wouldn't be much trouble, she knew. They were almost asleep the minute she laid them in their beds.

Ellen and Danny met downstairs, and walked outside in the cool night air.

"Are the children asleep?"

She nodded. "Yes, I think ye were wonderful with them today," she told him. "Matt loves ye already." They walked along the dark streets, alone except for a few shopkeepers still closing their stores. "I want to tell ye now all about why I brought Matt and Elizabeth," she began.

"I've only one question about that, Ellen." Danny turned to face her. "Did you love their father? It's all I want to know." The thought had been tearing him apart ever since he'd read her letter. He'd been afraid to ask, afraid the answer might be yes.

"No, Danny," she told him honestly. "I never loved Colin. I worked for him, and I cared about his family, but I never loved him. He wanted that," she admitted, "but I never did. I told him I was promised."

They walked on, a silence between them. Danny was strangely distant. "Do ye mind the children bein' here?" she asked.

"No," he said quickly, and she saw he meant it. "I like them, both of them."

"Then ye're not mad about my bringing them?"

"No, of course I'm not mad."

"Then, what is it that's standing between us, Danny? Why have ye been holdin' yerself away from me like a

197

stranger?" she asked. He looked at her so oddly. "Ye haven't as much as kissed me since I've been here, or held me close, as a man would who loves a woman. Is that it, then? Have ye stopped lovin' me, Danny?" Her heart was pounding wildly at having dared so much. Now that she had said it, she couldn't look at him.

"Not love you!" he said, and pulled her to him. There was something of such urgency in his eyes that it frightened her, something she felt within herself too. "Come here," he said, and took her by the hand into the dark passageway between two stores. She could scarcely see his face or anything else in the dark alleyway, but she could feel his presence beside her, like part of her own breathing. "Don't you know how much I want to touch you, Ellen?" he asked, the tips of his fingers touching her face like sparks against her skin. She found she couldn't breathe.

"I . . ." she tried to tell him how she felt. I need to know if it's the same between us, she wanted to say. I need to feel your arms around me. I need to know you still want me, as much as I want you. "Danny . . ." she tried to tell him, but his arms went tight around her, crushing her to him. His kiss was hot against her mouth, and all the words she might have said were lost.

"You think I didn't want to touch you, didn't want to hold you?" he asked. "It's all I thought about since the minute you stepped off that ship, and before that too." His hand touched her breast, and a shiver of such longing shot through her, she cried out in its intensity. "Oh, God, Ellen. Can you doubt I want you?"

She pushed away from him. "Take me back to the hotel now, Danny, before we spoil what we've waited so long to have. Take me back now."

They walked back in silence, afraid to touch each other for all the feeling that was so close to the surface in both of them. In the hallway, outside her hotel room door, he said, "I love you, Ellen. I hope you know that. I've said nothing tonight about the wedding, because I didn't want to rush you, but . . ."

"I don't need time to think, Danny. I'll marry ye tomorrow if the Church will have us," she told him.

"You're sure?" he asked.

"Very sure," she answered, kissing him with the look in her eyes. "I want nothing more than to be beside ye for the rest of my life. Now go to bed, man, and sleep." She brushed her lips lightly against his.

"I'll never sleep another night until I have you lying beside me as my wife," he answered her.

She went inside her room then, and closed the door. The children were asleep, and all was still. Something had happened to her this night that had changed her life forever. She had come so far, and now she was sure. In this place where she was a stranger, she had found the love her life was meant for. All the times when life had seemed hopeless, all the hardships she had struggled to survive, now were lifted from her spirit by the love of this one man. She opened the window and stared out at the night, the fat yellow moon, and the sky full of stars. Her world seemed as hopeful as those twinkling stars lighting the dark skies of a distant Earth.

They were married the next morning in the Mission founded by Father Junipero Serra. It was called St. Francis de Assisi de Lugeuna de Nuestra Senora de los Dolores (St. Francis of Assisi of the Lake of Our Lady of

199

the Sorrows)—quickly shortened by the populace to the more familiar Mission Dolores. Spanish in design, it was strange to Ellen, as was the Spanish priest who married them.

"How did ye convince him to marry us today?" Ellen asked after the ceremony was over. "I thought there would be banns to be read."

"Oh, we've already done that." Danny laughed at her surprised look. "Well, when I knew you were coming, I just planned it as though it was going to happen. I explained to him how you were there with the three children, and that we needed to live together as soon as possible."

"Danny! Ye didn't say it like that, did ye?" she asked, wondering what the priest must have thought of such a statement.

"Well, my Spanish isn't too good. Don't worry. He was glad to see us getting married. High time, he thought."

"Daniel O'Mally! Ye didn't let him think they were all ours?" she demanded, amazed at his deception.

"I didn't say they were, and I didn't say they weren't. Whatever he thought, they are ours now, aren't they?" He smiled at her, full of fun and happiness on this day he had waited so long for. "Here, let me see that," he said, taking the marriage license from her hands. "Ellen Gwenhara O'Reilly. Pretty name."

"Danny, I should have told ye before. It was just, with Caitlin and all, I was afraid to let anybody know who I was. I wanted no shame to come to my family, and I . . ." She faltered.

"And you didn't want Caitlin's father to find you," he finished for her.

She shook her head. "No. I'll tell ye about it now, if ye

200

want t' know," she offered, feeling the shame of that time come over her again.

"Do you want to tell me?"

"No, but ye have a right to know, an' I will if ye ask me."

He thought about it for a minute, watching her face. "Was he married?"

"Married, and with children of his own." Her voice trembled.

"Did he know about Caitlin?"

"No, he never knew. I was gone before anyone knew."

"Only one thing more, Ellen. Only one thing I have to know," he said. "Do you love him still?"

"No," she said quickly, very sure of her answer. "I love only one man, an' he's standin' here beside me."

"Then I need to know nothing else," he told her, and kissed her.

They spent their day looking through the town. Danny showed Matt the gold exchange, where the miners brought their nuggets and dust. Matt was excited with just the thought of finding gold, and anxious to try it.

They drove the cart along the wharf, looking at the ships in the harbor. "Why are there so many ships crowdin' in?" Ellen asked.

"They've been abandoned by their crews," Danny explained. "They sit dead in the water, their timbers rotting away. A great loss it is to a city so short of wood. The old ones are trapped by the new, till none can move. What trade vessels we have must pull up to a pier built farther out to sea, and can never attempt the harbor at all."

"They're like a forest," Ellen said, "comin' out of the water."

Danny drove on. Along the boardwalk were the abandoned hulls of ships pulled up on shore, like the Hotel Niantic and the Boatswain Warehouse. "When they first brought them ashore, it was for temporary use only. Then the town grew up around them, and now they can't be moved," Danny explained.

There was a lot to see of this city, so much that was new and exotic. Mostly it was saloons and gaming houses. There was a roughness to the town that frightened her. "When will we go home, Danny?" asked the bride of one day.

He looked at her, surprised at her eagerness to be away. "I thought to give you a week in the city before drawing you back to the old cabin where Mac and I work our claim. It's there we must keep this winter. We've the diggings to play out, and then we'll think what to do in the spring. Mac's there now. He's built a separate cabin for himself, so we could have a bit of privacy."

"I'm glad of that," she said, "but, Danny, couldn't we go back the sooner? I'm anxious to see it all—the cabin, and the claim, and all ye've been doin'. To tell the plain truth, I'm that skitterish in that hotel room, with so many drunken miners yellin' and singin' so loud. I can't sleep for thinkin' one of them will shoot off a gun right through the floor of our room. Couldn't we go back right away?"

"Well," he said, pleased at her reaction, "if you've a mind to go, I'll not delay us. Only let me show you the lots and bits of property I've bought about the town. We'll have our supper here, and stay in the hotel tonight. In the morning, we'll go." He was surprised and pleased at her eagerness to make them a real home. The town was wearing on him as well.

He drove them to a stretch of beach, the water lapping the shore at low tide. "I own ten of these beach lots. Bought them cheap, at twelve dollars apiece. McTaggart insisted. Believes they'll be valuable one day. He has a good head for business as a general rule, so I went along. I'll admit I wasn't sure about these bits, though. They go awash at high tide. Still, there's money in them. The gaming tents rent the space during the day, and pack up before the water's rise."

"If there was just a way to hold the water back," said Ellen, thinking aloud.

"That's a woman's way of thinking," he teased. "Hold back the sea, would you? Come on, I've something else to show you."

He pointed out several empty lots on Kearny Street. "We own these. A business district's building up here, and when it does, prices will go up as well." He showed her the mercantile, where he held an interest, and the saloon which was rented out on his land. There was a partnership in a lumbermill too.

She was amazed. He had done so much with the yellow dust. Unlike most of the miners she had seen, who threw their money away on drink or gambling, or hoarded it, afraid to spend an ounce, Danny had invested in the town. The growth of a city was due to men like him.

"But ye're rich!" Ellen said, in honest surprise.

"Oh, not rich"—he shook his head—"but we'll do. Come on. I've saved the best for last." He had a look about him, like a little boy with flowers hidden behind his back.

He drove them to a hill overlooking the bay, high above the business district of town and far away from the gaming houses and saloons. Workmen were finishing the third story of the wooden Victorian house. Open fretwork decorated the second story and the frame above the door. There was a wide porch on the first floor, and a fenced-in balcony on the second. Both overlooked the sea and the ships in the harbor. Diamond panes sparkled in the windows, and a cutout on either side of the gables was in the shape of a shamrock.

"It's to be our home one day," he told her. "Do you like it?"

"Are we as rich as that?" she asked, still staring at the house.

"Do you like it?" he asked again, ignoring her other question.

"It's got shamrocks at the top."

"Well, it's Irish that'll live in it, so why not? When the workmen are done, we'll paint it a lovely cream color, and all the doors and windows will be green. I wanted it finished before you came, as a present for you for waiting so long. I'm afraid it's not ready yet, and we'll have to spend the winter in the cabin by the claim. Do you mind too much?"

"Oh, Danny, ye are such a sweet fool. I love ye for it. I can't believe this," she said of the house. "I'm glad it's not done, an' I'll have some time t' get used to the idea. It's a beautiful house, Danny. We'll have a fine home here, all of us, an' I'll be the best wife I know how to be to ye. Ye deserve it. Shamrocks!" she said again, and started to cry.

"Here now, I didn't mean to make you weep. That won't do on your wedding day. Come on, we'll go now. I only wanted you to see it."

"I love ye, Danny," she said so softly the children couldn't hear. "I love ye more than ye'll ever know."

He took her hand then, and held it. "We'll have a fine life, Ellen. I promise you that. I want to give you everything. I want—"

"Shh." She laid her finger against his lips. "Ye need promise me nothing, Danny. If ye love me, I have all I need. Take me back to the hotel now. The children are tired, and . . . I want to be with ye." The look in her eyes was that of longing, and she did not try to hide it.

The girls were tired, but Matthew was so excited to be in San Francisco and see all the newness of the place, he had no thought for sleep. "We'll be leavin' here early in the mornin'," Ellen told him. "It's a long way to the cabin, and ye must get yer rest."

"Where are ye goin'?" he asked, seeing she meant to leave the room.

"It's my wedding night, Matt. I'm goin' to spend it with my husband. Ye'll be all right here with the girls, won't ye? We're just down the hall if ye need us."

He looked up at her, made shy by this turn of events. "It's hard to think of ye as a bride, Ellen."

"I thought it was Mother now."

"Oh, it is," he said quickly, "but tonight, ye're a bride, aren't ye? I can hardly call ye Mother tonight, can I?" He smiled at her, and she kissed his cheek.

"Good night, ye lovely boy," she whispered.

"Good night, Ellen," he said, and hugged her with all his might. "We'll be fine, don't ye worry."

"I know ye will," she told him, blew him a last kiss, and was out the door. She walked down the hall to her husband's room, each step like a memory of the journeys of her life that had brought her to this moment. She knocked softly at the door.

Danny opened it at once. The change in his looks made

205

her stare. The beard was gone. "Why'd ye do it?" she asked, truly surprised.

"I didn't think you liked it," he told her, and closed the door after her. "Besides, I rubbed your face red the other night."

"Well, I . . ."

"You didn't like the beard, now did you?"

He looked so much like the Danny she remembered, but older. "Ye might have kept it," she said. "I didn't mind it."

"Ellen, tell the truth. You didn't like it," he insisted.

"Well, I like ye better as ye are," she admitted, and touched his face with her hand.

He drew her to him then, kissing the inside of her hand and pressing his lips to the pulse at her wrist. "You coming to my room like this," he said, "it's like we're lovers, meeting in secret."

"Be my lover, Danny," she whispered, and stood trembling as he drew her dress from her and slipped it to the floor.

"For this one night," he said, "we're only that, Ellen. Lovers. You're so beautiful, woman. You take my breath away." He bent his head and kissed her breasts, and heard the sharp little intake of her breath.

"Promise ye'll always love me, Danny." She held him from her for an instant. "Promise."

"Until the day I die, Ellen," he told her, meaning the words with all his heart, "and after, if there is a God."

Chapter Twenty-One

The two cabins of the O'Mally-McTaggart claim were high in the foothills, near the riverbed where they worked the gold. The ore vein was higher up the mountain. Winter snows and spring rains brought the nuggets and dust downstream and trapped them along the banks, beneath rocks, against the roots of a tree, and within the silt of the river channel. A rise of smoke came from the McTaggart cabin.

"That'll be Griffin cooking his supper," Danny told them. "He isn't expecting us for a week yet," he added, hoping his partner was dressed in something more than his long underwear and his pipe, his usual evening wear.

"That's close enough!" a voice shouted from the cabin. "This is private property," he said, his thick burr whirring. "Announce yourselves, or feel the sting of my rifle!"

"Danny, what's the matter with him?" Ellen asked, alarmed by his words.

"Nothing. He's just protecting the place. He wouldn't shoot at anyone unless he saw that they meant trouble.

It's just a threat, really, to scare away claim-jumpers. Don't look so worried. He's safe enough." Ellen didn't look so sure.

"Ye've never shot at someone up here, have ye, Danny?" she asked, horrified at the idea.

He didn't exactly answer, but brushed the back of his ear as though it troubled him. "McTaggart! It's Danny," he called out. "You learn a lesson from this, Matt. This is a new country, and things are done different here. Never sneak up on a cabin in these mountains. Men are nervous about their claim, and would shoot a man to protect it. Always call out, like I did. Understand?"

The boy nodded, impressed by this little drama. He liked the element of danger. He couldn't wait to meet Griffin McTaggart.

"Dan'l? You're back early, man. Wasn't she there?" he shouted.

"She's here beside me, Mac."

"Weel, come ahead in," McTaggart shouted back. "You might have warned me, though," he yelled. "I washed my britches, and I'm sitting here in nothing but my red underdrawers and my boots."

Danny was embarrassed, but Ellen, relieved that they weren't about to be shot, laughed and laughed. "Come on over when you're decent," he yelled, and drove the wagon up to the cabin.

It was fine to look at. Its logs were well joined, and needed little caulking between the timbers. Being a carpenter, Danny had done a better job of it than most. It had a peaked roof, to keep the weight of the winter snow from caving the cabin in, and a railed-in porch, just so Danny could sit out at night and watch the stars. There were four good-sized rooms, and a shed for the cow. A

208

perfectly plain, rough-hewn mantel was set above the hearth, but it fitted the setting it was in. Ellen liked the cabin at once. And when all was unpacked, and she had set a coverlet on the bed, a cloth upon the table, and a lamp on the mantel, it did seem a proper home.

Danny lit a fire in the roomy hearth, and good, satisfying warmth filled the rooms of the cabin. Ellen set out a quick supper of hot tea, dried beef, stewed apples, and hot biscuits. The children had fresh milk, still warm from Bess.

Griffin McTaggart came to the door when the smell of stewing apples and baking biscuits became too hard to resist. "There you are," Danny said to him, good-naturedly, "after all the supplies have been carried in."

"I didn't want to intrude," McTaggart answered. "I thought I'd give you time to settle."

Danny noticed the man had brushed his hair and beard and put on a clean shirt for the occasion. "You look grand, Mac," Danny observed wryly.

The Scotsman leveled a calculating eye at him. "I see you've done somewhat to your face, Dan'l. It looks naked as a skinned rabbit. Weel, are you going to invite me in?" he asked, in a hushed voice.

"You never needed an invitation before. Don't be so damn silly, come on in."

McTaggart stood like a wooden Indian at the door and pointed his head in Ellen's direction. Danny was amused by his friend's shyness. One thing Griffin McTaggart had never been was timid. He had seen him charging like a wild man out of their cabin, shooting buckshot at three men who dared to try to steal their claim, sending them riding hellbent down the trail, howling for their lives. This side of him was new.

"Look who's at our door, Ellen," he said loudly. "It's Griffin McTaggart, coming to pay a call. Shall we invite him in?"

Ellen turned away from her baking, and saw this rough-voiced, lank-limbed man, swathed in red hair and red beard, staring down at his boots like a schoolboy meeting the teacher. "Come in, Mr. McTaggart," she offered. "Ye're very welcome here."

McTaggart stepped inside then, wiping his feet carefully before putting his boot to her clean-swept floor, something Danny had never seen him do before. "Griffin McTaggart," Danny said formally, "this is my wife, Ellen, and our children Matthew, Elizabeth, and Caitlin."

"I'm happy to make your acquaintance, ma'am," the Scot said politely.

He seemed so different from what Ellen had imagined when he had shouted at them on their arrival. He was a gentleman, and more than a little in awe of her. She liked him immediately.

"Ye're most welcome at our table, Mr. McTaggart. Will ye stay and share our meal?" she offered. "It isn't much, as we've only just arrived, but the apples are nice. I'd be happy if ye'd stay," she encouraged him.

McTaggart nodded his acceptance and sat. Danny produced a bottle of fine Scotch whiskey, a surprise from San Francisco. "Will you have a drop with us, to mark the day?" he asked his partner.

"I wouldna' mind a wee dram." He seemed to relax visibly as Danny poured it out. "To your new family." The Scotsman held his mug in a toast. "May you have nothing but happiness from each other."

Half a bottle later, McTaggart was telling them about

210

his father, Angus McTaggart, and Angus's whiskey distillery, and his mother, Hannah Gray McTaggart, a practical, Free Kirk Presbyterian woman, bent on endowing her sons with the values of a good Scot's thrift and industry.

"She was a good cook, my mother," McTaggart told them. "Never did a Sunday pass withoot a platter of hot scones or bannocks filled with jam. For a special night, she made the black bun or a ginger cake. Christmas was the Dundee, filled with fruit, and nuts, and whiskey, then iced all around. Then the puddings," he added, getting caught up in his remembrances, "the black and white, the mealy pudding, and the Haggis."

The children listened with rapt attention to his tale. His quaint accent, and his enthusiasm for his story, made him the perfect weaver of dreams. He set them all imagining the steamy dishes. Ellen could almost taste the puddings.

Later, the bottle was well and truly empty. "I've had a fine night," Griffin said. "I hinna had such a merry time since I was back in Sco'land. I thank you for the meal, ma'am," he said to Ellen. "I'll say good night to one and all." He stood unaffected by the great amount of whiskey he had drunk. The only noticeable difference in his behavior was that it had relaxed his nervousness and loosened his tongue.

"He ought to be passed out drunk," Ellen whispered to Danny, amazed at the man's capacity for liquor.

"Never. He grew up on it. It's like his mother's milk," Danny whispered back.

With quick good-byes, Griffin was gone, crossing to his own cabin. "I like yer friend," Ellen said when he was gone. She put the girls to bed, and Matthew helped her clear the table. "He seems a fine man."

"I like him too, Father," Matt spoke up boldly. "Has he really shot a claim-jumper?" he asked excitedly.

"That's enough questions for one night," Ellen said, stopping Danny before he could answer. "Go on now, and get ready for bed, Matt. We've had a long day, all of us."

They were alone then, and when the dishes were washed and the dough set out for the morning's baking, Danny banked the fire, and they went to bed.

"Did you hear what the boy called me?" he asked.

"He called ye Father."

"Yes, he did. It surprised me a bit. Sounded odd to my ear, someone calling me Father."

"Do ye mind?" she asked.

"No, I don't mind at all. I'm happy he wanted to."

"Well, it might have been because ye introduced him as yer son to Griffin McTaggart tonight," she explained, to his puzzled look. "Remember, ye said, 'This is my wife, Ellen, and these are our children.' He admires ye, Danny. I think he's tryin' hard to belong."

They lay in each other's arms, listening to the silence of the night and thinking of all they had said.

"It's quiet here," Ellen spoke.

"It's a lonely kind of quiet," Danny said softly, "when you haven't anyone to share it with. I used to lie here in this very bed, staring at the ceiling, dreaming you were here beside me." He turned to her. "And now you are." His hand reached across the dark between them, and touched her. She lay quite still, tingling beneath his touch. She felt the whole of her body drawn to him, as though their passion were a magnet.

"Do ye know what I want?" she said quietly.

"What?" he asked, aroused by the possibilities of the question.

"I want to have yer child, Daniel O'Mally. I want to give ye a child of yer own. Not just for ye, though. I want it for myself too, an O'Mally child."

He held her close to him, silent, so moved by her words he didn't trust himself to speak.

"Danny?" she whispered, tracing the outline of his lips with her finger.

He couldn't see her in the dark, only feel her touch against his skin. Her lips were soft and gentle, lightly kissing his eyelids, his lips, his chest.

"Danny?" she said again, wondering why he didn't speak. "I hoped ye might want a child too, but if ye don't—if ye think we've got too many bairns now, I understand."

"Shh," he said. "Be quiet, woman." He held her face between his two hands, and in the dark he pulled her to him, kissing her. Even in this moment of wanting her, he realized how precious she was to him, more precious than the gold that had taken him away from her, more precious than the desire for her which he felt like a hot wave awakening his senses. She was all that was good and fine in him. "Nothing would make me happier than to have ten children with you, Ellen O'Mally. Come here to me," he said, his voice husky with need, "let's begin now."

In the second week of December, the river froze, and snow fell for days at a time. Forced into a time of rest, Danny looked around him, and knew that his days as a miner were nearly over. His business interests in San

Francisco were making him a rich man, growing larger every year. San Francisco in 1851 was a growing place. A bold man could profit in the making of such a city. It was rugged and newly rich, like Danny himself.

Something troubled him about it, though. It wasn't enough, owning land and interests in business. He wanted something he could be a part of. In the quiet days of late December, a kernel of thought seeded in his mind. Land that is newly building needs lumber to raise its cities, lumber to fashion its houses, schools, churches, and stores. There was no doubt that cities would grow up—were, in fact, already growing up—around the gold fields. Not far away, as though planned for this very purpose, verdant forests lay waiting for the touch of an axe, the rasp of a saw. Oak, redwood, fir, pine, and birch—all were waiting for the right man to yield their treasure to. In his mind, the dream built upon itself, catching like the wisps of a fire to the gathered kindling of his thoughts. He would need men to work as loggers, and teams of horses to draw the heavy lumber down the mountains. He would build a sawmill, where clean planks of virgin wood could be fashioned for the cities of tents and shanties.

The more he set the vision spinning through the labyrinth of his mind, the more determined he was to see it happen. The miner's game was a frail one, floating on the whim of chance. Timber was solid, strong. It was hard won, but a lasting wealth, a proud legacy to leave a son. Surely there would be sons between him and Ellen, many of them. He sighed a heavy sigh. It was a dream to linger on.

Christmas came, mantled in a morning of cold, bright sunlight. There was no Mass to attend, no priest to bless the day, but it shone brilliantly among its fellow days despite the lack of ritual. It was a day of celebration.

A gift of two fat roasting hens came from McTaggart, who would not say how he came by them. He brought real apples too, from the faraway Sacramento Valley, one for each of the children's stockings, and enough left over to make two pies for their supper. They had sweet potatoes, bursting from their skins in slits of bubbly, sticky, caramel. Ellen made a sage and onion dressing for the roast chickens, and soft, fragrant rolls with buttery brown heads.

Besides the wealth of food on the table, there were Christmas gifts for each of them. Danny and McTaggart had slipped into Selby Flats early in the week, and made their special purchases. In a big, bright box, there was a doll for each of the girls, with eyes that opened and closed and real hair, curled in ringlets and held with bright blue bows. The dolls were made of bisque, with painted blue eyes and rosy cheeks. Each of them had a new dress for Christmas, from a bolt of cloth that Danny had brought. Matthew got what he wanted: a pair of the new denim pants that the miners wore. As a special surprise, Danny said to Matt, "I've something for you that I've kept hidden over at McTaggart's cabin. Do you want to go and see what it is, son?"

"For me?" Matt asked. "But I've already had my gift."

"It's a special one, just from me to you. All right?"

Matthew nodded, then shouted to Ellen, "We're goin' 'cross to Mr. McTaggart's cabin, Mother. I've got a present!"

Griffin followed them across the snow. "It was the queerest thing," he said to Matt. "In the verra early hours, I heard this frightful din. I got up oot of my bed, but I dinna' see a thing. Then I tripped over this bundle lying on the floor, and went crashing aboot, and landed on my duff, hard as a rock." Matt laughed at the way Griffin was telling it. "And who do you suppose it was for?" McTaggart said.

"For me!" Matt shouted, as excited as he could be.

"For you? Weel, I dinna' doot you're right. You'd best go in with him now, Dan'l, and show him what it is."

"Come on, son," Danny said, opening the door to Mac's cabin.

As soon as he opened the door, out jumped a black and brown ball of fur, yipping and yelping and throwing itself at first one set of legs and then another.

"A dog! My own dog?" He scooped the puppy up, and it licked his face. "It's really for me?"

"Of course it's for you," Danny told him, smiling at the happiness such a small thing had brought. "I had a dog when I was your age, and this pup fair begged to come home with me," he said of the wiggly bundle in Matt's arms. "Look at him," he added, "doesn't he strike you as a dog with a mind of his own?" The puppy was chewing on Matt's collar.

"Does Mother know?" the boy asked, looking worried.

"No, I've kept it a secret," Danny told him.

"What do you think she'll say?" He could just imagine her not liking dogs.

"Well, being a mother, she'll probably say, 'I won't be having a dog running loose in my house. It has fleas, and it barks, and it might even bite. What ever possessed ye to buy such a thing, Daniel O'Mally?'" The boy's face fell. "And then I'll say, 'What possessed me is that he's a boy, and a boy needs a dog, and that's the end of that.'"

216

"Ye will?" Matt looked up, his whole face alight with joy.

"I surely will," Danny said. "Now, let's take him home."

It was a lasting day, a day bright in the present and golden in the memory. Danny had a gift for Ellen as well, a gold nugget he had found, hung on a chain of openworked gold. There were tiny nugget earrings to match. He had wrapped them in a silk scarf, a gift that had come all the way from China.

For Mac, Ellen had made a wool muffler and a pair of good wool socks. There was also a new briarwood pipe, and six initialed handkerchiefs.

For Danny, she made a scarf as well, and a jaunty pair of argyle socks done in red, black, and blue, six initialed handkerchiefs, and a pair of woolen mittens.

"I feel as rich as six bowls of cream," Danny said, smiling at her and holding out his pair of red mittens for all to see. That night, he spoke his mind to Mac about the selling of the claim and the dream of the lumber mill.

"It sounds a good thing for a man to do," McTaggart agreed. "I wouldna' mind swinging an axe now and again. Could you go a partner, or weel you have it all to yourself?"

"You mean you're interested?" Danny asked him, genuinely surprised. In his mind, it was always his alone, his mill, his lumber, his dream.

"I am. You're right that it's time we quit the mining," Griffin said. "We've had our go at it, and we've done weel enough, but this idea of yours, Dan'l, it sets right with me. I've got a good feel aboot it. I'm ready for something more permanent in my life. What do you say, man? Will you have me as a partner, or do we go our own ways?"

It seemed Danny had heard this before. "Mac, I remember saying once we made a good team, didn't I?"

"You did."

"And so we do," Danny declared. "Let's have a drink on it, to mark the partnership."

"You've got another bottle of Scotch?" McTaggart asked, his interest peaked.

"It's Christmas, isn't it?"

"It is that."

"And we're sealing a business arrangement, aren't we?"

"We are."

"Well, then, I think a drink's only right," Danny suggested, bringing out a bottle of twenty-year-old Scotch.

"Dan'l." McTaggart cocked his head back and eyed his friend. "Sometimes I wonder aboot you." He pulled the bottle closer to his side of the table. "Are you sure you weren't born a Scot?"

On that day, the O'Mally-McTaggart Lumber Company came to be, no longer a dream but brought into the light. Its beginning, from the kernel of one man's thought, would grow into a feasible plan of business.

A light snow fell that night, frosting the windows and coating the ground with white. The world seemed gentled on this special evening. A feeling of warmth coursed through Danny, looking about him at those who made up his world. The scene was dear. All the chicken, stuffing, and applie pies had been eaten. All the gaily wrapped presents had been opened, and the small clutter of their paper and ribbons remained a colorful display on the floor. Mac had sung his last Scottish lay, then trudged home, three-quarters-full bottle under his arm, a happy, if none too sober, man. The girls played with their new dolls; Matthew's puppy was curled up in his lap. It was so beautiful a scene, Danny hated for the night to end.

Ellen put the paper and ribbons away, and the children carried their presents with them to their beds. Danny kept the fire going well late into the night, for the snow was falling heavily now. At last, he and Ellen climbed into their bed, exhausted with the day's pleasures.

"I've another gift for ye, Danny," Ellen whispered, "something I've been saving out. I hope ye'll be pleased. I'm going to have a baby."

He held her close to him and whispered, "I love you so, Ellen. I love you." His mind was racing. It'll be a son. A man with a lumber company needs sons.

As though granting a Christmas wish, in seven months' time, Seamus Rourke O'Mally came to be. And even as Danny had hoped, they never stopped at one, but four strong sons were born to them in time. Sons to build a legacy for. Sons to carry on the dream.

Part Three

Brendan and Caitlin
The Heirs

Chapter Twenty-Two

Ten years had passed since Ellen O'Reilly had fled into the night. Even now, in odd moments, Dougal still thought of it, that dark time when he had almost lost his family. That part of his past was a question to him now, nothing more. What happened to Ellen? What had he done to her life? The O'Reillys had never heard from their daughter again, that much he knew. He had a letter from them every year at Christmas. It always had the same words at the closing: "Of Ellen, we have heard nothing."

Dougal's son Brendan, a young man of seventeen, came into the room, interrupting his father's thoughts of so long ago. Dougal glanced up, thinking how suddenly his son had become an adult and how proud he was of him. Brendan would inherit O'Shay Shipbuilders one day. The boy had a fine mind. At seventeen, ships and the sea were everything to him.

"Have you thought about what I mentioned to you, about my signing on with Captain Janders?" Brendan asked. He was taller than his father, but always deferred to him.

"It was in my mind that ye'd go to Trinity College," Dougal answered, "then come home and run the business with me. This idea of goin' to sea's a dream, Bren, a dream ye've had since ye were a little boy, coming down to the shipyards with yer da. Ye hung around that place, talking to shipwrights and sawyers, listening to their yarns."

"It's that life I want," Brendan insisted. "You know I want no part of college. You have Jamie for that, if you must have one of us there. The oceans of the world will be my teacher and my books."

Moira O'Shay listened with great interest to the conversation between her husband and her eldest son. She was in the nearby room, where she sat and mended a dress of her daughter, Bronwyn. Her needle darted nimbly in and out of the cloth. Her thoughts, like the fingers that drew her needle, were racing. What had just been said worried her. Dougal could be stubborn when he felt he was in the right. Brendan was like him, stubborn too, and impulsive. She listened as their argument ended, listened as each walked away angry. Putting her sewing down, she went to find her husband.

He was in the garden, cutting the dried blooms of roses off the bush. It was a thing he did when he was angry, or worried, or frustrated. She suspected he was a little of all three at that moment.

"Don't cut it back too far, or we'll have nothing left of it," she said to him, crossing the yard to where he stood.

"Oh, it needs a firm hand now and again. It'll be the better for it. It's growing wild," he said, still snipping.

"But if you cut it back too far," she persisted, taking his hand away from the bush, and holding it in her own,

224

"you'll destroy it. A thing must have the freedom to grow as its own nature guides it."

He stared into her eyes. "Are we discussin' roses?"

She smiled, drawing him away from the flowers. "We have to let him go, Dougal. He's our son, but he's grown up now, with a life of his own and a right to live it as he sees best."

"Being a sailor?" Dougal stormed at her. "His future's here, where he belongs. What else did I do all this for? He wants no part of it, he says. No part of it! No, he'll stay here and do as I tell him."

"He'll go anyway," she said softly. "If we let him go, he'll come back to us. If you force your will on him, he'll run away. If that happens, he may never come back. He has a mind of his own, like you," she pointed out. "I love him too much to lose him forever, Dougal. I'm asking you, do this thing for me. Let him go with your blessing."

"He'd never go without my leave," he said, but he believed her words. She was the boy's mother. She'd always known him better than Dougal had.

"I know my son," she said quietly. "He's not a child anymore. He loves you, but he'll go just the same. He feels it's time for him to make his break from us. He's ready, even if we're not."

It was a hard thing for Dougal to do, give up the son who was his best hope. Something defiant in him still wanted to force the boy to his own way of thinking. This was just a whim, surely. He looked at Moira, and saw worry standing in the corners of her eyes.

"All right. All right," he said, laying his hand gently against her cheek. "Don't look like that. I won't have ye frettin' over it. It may be he's more determined to do this than I thought. I'll speak to him tomorrow, tell him I've changed my mind."

It wasn't in Dougal to refuse anything Moira asked of him. It hadn't been since Ellen. He had never told Moira, had never wanted to burden her with the cleansing of his own soul. Through the years, he had tried in every way he knew to make up to her for the wrong he had done. There was nothing she could ever ask of him that he wouldn't do, even this—even giving up his son.

"Promise me you'll tell him tonight, Dougal. Don't wait until morning. Promise?" Her eyes implored him.

"Fine," he agreed. "If ye feel that strongly about it, perhaps it's better done now. We'll both sleep easier knowing how it's decided. I'll go and tell him." He walked slowly back into the house.

Moira watched until he was gone, then followed her husband into the house. She walked quietly up the stairs, and into her son's room. She could hear the sound of their voices downstairs. She walked over to Brendan's bed, reached under it, and pulled out the traveling bag she had found there that morning. It had been empty then. She opened it, staring at the belongings her son had packed, ready to leave them. He mustn't see me here, she thought, putting everything back as it was. Her hand trembled as she closed the door to his room. They had come so close, so close to losing him forever.

"Have a care where you put that thing, man," barked the captain to the young man before him. It was Brendan's first voyage. He carried his sea chest high on one shoulder. A satchel of books hung from his other hand.

"What's that in your hand?" asked Captain Aloysius

P. Janders, blocking Brendan's way and openly scrutinizing every hair on his head, every particle of dust on his boots.

"Books, sir."

"Books, eh? If you have time to read those while working on my ship, I'm not doing my job." He stood aside then. "You may come aboard, Mr. O'Shay."

Brendan stepped onto the deck of the *Wraith of the Seas* on June 14th, 1862. The *Wraith*, a tea clipper, registered 750 tons, and carried a cargo of wool cloth, British pewter, cases of Scotch whiskey for those British subjects living in China, and other manufactured goods not easily found in the Orient. Her course was set for Yokohama as her first port, then a run to Saigon for a cargo of rice, and a race to Foochow Harbor for the tea.

Given a hammock to sleep in, and no more than a piece of deck to cleat his sea chest to, Brendan spent his first night aboard the *Wraith* wondering if this would be the adventure he'd dreamed of. He awoke at eight bells to find that the deck had to be holystoned smooth, the standing rigging freshly tarred and rattled down, and the yards of brass burnished. The voice of Captain Janders shouted, "Bend sail!" as the billows of white canvas sheeted against the wind.

In only a few days, Brendan's pale skin was burned a copper bronze by the glare of the sun. He worked, shirtless, high on the spar, with only a footrope to steady him.

In Saigon, the native stevedores carried the sacks of rice onto the ship. Although a diminutive people, they bore the heavy burden, ignoring the steam bath they lived in. For Brendan, all of the sights and sounds of this country were exotic. Captain Janders had been right. He had no time for books. There was too much to do, hear, and see.

The monsoon season was upon them on their run to Foochow. Brendan quickly learned, as all sailors did, to get wet and stay wet in this part of the sea. It was far better than trying to keep dry, which was useless anyway. A fierce wind blew up, rocking the ship with sickening force as the torrent caught the sails. Seeing the waves wash over the deck, one of the crew grew bold enough to approach Janders himself, who was lashed to a cleated deck chair near the wheel.

"Wind's blowing right hard, sir. Shall I lower the skysails off her?" This was a hopeful wish, these sails being up to catch the terror of the wind and sent them flying over the foaming waves. The *Wraith* could make good speed in this kind of wind, if the man who captained her had grit enough to give her her head and sail through the hellish wind.

"Is the bowsprit clear of the water?" Janders asked him coolly.

Hope dwindled in the deckhand's heart. "Now and again she surfaces, sir."

"Nothing to worry about then. Leave the sails be."

The wind grew to the force of a cyclone, with the *Wraith of the Sea* set in the middle of it. It screamed in their ears. Life and death was held in the balance of the pitch of the hull. It was the most exciting moment Brendan had ever known.

By morning, the heart of the storm had passed. Janders was out early, going among his crew, ordering the sails checked for rents and the general debris removed. The men were dull-witted with exhaustion. More than one of them swore never to sign on in these waters again. It was always so. Most men were not suited to the savagery of a monsoon.

"And you, O'Shay. What did you think of our storm?" he asked Brendan.

The young man looked at him, his eyes still reflecting the flash of excitement he had felt. "'Twas grand, Captain. It was screaming, howling at me, knocking me from my feet. It damn near swallowed us up, spars, masts, sails, and all. Such a fury I've never known. I felt alive all over, every inch of me tingling with raw nerve. 'Twas grand," he said again, as if that said it all. To Janders, it did.

From that moment on, Janders gave generously of himself in time and experience to make Brendan the fine seaman he was meant to be. It would be keeping a bargain with the mistress he had loved for over thirty years, the sea. He could train Brendan, teach him all the natural wisdom Janders himself had paid so dearly to learn. The sea was a cool, jaded love that consumed your days and lit your heart with fire. The sea was that for a man the likes of Aloysius P. Janders, and would be, as well, for Brendan Michael O'Shay. It was as though a son of his own kind had been given him. Not those namby-pamby boys his wife had given him, unfit to bend a sail, but a boy so like himself that he rejoiced in him.

"Break out the rum!" he called to the steward. "A noggin for all hands!"

After the night's wreckage, the surprised seamen saw nothing much to celebrate, but there was never a group of men less likely to turn down a nip. They soon were singing, awash with good feeling toward one another brought on by Jamaica rum. In that happy hour, Brendan knew he would never be his father's first hand again.

Foochow was a heady place. Its harbor was lined with clippers, each jostling to be among the first to load the tea. Sampans brought the fragrant tea leaves down the Min River, and porters and tea chops fitted the graceful clippers with maximum loads. The red tea chests were stored in every corner of the ships, permeating the air the crews breathed. The dock handlers were kept busy day and night, working in shifts. All was carried out in a rush, racing for every second of advantage. A sizable prize awaited the first clipper to reach London dockside, and a wealth of glory awaited the man who captained her.

On board the *Wraith* all was in preparation for speed. Needed repairs were made. The chafing gear and stunsail gear were overhauled and sent aloft. Ship's carpenters were over the side, dressing out the chain plates along her hull with three-inch pine planks, thought to prevent drag in the water when the ship was well healed. In every breast, fever-pitch excitement grew.

At last, loaded with tea chests in the hold, the lazarete, the forepeak, and even the galley, the *Wraith of the Seas* was ready to sail. Leaving the Pagoda Anchorage, the clipper was towed out to sea. Well outside the outer knoll, the China pilot was discharged, and the two ropes cast off. Every kind of flying yard was hung, eager to catch the strong winds of the Indian Ocean. The clipper *Sir Lancelot* was spotted ahead. An extra jib was set up at once to overtake her. All hands manned their posts, sheeting the sails as needed. The *Wraith* caught up, and bow to bow the two clippers ran, a vision of majesty to fill the eyes.

Janders called Brendan to the wheel, and showed him how to set their course. He stood beside him, and told him how to hold the wheel steady in high winds. He spoke of the doldrums and the trade winds in these seas. Eagerly, his pupil stored the knowledge away, like some enormous text, implanted all the more firmly in his mind because of the reality of the sea all about him. The knowledge would serve him well in future years, when gales threatened to wreck his own ship and cast all hands awash to a watery grave. The words of a master sea dog like Janders would echo in his mind, and bring him safe to shore.

The strain of the long-term tension wreaked havoc with the nerves of the crews as they neared the Thames. Each captain raged demands at his men, ever increasing in volume.

"Sheet the skysails! Raise the topgallant! Look smart, you on the crow!"

Even to the last hundred yards, the race was contested. The *Sir Lancelot* drew well, and threatened to pull ahead. Janders maneuvered the *Wraith* in such a way as to cut across the *Lancelot*'s bow, making the *Wraith* dock first, winning the cash prize and a higher bid for its cargo of tea. One hundred and three days of travel had brought them three-fourths of the way around the world.

The tea was unloaded, the crew paid out, and there was a short rest in port. Then on to Ireland to pick up a cargo of goods and rugged Irish men to crew the ship, men eager to be free of their oppressive poverty.

As they anchored in Dublin, the gray-haired man could be seen from the deck, waiting in the stiff wind and chilling sleet for his son, his eldest and his heir. To Brendan, the sight of his father was startling. He's not young anymore, thought the son, in sudden notice of the man. How can I tell him I want no part of the life he has planned for me?

Brendan needn't have worried, for Captain Janders saw to it that Dougal was informed in no uncertain terms of what his son was, could, and ought to be. He left no room for doubt in Dougal's mind.

"He's more like me than I was myself at his age," he said. "A man like that, you don't waste behind a desk."

Dougal had only to look at Brendan to see that this was so. In the end he agreed, without Brendan's having so much as fired off a shot from his own cannon. After only a fortnight's visit, Brendan was signed on again, and sailed with Janders to the Hawaiian Islands to load whale oil and copra, and swim naked in dreamy lagoons with soft-eyed island girls.

Chapter Twenty-Three

While the son of Dougal and Moira was becoming a man, and learning to navigate the oceans of the world, the daughter of Dougal and Ellen was becoming a young woman, in a land as raw and green as the new timber in her father's lumber mill. Caitlin O'Mally, as she was known, was what her mother called strong-willed but her brothers called hard-headed. Only in a place like the California of the 1860's, and only in a family such as hers, could a girl like Caitlin have come to be. A free spirit thrived in California, affecting both young and old alike. It was a place where riches could be had by simply digging in the ground, where a man could build an empire by following a dream such as logging, where a young woman could grow up feeling free to speak her own mind. Impulsive, opinionated, and willful, Caitlin O'Mally had been given the freedom by the family who indulged her, cherished her, and allowed her to be the daring, intelligent woman she was meant to be.

From 1861 to 1865, civil war divided the country. Secessionists in California bid to influence the state to the Confederacy's cause. The majority of political opinion was pro-Southern. A deep split divided those who followed Senator Gwin, a Democrat and a supporter of slavery, and those who favored Senator Broderick, who championed the Union.

Although no conscription was mandatory in the state of California, some men chose to enlist in support of their nation. A strong feeling of obligation to his adoptive country led twenty-one-year-old Matthew Muldair to join the California Cavalry in Virginia. Matthew had never forgotten the signs he had seen as a child in the shop windows of Boston—"No Irish Need Apply." The concept had been born then that would guide his actions for the rest of his life, that it was wrong for men to discriminate against other men because of their nationality, race, or religion. The idea of slavery for any race of men was something Matt could not abide. The love he bore his country was fierce, as fierce as his desire to uphold its honor.

Distant as California was from the battlefronts, it was only through Matthew's letters that the family kept contact with him or had knowledge of his whereabouts. To his brothers, Seamus, Griffin, Connor, and Pat, Matthew was the hero of their boyhood lives. He lived the battles they played in their pretend forts. His was the life they dreamed of. To Danny and Ellen, he was simply their son, whose welfare they worried over and whose life they prayed for. The time between each letter was long, the thoughts that he had been killed or injured hard to put away. To Caitlin and Elizabeth, he was the brother who was truly their friend. No one in the family understood the special relationship they had with each other as well as Matt. He knew the reasons for Elizabeth's shyness, as well as the sensitivity behind Caitlin's brashness. He was the brother they both turned to for support, the one person they each trusted with their secrets.

Caitlin read and reread each of her brother's letters, wanting to be a part of what he was doing. In the first year of the war, his letters were cheerful, advising them that the war was sure to be over soon. They were letters a boy wrote, excited to be away from home, to be involved in something so noble that he believed in. He wrote:

Dear Family,

Our men have come forward in great numbers to serve their country. We far outnumber the Confederacy. Our cause is just, I believe that to be true.

There is some sickness in camp. Some of our men have dysentery or malaria. They are felled without ever having seen a battle. The quiet we know now is frustrating. We are anxious to be about this war, to see the rightful conclusion to it, and to return to our families.

I know you will do everything you can to support our cause. The Sanitary Commission is an excellent idea, for many of the men are ill and need nursing. I am well and in excellent spirits. I pray you are the same.

Your son,
Matthew

As the war progressed, the letters became less frequent. Rumors of the South's victories arrived in

California, greeted by Secessionist newspapers with bold headlines: LEE VICTORIOUS—UNION ARMY ROUTED. Matthew's letters, when they came, reflected the mood of the war.

My Dear Family,

I have seen too much death today. It hardly matters to me at this moment whether the uniform is blue or gray. The man in it is American. How have we come to this? What honor is there in killing your own countrymen?

Forgive my bitterness. We fought all day in a field I don't even know the name of. I am exhausted in mind and body. It didn't seem I would live through this day. Many of our men didn't. The smell of blood is in our camp. It is on my uniform, on my boots.

If being in this has taught me anything, it is the senselessness of war. What purpose has all our fighting served but to kill sons, husbands, fathers. When this war is ended, our nation must find a way to mend the terrible wounds we have given it. Sometimes, I cannot think of these gray-clad soldiers as any but our own men. I am sick of this war.

A man I lived beside for the last two years died today. Jared Taylor was my friend. He planned to come to California with me after the war. What did he die for? What noble purpose? One minute he was riding beside me in our troop, and the next, he was lying on the ground with half his head blown off. Jared was twenty-three. There is no one to mourn him but me. No one to remember his name. I mourn Jared Taylor. I mourn all of us.

Your son,
Matt

Such letters from Matthew raised a new sense of awareness in all the O'Mallys. The ugliness of war was no longer distant from them. One of their own was suffering, and men he was fighting beside were dying. Each of them found a way they could help. Ellen and her daughters put their energies into the newly formed Sanitary Commission, an organization based on the British Sanitary Commission, which had been very effective during the Crimean War. Its purpose was to provide nurses, medicines, and funds for the Union soldiers. Caitlin and Elizabeth rolled bandages, knit socks and mufflers, and put together packages of soap, tea, razors, and a few other necessities for the men. Danny was a major contributor for its fund-raising events. Dances were held, with expensive tickets of admission. Auctions provided needed means of raising money. One bag of flour, sold and resold so many times across the country, brought in a total of $40,000. California alone contributed $1,234,000 to the organization, one quarter of the national fund.

Their own lives went on, despite the war. The American River Logging Company, as the O'Mally-McTaggart partnership was called, had become one of the leading lumber suppliers of ever-growing San Francisco. Employing hundreds of men, mostly Irish, it was itself a boon to the economy. It had prospered with the country's need. By 1863, it was providing lumber not only for the city and the mines, but also for the railroad.

A massive project was taking place to connect the nation by rail. Railroad barons—Charles Crocker, Leland Stanford, Collis Huntington, and Mark Hopkins—imported 15,000 Chinese laborers to lay track across the country, with the ultimate goal of joining the Central Pacific line to that of the Union Pacific. Such an undertaking needed lumber. American River Logging supplied them with their needs.

The Chinese brought in to build the railroad, to blast an opening through the mountains and lay endless miles of track through the blistering desert, were paid so low a wage no other group would have considered working for it. Even so, they were resented for taking the jobs other groups felt entitled to. Their unique appearance and beliefs made them alien to the white population. Unlike their European counterparts, the Chinese men rarely brought their families to California. In the squalor of the Chinatowns they were segregated in were opium dens, gaming houses, and places of prostitution. Sanitary conditions were deplorable. Ill feeling from native Americans and European immigrants against the Chinese often built to violent levels.

Drawing upon the influence of her brother Matthew's belief in the equality of man, Caitlin, seeing the abuse of the Chinese, slowly formed her own belief that not only were men equally valued by their Creator, but that those who had much should help those who had little. It was an ideal she nurtured through the war years as she grew to adulthood. It was the one thing she and her father often fought over.

"Why won't you hire Chinese for the logging?" she asked him. It was a question that had come up before.

"You know the answer to that, Caity." He tried to be patient with her. In many ways, she was his favorite among the children. "My men are Irish and European. They won't work with Chinese. It's as much for the sake of the Chinese as for my own crew that I won't hire them. There'd be murder to pay for it if I did." He admired his daughter's tenacity, her loyalty to the underdog, but he knew what his men would stand for, and what they wouldn't. "Most of the Chinese don't even speak English," he explained.

"They could learn," she insisted. "We could set up a school to teach them. Elizabeth and I could give them lessons."

The very idea horrified him. "Now that's enough of such nonsense," he said, ending their conversation abruptly. "Just put that idea right out of your head."

She didn't put the idea out of her head. It grew, and with it the certainty that it was what she should do. When Matt comes home, she thought, he'll help me. We'll do it together.

By 1864, the Confederate Army had been cut off from its supply lines by Union blockades. Matthew's letters told of the pitiful condition of the Confederate soldiers.

21 November, 1864

Dear Father, Mother, and All,

We have been in a skirmish today, the third one this month. In each, the soldiers we fought against were scarcely fit for battle. Their uniforms are in rags, their feet are bare, even in the snow. My heart tells me it is wrong to kill such men who hold out so valiantly against such great odds. There is sickness in their camps, as there is in ours, but we have some medicines still. They have none. Dysentery kills more men than bullets.

It is my hope that we will be home by Christmas, for the war seems to be drawing to an end. The men we fight against are starving. How much they must believe in their cause, to go on fighting when there is so little left. Were we one army, fighting against a common enemy, I believe we would be undefeatable.

You will not know me when you see me, for I have grown some, and I am thinner now than I was when I left home. I know my brothers and sisters have changed too, and I am anxious to see them again. I miss all of you, and send you my love.

Matthew

It was not to be that Matthew would be home for Christmas. For the next four and a half months the armies of the Union and the Confederacy continued waging a war that even the common soldier knew was hopeless. So hard pressed were the men of General Lee's army by starvation, scurvy, malaria, and dysentery that 200,000 of them were absent without leave by April of 1865. They had seen what the generals refused to see. The war was over. They had lost. They took what was left of their lives and went home.

It was spring, not Christmas, when it ended. Spring, a

beginning of new life, was the background for the surrender by General Robert E. Lee of the Confederacy to General Ulysses S. Grant of the Union. On April 9th, at Appomattox Courthouse, Virginia, the war officially ended. It was time to go home. Time for life to begin again.

Chapter Twenty-Four

"You've come home with some fool ideas, Matt"—Danny turned on his son—"and this one's the most foolish of all. You've been listening to Caitlin. She's been preaching this at me for two years now. I thought you'd have better sense." It was hard for Danny to argue with Matt. He respected the man, admired him for the way he had fulfilled his duty to his country during the war. The war had been over for a year. At twenty-six, Matthew Muldair was a man Danny was proud to call his son. He was honorable, intelligent, hard working, and caring. He was everything Danny wanted his son to be. But now, through Caitlin's influence, he was serious about opening a school for the Chinese.

"Caity's right about this," Matt answered his father. "She's a bright young woman. She won't close her eyes to what's happening to the Chinese in San Francisco. She sees that their children are not welcome in schools. She sees the abuse they receive from nearly every other element in this town. You don't have to be a man to see all of that, Father. I admire her for what she's trying to do. I think you should be proud of Caity for feeling as she does." Danny rewarded him with a raised eyebrow for that remark. Matt chose to ignore the look and continued.

"I'd be dealing with the men. They could come to me in the evenings at the warehouse. I could teach them English there. Caity only wants to teach the children and their mothers. What would be the harm in that?"

"What would be the harm!" Danny turned and faced Matt. "I'll tell you what the harm would be. The resentment of this town. You're not a priest, Matt. See things as they really are. The men who work for me are Irish, or European. They've no love for the Chinese. If it wasn't for the Chinese, they'd have had jobs on the railroad. That cost them food on their table. They'll not appreciate you bringing in those men right beneath their very noses, and catering to them. I know my men, Matt. They won't stand for it."

"Then I'll do it somewhere else," Matthew said quietly. "If you're going to let men like that prevent you from allowing freedom for every man in this country, then you might as well have stayed in Ireland under the thumb of the British."

"I'm not saying I agree with them," Danny argued. "I've seen some things that turned my stomach too."

"Then take a stand against it," Matt insisted. "You're a powerful man in this town. Your support would lend respectability to the idea. We're not asking for so much, anyway. We only want to teach them English. As it is, they're cheated all the time because they don't understand our language."

"I sympathize with what you're saying, Matt. I know you want to help them, and that's fine, a noble thing." He

243

started to say more, but looked up at Matthew and saw something in his son's eyes that stopped the words from being spoken. He saw himself as Matt was seeing him at that moment, and he didn't like it. What he was telling his son was to take the coward's stand, ignore what he saw, let it go. Through Matt's eyes, eyes that had seen so much struggle and suffering for the right of freedom for all men, Danny saw how his own inaction, his own attempts to prevent his children from doing what they saw as just, must look to them. It made him ashamed.

"You needn't go anywhere else," he spoke up, looking into Matt's eyes. "I'll let you use the warehouse in the evenings, as you said."

"But I thought," Matt began, "the men . . ."

"Well, they won't like it, that's true, but it's my warehouse. I'll do with it as I see fit. I expect I have some rights too. It's a good thing you're doing, Matt. Your reasons for it are fine. I'll help you if I can, with supplies and such." He was embarrassed by the way Matt was smiling at him. It made him feel caught out at doing something right. "What I should be supplying you with is guns," he said, only half jokingly. "You'll meet resistance, you know."

Matt nodded. He knew the way men reacted with prejudice. He'd seen enough of that during the war. The thought of that wasn't going to stop him, though. "I can't wait to see the look on Caity's face. She won't believe me when I tell her that you've come around to our way of thinking. I'm glad you did," Matt said softly. "I remember the first time I met you, coming off the ship out of Ireland. I was scared of what you'd be like. You were something. There you were, looking hard as a mountain, but you were good and gentle with me. I was so proud of you, of what you'd done, of what you were. Through all the years, I've respected you, loved you, but I've never been prouder of you than I am right now, today."

Danny was quiet, thinking. It's all right, then. I haven't lost him. What Matthew Muldair thought of him meant a great deal, more than he had realized.

"I haven't said I agreed to Caitlin's running a school. She's got no business doing such a thing. She ought to be married, with children of her own to tend to. Too much time on her hands, that's the problem with Caity."

Matthew laughed. "You don't know what you're in for if you mean to stop her. She's ten times stronger-willed than I am. She'll have her children's school, if I'm a judge, and none too long from now, either. Caity's beautiful, but she's not meant for marriage. Not yet, anyhow. She's got a cause she believes in. God protect the poor man who gets in her way when Caity has a cause."

Danny looked at him, winced at the bold truth of his words, and sighed.

Unknown to her father, Caitlin O'Mally had already begun her school. At eighteen, she was, as her brother described her, a beautiful woman. She looked the way Ellen O'Reilly had looked at the same age: dark-haired, pale Irish complexion, lovely blue eyes that drew everyone's notice, and a figure even the hoop-skirted fashions of the day could not conceal. Caitlin was all that Ellen had been, and more. There was pride of family in the way she carried herself, and pride of self in the direct look of her eyes. Where Ellen had been shy, Caitlin was

245

unafraid. She was comfortable with her place in the world.

With Matt to befriend her should she fail, she began actively seeking out Chinese students for her school as soon as he was back from the war. Had her father known her plans to drive her own carriage into Chinatown alone, a fact even Matt wasn't aware of, he would have locked her in her room for her own protection. Any woman alone in San Francisco's Chinatown was courting danger—a young, beautiful, white woman alone would have to be insane. Stories of kidnapping, forced prostitution, and slave girls in the Chinatown of the 1860's were not exaggerated. So many criminal cases of prostitution came up before the court in 1866 that an entire jail was set up for Chinese prostitutes alone. It was foolhardy, she knew, going alone, but it was the only way she could think of to let the parents know about the classes she intended.

She drove slowly through the unpaved streets in her first mission into the Chinese community. Men stood outside their houses and shops, staring at her with hard eyes of suspicion. No one spoke. She gripped the reins more firmly and drove on, looking for signs that would identify a place of business. What signs she saw were in Chinese. There was no way for her to tell what business she would be walking into. Her greatest fear was that she might mistakenly walk into an opium den, or a house of prostitution.

There were children at the shop doors. None of them smiled at her. They stared with solemn eyes, distrusting her for the color of her skin. This must be how they feel, she thought, when they come into our side of town. She was the alien here.

The strong scent of lye soap brought her to a halt outside what was obviously a laundry. Three little girls looked out at her from the doorway, the oldest about six. They stared in fascination. It wasn't often they saw a white woman at their door. They vanished as Caitlin approached.

"Hello?" she called into the dark room. The sharpness of the lye stung her eyes and made them water. Even breathing was difficult as she inhaled the fumes. "Hello, is anyone here?"

A young man, perhaps in his early twenties, stepped out of the back room. He wore a blue cotton shirt and pants of the same material. A long queue hung down his back, beginning beneath a skullcap.

"I am Ming-Low. You want laundry?"

He spoke English. It was broken, minimal English, but enough to understand her. She looked around the room. A heavy cauldron set on a tripod stand held a load of soaking clothes. In the back room, she could see a woman ironing. The woman was going to have yet another child, and very soon, but was vigorously ironing. Beside her, at a low table, sat a boy of about seven, wrapping bundles of ironed clothes into paper and tying them with string. Four children in a two-room house, and another on the way. It seemed to Caitlin she had come to the right place.

"My name is Caitlin O'Mally. I'm here about your children," she began. The woman in the back room stopped ironing. So she understood English too. "Do your children speak English?" she asked Ming-Low.

This was something the man clearly had not expected. He stepped back, as though she were threatening him. "You missionary lady?" he asked.

Caitlin knew what he meant. A few of the churches in

San Francisco had tried teaching English to the Chinese, with the added intention of teaching them Christianity as well. The Chinese had come at first, until it was clear what was expected of them in the way of converting to Methodist, or Presbyterian, or Catholic beliefs. It soon became obvious that this was the main objective of the teachers, and the Chinese stopped coming.

"I am a teacher," Caitlin explained, which wasn't exactly true. "I want to begin a school for the Chinese children, to teach them English and simple mathematics. I want to teach them a little about this country," she added, hoping to sway him. "I will not teach religion. I am not from a church, and no one will ask your child to learn any religion. I promise you that."

The woman in the back room took the boy by the hand and led him into the outer room. She stood beside Ming-Low, silent, but listening to all Caitlin said. She was not pretty in any recognized sense. Her face was almost square. Her hair hung in untidy strings down her face. Her dress was of the cheapest material and poorly cut. Her feet were bare. Caitlin felt sorry for her at once.

The boy , in contrast, wore a blue jacket of finer goods, blue trousers, like his father, and shoes. His hair was neatly combed, and he looked well nourished. His skullcap was of fine embroidered material. A queue of glossy, dark hair hung down from it.

"My children not need school," Ming-Low said as much to the woman beside him as he did to Caitlin. The woman had not even looked up, but did not move away either. "I go back to China soon," he explained. "Not need English there." He had dismissed her idea, and began to walk away.

This was the reason so many Chinese refused to learn

English, refused to become Americanized, refused many of the responsibilities of a citizen. They planned to return to China. America was a visit. They came here to work, to earn money, and to return home as quickly as they could. They did not often bring their wives or families with them. This was not their home. Those who died had their bodies cremated or embalmed and sent back to China. They looked at their stay here as temporary. What good would English be to a boy in China?

"You have been here how many years?" Caitlin asked.

"Eight years I stay," Ming-Low replied.

"I think you will stay many more years," Caitlin said softly, not wanting to anger him. "In that time, your children need school. They need to learn English so that they will not be cheated. Would that not be best for them? There are many who would cheat the Chinese.

"My school would cost you nothing," she told him, thinking that this might be why he held back. "It could only help your children to learn the language of the country they live in."

"Where you teach this school?" Ming-Low questioned her. His eyes were full of distrust.

"I'm not sure," she admitted. "I'm finding my pupils first. Then I will find a place for a school. Does your wife understand English?"

"Not wife," Ming-Low looked at the boy's mother. "She nothing," he explained. The woman's head bent lower to the floor.

"But these are your children?" Caitlin asked, confused.

"Oh, yes," Ming-Low answered. "My son," he said, taking the boy's hand from his mother's. He seemed proud of the child.

"And the girls?"

He brushed his hand in their direction, as if they were of no consequence. "Girls this one's daughters. They nothing," he answered, dismissing them.

This attitude infuriated Caitlin, but she kept her anger under control. "I would like to educate all your children—your son and your daughters."

This was too absurd a notion for Ming-Low to contemplate. Imagine, teaching useless girls. Such a thing would only bring him ridicule and loss of face in his community. Besides, the girls helped in the laundry, as did their brother. Although they were young, every hand was needed to survive. This American woman was persistent.

It was true he had been here longer than he had planned. First, there were the years working on the railroad, paying back the Chinese company for his passage over. He worked three years for no wages other than his food and clothing. At the end of that time, he had no money to return. He then began the laundry, eking out a living doing both washing and ironing and delivering laundry to the shopkeepers or men in boarding houses. After a while, he saved up enough to buy the woman, Soong-Tse. With her help, his business had improved. He worked her very hard, as he did himself, but she was uncomplaining. She was grateful that she had escaped the disgrace of becoming a sing-song girl. She was not pretty enough for that life, and so she had been sold to Ming-Low at a small price. When he returned to China, as he promised himself he would, he did not plan to take Soong-Tse or her daughters with him. The boy, he would take. His son was all that pleased him in the world.

It was that special fondness for the boy that swayed his

thinking. It would be a shame for a boy as handsome, quick-witted, and blessed with a serene spirit to grow up ignorant. Ming-Low had to admit it might be a very long time before he managed to save up enough money for two passages to China, and enough to live well when he got there. Soon there would be another child, perhaps another son. That would mean yet another ticket. Lastly, he thought, with only Chinese children in the school and no American children, how much evil influence would he really be exposed to? It might be safe enough.

"Will you allow me to teach your children?" Caitlin pressed. She wanted to appeal to the woman who stood silent and barefoot beside the boy, but she didn't dare.

Ming-Low stared at Caitlin for a long, uncomfortable moment. He seemed to be deciding. "You teach son," he agreed at last. "You say when. I bring."

"And your daughters?"

He looked insulted by her question. "Daughters? Never."

That was the answer Caitlin had expected. She felt it unwise to push the issue any further. If she made him angry, she would lose the boy as well.

"Will you tell other families you know that I will teach their children as well? In one week's time, I will come back here and tell you where our school will be held. Will you do that for me, Ming-Low?"

He nodded, and bowed deeply to her. Their conversation was at an end. Ming-Low returned to his work. The woman, who was not his wife but who had borne him four children and was soon to bear the fifth, went back to her ironing.

Caitlin walked outside and climbed into the buggy. As she picked up the reins and clucked her tongue at the horse to urge him forward, the three daughters of Ming-Low appeared at the door of the laundry. They ran after the buggy until the swiftness of the horse left them far behind.

"Good-bye," Caitlin called to them, and waved.

They didn't respond, but stood in the road, staring after her. Did they, like their mother, understand English? Did they understand that I was trying to help them? she wondered. Their faces were so very solemn. Did they believe what their father said, that they were nothing? One day, Caitlin thought, looking back at them. One day.

The Sisters of Mercy Orphanage was located on Dupont Street, directly between the heights of Washington Street and Chinatown. The day after Caitlin met Ming-Low and his family, she went alone to see Sister Judith, Reverend Mother of the Sisters of Mercy Convent and Director of the Orphanage.

Caitlin was looking forward to seeing Sister Judith again. She had met the indefatigable nun while working beside her for the Sanitary Commission during the war. The job of rolling bandages and packing aid boxes was tedious and mind-numbing. Sister Judith had relieved their boredom by recounting vivid stories of her girlhood in Ireland. She'd been far from a saint then, always in trouble with either her parents or her priest. Too daring, too adventurous for a girl, she was the last pupil in her class who would have been expected to consider the religious life.

Quick to act when needed, and quick to speak out, like Caitlin herself, Sister Judith became a kind of heroine to her. Caitlin admired her. She was a woman who did things that needed doing. Not only did she give up her quiet life in Ireland and bring her sisterhood of nuns from Dublin to San Francisco in a time when it was a rough town of miners and sailors who resented their presence for reminding them too keenly of their sins: she eventually proved herself to those same men by nursing them through the cholera epidemic of 1854, risking her own health and that of her nuns, and thereby gaining the men's respect.

To Caitlin, Sister Judith's most admirable success was the founding of St. Mary's Orphanage and Infant School. Lacking the organizations of older states with longer histories of charitable development, California, still shaking itself free of miners' dust, had no state-provided homes for its orphaned children. Sister Judith had gone out herself, among the men who'd made their fortunes from the riches of the state, and collected enough money to build and run the badly needed orphanage. For Caitlin O'Mally, this was the kind of success she wanted for herself. Far greater than accumulated wealth, this success was of the spirit, the hard work of her own hands. Caitlin wanted a chance to prove herself just as Sister Judith had.

"Caitlin O'Mally," the Reverend Mother greeted her warmly. "How good to see you again. Come and sit beside me. You've not come about joining our religious life, have you?"

"No, Sister."

"I thought not, but God can often surprise us. How are you, my dear?"

"I'm well, thank you, Sister, but I've come to you with a problem, one I hope you will be able to help me with."

Sister Judith smiled. "That is the nature of my life, I suppose. People come to see me only when they have a problem. Tell me, what have you come to see me about, Caitlin? I'll help you if I can." She smiled encouragingly.

Caitlin had carefully worked out exactly what she would say. It wouldn't be a lie, not really. She simply wouldn't tell the whole story.

"You know my brother Matthew is back?" The answer was a nod. "My father and Matt decided that it would be a good idea to provide a free class to teach English to the Chinese men of San Francisco. Father offered Matt the use of one of his warehouses to hold the classes in."

"That's a wonderful idea." Sister Judith seemed genuinely pleased. "It's very much needed, as your father must be all too aware."

"Yes," Caitlin answered, feeling more nervous by the minute for the mild deception she was attempting. "It is very necessary. For my part, I'm beginning a school for Chinese children, and their mothers, if they wish to come. Our public schools won't accept them. How can they be expected to better themselves in this country if they can't speak English? I've seen too much prejudice and abuse directed at them. I want to do something to help. I can't close my eyes to such injustice."

Sister Judith was surprised at such an ambitious undertaking by the daughter of a very well-to-do family. Girls of such a station in life were usually content to donate money toward charitable endeavors, never thinking to involve themselves personally. She looked at Caitlin again, seeing willful determination in the young woman which reminded her of herself at that age. She saw too the great possibilities of someone of Caitlin's fine

254

reasoning, courageous character, and strong sense of fair-mindedness.

"Caitlin, as much as I admire your motives for such a project, I must tell you that this is a thing that will not be easily done. The Chinese of San Francisco are very much a closed society. They still consider their homeland to be China. Many of them don't want to learn English, or American ways. I doubt they would even speak to a young woman like you about such a thing as a school for their children. You are a woman, don't forget. They have very little value for women."

"But I have spoken to them already." Caitlin rushed on with her story, eager to tell it. "I went to Chinatown yesterday, and made arrangements."

"Caitlin! You went to Chinatown by yourself?" Sister Judith asked, staring in frank surprise.

Careful, Caitlin thought. "My father would never have allowed me to go alone," she answered.

Sister Judith's hands folded into a little prayer temple as she pressed the tips of her fingers against her lips. In her years as Reverend Mother of the Convent, she had learned to detect a lie, even a small one. Her best instinct told her she was hearing one now. Caitlin had lowered her head when speaking about her father, as though hiding some deceit.

Had she really gone into Chinatown alone? Was she that daring? If she was, it was a very dangerous thing to have done, a foolishly brave thing—the very sort of thing Sister Judith might have done herself. Of one thing she was absolutely certain, and that was the sure hand of God moving in this, sending this girl to her. She felt His presence in what Caitlin had done. She remained still and

255

quiet, pressing her fingertips together, and listened with both her ears and that sensing part of her spirit to what Caitlin had to say.

The story unraveled. Caitlin told about Ming-Low and his family. "He lives with a woman who is not his wife," she explained. "They have three daughters and a son, with another child due very soon. I told Ming-Low that I wanted to teach his children English, so they wouldn't be cheated in the shops. I said I would begin a school for Chinese, that it would be free, and that it would teach no religion. He thought I was a missionary," she remarked to Sister Judith. A smile at the delightful improbability of that passed between them.

"At first, he wasn't interested. He said his children worked with him and he needed their labor, that he couldn't spare them. He loves his son, Sister. I told him it would be a terrible thing to have so fine a child grow up ignorant. It was his love of the boy that changed his mind," Caitlin explained carefully. "He agreed not only to bring the boy, but to tell other families in Chinatown about my school. They will meet me at his house next week.

"I asked about his daughters," she continued, "but he refused, and said that they were nothing." She paused, remembering the anger of that moment. "I had to let them go, or lose the boy as well, but I won't ever forget them, or give up on them either. I have to be patient. One day, I'll have them as well."

She was still for a moment, then spoke more calmly. "That's why I'm here today, asking for your help. I was hoping you might let me use a spare room at the orphanage for my classroom. It needn't be much of a room. I doubt there will be too many."

Now it was Sister Judith's turn to draw a deep breath. She was amazed at what this girl had done. The Church had tried for years to approach the Chinese with offers of aid, but had always been rejected. In one afternoon, Caitlin had gained their trust with a simple offer to teach their children English.

"I'm very proud of you," Sister Judith said to her. "You'll have the classroom. I give it to you gladly. I won't say anything about this to anyone else just yet." She met Caitlin's eyes. A look of understanding passed between them. "Promise me you will be careful," she stressed. "I will give you as much support as I can, and if it counts as anything to you, my admiration."

Later that day, Caitlin found the opportunity to speak to her father. It was important that he approved of her working at the orphanage. She could only hide that from him for so long.

"I saw Sister Judith today," she began innocently.

He looked up from his paper. "Did you? How was it that you saw her?"

"I just wanted to talk to her. I hadn't seen her in so long. She's always been so nice to me."

"She's a fine woman," Danny agreed. He picked up his paper once more.

"Sometimes I feel so useless here," Caitlin went on. "I feel as if I'm going to suffocate in this house. I need something to do that's helpful to someone else."

"You know there's much you could do to help your mother."

"That's not the kind of thing I mean, Father."

Danny looked up from his paper once again. "Is there

something you want to tell me, Caitlin?"

"Sister Judith says I can work with her at the orphanage," she blurted out. "I just can't bear to be idle any longer."

"Sister Judith agreed to this?"

She nodded. Silence was her best defense. Words could catch her out.

Danny looked at his daughter. She was eighteen. At her age, he had been working for several years. It must be hard on her, this time between the age of child and wife. Too little for her to do. Such confinement would drive him mad. What safer place for her to occupy her time than with the Sisters of Mercy? What harm could there be in that?

"Well, if Sister Judith thinks she could use you, and if you genuinely want to go there," he began, "I won't refuse you. It might be the very thing for you to do. You have my permission, Caitlin. I'll see to it that you have the horse and buggy when you need them."

Caitlin smiled, and had to bite the inside of her lip to keep from shouting her hurrah out loud. I've done it! Her mind sang over and over. I've done it!

That had been the beginning. The next week, when Caitlin O'Mally returned to the house of Ming-Low, six Chinese children, all boys, were waiting outside— waiting to learn. They bowed when Caitlin, their teacher, stepped down from the buggy.

Chapter Twenty-Five

By December of 1867, Caitlin's Chinese school had grown from six pupils to thirty. The children, all boys, ranged in age from six to fourteen. They had made remarkable progress in one year's time. Their verbal skills were good, and their reading abilities improved daily.

Word had spread quickly in the Chinese community that Caitlin O'Mally was a woman of her word. No religion was ever taught in her school, and no fee was ever charged. The sons of Chinatown's merchants came to her classes, wanting to learn.

The one regret Caitlin had was that still, after a year, not a single girl had been enrolled in her classes. She had spoken to families with daughters time after time, to no purpose. Fathers flatly refused to educate their daughters. It was pointless to try to convince them. Yet the three daughters of Ming-Low stayed in Caitlin's mind. She had promised herself that she would help girls such as these. Impatient as always, she decided she'd waited long enough.

It had been a long time since she ventured into Chinatown. A year had made little difference in the place. She noticed a few more stores, more people milling in the street, but little else. She was looking for something. There! In the alley, behind the Chinese Pagoda restaurant, was the house she was looking for.

Caitlin had given up asking the parents of her pupils to bring their daughters to her class. Instead, she had asked the older boys for the names of other families in Chinatown who had daughters only. Such a family might be willing to educate a girl, she thought. That was her hope when she knocked on the door.

A young, and very attractive Chinese woman answered. Her hair was coiled in beautiful loops, held by jade combs. Tiny pearls of jade hung from her ears. She was small, under five feet, with painted eyes and painted lips. Caitlin stared, knew she was staring, but continued to do so. She hadn't known what to expect, but it certainly hadn't been this. The woman's robes were silk, embroidered with gold thread.

"Yes?" the Chinese woman asked, puzzled by Caitlin's silence.

"My name is Caitlin O'Mally," she began. "I'm a teacher. I teach a school for the Chinese of this community. I was told that you have children that might be old enough for my class."

"Who says this?" the woman asked.

"Some of the older boys in my class gave me your name," Caitlin explained. "They gave me the names of other families as well."

The Chinese woman's eyes lowered so as not to shame Caitlin. "I fear boys play tricks on teacher," she said carefully.

Caitlin began to feel uncomfortable. She began to think she knew what sort of house this was. Could boys as young as fourteen know of such a place? Was this their way of telling her they didn't want girls in their class? If it was, they had made a big mistake.

"Then you have no children?" she asked, angry as she had ever been in her life at these boys, and at their parents who had made them this way.

"Oh, yes," the woman answered. Realizing that she must appear rude standing in the doorway, yet unsure that she should invite this white woman inside, she felt acutely uncomfortable. She debated about the propriety of such a thing. Would the white woman's honor be diminished by coming inside her house? At last, good manners won out over such caution. "Please," she said, standing to one side, "you come in?"

Caitlin hesitated only a moment, then stepped quickly into the house. The room was sparely decorated, but small lacquered tables shone with light from the window. A large red vase rested on a low, black table. The patterns on it were brilliant blends of gold, sapphire, and emerald. The design was exquisite, and from the crazing of the glaze, looked antique.

"Please," the woman spoke as a hostess, "I offer you tea?"

Caitlin nodded. She listened as the woman called softly in Chinese, and a lovely young girl of about twelve appeared.

"Eldest daughter, Sui-Szi," she said, introducing the girl. She spoke again, rapidly, and the girl disappeared— to prepare the tea, Caitlin supposed. In a moment, she returned with a tray holding a teapot and two handleless cups. Her eyes were cast down the entire time, never daring to meet Caitlin's.

"She is lovely," Caitlin said. The woman did not respond to the compliment. To be a Chinese woman, and be beautiful, was not always a blessing. "You said you have other children, Mrs. . . . ?" Caitlin faltered.

"I am called My-Ling. Sadly, my children, all daughters," she reported.

"I'm very glad to hear that. Girls are exactly what I want for my school. At present, we have only boys, but that's something I intend to change. If you would allow me to teach your daughters, My-Ling, then other families might follow your example and allow their daughters to attend school too. In this country, both boys and girls are educated."

The Chinese woman looked meaningfully at Caitlin, as though speaking to a slow child. "Other families not send children to school with daughters of prostitutes." She looked embarrassed. "You find other daughters, maybe." She said it simply, as though the logic must be clear, even to Caitlin.

The logic was all too clear. "My-Ling, do you want your daughters to live as you do? Do you want them to be prostitutes too?"

It was a hard question. "There is little choice," the mother answered quietly. It was a truth she had learned through her own life.

"There is a choice," Caitlin insisted. "Let me educate them. They can work in shops, in factories, in people's homes. There would be a real life for them. This is a new country. Give them a chance. Their lives need not be like yours. What mother wouldn't want her child to have a better life than her own?"

My-Ling rose, and bowed formally to Caitlin. "In

China, where I was born, my family is poor. Daughter is a burden to parents. They sell daughters to be prostitute. I am thirteen when sold. My mother said to me, that day, to her I am dead. In China, children of prostitute lower than nothing. You say, you save daughters of My-Ling from such life. For this, I give all I possess."

Never in her life had Caitlin been more certain that she was doing the right thing. "You need give nothing," she said, "only bring them. Promise?"

The woman stood straight, eyes welling with unshed tears. She nodded her agreement to this white woman who had come into her life unasked and changed the course of her daughters' future.

Caitlin gave My-Ling the list of names the boys had given her.

"These other women," she asked, "are they like you?" My-Ling nodded. "Then, will you speak to them for me? Tell them that it doesn't matter what they do. Their children will be treated as my pupils and the equal of every other child in my class. Will you say this for me? Will you help me?"

It had been a long time since anyone had spoken to My-Ling as they would speak to other women. That was a gift Caitlin was unaware she was giving. She had treated My-Ling as she would have treated any mother.

"I will," the mother of three daughters said solemnly. "You need only ask. I will always help you."

Caitlin left Chinatown, her heart gladdened that at last, there would be girls for her school. From small, dark rooms all over the city, the daughters of Chinatown would at last come forth. One day, Caitlin vowed, the other daughters would come as well, those of such men as Ming-Low. She hated that she couldn't reach them. This was a day for joy, and not for sadness. On Monday, there would be at least three girls in her class, the three daughters of My-Ling—the prostitute.

"You've done what!" Danny's anger carried in the sound of his voice. He stood across from Caitlin, face suffused with red, eyes glaring like sharp needlepoints of stabbing fury. "You've carried on this deceit for a full year? You've gone into Chinatown several times alone? Didn't you realize how you were risking your life? How could you have been so foolish!"

"Danny, don't get so excited," Ellen said, trying to calm him. It was always this way between Danny and Caitlin. Sometimes it developed into raging, screaming battles. Caitlin always knew just how to provoke him. "Please, come and sit down. She's promised not to do it again, haven't you, Caitlin? You'll not make it any better by all this shouting."

"I wouldn't have had to deceive you if you would have just allowed me to teach my school openly," Caitlin reminded her father. It was a point, she quickly saw, she might better have kept to herself, for it angered him all the more. This was a time for backing down, but backing down was not a thing she had learned to do. She stood her ground firmly, as she always did, which so infuriated her father he might have struck her had not Matthew stepped between them at just that moment.

"I don't see that any real harm's been done," he said, trying to reason with Danny. "Her intentions were certainly in the right place. You remember what Sister Judith said about how much good Caity's done? It's fear for her safety that's got you so upset. I understand that.

She mustn't put herself in such danger. Now that it's out in the open, though, there'll be no need for her to ever go alone again."

Danny pounced on that remark. "Oh, she'll never need to go again," he said, "for this is the end of that Chinese school. She obviously doesn't know what's safe, and what isn't. Her logic can't be trusted."

Caitlin opened her mouth to say she would go no matter what he said to the contrary, but before she could speak such inflamed words, Matthew took her part again.

"Of course, you could do that," he said slowly and calmly, "and Caitlin would have no choice but to abide by your wishes. But I'd hate to see that happen, for those children's sakes. They've gained so much from her teaching. It really is a blessing she's giving them, even if she has gone about it in the wrong way."

Danny visibly calmed with Matthew's words. He mulled over what he was saying, the storm of his anger easing away from him with the stabilizing normality of Matt's voice.

"I wonder if there isn't another choice," Matt said. "One that satisfies everyone. What if she promised never to go into Chinatown without one of us again? Wouldn't that serve to protect her? Now that it's openly known, there's no reason for her to break her promise. Remember, Sister Judith told us that Caitlin is performing an irreplaceable service for those children."

Caitlin had the good sense to remain silent while her father thought this over. It was a tight, uncomfortable moment.

Ellen touched her husband's arm gently. "It seems safe enough, Danny. To be honest, I'd hate to see the children's school closed. As long as Caitlin will respect our wishes, I see no reason to force her to stop what is really an admirable work. She's doing something a lot more useful than most girls of her age. She will promise, and mean it, won't you, Cait?" There was nothing Ellen hated worse in the world than these quarrels between her husband and Caitlin, the child of her heart.

Every pair of eyes focused on Caitlin. She looked around the room, noticing Matthew's small smile of warmth and encouragement, her mother's worried parental frown, Elizabeth's guilty, downcast eyes, and her father's hard look of immovable rock.

"I'm sorry you found out the way you did," she began. "I would have liked to have told you myself. I only risked what I did because I knew it was important. I'll promise you, though, since you've asked it, that I will never go into Chinatown without one of you beside me again. You may believe that, Father. I would never break a promise to you."

"You can be a willful, difficult girl, Caitlin," Danny chastised her. "If it weren't for that letter arriving here from that Chinese woman, there's no telling how long this might have gone on. You're good at keeping secrets, I see that. I don't want to be too hard with you," he said, softening, "but this is a matter of putting yourself in serious danger. If I accept your word, you'll promise never to go there alone again?"

"I promise," she swore.

"All right then, that's the end of it. I'll not say another word against it. You can count yourself lucky, my girl, and you can stop giving your sister that look too. She had no idea what was in that letter when she brought it to me. She'd hardly have been the one to betray you if she'd realized, and you know it." He walked out of the room, and Ellen followed him, leaving Caitlin with Elizabeth and Matthew.

"Don't hate me, Caitlin," Elizabeth said. "I didn't know."

"You might have ruined everything," Caitlin snapped.

"Well, you should have told me what you were doing. Then I could have kept your secret. How was I to know?"

Elizabeth was right. Caitlin knew it, but was still too worried to think clearly. She wanted someone to blame for her ill luck. It wasn't Elizabeth's fault that My-Ling had written a letter of thanks and addressed it to the O'Mally family. Fate had chosen that Danny should know.

"You constantly surprise me, Caity," Matt said to her after Elizabeth had gone. "You were pretty impressive with Father, you know."

"If you hadn't spoken up when you did," she admitted, "I would have said too much. I'm still learning not to explode whenever I feel like it. I'm very glad you were here. He listens to you. He thinks I'm a fool who needs a caretaker. Why does he have to be so stubbornly rigid?" she demanded, her voice hard with emotion.

Matthew held her in his arms, and she felt the anger drain away from her. "You know, we're much alike, you and I. We're not the same blood, but we've like minds. I understand what you're trying to do. I want to do it myself. You have to realize that he's protective of you. He's doing what he thinks is his job as a parent."

"I'm not a child."

"I know you're not. Sometimes I think you're more self-reliant than any of us. He loves you, Caity, that's all. Don't be angry with him for that. And don't make Elizabeth go on feeling as you have. None of this is her fault. She'd never do anything to harm you, and she doesn't deserve to be hurt this way."

A calmness came over her as she stood with Matthew. Only with him did she feel a kindred spirit, and understood. Thoughts began formulating in her mind. This wasn't the end of her helping the Chinese, not by a long shot. She had a plan.

"Where's Elizabeth? Where did she go?" she asked, suddenly intent on finding her.

She left Matthew standing, staring after her. Now what's she up to? he wondered. With Caitlin, you never knew. Of one thing he was certain; she wasn't about to give up easily. He had to admire her for such determination, and for her strong sense of right. In fact, he admired her for quite a lot. She was by far the most interesting woman he knew.

Elizabeth was sitting by herself at the table beside the scrub oak. That she was still upset by what had happened was obvious. She was sensitive to other people's feelings—too sensitive, Caitlin often thought. It was always Elizabeth who made the effort to mend their quarrels. She hated the arguments, hated the separation they caused. As Caitlin approached her now, she was sorry for her angry words. Elizabeth was unfailingly loyal, if timid and unadventurous. When she loved, she loved forever.

"Don't sit and sulk," Caitlin told her. "I've got an idea how you can help. That'll make you feel better." Caitlin was a firm believer in the healing power of action.

"I'm not sure I want to help," Elizabeth said, her pride still hurt from the earlier accusations.

"Of course you do," Caitlin insisted, ignoring her sister's mood. "I'm going to need your help. Come on," she urged her, "I'm sorry about before. I know it wasn't your fault. Really. Elizabeth?"

"What is it you want me to do?" her sister asked, having held out as long as she was able. Of the two personalities, Caitlin was the stronger. She always had been. Elizabeth was sensitive and gentle. She had never been defiant in her life.

Caitlin's face reflected her own sense of excitement. "I've thought of a way that we can meet a lot of Chinese families all at once. That's why I need your help. There may be too many for me alone."

"Caitlin! You just promised Father you wouldn't do this anymore." Elizabeth was horrified as much with the lie as with the implication of her own possible involvement.

"That's not what I promised at all. I promised I wouldn't go alone to Chinatown again, and I won't. I won't have to. We'll go down to the wharf. We'll meet the ships as they arrive, and talk to the Chinese families right there about the school. You could meet one ship, while I meet another."

Elizabeth had the look of someone whose air had been cut off. "Oh, Caity, I couldn't. I just couldn't." She held her hand to her throat, a look of horror on her face.

Caitlin stopped, surprised, and stared at her. She hadn't expected so strong a reaction. She knew Elizabeth was timid, but this sort of weakness bothered her. "All right," she said, giving in, turning away in despair at her sister's crippling shyness. "Just be sure you don't say anything to anyone."

"Cait, do you think you ought to? Please don't do this. It's so dangerous down on the wharf. I want to help you. I do. I'd just be too afraid. You and Matt are the brave ones. You're more like him than I am, and I'm his natural sister. I wish I were more like the both of you, but I'm not."

Caitlin's fierce anger softened, as it always did toward Elizabeth. Perhaps it was that she had lost her natural parents so early that made her such a gentle soul. Whatever the reason, it was her nature, and it wasn't going to change. It was no use being hard with her.

"Do you really want to help me, in another way?" Caitlin asked.

Her sister nodded, miserable with her own lack of nerve.

"Good, then you can teach the school on the days that I go to the wharf. It will free me to go."

To Elizabeth, the idea of teaching the school was almost as bad as going to the wharf. It meant direct contact with people she didn't know, people she feared. The thought of standing up and speaking in front of a roomful of staring children terrified her. She kept it to herself. She feared the loss of Caitlin's friendship more. Pushing her shyness a distance from her, she said, "Yes, I could do that."

Caitlin hugged her, a warm reassuring embrace. "Could you? That's wonderful! We'll start tomorrow."

Tomorrow! Elizabeth thought, a tight knot of fear hard in her stomach. Tomorrow!

Chapter Twenty-Six

Captain Brendan O'Shay was known to his men as the Celtic Cannon, for the temper of his Irish nature was liable to explode at any man unfortunate enough to have provoked it. He was a hard captain, he knew, demanding of his men, but winning their admiration and loyalty by his fair-handedness and expert seamanship. He was the kind of captain who got his crew home to port with no deaths to any on his ship. Men signed on with him again and again, for though he required excellence of them, he returned it with decent wages and fit food—and he was just.

At twenty-six, the five years' apprenticeship with Captain Janders had taught him well. In those years, he'd learned more than navigation. He'd learned men. He could spot those who were harbingers of trouble. No matter how skilled the man, Brendan refused to sign him on if he looked to bring a problem to his ship.

With Captain Janders's recommendation, at twenty-four he had become the youngest commissioned captain of the Blackwell Line, given command of the clipper ship

Berengaria, a British cargo and passenger vessel. In the following two years, he'd quickly gained the respect of his superiors by finishing first in the tea race from Foochow Harbor three times running. He knew his ship, and sailed her as no other man could.

The harbors of the world were home to Brendan O'Shay. He followed the trade lines, unloading 100-pound sacks of rice in Japan, fragrant tea leaves from China in London, and bolts of rare silks for the European market, picking up a cargo of whale oil and copra in the Hawaiian Islands and then heading for the California coast, to deliver his human cargo of sixty steerage passengers of Chinese.

The Chinese on board lived in a state of controlled squalor. Their meals were frugal, their comfort minimal. It irked Brendan that his ship, the *Berengaria*, so clean of line, should carry a cargo as offensive and foul as human beings packed in close quarters for a long journey could be. He felt pity for these people, for he saw them as such, and not as simply ship's ballast, as had other captains he had known. Their agonies were painful to him, their small triumphs joyful. When a Chinese woman on board gave birth to twin sons, while making the Atlantic crossing, he sent a bottle of good whiskey to the father in honor of the event.

He had seen many people of the world, and knew the Chinese to be neither better nor worse than any other man born of woman. As far as their women were concerned, his tastes ran more to the native Hawaiian girls with their inviting eyes and willing smiles. He thought of himself as a connoisseur, sampling the lovely flowers of all the races, like exotic wines.

*　　　*　　　*

San Francisco of 1868. The city always awakened his sense of excitement. After so long a journey, it was a welcome spot to harbor in. It had grown tremendously in the eight years since Brendan had first seen it aboard Captain Janders's ship. It had been a city of tent and wood before the earthquake of 1865. Fire had leveled it again and again. Now, Brendan noted, the buildings were of brick. Years of hard lessons had brought this fantasy-loving city to its senses. It was no longer a town of pitched tents, but of solid houses built for permanent dwellings.

It was also a place where loneliness could be eased with the price of a coin. Brendan's crew looked forward to the French women of Jackson Street. The restaurants there were well known for their upstairs rooms. San Francisco always meant shore leave for the men of the *Berengaria*. Although it was true that many of the men returned to the ship with their pockets empty and their heads aching from the whiskey they had drunk, those same men wouldn't have missed it for anything. Brendan knew this, and always gave them free rein.

Barbary Row had grown up amid the beauty of the city. It was a place to shanghai a sailor, buy a woman, pick a brawl, sample an opium den, and most odious of all, a place of Chinese and white slavery. Women were known to disappear here and never be heard from again. Some unscrupulous captains were willing to be the bearer of such illicit merchandise to foreign shores, where high ransoms were paid by men with dark and piercing eyes. Often as not, however, a Chinese girl was spirited away to the back of a shop, heavily drugged, and sold at her keeper's discretion. It was a place to be wary of, and passengers aboard Brendan's ship were always well warned of such dangers for their own protection. Unlike

273

many ship's captains, Brendan refused passage to Chinese women who were not the legal wives or daughters of the men they traveled with. He wanted no part of the slave-prostitution trade so much in evidence. The business was hugely profitable, and therefore, extremely dangerous. It was to that purpose that he spoke to the Chinese on board his ship before they departed.

Carrying their weighty bundles, they made their way down the ship's ramp. The day was foggy and cold, like many in San Francisco, and they shivered in their thin cotton shifts. Families kept close to one another, fearful that they would become separated in this great, foreign city. Brendan watched them go, then turned his attention to the replacement of a frayed rigging.

A few minutes later, he overheard the beginnings of a scuffle nearby. Two drunken sailors were ragging a newly arrived man and his family. They were lifting the Chinaman's queue, and making lewd gestures to his pretty wife. The wife held the hands of her two small sons, who had begun to cry from this bullying. Such sights angered Brendan, but it was an all too common occurrence. The Chinese in particular were often the target of such abuse. A man must be man enough to take care of his own, thought Brendan, and resolved to stay out of this explosive situation. If he challenged all such harassment, he would be doing nothing but that. He kept his eye on it all the same, just to see that it didn't get too ugly.

Just then, a young, well-dressed white woman intervened on behalf of the Chinese family, and a true incident began to develop.

"Mind yer own business and be on yer way," the

rougher-looking of the two men said to the woman.

"You cowardly sots," she railed at them. "Are you such great, brave men that you need to frighten little children? You're drunken fools, the pair of you. Leave this man and his family alone, and get out of here."

"A spunky lil' thing, ain't she?" the same man who had spoke before said to his partner. He turned his attention away from the Chinese and toward her. It wasn't often he saw someone like her on the wharf. "She's a pretty piece," he said, lifting a fingerful of her hair. She hit his hand away, which only served to make him laugh. "Feisty, eh? Come here, my gingery girl," he said, pulling her roughly to him, "let's have a kiss." He pressed his foul-smelling face to hers, knocking the flowered bonnet she wore into the grime of the street. Before his lips touched her, she sunk her nails into his cheek, in an effort to free herself. He howled in genuine pain, but didn't release her.

"You hold her, Yarby," cried the wounded man. "I'll learn her to be a she-cat. Want to play rough, do you?" he jeered. They began pulling her into the dark shadow of the alley, leaving the Chinese family alone at last in favor of their new plaything. A cruel hand was clamped over the woman's mouth to silence her, but barely into the alleyway a loud yelp broke from that man as her small white teeth tore into the flesh of his hand. The sound of a heavy blow followed.

This was too much, even for a man bound to keep to his own affairs. A woman as brave as that one had been, handled as brutally as those two would—no, that couldn't be allowed. Snatching up two belaying pins, he ran down the ramp, and after them. He grabbed the Chinaman by the arm, and shoved the wooden club into

275

his hands, saying, "She saved your skin a moment ago. If you're a man at all, you'll move to help her now. Understand? It's not as good as a shillelagh," he said of the wooden cudgel, "but a smart crack across the skull will douse their lights." He acted this out for the man, and was rewarded by a broad, understanding grin from the Chinese. "Come on then," he called, and they went into the alley, holding the pins high before them.

In the shadows, one of the men held the woman pinned in the filth of the alley, while the other roughly forced his hand under her fitted jacket, rubbing it across the bodice of her gown. She struggled desperately against them both.

"Hurry it up, Reese. I want a turn at her too, you know," said the man who held her down.

"Hold still, you teasing slut," the groping man ordered, "or I'll clap you another one you won't forget!"

The thought was his last, for Brendan's belaying pin cracked down on his head, and a world of lights exploded before his eyes. His body fell over the girl in a grotesque parody of lovemaking. The man kneeling on the girl's arms scuttled back like a crab, and ran down the alley. The Chinese gave chase, and the satisfying sound of a loud crack and then a fall was heard by Brendan and the girl. As they listened, three more cracks were heard, which Brendan took to be repayment for the personal insult to the man and his family. He would have done the same himself.

"Good man, Chopsticks!" Brendan shouted, as he kicked the body of the unconscious sailor off the girl.

The woman before him—and she was a woman, he saw, and not a girl—had blood trickling down the corner of her mouth and a swelling beginning on her cheekbone, just below her eye. Her dress was torn at the bodice, and the hem of her skirt was thrown high.

"Let me help you up," he offered, stretching out his hand.

Up she came in one movement, fighting mad, pulling her clothes more modestly about her and roughly brushing the wisps of hair from her eyes. He thought she might cry, but when he looked more closely at her face, he saw that her eyes were not only dry, but filled with cold, steel-blue fury.

"Give me that," she said of the belaying pin in Brendan's hand.

When he didn't move quickly enough to suit her, she took it from him, and started beating the unconscious man about the body with it. It so startled Brendan to see her do this, his reaction was frozen. He simply stared at her until, after a long moment, he realized he'd better stop her.

"I'd go easy on that," he said with a relaxed casualness he didn't feel. "You don't want to kill him." She looked at him, not at all certain that she didn't. "That could get messy," he added while she was thinking. "There'd be an inquiry for sure. A lot of questions." She dropped the club and stepped back, all the fire gone out of her.

"Come on," he said to her, seeing the trembling of her hand. "Let me take you out of here." She kept glancing back over her shoulder at the men on the ground, as though one of them might leap up and attack her again. Brendan doubted there was enough life left in either man to bother about.

When they came out into the brighter light of the street, the woman drew back into the shadows, ashamed to be seen as she was. Her fingers kept trying to pull the cloth together, as though she could weave it whole again. Now she looked as if she might cry. She looked helpless and afraid. He was moved to pity by her sense of shame.

"Stay here," he said. "I'll go and get a carriage. You mustn't even try to go home as you are," he told her. "Chopsticks, you stay with her until I get back. Understand?" The Chinese nodded.

It didn't take him long to hire a buggy. She was still there when he stopped before the alley, got down, and helped her in. If anything, the shaking was worse now than before. So she wasn't as tough as she seemed. She needed gentleness.

"That's all, Chopsticks," he said to the Chinese. "You did well. You were brave. You'll make a fine American." He doubted that the man knew what he was saying, but he bowed, gathered his frightened wife and two small children to him, and hurried away from this scene of trouble.

"My name is Brendan O'Shay," he told the woman, trying to calm her fears by the easy tone of his voice. "I'm the captain of that ship over there, the *Berengaria*." She seemed to be breathing too fast, and her color was chalky. "You're all right now. Take a deep breath or two. It's all over." He tried not to look at her too long, for she was so obviously embarrassed by her appearance. "Where can I take you?" he said at last. She didn't seem to understand. "Shall I take you home?" he asked, almost hoping she would cry instead of this trembling silence.

The question seemed to jolt her into awareness. "No! I don't want to go home. I can't go home like this." Panic threatened to engulf her.

"All right," he agreed quickly. "Steady on. Why don't

278

you just tell me your name." He couldn't help noticing how beautiful her eyes were, even after what she'd just been through. They were blue eyes, blue eyes against the dark swirl of her hair.

"Caitlin O'Mally," she said softly.

What he said aloud was, "Irish too?" What he thought to himself was—beautiful and Irish too. "Both of us Erins, are we? That only makes me happier that I stepped in to help you. So, where shall I be taking you, Caitlin O'Mally?"

"Do you know Washington Street?"

"I know it well enough," he told her, thinking she must be a housemaid from one of the big houses on the hill.

"There's an orphanage there, Sisters of Mercy Orphanage. Could you take me there?"

He looked more closely at her. "Surely you're too old to be an orphan, aren't you?"

"Of course I'm not an orphan. It's where I work. I teach school there."

"At Sisters of Mercy? You're not a nun, I hope, not the way you're dressed." The thought appalled him. If she was from a convent, what on earth was she doing on the wharf?

"I teach English to Chinese children," she explained. "That's what I was doing here, trying to speak to Chinese families about letting their children come to my school."

"You do this all alone?" He was amazed at her nerve, and her foolhardiness. He knew the kind of men who hung around a wharf, and the dangers possible for a woman like this one.

He gave the horse a slap of the reins. By the time they had reached Washington Street, she had calmed considerably. When they reached the orphanage, she was perfectly normal, as though nothing untoward had happened.

"I'll just see you inside," he said.

"You needn't trouble yourself, Captain O'Shay. I'll be quite all right now."

"I insist," he said firmly, making it impossible for her to refuse him.

Now what am I going to do? she wondered. How can I tell Elizabeth a lie when he's standing right there? Oh, why doesn't he go away?

Elizabeth Muldair caught sight of Caitlin while she was still across the playground. Even from that distance, she could tell that something was wrong. She left the children staring after her, and ran across the grass.

"What's happened? Caitlin, you're hurt. Oh, dear God, what's happened to you?"

"Now stop fussing, Elizabeth. I'm all right. I just had a fall, that's all. The horse and buggy got away from me. It was stupid really. I feel such a fool. I'm usually such a good horsewoman. This gentleman saw everything and offered to help me. Captain O'Shay, my sister, Elizabeth Muldair."

It was so obviously a lie. Elizabeth tried not to stare at the cut on Caitlin's lip, or the purpled swelling below her eye. It was horrifying to think of how they'd come to be there. Worse were the tears in Caitlin's dress, at the neck and bodice. It was clear she'd been through something terrible. Elizabeth put her arms around her sister protectively. She felt it as Caitlin began to tremble, even as she held her. Something fierce in Elizabeth, something she had never known was in her, was outraged at what had happened to Caitlin. She wanted to shelter her sister, wanted to hurt anything that hurt her.

"Oh, Caity," she said, feeling her pain as if it were her own, "you might have been killed."

At Elizabeth's words, Caitlin's hard-earned courage broke and she began sobbing. The reality of what had nearly happened to her was at last felt with full impact, and the terror she had held back by force of will came through.

"Cait, oh, my poor Caity," Elizabeth said, trying to comfort her. "Come on," she urged her. "Come inside for a few minutes and lie down. I'll help you clean up, and we'll fix your dress so no one will notice." She supported Caitlin as they walked toward the school.

"Do I look awful?" Caitlin asked, fearing what her father would think, what they all would think.

"No. You look fine. I'll help you with your hair and your dress before we go home. Father won't have to know. Please don't worry. It'll be all right. I promise you. Everything will be all right now."

"Captain O'Shay," Elizabeth called back. "Could you please wait there for just a moment? I would like to speak to you."

Brendan waited, wondering what he should say when she came back. Would it be better to tell her everything that really happened, or keep the lie the woman had invented? He didn't have long to wonder, for Elizabeth returned as quickly as she had promised.

"Captain O'Shay, I'm only going to ask you one question about what happened to my sister. Was she raped?"

Brendan hesitated. This woman had seen through everything. It seemed pointless to worry her unnecessarily. "No, Miss Muldair, she wasn't."

"Thank God for that." Elizabeth breathed a sigh of relief. "Captain O'Shay, I'm not certain of your part in this, only that my sister and my family owe you a debt of thanks. I know they'd like to offer it to you in person. Would you consider dining with us this evening?"

His first reaction was to cut and run, but something held that back. The fact was, he wanted to see how Caitlin O'Mally would handle the situation. More honestly, he simply wanted to see her again, wanted to see both of these women. Elizabeth Muldair was not the beauty her sister was, but there was a graceful strength about her that drew him to her as well.

"I'd be honored, ma'am. What time would you like me there?"

"Eight o'clock?"

"Eight o'clock, then. Good day, Miss Muldair." He turned to go.

"Good day, Captain O'Shay. And Captain O'Shay," she added, "you will keep to Caitlin's version of this, won't you?"

"You need have no fear of that account. I'll keep it to just what she has said. Miss Muldair, there's something I just don't understand. What was she doing there in the first place?"

Elizabeth looked up. Her eyes met his for a moment. "Being a Christian, I think."

Chapter Twenty-Seven

"I can't believe you did this," Caitlin said to Elizabeth. "You invited him home to dinner? How can I possibly explain him to Father?"

For once in her life, Elizabeth stood her ground against Caitlin. "Tell him just what you told me. Captain O'Shay has agreed to stand by whatever you say. I'm certain he'd just as soon not explain to Father what really happened. He seemed like a very sensible man, and after all, you owe him some show of gratitude for helping you, don't you think?"

Caitlin looked far from certain. "All right, but you stay close by, and if I get in trouble with my facts, help me out. I just hope he has the sense to say nothing about the wharf. If he just wouldn't say anything at all," she sighed. "I know you did this for me," she said in a kinder tone to Elizabeth, "but really, I wish you hadn't."

Elizabeth kept her silence. She didn't argue Caitlin's reasoning, but the fact was, she hadn't invited Captain O'Shay to dinner because of Caitlin at all. She had invited him for herself. It was an astonishing feeling, but she found him the most attractive, interesting and exciting man she'd ever met. She wanted to see him again. Something very new in her was strong enough to do that, no matter what Caitlin thought.

The general alarm over Caitlin's condition had settled by the time of Captain O'Shay's expected arrival. The family had accepted Caitlin's explanation of what had happened to her. More careful scrutiny of the tears in her clothes, and the bruises on her face, might have led her mother to suspect something more, but fortunately for Caitlin, Ellen was not at home. She had gone to stay the night with Rachel McTaggart, Griffin's wife, who had taken ill after the birth of her fifth child. There was no one to see through Caitlin's lie. She didn't seem too badly injured, and for that they all were grateful. They were anxious to meet this captain who had helped her.

Danny had said, "You might have known he'd be Irish."

Elizabeth sat by the window and listened for the sound of the carriage on the road. All her senses were heightened. This feeling was new to her, like nothing she had ever felt before. From one moment to the next, she first felt ill with nervousness, and then light enough to float with heady expectation. She had dressed her hair with special care, putting her best combs in, and worn her prettiest gown. She had glanced in the mirror before she came down, something she rarely did, and thought, I look pretty enough. Even so, she knew she was dull in comparison to Caitlin. They were different types. Caitlin had a beauty easily observed. To see Elizabeth's, you had to look carefully. It was a reality Elizabeth had always known, and that had never troubled her—until now.

"I see his carriage! He's here! He's here!" called Pat,

the youngest O'Mally son.

"Settle down then, Pat," said Danny. "I'm sure the man knows how to pull a doorbell, just like everyone else. Go and tell your sister our company's arrived, will you? There's a good boy."

A servant opened the door. The girl came in to announce the visitor's arrival, as if none of them inside the room knew.

"A Captain O'Shay is here, sir."

"See him in, Martha," Danny said.

Brendan had the look of a man stunned with surprise. He had never expected the home of the girl on the wharf to be a place like this, with servants and the look of money everywhere in evidence. What was a girl from a home like this doing there? What was she doing teaching Chinese children? Why had she needed to lie? There wasn't time for him to sort out the answers, for Danny was there, with his hand stretched out to him in welcome.

"Captain O'Shay, I'm very happy to meet you. I'm Caitlin's father, Daniel O'Mally. My daughters tell me we are greatly in your debt."

"Not at all," Brendan protested, "at least, no more than a dinner in this house will amply repay. How is Miss O'Mally? Is she feeling better?"

"Oh, Caity's fine. Got some bruises, but nothing too serious. She's tougher than she looks."

Tougher than you know, thought Brendan. I wonder if you'd think it was nothing serious if you knew the truth about today. The woman beating that drunken sailor with the belaying pin was more than tough. She was courageous, and she was fierce.

"I'm happy to see you could join us, Captain O'Shay," Elizabeth Muldair said, speaking up.

Brendan turned to look at her, noticing the change from the afternoon. She can be very attractive when she wants to, he realized. If it weren't for her sister, it might be her I'd be here for.

"My mother won't be able to join us this evening, I'm afraid," Elizabeth said. "One of our friends, Rachel McTaggart, is ill, and she has promised to stay with her tonight. Mother says to give you her thanks, and her regrets that she cannot say them herself, in person."

"There's no need," Brendan answered, enjoying the looks this shy girl was giving him. She had made quite an effort, he was sure, to be attractive to him. You look as if no man has ever kissed you, he thought. I wonder, Elizabeth, would you like to be kissed? What is that message I see in your eyes?

"Captain O'Shay, I see you've arrived," said a voice from the staircase.

Brendan turned away from Elizabeth and saw Caitlin, and all thoughts of the shy girl vanished from his mind. Caitlin O'Mally stood against the rich mahogany backdrop of the staircase wearing a dress of burgundy velvet. Creamy Belgian lace trailed at her wrists and in the cascading folds of her skirt. Her dark hair, pulled back from her face by ivory combs, set off the pale beauty of her skin and the deep blue of her eyes.

"Miss O'Mally," Brendan acknowledged her. She was breathtaking.

"So." Danny broke the too intimate silence of the moment. "Come and sit at our table. We'll have a fine meal, and then, you can tell us about Ireland."

In the course of the evening, Brendan met Danny's sons, Seamus, Griffin, Connor, and Pat—and Matthew Muldair, a strangely quiet man. Apparently, he and

Elizabeth were natural brother and sister. There was a family resemblance between them that set them apart from the others, obvious to even the casual observer. There was a story about those two he might like to hear one day, but this night, his mind was only on Caitlin.

After a meal of prime roast beef au jus, buttered and parsleyed potatoes, a course of three vegetables, each prepared and seasoned to perfection, and ending with a chocolate cake so rich he had to wash it down with hot, sweet coffee, Brendan and Danny retired to the library, where Danny opened a bottle of French cognac.

"I haven't really thanked you properly for what you've done for my daughter," Danny began.

"I thought we'd covered that." Brendan had hoped to stop him from such a speech. He felt guilty lying to the man. "It really isn't necessary."

"Oh, it's necessary, all right," Danny insisted. "My children mean more than anything in the world to me, excepting their mother. Just the thought that Caitlin might have been badly injured . . ." He didn't finish his thought, as though it was too painful to consider. "I want to show my thanks in some measurable way. I've been thinking, just what can I do to repay this man? Would a gift of money insult him?"

Brendan laughed at that. "I've never been insulted by the offer of money in my life, but no, I wouldn't accept it. I hope you didn't expect me to. There is something else I'd like to ask of you."

Danny sat back, more comfortable now that he thought he would be able to pay his debt to this man. "You have only to tell me what it is," he offered generously.

"I'd like to see your daughter again, perhaps take her

to dinner at one of the restaurants in San Francisco. Would you have any objection to that?"

It certainly wasn't what Danny had expected. He was silent for a long, thoughtful moment. "I'm not in the habit of bargaining for my daughter," he began. His first instinct was to say no, flatly. What would Ellen think of such an idea? He knew the answer to that well enough. Still, there was something fine about this young man, this young Irish man. He was a gentleman, he'd proved that to Caitlin this morning, and at dinner, he'd shown himself to be an intelligent, well-educated, properly brought up, and thoroughly charming man. Even Elizabeth seemed smitten with him. Caitlin could do a lot worse for herself than this one. Added to that, he was already a captain at his young age, which said something about his ability and his future. It had troubled Danny that Caitlin had never taken an interest in any of the young men in San Francisco, although many were interested in her. It was time the girl settled down and began thinking of herself as a wife and mother. This business with the Chinese school was ample evidence of that. A married woman would be too busy for such things. The whole idea of Caitlin teaching there still rubbed Danny the wrong way. A man like Captain O'Shay might be just what his willful daughter needed.

"It's Caitlin you'll have to ask, of course, but I've no objection. Where had you in mind to take my daughter? Not one of those French restaurants on Jackson Street," Danny warned him.

"No, of course not. I wouldn't want to run into my own men," he said, then he and Danny laughed over that.

"All right, then. What are you sitting here with me for? Go on with you, go and ask her," Danny said to him.

Brendan left him then, and Danny sat on, alone in the library, sipping the fine cognac. A sense of sadness came over him. It wouldn't be long, he knew, until he'd be losing this daughter. If he lost her to a man like O'Shay, the blow might not seem as hard. Another thought, equally troubling, came on the heels of the last. I'm getting old, he realized. He'd noticed the sharp contrast between him and young O'Shay. The man was in his prime, in his twenties, and the comparison was almost painful to recognize. The cognac created a warmth in him, easing the acceptance of even this.

Where did my life go? he thought. Still, I've done what I wanted. That's more than most men can say. I've followed my own dreams, and I've won. Life, that fine, challenging game, was drawing to a period of quiet. How he resented that. His children's adult lives were just beginning, and his . . . ? He cradled the cognac snifter in his hands, and sighed.

The City Hotel was at one time the best restaurant San Francisco had to offer. In 1868, it was still considered one of her best. Brendan ordered them a supper of crab salad, steak Del Monaco, and a wonderful clam chowder with crusty French bread.

"I want to thank you for keeping my secret the other night," Caitlin began. "My family worries enough about me as it is, without that incident added to it. If he knew, my father would force me to stop teaching. I'm very grateful to you for what you did at the wharf, and after."

Brendan couldn't get enough of looking at her. She was more beautiful every time he saw her. There was something else about her that drew him to her. She was magnetic, passionately alive, with a need to be something special. He was captivated.

"What do you want to do with your life, Caitlin?" he asked suddenly.

"Me?" It wasn't a question she'd often been asked. People usually assumed she would marry and rear children as her mother had. Beautiful women married. It was another sign that this was a different sort of man, that he had noticed that she was an individual.

"If you really want to know," she answered, in a tone of all seriousness, "I want to be a woman who gets things done, not a pretty little wife filling up a boring house with boring children. I'm teaching the Chinese school now because I see a need for it, and because no one else will. I want my life to count for something."

Brendan was impressed with her forthrightness. "You're not concerned at all about what anyone thinks of you, are you?"

"I won't let such people stop me, if that's what you mean." She realized she had been angry when she spoke, taking that anger out on him. He had drawn that response from her, as though he knew it was there. "You must think me quite a devious woman, Captain O'Shay."

"Hardly," he said. "I'd say a remarkable woman."

He hadn't said beautiful. She liked that. He saw her more for what she was than what she looked like. It wasn't a secret to her that men thought her pretty. She'd heard that compliment often enough, and after a while, it had become meaningless. He had asked her what she wanted to do, and that was a compliment too, and worth more. For the first time, she really looked at Brendan O'Shay, saw the strong line of his jaw and the deep sea-blue of his eyes, intelligent eyes. There was a bearing of strength to the man that attracted her, and held her interest. He was handsome, she saw, very handsome.

"Tell me about Ireland," she suggested.

"Ireland? What do you want to know?"

"It's where I was born. I was so little when I left, I don't recall any of it. Tell me something about it, so I'll know it, like you."

It was an intriguing idea, describing Ireland to a woman who'd been born there but didn't remember it. He wondered what he could say that would explain the feeling of country that Ireland left in a man. How could he give her that sense of a belonging place that he knew for himself?

"When I go home, after months at sea," he began, "the first thing I notice is the green of the land. I see it from the ship, and a longing comes over me to breathe it in, like a lush perfume. We're a part of the ocean, separated as we are on an island. The mists that rise up from the warm currents and the cold swallow us up whole.

"She's an ancient place. Her history clings to her in her people. Look at us closely and you can see all the invaders that ever came to her still living there among the faces of Ireland. The dark-haired ones, like you and I, were Celts, the blond Danes, the red-haired Norsemen, and the pale-skinned Englishmen—all living side by side. Her gods were ancient too. The places you'll see on that little bit of land, where men worshipped in forest groves, or beside huge slabs of stone—places the heart of you feels a kinship with. Religion has as much a hold on Ireland as life itself. It'll never be separate from her.

"There's a sound to Ireland. Music and poetry, which is only really songs without the music, are inherent to the

291

place, second only to religion. The people have a music, even to the way they speak. You'll hear it all over the land; mothers singing to their babies, men joining in a song in the pubs, bards of ancient days playing music for the High King, poets and writers of stories that carry the mind along like a song plying their trade among those who'll listen. We're a wordy people. Always have been.

"There's a cottage I always go by when going home. An old man lives alone in it, farming the land. I stop in each time and pay him a visit, as much for myself as for him. I always have that little bit of dread, going up to the door, wondering if he'll be there still. He has this wonderful, weathered face, lived in like a good boot, or a coat you've grown comfortable with. It fits him. You can't help noticing that, and the eyes that look clear enough to see to his soul. I've no idea how old he is. He's never said, and I've never asked, but he's seen a bit in his day. We sit in his cottage, and he makes me a mug of tea that he pours whiskey in, and we talk. He's like the land, you see, a homeplace, going on as usual, drawing me back like some mystery I've a longing to find the answer to, seemingly ancient as the stones."

Caitlin O'Mally, born of Ireland, child of California, felt that she had come home. The image he'd spun so ensnared her, she would be forever caught by it. She felt the tug of the place, felt a part of it—and by his own telling, a part of Brendan O'Shay as well.

Chapter Twenty-Eight

Brendan held the *Berengaria* in San Francisco a full two weeks, seeing Caitlin every day of that time. A sense of urgency commanded them both. Time was their enemy. Time would take him far away. Time would loosen the hold of their feeling for one another. Time together was therefore precious.

"How long will you be gone?" Caitlin asked, feeling the hurt of his absence already a part of her.

It would be eight months at least. That was a fact he didn't want to tell her. "Longer than I can bear to think about," he said instead. He had never felt this, the pull of a woman that was stronger than the pull of the sea. Always, before, he had been glad to be away from every woman he had met. Not this woman. To part from her would be the hardest thing he had ever done.

"We still have a few days," he told her, failing at the comfort he tried to give. It only made their parting seem more real to her. In a few days, he would be gone. In a few days, she would be alone.

"I wish I were going with you," she said to him,

unafraid of what he might think. "I do. The idea of months without you . . . Do women ever go aboard with the men?"

"Passengers do, of course, and sometimes a captain will take his wife along. It's a privilege of rank, though not often used."

He was silent so long, she grew afraid of what she had said. Have I dared too much? she thought. What will he think of me? For the first time in her life, she was worried over what someone thought. One someone. She started to excuse her words, to find a way to take them back, when Brendan spoke up, stopping the utterance before it formed on her lips.

"Did you mean it just now when you said you wished you could come with me? Would you do that, then? Would you leave it all and come away with me?"

The shock of his words, coming on the heels of her own admission, stunned her into silence. Her heart was beating wildly. Her body felt hot with fear, and hope, and longing.

"I'm asking you to marry me, Caity. Marry me before I sail. Will you come with me, and be my wife?"

"Yes," she said, a single word, as calmly as if she had been expecting the question all along, as if her heart were not ready to burst with mad joy, as if she only loved him—denying the sweet torment of her own passion, her own desire.

"You're going to marry him?" Elizabeth asked, not yet willing to believe what Caitlin had said. Something of a little flame of secret hope that she had kept alive within her, hope that one day Brendan would begin to notice her, began to shrivel and die. "You've only known him two weeks," she heard herself say, sounding foolish even to her.

"It's long enough to know you're in love," Caitlin said to her.

Yes, Elizabeth thought, it is. Long enough to be absolutely sure. As sure as she was herself. Something in her raged at this unfairness, at this treachery life had dealt her.

"Say something," Caitlin urged her. "Tell me. What do you think?" She was so happy. So excited. She was in love.

"I think it's wonderful," Elizabeth said, smiling. "How are you going to convince Father? You don't really think he's going to let you just sail away, do you?"

"That may be a problem," Caitlin admitted.

"What will you do if he says no?" Her heart knew the answer. It's what she would do herself.

"I'd go anyway."

"Of course you would," Elizabeth agreed. "Do you love him, Cait? Do you love him very much?" She had to know. It hurt to think about someone else loving him, but if Caitlin was going to marry him, she had to know. "He's not just romantic to you, is he? You really love him?"

Caitlin's eyes crinkled as the corners of her mouth turned up. "Why, Beth, I think you love him a little yourself. Look at you. You're full of concern, but it's all for him. Doesn't it matter to you whether he loves me?" she teased.

"You're my sister," she said. "Of course I care." She let the question go. It might be better not to know. "Speak to Mother about it, before you ask Father. She'll know how to help you convince him. She's like you, always has been." She rose, and started to walk out of the room.

"Where are you going? What's the matter with you?" Caitlin called after her.

"Leave me alone, Cait. You asked me if I loved him. You're quite right, I do. Now, will you leave me alone?" She hurried away, shutting the door between them. Shutting the door forever.

I hadn't realized how strongly she felt, Caitlin thought, feeling the weight of her sister's unhappiness on her own heart. Poor Beth, never brave enough to fall in love with any man, and now . . . with Brendan, of all men— Brendan. Damn the fates for being fools and complicating all their lives!

In all the years Ellen O'Reilly O'Shay had lived in San Francisco, amid the wind and fog, the summer's scorching heat, and the populace of dreamers—for everyone who came to California came with a dream— she had never forgotten the green hills of her home. Her sons had been born here, in this new land. It was all they knew. But to Ellen, the small, thatched-roofed cottages, the smell of peat on the fire, the sight of her mother and the other women, in their shawls, going down the road for Mass in the morning—all of it sometimes made her heart ache for the familiar land of her childhood.

Her children spoke no Gaelic, their voices held no lyric lilt, but repeated the flat, Americanized English they heard about them each day of their lives. I must be getting old, thought Ellen, to be musing about times gone by. Indeed, she did feel old some days, with Matthew grown and working among the men, and Caitlin teaching school to the Chinese. Of her own four sons, Pat, at thirteen, was nearly a man. The others, Seamus, Griffin, and Connor, worked with Danny and Matt. No one really needed her.

Her fine face had not been badly touched by age, although gray was beginning to show itself among the smoky black color of her hair in her youth. The bearing of five children had taken its toll on her figure. She had never been fat, but her bosom was heavier, more matronly, and her waist would never again fit into her wedding dress.

"I'm not so bad to look at, after all these years," she told her too honest mirror. "Who wants a thin slip of a girl? A body my age should have a lived-in look."

"Heartbreaker," said Danny, stepping up behind her, their faces meeting in the glass.

He too had aged. Nothing of the young man he had been when they first met was left to him, except in that image his wife had of him, the memory of that man she had fallen in love with. He was a self-made man, and had the look about him. He was strong, in a land of strong men. Mindful of his family, as other men were mindful only of themselves, he loved them all with reasonless joy, and loved this one woman for the last twenty years, more now than on the day he'd married her. He bent his head and kissed the nape of her neck.

"Have ye been happy then, Danny?" she asked, the thought coming to her as suddenly as the memories.

"Happy? What a question. A man could bear no more happiness. I've everything I ever wanted here in this room, and the whole of the world besides."

That was how they were, more needful of each other

than of anyone or anything else on earth. Both of them knew it. It was a love that had sustained them through the many tragedies of their lives, like the stillborn daughter Ellen had miscarried, far into her sixth month. A girl. Dearly had she wanted to give Danny that child, a daughter of his own. God had not allowed it. Caitlin and Elizabeth were the only daughters Danny would have, as though an all-wise God had ordained it from the start.

Ellen named their fourth son after her father, changing the Irish Padraic to the more common Patrick. The name change was as much for herself as for the boy. She could never have called the child Padraic. That was her father's name, and only for him. It hurt her still, the loss of her family in Ireland. She often wondered about them all, especially her mother, Kara, in their little cottage. She was a stranger now to them all. The years had been too long.

The girl who had been Ellen Gwenhara O'Reilly was no more. There was no trace of her here, in this ornate Victorian house that was Ellen O'Shay's home. She thought about her brothers and sisters, about Connor, her sisters Kathleen, Maggie, and Mary Elizabeth, her brother Pat, and the baby, Brian Andrew. He'd be grown by this time.

It's a wonder how we all lived under one roof, she thought, so small was that house. She remembered the days of her girlhood, when all ten of them crammed their days into that four-room cottage. I hope they've added another room by now, she thought. It seemed almost incomprehensible to her living like that, where here there was so much space. One day I must go back, she mused, when the children are older and can manage without me.

"You're a poor liar," she said to the vision of herself in the mirror, "for if the truth be told, it was never the children holding you back, then or ever. Quite another reason indeed."

It was something she couldn't deny. Within her, where no mind's thought had touched nor any memory faded, was that achingly sweet love a young girl had felt, a lifetime ago, and the burned hollow in her heart that love had left when it ended. In all the years that had passed, she had never written to them, or in any way tried to contact the man who had been so much to her so long ago. It was easier done in America, half a world away, than in Ireland, where she had first met him. Would all the memories come flooding back, erasing years with their sharpness? How easy it might be to ask about him. Her mother might offer it as a bit of news. She might say that Dougal and Moira were married no longer, or that an illness had turned him into a cripple. Or worse, that he was dead. It was one thing to bury a man in your heart, but quite another to know that he was truly dead.

It was a fire she had tried to burn out of her, but all the years, all the love she bore her husband, her children, could not entirely put it out. It was but an ember of that old love, but it burned with the ferocity of a live coal. For years, she had berated herself for its presence as an unwelcome claimant to her heart. With the passage of time and the security of her marriage to Danny, it became more like an old friend, an old memory, a place to visit now and again when the world left her low. If that living ember were struck from her with the certain knowledge of Dougal's death, then a very real part of her would die with him.

And so, she had never gone back. Never written to any at home, even to let them know she was alive. In truth, that life was dead to her.

And now, into this controlled peace of her life, fate brought Brendan O'Shay. When Caitlin first spoke his name to her, her heart had stopped—really stopped—for so long, she thought she was dying. It cannot be the same boy, she told herself. That Brendan would surely be too young to be the captain of a ship. It wasn't long before she met him, saw for herself, and knew the truth.

Her decision had been a hard one. Shall I tell Danny that this man is the son of the man I loved? Shall I hurt him that way, bring back old pain? Shall I tell Caitlin she mustn't see him ever again? Tell her that the father she loves is not her father at all? Or, shall I remain silent, hoping that time and distance will do my job for me? She chose the latter. It may have been the coward's way, but it hurt fewer people. Only she would be tormented with the fears of her secret coming to light. Only she would be plagued by her own guilt. It was better so.

"What is it, Caitlin?" Danny asked, seeing she had something to say to him. He had been sitting alone in the library, not thinking, only sitting. He welcomed her interruption.

"I have something I want to tell you, Father," she began. She had chosen to go against Elizabeth's advice and gone first to her father with her news. Because Elizabeth had suggested just the opposite? Perhaps.

"Come in and sit down, Caity. Well, what is it you want to tell me? I've a good ear for listening today. Not

300

another thought in my head. What is it, Cait?" he said more gently. He saw it was difficult for her.

"Brendan's asked me to marry him," she said straightforwardly. "He loves me, and I love him. Neither of us can bear the idea of a long separation. He's asked me to marry him before he sails next. He wants me to go with him when he leaves."

Danny's forehead puckered in a frown. He'd seen that young O'Shay liked Caitlin, and that she liked him, but the suddenness of this proposal worried him. "You're not having to get married, are you, Caity? That's not the why of this rush, is it?" He liked O'Shay well enough, liked him very much, in fact, but if he'd gotten his daughter with child before her marriage, he'd beat him to the ground with his own hands.

"Of course I'm not having to get married," Caitlin answered, hot with indignation. "It's not like that at all. We'd never," she said, hurt that her father would think such a thing.

"Oh, I am sorry. I've put my foot in it, haven't I? It was just the suddenness, and you wanting to go away so soon after the wedding. It's the way a father's mind works. Enough about that. Tell me, what have you said to him in answer? I know well you've not waited for me to decide for you."

"I said yes," she told him.

"Did you?"

A silence fell between them, a cold, dead silence.

"You're not angry?" she asked at last.

"Angry? No, girl. Only sad to be losing you. He's a fine man, Brendan O'Shay. I couldn't have picked a better one for you myself. Do you love him, Caity?"

301

"Yes," she answered simply.

"That's my good girl," her father said, putting his hand to her cheek. "That's what keeps a marriage whole. Remember that. Nothing else will bind it."

"I'll remember."

"Have you told your mother yet?"

"Not yet. I wanted to tell you first," she confided. It was a gift she gave him.

"You'd best go and tell her now," he urged. "She'll have my scalp for knowing before she does. Go off with you, then. Go and tell her the news."

The door to her mother's room was open. "Mother?" Caitlin called softly.

"Come in, Cait. I'm just having a lie down."

Ellen was in bed. In the warm of the afternoon her hair, which she always wore up, was down, long and straight across her shoulders, giving her the look of someone Caitlin didn't know. She'd never seen her mother look like this.

"Are you ill?" she asked, ashamed that her first thought was that if her mother were truly ill, her wedding might have to be postponed.

"Not ill really," Ellen answered, "just unwell. I'll be fine again soon." As soon as that man leaves San Francisco, she thought. "Was there something you wanted to ask me?"

"Something I wanted to tell you, Mother," Caitlin said, making the distinction. "I'm going to be married. Captain O'Shay has asked me to be his wife, and I've accepted."

Ellen sat up as though someone had plunged a knife in her back. "What! Caitlin, listen to me, you can't marry

302

him. He isn't for you, my girl," she said, slipping into a thicker dialect than she normally used. "You mustn't even think of it. Do you hear me? I'll never allow you to marry him. Never!" She got up from the bed, paced around the room frantically, working her fingers into knots, and breathing heavily. "Promise me," she said to her, "promise me you'll stop this now, Caitlin, before it's too late."

"Too late for what? Why should I stop it? What's come over you, Mother? I'm twenty years old. I have a right to be married. Why are you so against it?"

Her mother's eyes were wild with panic. "I never thought it would go this far. I've been afraid, since the first day, but I swear, I never thought it would lead to this. Please! Please, Caitlin! Don't make me tell you this. Ye cannot marry him. Believe me."

Now Caitlin was afraid. Something was terribly wrong. Something that would spoil her life. The look on her mother's face terrified her. What was it that would do this to her? What could be so awful?

"Why mustn't I marry him? Tell me if there's something to tell! What is it?" She stood in front of her mother, facing her. "I want to know," she insisted.

Then Ellen crumpled before her eyes, caved in. She slumped to a chair, all of the fight gone out of her. "I never wanted you to know," she said, tears brimming in her eyes. Oh God, she thought, what game have I been playing with my daughter's soul? "Sit down, Caitlin. I've a story to tell you.

"I was your age once." She smiled. "And I was in love. Not like you are—another kind of love."

"With Father?"

303

"No. Before I met him, there was another man. I was working in his house. He was married. His wife was going to have another child. I was a temptation in his love for her. We sinned against her, and against ourselves. We became lovers."

Caitlin couldn't breathe, the air had grown too close around her.

"When she bore her child, she nearly died. I wanted her to die, thinking he would marry me. Can you believe that of me? He told me then that it was her he loved, that he would never leave her. Even if she died, he said, we would never be together. I ran from him, ran from everything I knew. I wanted to die. But I didn't die."

Caitlin wanted to stop her from saying any more. She wanted to shout at her, but no sound would come.

"I would have died, I think, if I had not met your father. He took me in, cared for me. He was there when you were born, delivering me of my child of another man. Later, we fell in love. I put the past forever behind me, never naming who the man was, even to him. We came to California, and we married. I never thought my secret would follow me here. I never thought it would destroy my own child!"

Caitlin could stand no more. She stood up to run from the room. She wasn't Danny's daughter? No wonder he had asked her what he had, about her and Brendan. He thought she was like her mother. What more was there to tell? She was desperate to escape her mother's words.

"Don't go!" her mother pleaded, in a voice small with fear. "You must listen. Dougal O'Shay was my lover. Brendan is his son. He's your natural half-brother, Caitlin. You can't marry him now or ever. He's your brother!"

The room was white. Panels of white filled Caitlin's eyes.

"Caity?" she heard a voice calling. Someone was speaking to her. What did they say? She heard it clearly now—"Oh, God, what have I done!"—before she felt herself fall, into the panels of white, into the pure, pure white.

Chapter Twenty-Nine

Brendan stood bareheaded in the pouring rain, his entrance into the house blocked by Matthew Muldair standing in the open doorway.

"I've come to see Caitlin. I won't leave without seeing her," he said, trying to hold onto the reins of his anger. "What's happened to her? Why won't she see me? Why doesn't she answer the messages I've sent?"

Matthew made no move to allow him in. "I've already told you, you can't see her. She doesn't want to see you. You must take that as your answer, Captain O'Shay, and for God's sake, leave her alone."

"What is it? Who's at the door?" asked Ellen.

Matthew tried to close it, but Brendan pushed the door open. Ellen stared at him, eyes wide with alarm.

"I'm going to see Caitlin. One way or another, I'm going to see her, today." Brendan stood ready to fight Matthew, or anyone else, if he had to.

That was one thing Ellen didn't want. "I don't want my daughter to hear any of this, Captain. She's been quite ill. It would be better if she didn't know you were here."

"I'll march upstairs and find her myself, if I need to," Brendan threatened. "I've a right to know what's happened."

Ellen saw that he meant it. "Very well, Captain. Come into the library with me. My daughter mustn't know about this. I'll tell you what I can."

Matthew stepped between them. "You don't have to do this, Mother."

"It's all right, Matt," she said to him. "The time for secrets is over. Please, leave us now. I want to speak to Captain O'Shay alone."

The two men's eyes met, a burning anger held between them. There was hatred in that look, the kind of look men have before they kill. Matthew fought hard to control his temper. He stood his ground with O'Shay, daring him with his eyes to make one move toward the stairs.

"Matthew, please," Ellen asked again, more strongly than before.

He turned then, and walked away, his blood hot with hatred inside of him. His hands were clenched into fists at his side, and his pulse pounded in his brain. He heard the sound of the latch catching as they shut the library door.

"Sit down, Brendan," Ellen said to him, reverting to the name she had called him when he was seven. He continued to stand. "I see you're not going to make this any easier for me. I'm not going to tell you everything. I don't think I could bear to do that again. I'll only tell you what you need to know." She tried to pull her thoughts together clearly, tried to think of what to say to him.

"Caitlin has told me of your proposal to her," she began.

"My proposal, and her answer of yes," he added.

Ellen nodded in response to this, a small, tight movement of her head. "My daughter has told me everything. She thought herself deeply in love with you, and planned to fulfill her agreement to you in marriage."

"Planned?"

"I'm afraid there cannot be a marriage, Brendan. There can never be anything more between you and my daughter. Caitlin is—"

The door to the library opened. Caitlin stood in that space, her face a hard mask, her eyes stony and cold.

"Caitlin!" Brendan started toward her.

"I thought it was your voice," she said, stepping into the room. "No one told me, of course. They wouldn't want me to know, would you, Mother? Mother likes her little secrets, don't you?" Her eyes looked with hatred at the woman she had loved for twenty years.

"Caitlin," Ellen tried, "you mustn't stay here. Please go back to your room. I'll explain everything to Brendan."

"Explain what?" he demanded.

"Hasn't she told you? Her little story? I'll tell you myself, then."

"Don't do this, Caity," Ellen begged her. "Please don't do this."

"I don't care a thing about her story, Caitlin. I came to see you." Brendan tried to take her in his arms. "As long as you haven't changed your mind about marrying me, nothing else matters."

For a moment, the Caitlin he knew was back, with eyes he loved, the Caitlin who had loved him—a softness about her mouth—her body warm against his—and everything would be all right. Except it wasn't. It wouldn't ever be again.

She pulled away from him as though he'd struck her. "She's quite right, Bren." Her voice had gone low and flat. "I can't marry you. Something I didn't know has changed it all. I never meant to hurt you," she said, her eyes lifting up to his with a sadness he could not penetrate.

"What have you done to her!" he shouted at Ellen, who was holding her hands in two fists, hard up against her mouth. "Caitlin, listen to me." He tried to hold her in his hands. "I love you! Do you hear me? I love you."

"Oh, God!" Ellen whispered.

But, it was Caitlin he heard, Caitlin who screamed, "No! Don't touch me! Don't ever touch me again! I'm your sister! Do you see now? I'm your sister!"

Matthew threw open the door. Brendan saw him—and didn't see him. Nothing made any sense. He watched Matthew cross the room to Caitlin, pick her up in his arms, and carry her out of the room and up the stairs, away from the madness Brendan was lost in. What had she meant? His sister? That couldn't be. How could she be his sister? It was a lie. All of it was a lie. He'd tell her. He'd tell her that it wasn't possible. He'd mend everything between them. He'd go now . . .

Then Ellen stopped him, and told him the truth he didn't want to hear. Told him about her and his father, about the child they had together. Caitlin. And when he knew that truth, he also knew nothing he could do would ever mend that love now lost to him—forever.

The night before the *Berengaria* was due to sail, Brendan had a message, delivered to the ship by a Chinese boy. It was from Elizabeth Muldair. It read:

Captain O'Shay,

    If you are able, please meet me this evening at the classroom of the Chinese school. I will be working there quite late correcting papers. I feel it is important.

                                     Elizabeth

He wasn't going to go. What point was there to it? He was sure he wasn't going to go, until he found himself in the hired carriage following the road to the school.

Strange, he thought, for timid Elizabeth to be here so late. Had she taken over Caitlin's work for her? He would have expected Elizabeth to close the school as soon as Caitlin fell ill. Ill, that was a word. Ill in mind and spirit. Ill, with the will for life taken from you. He knew such illness too. Knew it as an added flesh upon his skin, weighing him down. Poor Caity. Poor Brendan. Poor damn fools.

Elizabeth was alone in the building, marking papers by the light of a lantern. She looked up at the sudden sound, the crunch of Brendan's boot on the gravel outside the door.

"I'd almost given up that you would come," she said instead of hello. "I'd promised myself that when this pile of papers was finished, I'd go home. Like a bargain, you see?"

He stood, waiting at the door, waiting for her to tell him why she'd sent for him.

"I'm glad you came, Brendan. I've wanted to talk to you about what's happened, ever since that day, but . . ."

"There wasn't really anything to say, was there?"

"Come inside, please," she said. "Let me look at you."

He walked into the room, sat down on one of the

310

children's chairs, wondering why he'd come. "How is she?" he asked, in spite of his firm resolve not to. It wasn't easy to kill a feeling that had worn its way so deep in your heart.

"She'll be all right in time. I'm not worried about her. It's you I'm worried about. You look awful."

"Do I?" he asked, smiling wanly at the unimportance of it.

"Yes, you do. I hope you won't let this go on much longer, this wallowing in self-pity. Nothing good will come of it. I know it was a hard thing, for both of you, but it's ended now, and you have to find a way back to the living. Come back yourself. Come back to all of us."

He stood up. "Is that what you sent for me to say? I'm leaving early in the morning, I'd better go now." He rose to walk away.

"Wait!" she said in such a voice that he turned and stared at her. "That isn't why I asked you here. I wanted to see if you were all right, that's true, but I wanted to tell you something too. Please, just for another minute, would you come back inside? Please?"

He was anxious to be away. Whatever she had to say wouldn't matter anyway. What point was there in picking through his feelings? He looked at her to tell her that, and saw something in the way she looked at him that brought him back into the room. What was it? He'd noticed it the first day he met her, and there it was still.

"I don't know how to say this," she began. "I haven't had any practice at such things." He was staring at her, his eyes frowning in confusion. "I want to tell you that I'm sorry you've been hurt this way. That I care for you. I care about what happens to you. This won't make any kind of sense to you now, but I want you to know that

311

when you return to San Francisco, I'll be here."

He stared at her, trying to put some other meaning to her words, but saw there was none.

"Only remember what I've said," she told him. "I don't want you to forget me. I know I will never forget you." She leaned across the space between them, and kissed him.

"Elizabeth, I . . ." He couldn't think what to say.

"Don't say anything now. I couldn't let you go away—maybe forever—without at least telling you how I feel. I don't care how it makes me look. Think about what I've said"—she gathered her things to leave him—"and after you've thought, if you want me, I'll be here. I love you, Brendan. Come back to me." She walked away from him, out of the room, out of his life.

The *Berengaria* sailed out of San Francisco Harbor on the morning of February 10th, 1868. A hundred thoughts beset Captain O'Shay as he piloted his ship away from the submerged reef and kept her from heading into the wind and against the rock barriers jutting out from the shore. A hundred thoughts of wind sails, water supply, the men of his crew, and the passengers who sailed with him. Thoughts of Caitlin, and saying good-bye. And one other, new and confusing to him still—that image of Elizabeth Muldair saying, "I love you. Come back to me."

Chapter Thirty

The sudden death of Daniel O'Mally took place as the result of an accident at the tree line of the American River Lumber Company. Danny and his partner, Griffin McTaggart, had been making their monthly inspection of the logging camp. The men at the base level were throwing a party, celebrating the end of a two-week stint of work in the high camp. The foreman had supplied the whiskey, and they were more than a little drunk. It was hard work, exhausting work, and it was company policy that the men have such a reward at the end of each high-camp shift.

The men's voices were loud in their celebrating. Music of a sort, from a few harmonicas, played hauntingly through the night, making it impossible to sleep. Some of them were dancing, some merely keeping time to the music with a stomping foot. No firearms were allowed in camp, but that didn't prevent the men from finding other means to wake the spirits of the mountain. With enough liquor in them, they whooped like red Indians. One man even gave a Rebel yell. That was either very brave, or very foolish, Danny thought, in a camp full of many Union sympathizers. He listened, but he only heard it once.

"They're in a rare good mood," McTaggart remarked, sucking hard on the stem of his briarwood pipe. The fine red of his hair and beard had turned a sandy shade with age, salted as it was with gray. He had a respectable look about him, like a laird, the gentleman in the workers' camp. There was nothing left to show of the man who had slogged through the swamps of Panama, nor the man who had worn a week's layer of silted dirt every Friday night in the gold fields of California. He had taken on a proper look. His wife, Rachel, saw to that.

When he married a Scotswoman sent over by his mother, Hanna McTaggart, with a note of strong advice to her son concerning marrying one of his own kind, Griffin's life as a carefree bachelor had taken on a sudden change. Almost overnight, it seemed, as if by none of his own doing, he had become a conscientious, kirk-going, civic-minded citizen. And he was sober. Rachel McTaggart had wasted no time in producing six children. The first year they were married, there was Lauchlan, followed a year later by Angus. Alistair arrived not quite eleven months after Angus, after which Rachel took a two-year rest before giving birth to Ian. With four sons assuring the continuity of the family name, she changed her preference and bore two girls. Anne, and a year later her sister, Deborah.

Griffin, asked what he thought of all of this, said only, "I expect she knows what she's doing." She did.

After producing six children in seven years, Rachel McTaggart concentrated her efforts on making her husband the man she wanted him to be. With whirlwind speed and efficiency, she rid the man of every evidence of his natural state.

It was with some degree of longing then that Griffin asked, "Do you ken it would embarrass the men if we were to have a round or two with them?"

"It wouldn't be the first time," Danny reminded him.

"No, verra true," McTaggart replied, as though weighing and considering the facts.

Danny smiled, and waited for the usual outcome of this decision. Rachel McTaggart might have her way at home, but when he was in camp, and free of her scornful judgments, the man did as he pleased. That usually meant a bottle.

"Are you coming doon, then?" he asked, wanting a friend beside him if he was going to make a fool of himself.

"You go on," Danny urged him. "It takes you longer to loosen up. That Scot pride of yours, I expect. I'll be along in a while."

"I'll just do that," McTaggart came back at him, firing up, ready for a roaring drunk. "It may take me a while longer to get where I'm drinking to," he pointed out with some sense of satisfaction with himself, "but I stay there and enjoy the view when I've got where I'm going. Never been known to pass out, like some I could mention."

He was off then, hurrying down the hill to the noise of the camp. Danny watched him go, feeling a sadness he couldn't explain at the sight of Griffin's long legs taking the hillside in four easy strides. It was an all too familiar feeling of late, this unreasonable sadness at the small events of his life.

The camp was too noisy for him. The idea of carrying on a night of high drinking with McTaggart sounded like a boy's game he didn't want to play anymore. This thing between Caitlin and O'Shay had got him down more than he liked to admit. He felt her pain over it, as though he had somehow been responsible for what had happened. The truth was, this sadness he carried was more than just grieving over Caitlin. It was a hollow within himself, growing wider with every day. It had come between him and Ellen, like nothing ever had before. It had come between him and his friends, all those he cared about. Sometimes he had to be alone, all alone, or he might break down and cry with the overwhelming sense of hopelessness he carried within him. He felt that now, and knew he had to get away to the quiet of himself. Only then did he feel that he could breathe, did his heart beat calm and easy in his breast. Only then was he at peace.

He scrawled out a quick note, and pinned it to Griffin's blanket. It read:

> Decided to ride up to higher timber. I've a longing to hear the sound of silence. Doubt you'll know I'm gone before morning. I'll camp out there, and make my way back sometime after breakfast.
>
> Danny

He saddled his horse, and rode slowly out of camp. The horse was a good mount for the soft dirt of the forest floor. It was dark between the trees. The snap of twigs beneath his horse's hooves and the soft thud as the weight of her shoe hit the bare ground were the only things his senses were certain of. In the break between the trees, the heavens opened, and he could see the stars, clear and brilliant white flashes of light. He stared at them. The beauty of that instant stayed with him, up the harder climb of the trail. He would camp at the lower summit. It would be clear there, a place of quiet night, with just him and the stars. He was looking forward to it, feeling better . . . so much better—when he felt the horse begin to slip. The side of the mountain moved away from him, pulling the earth from beneath the horse's hooves. He felt himself begin to fall. The night swallowed everything up in a cloak of black. There was nothing he could see to grab, to save himself. He fell, free of but keenly hearing the wild scream of the horse. A long way, he fell. No sound came from him. No cry. He felt the jagged spine of the rock, the lightning knife of pain in his back and neck. The sound his neck made when it snapped—then the agony of pain was no more.

Above him was the canopy of sky. His last clear thought, before he slipped into his own dark night: My God, Ellen, the stars . . .

McTaggart found Danny's body. A search party was sent out after the second day when he didn't return to camp. His partner of nearly twenty years carried him across his saddle, his horse carefully stepping around the crevice made by the earth slide. At the base camp, the men made a temporary coffin for Danny. They loaded the coffin on the company lumber wagon, and brought him down the mountain, to home. Griffin McTaggart rode with him all that way, his partner and his friend. The hardness of death weighed heavily upon him, like the weight of the coffin. It was he who told Ellen, and Danny's sons. The boys cried for their father, but Ellen never wept. It was as though she didn't believe him, even with Danny's body in the coffin on the wagon. Someone

317

else told Caitlin and Elizabeth—Matthew, he supposed.

Griffin stood before Ellen, trying to form the words to tell her how he felt. She stared at him, waiting for him to explain. "I don't know what to say," he tried, but all else stuck fast in his throat. He turned quickly away before his own tears shamed him before Danny's wife—now Danny's widow.

It didn't matter. Ellen knew what he would have said, knew he had loved Danny as she had. Nothing mattered anymore. Not all the words, or even all the unspoken words, the silences that had gone between them. Danny was gone. And with him, her happiness.

In the time after Danny's death, it was Elizabeth who held the family together. His natural sons lost themselves in work, even young Patrick. It was how they dealt with the pain of losing him. Ellen closed herself away from life, refusing to see friends, never going out, as though she too were dead. The house was a somber, lonely place, with grief the master there. Elizabeth took charge of the household, seeing that dinners were prepared, that the servants continued their duties, that her mother was not allowed to simply sit and stare into the distance, as she would have liked to do. She badgered them all into living—painful, and often unsmooth, but living.

Only Caitlin and Matthew seemed not to need her comfort. Hurt as they both were, they found solace in each other. Slowly, Caitlin was coming back to them. There had been a time, right after Brendan left, that it seemed she would be lost, always, in the torment of her own injured spirit. Only Matthew had believed she was

318

strong enough to find her way. He did little else but care for her, willing her to return. Six months of refusing to give up brought her back among the living. What he had done was remarkable, but even he hadn't seen why he had done it.

When Caitlin was strong again, when she had learned to smile and laugh, he came to Elizabeth, as acting head of the house.

"I came to tell you I'm planning to go away very soon. It's time I began my own life, and I can't do that here."

Elizabeth's first thoughts were of her sister. "But Caitlin?" she asked, knowing how much he had helped her.

"Caity's well now. She doesn't need me any longer. I have to get away, for myself."

Elizabeth saw something in that instant, heard it in that single admission, that she had never understood before. It was the revealing of a quiet desperation. She knew, in that instant, with sudden certainty, that Matthew had helped Caitlin as much for himself as for her. And now that she was well, he was running away, before . . .

"You love her, don't you?"

He looked at her with eyes like a trapped animal, confronted by this secret of the heart. "Of course I love her, she's my sister."

"I don't mean like that," she pressed, refusing to let him hide from the truth any longer. "You're in love with her, that's what I mean."

"I'm her brother, or have you forgotten? I'm not another Brendan O'Shay," he added, cornered, and fighting back the only way he knew.

"It's not the same. You're not really her brother. We're Muldairs, you and I. You haven't even lived as her brother for years, with the war. It's true, isn't it? You do love her?"

There was no answer to that. To admit it, or rather to keep from doing that, was why he was leaving. "What does it matter?"

"It does matter," she insisted. "Don't you think she has the right to know how you feel? Tell her, Matt. Tell her before it's too late. Real love isn't easy to find. Don't be a damn fool. Take whatever chance you have, and risk it." She was angry, angry for all the dreams he was willing to give up. Real love was worth risking everything for. It made her hard with him, to think he so feared the cost he was willing to lose without even a fight.

"You've undergone a change," he said, smiling at her. "Look at you. Ready to take on the world, if need be. What's done this to you, Beth? What's brought you out of that comfortable little shell you used to live in?"

He's right, she thought, I have changed. I'm not afraid of anything anymore. She shrugged her shoulders at Matt, pretending not to know the answer to his question. But within herself, she withheld that secret, and thought she knew.

It was nearly nine when Caitlin found him in the library. "I've been looking for you all day," she said.

"I haven't been around much today," he admitted.

"Elizabeth tells me you're thinking of going away."

"That's right," he said, continuing to put a few selected books into a leather satchel.

320

"Would you have left without even saying good-bye to me?" Her eyes said she was hurt, and his heart rejoiced at that hurt, but hurt wasn't love.

"No. I would have said good-bye," he told her, wanting to say more, so much more.

"Why do you have to go? I need you here. Aren't you happy here?"

He turned to her then, wanting to take her in his arms. "You don't need me anymore, Caitlin. You're well now. You don't need anyone."

"But I don't want you to go," she cried. "I don't want you to leave us. Don't you care about that? Don't you care at all?" Tears glistened on her cheeks.

"It's because I care too much that I'm leaving," he tried to explain, then wished he hadn't. That would bring it into the open. Did he want that? Was Elizabeth right? Did Caitlin have a right to know how he felt?

She had stopped crying, and was staring at him. "What do you mean, you care too much?"

"Nothing," he said, trying to put the thought away.

"It isn't nothing. You said it's why you're leaving. You're going away because of me? Because of something I've done? But what have I done, Matt? Please, you must tell me. What have I done to you?"

All the holding back broke. He pulled her into his arms, as he had been longing to do. "Don't you understand? It's nothing you've done. It's me. I'm in love with you, Caitlin."

"In love?" The sound of her voice caressed the words.

"Elizabeth made me see it, when I wouldn't admit it even to myself. I've known for a long time how I felt, but never looked at it as I did today. She made me. She said I

321

ought to tell you, but I couldn't, not after all that's happened. I couldn't be the one to hurt you. I know I'm not a blood relative, but people would think I was, and what would that do to you? So I decided to leave. I thought if I went far enough away from here, I might someday forget the way I feel now." He was still holding her in his arms. She made no move to pull away. She was looking up into his face, her eyes telling him something. Something.

"Say anything, Cait, for the love of God. Whatever you say will be better than what my mind imagines you're thinking."

"I wonder if you know, Matt, how much you mean to me," she began. "Without you, these last months, I would have never been whole again, and strong. You were right when you said I don't need anyone anymore. I don't. I can be by myself. I'm not afraid of that."

He stepped away from her, hearing the good-bye in her words. What else had he expected, anyway? God, what made me tell her? Now, everything's ruined. Ruined.

She moved closer to him. "Matt"—she laid her hand against his cheek—"we're alike, you and I. We have the same dreams, the same beliefs. I always turned to you for support, and you were always there. I never knew what this feeling I had for you was. I never understood it, but I do now. It isn't need. It's love. I love you, Matt, I always have. I want you beside me." She touched her finger to his lips. "I never want to lose you," she said, holding him with her eyes.

He kissed her then, afraid, every second, that something would take her from him. He pulled her to him, tightly, holding her.

"Please don't go," she said. "Don't leave me. Ever."

"I may have to go," he said, knowing they must leave this place, "but you'll come with me. Marry me, Caitlin. Before God, I love you more than anything on earth."

She thought, for one instant, of that other love, a lifetime ago. That love could never be. She closed her heart to it forever, and thinking only of this time, this man, answered, "Yes, I will."

Chapter Thirty-One

Elizabeth was more alone than ever after Matthew and Caitlin left. They were married in a quiet ceremony in the chapel of St. Mary's. Elizabeth and Sister Judith were the only witnesses. No one else of the family attended. The O'Mally boys stayed away, out of respect for their mother's wishes. Ellen would not acknowledge the marriage, and when she saw that she could not dissuade them from it, refused to attend. For her, it was a nightmarish repetition of what had happened between Brendan and Caitlin. Brother and sister, again. Common sense told her there was no blood tie between them, but that did little to change her feelings. In her heart, Matt and Caitlin were both her children, hers and Danny's. Hadn't Danny cared for them as a father? Hadn't he loved them as his own?

Guilt sat with her in the long nights before the wedding, guilt and a firm resolve that nothing would ever dishonor Danny's memory. She had given him enough pain to endure in those terrible days when her secret had become known. Alone, she grieved over the sins of her youth, and in the dark recesses of her mind they seemed tied together, this union and that other.

Worse than that, worse than her grief at losing Danny, was her fear of losing both Caitlin and Matthew. Together, they would leave her now. To what? A widow's life. Her young sons were little more than boys, too busy in their own lives to notice the emptiness in hers. Elizabeth, that quiet young woman, could never fill this lonely life, Ellen thought, as Caitlin and Matt had. There would be emptiness now. She feared that emptiness. Feared too the memories that this marriage brought back to her, of Dougal and that other life, of Colin and the suffering she caused him, of Danny, her own Danny, and the secret that had lain between them always, and of her own child, Caitlin. What she had done had almost destroyed the girl. So much grief to them all.

Don't do this, she wanted to shout to them both, to Matt and Caitlin. Fragile in both mind and spirit, she could bear no more. Surrounded still by those who loved her, she drew herself inward, already pulling away from them, even before they were lost to her. Hardened by such thoughts, she set up a barrier against further pain, refusing to listen to either Caitlin or Matt. This sinking depression worked on her mind, but she said nothing, allowing it to grow and turn into anger.

"Don't let us part like this," Matthew had begged her, the only mother he had known since he was eleven. "We've been through too much together to let this come between us. I love you, you know that. So does Caitlin. All we ask is your blessing. I beg you," he said.

For answer, Ellen had said, "I regret the day I brought you here with me, Matthew Muldair. I should have left you to die, back in Ireland, with your father and sister.

325

Damn you for what you are doing to me."

Caitlin tried once more, on the day they left. "We're leaving now, Mother. Will you kiss me good-bye?"

Ellen made no move to touch her. She sat rigidly in her chair, refusing a glance that might weaken her resolve.

Caitlin crossed the room to her, bent down on her knees before her mother's chair. She put her head in Ellen's lap, her tears wetting the dark panels of the dress. In an anguished voice, she pleaded, "Mother, please! I can't leave you like this." Her back trembled in the wake of the tears she could not hold.

In that instant, Ellen's hand reached out to soothe and comfort her child, her firstborn. It lingered there, over Caitlin's head, wanting to stroke her fine, soft hair. Wanting to gather her into her arms. But in that same instant, the pain she could not bear, from what Matthew and Caitlin were doing, stopped her. Unseen, she withdrew her touch and let her hand drop once more into her lap.

Crying hard, Caitlin rose, kissed her mother on her cheek. Ellen could feel the tears against her own face, Caitlin's tears. She could feel them, though her heart was stone.

"Good-bye," Caitlin said. "I love you, Mother. Matt and I both love you. Good-bye."

Ellen heard them as they walked away, heard the sound of their muffled voices in the hall. A tightness drawn across her chest held her to her chair, the pressure against her lungs building, building . . . until she thought she could not breathe. The sound of her own heartbeats rocked her body, making her feel she was swaying. Dying. Go! She wanted to shout at them. Oh, God, will you go! Please, she thought, before I die here in

326

this chair. Before I run after you and call you back!

The door closed, metal catching metal. She listened for every sound, hearing the only sense of which she was aware. The crunch of the gravel as the carriage wheels bit into the worked path. The sound of the horses blowing as they pulled the weight of two people and their belongings in the buggy. Two people—one of whom she'd carried within her own flesh.

"Caitlin!" she cried. No one heard the sound. Her body went limp, and she fell against the arm of the chair, weeping. Her own tears, and those of her daughter's, mingled on her cheek and on the skirt of her dress. Her eyes were blinded by them. "Caitlin," she called out again, softly now. "My little girl. Oh, God, what have I done to us all? Caitlin and Matt? Danny? Gone . . . all of them, gone."

It was Elizabeth who found her there. Elizabeth who helped her to her room and cared for her through the long weeks after. Cared for her through Ellen's silence. Her mother had no need for words. The pain she lived with spoke loud enough in her eyes. Elizabeth cared for Ellen, as once Ellen had cared for her. It was her mother's life she meant to gain back, in whatever way she could. The O'Mally sons were too young to understand such grief. They couldn't think how to ease their mother's suffering. It was left to Elizabeth, who knew about such things. Elizabeth—who knew what rejection was, from her father—who knew what loneliness was, from all the years of crippling shyness, when she was too afraid to make a friend—who knew even what hopeless love was, from Brendan. She became Ellen's one companion.

Month followed month. The leafless trees of September, seen through the window of her mother's room, changed to the darker days of October, the gray rains of November, the cold of December, which lied and said the world was dead. Now the only teacher at the Chinese school, that legacy left to her by Caitlin, Elizabeth was glad to have a place to be free of the unlifting sorrow of the O'Mally house. The school, and her children, daily revived her. Her greatest happiness was the recent addition of the three daughters of Ming-Low, the laundryman, to her class. He had brought them one day, with no word of explanation for his change of heart. Many of the merchants brought their daughters now. That was Caitlin's doing, she thought. How she would have loved it. They were good pupils, learning quickly. She wondered if their brothers had helped them secretly at home. In all, there were twelve girls in her class. Soon, she would have to ask Sister Judith for one of the nuns to help, with a second room.

The day's lessons were over, the children gone home, and still she lingered in the classroom. She was postponing her time with Ellen. It was pleasant there, with the sun setting low in the sky, the softly blended colors coming through the multi-paned window across from her desk. She sipped the hot tea one of the nuns had brought her, and began reading Su-Szi's paper. The girl was a careful printer, unlike some of the boys in the class.

The door opened inward, and all she saw at first was his hand. But she knew—even at that instant, she knew it was him. "Brendan," she whispered, pushing back her chair and standing, as though he might disappear.

He came into the room, taller than she remembered. "Hello, Elizabeth," he said. "I'm back."

Slowly, slowly, he walked the distance between them,

his eyes never leaving her. Come back to me, she had said, and now he was here. What did it mean? His coming back was all she had dreamed of in the ten months since he had gone away. She had never let herself believe in the dream, never let herself hope that it could be. Now he was here. Was it for her?

"There's something you must know," she warned even before she could welcome him. She had to tell it first, before anything else. "Caitlin's married."

There was pain in his eyes, but he answered without taking time to think. "It doesn't matter. I didn't come back for Caitlin, Beth. I came back because of you."

It was hard for her to breathe. She couldn't speak. She couldn't think beyond the moment, beyond what he'd said. All of her was still, except her eyes. They searched his face, staring into his own eyes, unsure, but wanting to see truth there.

"Are you still that shy girl I first met right here, Beth?" His hand touched her cheek, brushing his fingers across them gently, leaving a trail of warmth across her face where his fingers touched. A shudder ran through her, as though something had taken all the breath from her. She lowered her eyes, unable to meet his any longer. "Don't look away from me, Beth," he said, lifting her chin with his fingertips. "You weren't shy the day I left. Do you remember what you said to me? I thought of it all the months I was gone, thought of what had happened between Caitlin and me, between Ellen and my father, and at last, of what you said to me that night. I was hurting when I left here, hurting with a pain I thought would never heal. But I did heal, Beth. As much as anything, that healing came from you, from your words to me."

She tried to look down, but his fingers would not let her move. She was held captive by the gentle pressure of his touch. She felt her face burn with his words, wishing he would stop. Wishing he would take her in his arms.

"Caitlin and I can never be," he said. "That's something I've had to accept. We were so much alike, willing to dare anything. Would such a love have survived?" His hand released her then, and it felt as though he pulled away in that moment, pulled away. The next instant he was back, saying, "I'll never know. It doesn't matter now. I came back to tell you something, Beth. That more and more, as the days went by, I found myself thinking of you, remembering the first day I met you, and that certain look in your eyes. That first day I remember thinking, if it weren't for Caitlin, I'd be here for her." He bent and touched his lips to hers, not really a kiss, only the barest breath of one.

"Brendan," she began, "I . . ."

"I want to get to know you, Beth. Don't say no to that. I've thought a lot about what you said to me when I left, of what those words must have cost you. You're not a woman who risks easily, I think. You're gentle and shy, with a loneliness that touched me from the first moment. For some unfathomable reason, you cared enough about me to dare tell me so. If you'll let me, Beth, I'd like to try to earn that love. Will you give me that chance?"

Something that was old in her, as old as that first love that had turned against her in her infancy, and that had been kept in secret shackles in that wounded place, broke free at Brendan's words. She knew he didn't love her as he had loved Caitlin. Perhaps he never would. But it was a beginning, a chance at happiness for both of them. Was

330

she willing to take that chance? She stepped closer, into his arms. Her kiss was his answer.

After that, she saw him every day. They met at school. Each afternoon, as soon as the children left, he was there. There was time for them. She made excuses to Ellen when necessary, but for the most part, no one challenged her whereabouts. She had long ago taken over the role as head of the house.

She met him secretly, innocently. For three weeks, she thought of nothing but that he would be there to meet her—in the morning, before class, in the evening, after school. And some days, she asked Sister Judith for a free day, to be with him. All this she kept from Ellen.

And one black, starless night, he took her in his arms—away from all the world, away from any eyes but their own. He pulled her close in his embrace, the warmth of his body against her own. Had he asked her, she would have done anything for him. She would have gone away with him, that moment, and never looked back. Or had he pulled her down onto the grass with him, his hands upon all that was her innocence, she would have welcomed him.

Had he asked. But he did not.

Instead, he kissed her, and as he felt the trembling of her lips beneath his own, a certainty began in him—a certainty that this woman, this trusting, loving woman, was all he would ever want in life. Her love had healed him, and more, had made him see that he could love again.

Her hands reached out for his, bringing them to her,

against the thin material of her dress. She pressed his palm against her, the warmth of her skin burning through.

"Love me, Brendan," she said, and in her eyes was the offer of all of herself, for just his love.

He left his hand against her breast, and kissing her again—a kiss that began at her eyes, her cheeks, her lips—he said, "I do love you, Beth. Not just for tonight, but for the rest of my life. You looked at me once, long ago, and I wondered, would she have me?"

"I would have Bren. I would have, then or now. I don't know what you want from me. Must I ask you again? I will then," she said. "I'll ask a thousand times, if you would have it. Love me." Her eyes were steady now, steady and honest in her want of him.

He'd never felt this way before, not even with Cait. Theirs had been a love kindled by passion. This feeling that he had for Beth, this was of a passion too. Different, though. It was a passion kindled by love.

"You need never ask me again, Beth, for the answer is yes, I love you. More than that, I want you desperately. I want you in my arms and in my bed. I want my hands here against your breast, where nothing comes between us. All of that I must have of you, and never would it be enough."

His final words scalded her, burned into her like a fire she would never find the means to put out. Her love would never be enough. That was what he'd said. She turned from him, shamed by the quick tears that stung her eyes.

But he turned her back again, frowning in wonder at the tears on her cheeks. "What is it?" he asked. "What have I done? It was only that I could never have only that. I must have you with me always, Beth. Can't you see how much I love you? Can't you believe me now? It's I who must ask you a thousand times, my Beth. It's what I wondered then, so long ago, and what I'm asking now. Would you have me?" Only silence for his answer. "Marry me, Beth. Say you'll marry me."

At last, clear voiced, she answered him. "I will," she said. "For all my life, I will."

Elizabeth Muldair went home to the O'Mally house alone. Brendan had wanted to come with her, to be with her when she faced Ellen, but she'd told him, "No, I need time to explain this to her in my own way. She's very fragile now, since Father died, and Caitlin and Matt left."

A look of pain had come over Brendan's face, and he'd made his only reference to Caitlin's marriage. "I never thought it would be Matt," he'd said.

Elizabeth could only guess at the hurt it caused him. Still, it was better that he understand. If there hadn't been Matt, she knew, Caitlin would have lived with that grief, alone, for the rest of her life. Would he condemn her to that? "If it hadn't been Matt," she'd told him, "it would have been no one. Be happy for her, Bren," she'd said, trying to make him see. "Be happy for them both."

"Yes," he'd said, giving her a smile. It was the last he ever spoke of them.

Ellen was waiting for her, worried that she was so late in coming home. "I almost sent the boys out to look for you," she told her. "You work too late and too hard at that school. You've missed your supper again," she said in mild reproach, "but I had Nancy keep a plate warm in the oven for you."

Elizabeth noticed that her mother was becoming just that, a mother again, worrying over her children, caring for them. That meant she was stronger, but was she strong enough? Ellen O'Mally had been through more than most women of her generation. She was a survivor. What made her strong enough for that? Something in herself, Elizabeth thought. Something at the core of her, a strength unbroken by any loss, any pain. She had it now, she realized, had it still. It would see her through this.

It was a strength born of her people, a strength forged in endurance, through invasion of their land, persecution of their religion, through famine and deprivation. It had kept them whole when the world crumbled about them.

"You shouldn't be out here in the cold," Elizabeth said to her. "Come inside, I want to talk to you."

"What is it, dear?" Ellen asked, when they were inside, sitting by the fire, their chairs pulled up close together. "Something's wrong, I see that."

"No, Mother," she said, not wanting to frighten her, "it isn't something wrong, but it is a hard thing I have to tell you. I think you're strong enough. You've been getting better each day, so much better." She stopped, trying to think how to say it.

"Don't be so scared of hurting me, Elizabeth. What harm could you ever bring me?" She reached out for her daughter's hand.

"I'm going to marry Brendan O'Shay," Elizabeth told her.

"What? But how?" Ellen struggled to understand. "You couldn't even have seen him."

"Before he left, ten months ago, I sent a message to

him then. He came to see me at the school."

"A message? How could you have dared do such a thing? You've never so much as gone to dinner with a man in all your life."

"I sent for him, Mother," Elizabeth insisted, "and he came. I told him then that I knew what he and Caitlin had was over, but that I couldn't bear to lose him from my life. I told him I loved him, that I had since the first day I'd met him. I asked him to come back, and told him that I would be here, waiting, when he did."

"I don't understand any of this," Ellen said. "Brendan O'Shay was in love with Caitlin."

"Yes," Elizabeth tried to explain, "maybe he still is. Maybe he always will be. But that love is lost, Mother, and can never happen between them. He's asked me to marry him. He says he loves me. I know I love him, and that's enough for me."

"I don't know what to say to you," Ellen answered.

"Say you wish us happiness. Say you won't hold any bitterness against us, as you did with Cait and Matt."

That was a hard lesson Ellen had already learned. Holding such bitterness against those she loved had only brought the pain of their separation more keenly to her. What she had done with Caitlin and Matthew was something she would never do again. Was this so different? Brendan—Dougal's son . . . and Elizabeth— although not her child, still her daughter.

"You've made up your mind, then?" she asked. "You've given him your answer?"

"How could I have said no, Mother? I love him."

Ellen thought about that, thought about the loves she had known. Could she have said no? No to Dougal? That had been beyond her. No to Danny? Never.

"You're leaving, then? He's taking you away?"

Elizabeth nodded. "As soon as we're married. He's taking me home to Ireland. I'm going back, Mother," she said to her, "to where I was born. I don't even remember it. Think, back home to Ireland."

Back home to Ireland, Ellen did think. A bittersweet longing filled her. Home to the earliest memories of her childhood, learning her letters at her mother's knee, learning about God in a stone church from a black-robed priest with a stern face and smiling eyes. She saw again, in her mind's eye, the faces of her sisters and brothers, the hardships and the small joys they had known. The poverty and the famine, she remembered. The face of starvation on the land. But it will be different for you, Elizabeth, she thought. Your world will be a better place. What would Colin and Annie have thought, she wondered, their daughter coming back home at last? How could she hold out against such a thing? It was not in her to do. All that fear and hatred had gone out of her when she lost Caitlin and Matt. One day, she prayed, she could make that right again. She'd not make the same mistake with Elizabeth.

"You're my daughter," she said, "and I love you. Whatever you do, and wherever you go, that will never change. If there's going to be a wedding in this house, we'd better see about making you a dress." It was an answer, all the answer she knew how to give. She had opened her heart to them, to them both, and let the beauty of their love come shining in. It was a beginning.

"You're my wife," Brendan had said to her that first night of their married life, when they were alone on the

Berengaria. "If ever I betray you, I pray God strikes me dead."

"Don't!" she said, holding him tighter to her, and kissing his lips as though to kiss away the words and the thought. She loved him so much more than she had known, and now that they were man and wife, more even than that. "I need no promises from you, Bren, only your love. That's all I'll ever need."

"That you have, my Beth," he whispered, "that, and evermore that." He took her in his arms again, and proved it.

Chapter Thirty-Two

Coming home to Ireland was for Elizabeth the second best experience of her life. She sat beside Brendan in the pretty bottle-green one-horse trap he had rented, and looked out on the passing land. California was so different from this, she thought. She loved it for its redwoods and its oaks, its mountains and its beaches. But this place, this was a land steeped in green. It was a place of growing things. Months of anticipation had keened her senses. She closed her eyes and breathed in the smell of it, an earthy, loamy kind of smell. Brendan might have a love of the sea air, but for her, land was the place for humankind, and this land more than any other. Looking out again, she saw acres of pasture grass separated only by hedgerows laid side-by-side, like a piece quilt, snug over the land. She liked to think of it like that, the green patterned quilt on top, and the land laying safe and warm beneath.

"My mother and father were born, and died here," she said softly, realizing that she too was part of this place, an heir to its wealth. She had the strongest sense that she was coming home. Her children would be born here, securing their own heritage in the first wailing cry of their birth. It made her happy to think of that, knowing she was already with child.

As they came into the city, she saw the two- and three-story stone houses, the manicured lawns, and the tailored, well-ordered flower beds. They turned the corner, and there was Dobbin Lane, and the O'Shay house.

For Brendan, seeing it with Elizabeth made it seem different. It was as though he were seeing it for the first time with her. The trees he had played on in his boyhood had grown tall as the red brick house, though he'd never noticed before.

"The chimney has a C on it," Elizabeth noticed.

"It's for Cleary," Brendan explained. "I'll tell you about it one day." That would be a story, he thought. Old Rebba Cleary and his mother, and how his father had come to this house on his birthday, to ask her to marry him. Old Mrs. Cleary, who his father had called a "black crow of a woman." This had been her house, and her inheritance had changed their lives. Where would we be now, he thought, if Rebba Cleary's son had lived, and not died of the measles? Odd thing, the hand of fate.

The front door of the house at 21 Dobbin Lane was painted green, a memory of another place, a cottage door. Brendan started to open it, but Elizabeth caught his hand. "Shouldn't we knock?" she asked, her eyes looking fearful as a trapped rabbit.

"This is home, Beth. You don't knock on the door of home. Don't worry," he said, stroking her pale cheek, "they're going to love you."

She followed after him like an obedient child, looking

at the hardwood floor in the entry and the richly grained paneling on the wall.

A large-bosomed, gray-haired woman carrying a tea tray came into the hall from the door leading to the pantry at the back of the house. She had a sweet face, Elizabeth thought, and a body that looked as comfortable as cushions. Her eyes lit up when she saw them.

"Oh, Mister Brendan! Lord love you. We had no word you was comin'."

"Hello, Martha. Shh, would you, woman. I wanted to surprise them."

Martha, who was no dullard, craned her neck to see around Brendan's shoulder, having a look at the woman standing behind him.

"I expect they'll be surprised, all right," she told him, her eyes full of the question she would not put to her lips.

"My wife, Martha," he said, bringing Elizabeth up beside him. "We were married four months ago, in California." The eyes looked unconvinced. After all, California was a foreign place. "Show her your ring, Beth. She's a suspicious sort."

Elizabeth held out her left hand, and a broad smile of approval covered half of Martha's face. "Ah, didn't I know you were married, then? You needn't have made the poor girl stand here, feeling she was at inspection, her first minutes in the house," she chided him as though he were still the little boy she had taken care of for all the years since that woman, Ellen O'Reilly, had left. "Welcome home to you, Missus."

"Well, now that you've been accepted by Martha, everything else is easy," he said to Elizabeth. "Here, I'll take the tray in to them," he said, taking it from Martha's hands. "Beth, you stay here. I'll bring you inside later, as my surprise gift. I always bring them back one, when I've been away at sea."

"Bren, no! Don't leave me out here in the hall alone," Elizabeth whispered. She was feeling the urge to run.

"You're not alone, Beth. You're with Martha," he reassured her, and quick as the words were spoken, was gone through the parlor door, balancing the tray before him.

"Don't you worry yourself a bit over it, Missus." Martha put a well-fleshed protective arm around Elizabeth's quaking shoulders. "The old couple are goin' to love a pretty little thing like you."

Elizabeth could have kissed her for her words, and let herself sag against Martha's ampleness. Maybe it would be all right, after all.

His mother was stitching a sampler, one of many she had around the house, and his father was reading the paper, when Brendan stepped into the room.

"Put it on the tea table, will you, Martha," Moira said without looking up from her stitches. "I'll get to it in a minute."

"Won't you let me pour you a cup, then, Mother?" He stood behind her chair.

"Jamie?" She turned her head to see. "Brendan! Oh, Bren!"

He put the tray down then, and came and kissed her, feeling that tug at his heart, as he always did after he'd been away, that she was the beginning of his world, and how much he loved her.

"But why didn't you let us know you were coming?" Her eyes searched over him. "How well you look," she said, satisfied.

"Welcome home to ye, son," Dougal said, hugging

him, his embrace still hard as wood bones. "Ye didn't come home at all on yer last circuit," Dougal said. "We were worried that somewhat had happened to ye. Later, we saw some of the men of yer ship, and they told us that ye'd stopped in Dublin only long enough to unload the ship and take on a crew. They said ye sailed again after only two days, leaving behind many of those men of yer ship who chose not to go out again so soon."

That had been in those first, hard months, after losing Caitlin, Brendan thought. He hadn't found the will to make himself come home then, home to the man whose sin had cost him so much pain. Those were dark days, when he had only himself to rage at and the peace of the sea to soothe him.

"We'd taken a few bad storms that passage," he explained, "and were running late with our shipments. I had to make the time up where I could."

"At least, we knew you were safe then," his mother said.

"I'm sorry that I worried you," he told her, feeling sorry for more, so much more. "I brought you back a present." He brightened. "I'll just go and get it." He walked out of the room, and came back a moment later, holding Elizabeth by the hand. "This is the present I brought you, Mother. My wife, Beth."

"Wife?" Moira said, looking for any sign that something might be wrong about this, but seeing only a nice-looking young woman staring back at her. She felt a moment of jealousy toward this unknown woman Brendan had chosen to marry. She would be his first love now, taking over that place in his heart that Moira had held so long. A moment later, that feeling was gone— replaced by a welling of sympathy for her. Her shyness was very real, as she was dragged in like a prize before Brendan's parents. How frightened she must be, Moira thought.

"Late on yer shipments, were ye?" Dougal repeated the excuse, furrowing his brow. "It wouldn't be this young woman had aught to do with it at all, would it?"

"Hush, Dougal," Moira scolded him. "What'll she think of us, with you making remarks like that before even a word of welcome?" She crossed the room to her new daughter-in-law, noticing the presence of Martha, standing in the doorway, observing it all.

"You are a surprise," she admitted. The girl had clear blue eyes, lovely eyes. Her bottom lip was trembling. Struck by the sharp poignancy of it, which filled her with such tenderness, she held the girl in her arms and kissed her on the cheek.

"You're welcome in this house, Beth," she said. "If Brendan loves you, then so do I. So will we all." She felt the trembling subside as she held Elizabeth in her arms. Looking to the doorway, she saw Martha—smiling.

"Come back to bed," Elizabeth said softly, holding the covers out for him. Her bare flesh beneath the quilt was invitation enough. They had just made love not twenty minutes before, and now she wanted him again. Surprisingly, she knew no shyness with him, but welcomed him always into her with a passion and sensuality unlike any woman he'd ever known. He looked at her, and was tempted.

"Leave me some strength, woman, to get a little work done, or we'll both of us starve to death in that bed."

"It's a lovely place to starve," she said, throwing the

covers to the floor.

"Temptress!" He went back to the bed, ran his hand along the smooth skin from her breast to her thigh, and kissed her—her mouth warm and covering his with little kisses of her own.

"I'll be back soon," he said, running his thumb across the tautness of her nipple. "You stay here, right here."

"You won't be too long?"

"No," he promised. He walked across the room and opened the door to leave. One last look at her, with the love for him in her eyes, made him almost turn around and stay, but there was something he needed to do. "Don't move," he told her, with a look that made her smile. Then he closed the door behind him, and walked downstairs.

His father was in the library, Brendan knew. He headed there. It had been in his mind to talk to Dougal about Ellen ever since he came home. The time seemed right. His mother was busy somewhere else in the house. They would be alone.

"There ye are, Bren," his father said. "I was lookin' for ye earlier."

"Were you? Well, I'm here now. There's something I've been wanting to talk with you about too since I came home."

"That'll be that secret I've been seeing in yer face, I expect," Dougal said to him. "I thought there was somewhat eatin' at ye. What is it, Bren?"

The look of concern in his father's eyes was genuine. This man loved him. Of that, Brendan was certain. What is the point of telling him at all? he thought. The words had a power of their own, and spilled from him almost against his will.

"When I was in California," he said, "I met a woman by the name of Ellen O'Reilly." The look in his father's eyes told him he had hit the mark.

"Ellen?" Dougal said, astounded and confused by the news. "Ellen's in California?"

"Sit down, Father." Brendan helped him to his chair. Dougal sat down, his legs too weak to support him, his face ashen.

"I know all about it," he told his father, "everything that happened between you and her twenty-one years ago. I've met her."

His father seemed to shrink, his body sagging inward into the chair. "Dear God!" he groaned. "How? What had ye to do with Ellen?"

"I met her through her daughter," he explained. "Ellen went out onto the road when she left you. She had nowhere to go, and no one to support her, so she worked when she could, and stole when she couldn't. At her lowest point, she met a young man named Danny O'Mally, who offered to take her in, until the birth of her child, Caitlin. Your child."

Dougal stared at him, then shook his head, trying to sort out the bits of this puzzle. "I never knew she was with child," he said. "She never said aught of it to me."

"O'Mally went to California in '48, after gold. Two years later, she followed him there, with Caitlin and two orphaned children. Elizabeth was one of those orphans."

Dougal's head felt light. He could feel his heart jumping wildly at the shock of Brendan's words.

"She married O'Mally in California, and they raised their children together. He did well in the gold fields, and in a lumber company afterward. She's had a good life with him. They were happy, I think."

"I never meant to hurt her," Dougal said. "I'd never in my life known a woman like her. She was young, beautiful, and for some unknown reason, thought she loved me. We were devious, the two of us—your mother, carryin' Bronwyn, never suspectin'. Then Moira was so ill, nearly dyin' with Bronwyn's birth, and me wantin' to die with her. Ellen said somethin' to me then—how it might be better if Moira died, that we might be together. I saw then what I'd done, and I railed at her for thinkin' what she did. I knew at that moment I loved only Moira, and this other had been a kind of madness. I suppose she saw it too, for she ran out of the house that night and I never saw her again."

Brendan touched his father on the shoulder. "Then, it was you who chose between them?"

Dougal looked up at him. "There was never a choice, Brendan. It was always yer mother I loved. This secret's haunted me for the last twenty years, never knowin' if Ellen might not turn up one day and ruin everythin' yer mother and me had between us."

"Then you never told Mother?" Brendan asked, wondering if she didn't have the right to know.

"Told her? No, never," his father said. "What would knowledge of that do but hurt her? Oh, I thought of it, many's the time, to ease my own guilt and ask her forgiveness. I found I couldn't do it, though. Knowin' how much pain it would cause her . . . I could never."

Brendan believed, and was touched by his father's words.

"Your daughter's married." He said it like a gift. "She's happy, I believe. He's a fine man." In that moment, he did believe it. He had found happiness with Beth. Surely Caitlin too had found the way to her own happiness. He chose not to tell his father about Caitlin and him. Dougal had been right to keep his silence. "I found I couldn't do it," he had said, "knowin' how much pain it would cause." Brendan couldn't do it either . . . never.

"I don't know what to say to ye, Bren"—Dougal tried to find the words to explain—"knowin' what ye must think of me."

Whatever feeling had brought Brendan into this room was gone now. The man before him was the father he had always loved, and always would. Nothing that had happened twenty-one years before could change that. There wasn't room in his heart for anger anymore.

"I think of you as human, Father, like the rest of the race of man, and far better than most."

"Ye don't hate yer father, then—do ye, Bren?"

Hate you? the son thought, feeling his own emotions tear at him. He looked at the sixty-five-year-old man who was Dougal O'Shay, saw the marks time had left on his face, saw the hair that had gone mostly white . . . when? Why hadn't he noticed? Did he hate him? The man who had held him on his shoulders, laughed with him, scolded him, and helped him when he needed it? He bent down, and kissed the crown of his father's head. Dougal clasped his hand, and Brendan saw the tears sliding down the old man's face.

"I love you," he said to him. "Nothing could ever change that." He walked out of the room then, too moved by the sight of his father's tears to remain.

Out in the hall, he found simply breathing to be an effort, hard won. Turning, he saw his mother standing at the far end of the hall, beyond the library door. The shock of seeing her there turned his legs to stone. By the look on her face, he knew she had heard what had been said. She gestured for him to come to her. He followed, and she led him outside, into the garden.

"Sit down, Brendan," she said. "I want to talk to you about what was said today."

That he had been the one to bring this knowledge to her, out of his own need for a kind of reckoning with his father, made him feel terrible. "I never intended that you would know any of this, Mother," he began.

"You needn't grieve over it so, Bren. I knew it all, long ago."

"Knew it?" His head came up sharply, and he stared at her.

"Oh, not for certain, at first. But after a while, I began to see the looks that passed between them, the sudden silences when I came into the room, the restlessness that kept your father from sleep. A woman knows. I felt it first, then knew."

"And you said nothing to him?" Brendan asked, wondering at this woman he thought he had known.

"No." She shook her head. "He kept it from me, and I let him. It was a secret that could only hurt us both if I brought it out into the open."

"But, didn't you feel . . . ?" He searched for the right words.

"Feel? Oh, I felt it all," she said. "The hurt that he would choose someone so much younger than I. The agony I went through each time I knew he was with her. The knowledge that I was carrying his child, and he was . . . with her."

He could see the pain of it in her eyes still. So, he thought, it hadn't been a simple thing for you to hide this secret, Mother. It wasn't out of indifference. "Then, why?" he asked. "Why did you let it go on?" He needed to understand.

"Because I loved him," she explained. "The thought that I might lose him to her was hard, but I held on to the belief that he had loved me once, and the hope that he loved me still. Only that love could bring us through, were it strong enough. Anything I could do or say would only damage that small chance. It was all I had, and I held to it. I loved him," she said simply, "and I believed he loved me too, even then."

"Through all these years since she left," Brendan said, putting his thoughts together like a great puzzle—this piece his mother, this piece his father, "you never told him?"

"No," she answered, "nor anyone else, save you. I couldn't let you go away thinking this of us, carrying this great secret in your heart. This thing we've kept so silent wasn't strong enough to separate us. Remember that.

"There's something more I want to tell you," she said. "I knew about the child, and kept it from him." She said it quickly, as though it cost her something in courage to tell. "Several years ago," she said, "I had a letter from Kara O'Reilly, saying she had finally heard about her daughter Ellen. She wrote that Ellen was living in California, and had a child, Caitlin, who was then almost thirteen years old, and four younger sons as well. She said nothing about the orphans, perhaps she hadn't heard about that. It wasn't hard to remember the dates of when Ellen left, and the age of her oldest child. I knew she was your father's. I burned the letter that same day, in a kind of terror that this child could do what her mother could not, take him from me. I've lived with the guilt of that, as Dougal has lived with his own, both of us hiding our secrets."

Brendan put his arm around her, to comfort her. "He knows now, Mother," he said.

"Yes." She brightened. "I'm glad of that." A visible weight seemed to slip from her. "You won't say anything to him—tell him that I know?" she asked.

"No, Mother," he answered her, gently.

"Not even if I should die before him," she added, and made him promise. "It would only hurt him to know. He's been the best husband I could ever have asked for, but for that short time. We've known a happy life together.

"I remember how proud he was of you, the day you were born, Brendan. You were his hope, and his future. How proud he is still. That kind of love never dies— remember," she said.

No, he thought, that kind of love doesn't die.

He walked away then, back into the house, up the stairs, and into his room, where Elizabeth waited. His wife. Home.

EXPERIENCE THE SENSUOUS MAGIC OF JANELLE TAYLOR!

FORTUNE'S FLAMES (2250, $3.95)
Lovely Maren James' angry impatience turned to raging desire when the notorious Captain Hawk boarded her ship and strode confidently into her cabin. And before she could consider the consequences, the ebon-haired beauty was succumbing to the bold pirate's masterful touch!

SWEET SAVAGE HEART (1900, $3.95)
Kidnapped when just a child, seventeen-year-old Rana Williams adored her carefree existence among the Sioux. But then the frighteningly handsome white man Travis Kincade appeared in her camp . . . and Rana's peace was shattered forever!

DESTINY'S TEMPTRESS (1761, $3.95)
Crossing enemy lines to help save her beloved South, Shannon Greenleaf found herself in the bedroom of Blane Stevens, the most handsome man she'd ever seen. Though burning for his touch, the defiant belle vowed never to reveal her mission — nor let the virile Yankee capture her heart!

SAVAGE CONQUEST (1533, $3.75)
Heeding the call of her passionate nature, Miranda stole away from her Virginia plantation to the rugged plains of South Dakota. But captured by a handsome Indian warrior, the headstrong beauty felt her defiance melting away with the hot-blooded savage's sensual caress!

STOLEN ECSTASY (1621, $3.95)
With his bronze stature and ebony black hair, the banished Sioux brave Bright Arrow was all Rebecca Kenny ever wanted. She would defy her family and face society's scorn to savor the forbidden rapture she found in her handsome warrior's embrace!

Available wherever paperbacks are sold, or order direct from the Publisher. Send cover price plus 50¢ per copy for mailing and handling to Zebra Books, Dept. 2556, 475 Park Avenue South, New York, N.Y. 10016. Residents of New York, New Jersey and Pennsylvania must include sales tax. DO NOT SEND CASH.